This Other Way of Knowing

a novel by

Mary Lou Bagley

Copyright © 2021 *This Other Way of Knowing* by Mary Lou Bagley

Published by Piscataqua Press
an imprint of RiverRun Bookstore
32 Daniel Street
Portsmouth NH 03801

ISBN: 978-1-950381-89-0

For **Bob**, there's a part of you in every good man in this story—
it cannot be otherwise

Melanie, your beautiful spirit fills these pages—
alive in the strong young women who inhabit my stories

Jeremy, ever my joy and delight—
I smile at the thought of you

Of corn & beans & squash, the way of the three sisters
The most important thing each of us can know is our unique gift and how to
use it in the world.... Being among the sisters provides a visible manifestation
of what a community can become when its members understand and share
their gifts. In reciprocity, we fill our spirits as well as our bellies

Robin Wall Kimmerer, *Braiding Sweetgrass*

Prologue

Insomnia has her sitting on her bedroom floor at two in the morning staring at the box.

It, or something else, has been calling her. Three times she has pulled it out from under the eaves. Twice she has pushed it back in place. But this time, the third time, she's let it remain in the middle of the room on the faded rug—her father's rug from his early years before becoming the famous painter, Maxwell Meader.

My little square of sanity. She can still hear him say it, though she was very young at the time. On those rare occasions when he invited her into his studio, she would sit on this rug. Laid out beneath the multipaned window in that large open room, it defined a smaller, separate space—sacred space.

As an unknown street painter, he'd rolled it up and carried it from room to tiny room in Europe, Canada, New Mexico, and finally back to family land in Maine. *Essential to living in this world, Magpie, is a place of safety, where you can be who you were meant to be. A place set apart. A simple square of cloth on a drafty garret floor will do. Sanctuary. Home to your truest self. Refuge.*

Chapter 1

"You okay? You seem distracted," Annie Foss asks as she sets her teacup on the table.

Margaret turns from the wall of windows where the flash of red, a cardinal on the wing, had drawn her gaze. "Sorry. I'm just tired." She tucks loose strands of auburn hair behind her ear, threads of silver shining in the sunlight, and returns to her chair. Absently, she rubs the pale scar over her left brow. "I haven't been sleeping."

"Oh?"

"Something's..." She searches the rafters as if the words to finish her thought were sitting there, just out of reach. "Something's off somehow."

"I wouldn't worry. When you least expect it, you'll have a dream or a vision and you'll know what's up." Annie leans across the table and pats Margaret's hand. "You can trust that your gift is back."

"You know me too well. Thanks." She leans back in her chair. "I took it for granted. Even wished it away at times. Then when it was gone—" She looks back to the windows, avoiding Annie's eyes, lost for a moment in the memory of the unaccustomed quiet, the absence. The emptiness.

"But it came back," Annie says again. "And a thirteen-year-old girl is alive because of it. Allisa Cates is home with her father because of you."

"And then it came back. Yes." Smiling with gratitude, she rises and carries their cups to the paint-spattered sink in the corner of the studio. "And I'd better get myself perked up and moving. I'm meeting Kenneth and the boys."

At these words, her golden retrievers, Sophia and Grace, scramble up and dance around her, their coats shining in the sun streaming through the windows.

⚜

Margaret stands at the crest of the hill watching Annie descend and cut into the woods toward her home. Thoughts of Jake, the childhood friend who married this girl from away, blur her vision, and she is back at his bedside, the air electric as he passes. Annie's strength in finding her way back to life, a life on her own, in just a few months still amazes her.

Watching her now—the elegance of her long-legged stride, the grace of her nearly six-foot frame, the easy sway of her calf-length wool coat— Margaret smiles. "Oh, to be tall and self-assured," she says aloud as she signals the girls to come.

Her cell phone rings in her pocket as she walks from her studio to her house. It's an unknown number, and she ignores it. Inside, she fills her water bottle and changes into her hiking boots. The phone rings again. The same number. About to decline again, something compels her to pick up.

"Is this Ms. Meader? Margaret Meader?"

"Who's calling, please?"

"I have to talk to Ms. Meader. Nobody else."

Noting the urgency, the catch in the woman's voice, she answers quietly. "This is she."

"Do you remember the woman who smashed her car into a telephone pole a while back? Hit her head and wandered away and they called you to—"

"Yes. I remember." A dizzying pain sizzles through her temple, forcing her to close her eyes.

"You still there?" The voice takes on a desperate note.

"I'm here. Her name was Molly. Molly…" She searches for the last name.

"Makepeace. You helped find me."

For a moment, Margaret is confused. Then she realizes what the woman is saying. "Molly? How are you?" Again, the stab of pain.

"I need you to listen carefully. Are you listening?"

"Yes." The pain worsens. Margaret bends forward, nausea rising.

"I'm about to go again, and this time I don't want to be found. Understood?"

Stunned, Margaret is unable to answer.

"Please." It's nearly a whisper.

"Talk to me, Molly."

Silence.

"How can I help?"

"By not finding me."

Margaret stands holding a silent phone, the pain ebbing, the nausea subsiding.

She weighs the wisdom of calling Jay Horner, the detective on the case back when Molly went missing. He was the one who called Margaret a week into the investigation. And he was the one who took heat from his superiors and ribbing from his peers for bringing in the "bat-shit-crazy lady." Even after she found the missing woman and helped resolve other cases including the recent case of a kidnapped teen, they teased him relentlessly.

Her thumb hovering, ready to scroll for his number, she looks at the time and pockets the phone. Kenneth is waiting. She'll call later.

⚜

As she enters the woods at the top of the far hill, Margaret's thoughts circle back to her initial experience of Molly Makepeace. The search had been difficult—the images indistinct, the process laborious. As she gazed at the scarred and twisted telephone pole for a last look before giving up, a flash of color across the field had pulled her focus. That fluttering scarf caught on the thorns of a wild rose bush, the first piece of physical evidence, led her on.

Molly was found in a convenience store three towns away with her head pressed against the glass door of a standing freezer unit, gazing at the ice cream. Margaret watched from Jay's unmarked car as two officers walked the woman out, her skin pale, bruises from the accident still visible on her sharp cheekbones, her dark eyes disturbingly empty. A sense of unease lingered for weeks afterwards.

Now this phone call, stirring the discomfort, raises questions. Were all the bruises from the accident? Where was she headed, and why?

She quickens her pace on the trail. Time to take Molly's plea, *Don't find me,* to heart. The woman clearly wanted to leave her husband. A sliver of guilt prickles. She helped send her back to him before. Time to let her be.

⚜

He stands at the top of the hill, waiting. The sight of him there, his dogs, Maxie and Gulliver, flanking him, lifts her heart and flagging energy. Sophia and Grace gallop toward them. Released by a simple nod of his head, the two black labs race to greet them halfway, and the circling and chasing and weaving begins. Kenneth is lost in laughter, head thrown back, wild gray curls dancing in the brisk wind as she approaches. She admires his lined and handsome face—the warmth of it, the ruddy glow, burnished by the sun and wind from a life lived out of doors, the hint of stubble scattered across his jaw and chin. When he greets her with those sea-green eyes, she is suddenly shy, self-conscious, aware of the flush brightening her cheeks. To recover herself, she looks out over the field of autumnal wildflowers spread below, the romping canines in the foreground.

"October in her glory," she says as she joins him. She is sixty-two-year-old Margaret Meader again—not the shy girl of a moment before.

They stand in silent communion with the natural world. The cloudless sky is bright blue. The sun heightens bursts of early color on the hardwoods and deepens the purple of the swath of blueberry scrub off to the right. The air is crisp, carrying the scent of apples and woodsmoke.

"Indeed," Kenneth says simply.

The dogs, alert to the stillness of the two, circle up to them, bumping and nudging each other and them. A crackling in the bushes at the edge of the woods has four bodies—two golden, two black—poised at attention, heads raised.

"Stay." Though spoken by two, it comes out as one curt command.

All is silent. Then the dogs visibly relax, tails wagging in playful anticipation. A man with a tall walking stick steps out of the thick undergrowth beside the path. His expression is unreadable as he approaches, but Margaret smiles in greeting and steps forward, the dogs dancing around her now.

"Hello again," she says, stopping just before reaching him.

He smiles, his dark eyes widening in recognition. Bowing slightly, he acknowledges her greeting with a nod. "Sister Grandmother. It is good to see you again. And your friends, of course." He bends to pat each dog in turn. "I have just visited your waterfalls. Beautiful in fall as well as summer. I was tempted to camp beside them and stay for a while."

"You're more than welcome."

"Afraid I must be on my way. Promises to keep and all." As he speaks, his eyes search behind her.

"Oh, sorry," she says. "This is my … friend, Kenneth. Kenneth, this is—"

"Wic," the young man says just as she realizes she never asked his name on their first encounter nearly two months ago. The sun glistens along the copper and gold of his outstretched arm as he offers his hand to Kenneth. "Wicasa."

They shake, each man taking the measure of the other. Kenneth nods, an easy acceptance in his casual stance.

Turning back to Margaret, Wic says, "I see you've found it."

She feels herself flush again, mistaking his meaning for an instant— aware of the unnerving proximity of Kenneth and the knowing look in the young man's dark eyes.

"What you had lost," he adds, rescuing her from her momentary fluster, "when last we met. It has returned, I see. The aura of emptiness has dissipated. You've righted yourself." He grins, looking at once like a little boy and a very old man.

She is back in the late-summer woods, meeting him for the first time. A strange yet familiar encounter. He came down the path, walking stick in hand, an agelessness about him, a distant look in his nearly black eyes. The dogs then, as now, relaxed into his presence.

"Lost?" he asked, knowing she was not lost in the woods but had lost something—something important.

She'd always had visions and dreams and simple "knowings." Those intuitive abilities seemed integral to who she was. And though they set her apart as an oddity to many, she'd never known life without them. Until last August. Suddenly they were gone, and she was trying to come to terms with that loss when Wic came along.

She smiles at him now. "Yes, it's returned, but I'm not sure I've completely righted myself. I keep waiting for the other shoe to drop, taking it away again."

His smile is beautiful, his voice warm and reassuring. "What if there is no other shoe?"

Her breathing settles. "I like the sound of that."

She turns to Kenneth, who has been taking in this conversation in silence. "This young man helped me to realize that my *second sight*, as our friend Sam Kingston calls it, does not define me. Without it, I am still me. Not diminished. Just different." She turns back to Wicasa, "Thank you for helping me get to that."

"I have carried your lesson of acceptance. It has helped others along my path. *You* have touched others along my way, Sister Grandmother. I am happy to know you are still carrying the gift. 'Other Wise' again." He smiles. "Namaste," he says, bowing with his palms pressed together at his heart.

As he turns away, Margaret sees him walking through a lush valley, mountains rising in the distance ahead of him. They are clothed in thick vegetation with moss-covered stone walls and terraces cut into their rocky heights. Overhead, a flock of small birds swirls, swiftly changing formations. *Murmurations.* The word slips into her mind as the cry of an eagle pierces the air.

The vision is gone along with the young man.

The dogs saunter several yards down the path after him, then return to nose around in the bushes.

"There's a place I'd like to show you," Margaret says to Kenneth, and leads the way into the woods. The trail looks much different from the day she first found it, so she takes her time searching for familiar landmarks. Finally, she sees the ancient stone wall littered with falling leaves and forest debris, and she follows it until it crumbles into nothingness. Sophia and Grace have raced ahead, knowing instinctively where they're headed, Maxie and Gulliver following.

As they slip into the narrow slice in the rock face, clouds pass over the sun, leaving them in momentary darkness. Then the passageway before them brightens, and Margaret follows the playful sounds of the dogs up ahead. As the walls open out, she turns to watch Kenneth's face as he takes in the beauty of this hidden cavern. Sunlight streams through the perfectly round hole in the domed ceiling. The ancient glyphs carved into the surrounding stone shimmer in the play of shadow and light as the walls curve outward and down. The waterfall cascading from the side wall sends water droplets up to glisten in the air. A breeze spirals in from the opening, shivering the leaves on a stand of birch trees and rippling the surface of the pool.

Kenneth turns slowly around. "I had no idea this was here," he whispers.

"I was coming from here on the day we met. I had just discovered it."

He looks at her for the first time since entering. "You mean on the day we literally bumped into each other."

They laugh at the shared memory. He was coming down from the ridge above, crosswise to her path, looking off to the side. She was in a state of reverie following her discovery of this place, walking with her head down. And they had run into each other, both nearly falling.

They'd exchanged a few words and parted, and she remembers now how buoyant and alive she'd felt going home. Then later, without knowing who he was, she hired him to build a new studio to replace the one gutted by a set fire. Reflecting on it now, she is still amazed that this highly prized, award-winning architect agreed to do the job.

One after the other, the dogs leap into the deep pool stretching to the back wall as Margaret and Kenneth settle on two rocks at its edge. Catching movement above, Margaret looks up to see a great blue heron glide overhead. As she watches it, the sky suddenly darkens and a gunshot pierces the air. Sharp pain sizzles through her skull. She tucks her chin and hunches forward as it intensifies.

Images flash, a flickering montage of color, light, and sound. A zigzag of lightning. A crack of thunder. A fat limb, thick with lichen and moss, crashes to the ground in an old growth forest. Raindrops pock the surface of a swampy pond. A baby cries. A woman screams. A twisted telephone pole leans, silhouetted against a white sky on an empty country road. A massive boulder rises from a snowy field. A horse rears. Its rider lies unmoving on the ground, head twisted at an odd angle. A hawk swoops and rises, a rabbit squirming in its talons. A woman, white-blonde hair to her waist, sweeps her arms skyward. Blousy sleeves cuffed at the wrists riffle in the wind. A stag leaps in a wooded distance, backlit by a nearly full moon. A chestnut-haired woman rocks a bundle in her arms, humming a lullaby, the lyrics familiar but just out of reach. An old woman slumbers, her tiny frame lost beneath the lumpy comforter that couldn't warm her in the end. Her mother's wrinkled mouth opens, her voice a paper-thin whisper. "I kept it from you. I thought it for the best. Forgive me." A final image hangs in the air. A black sketchbook tied with a rag. Empty darkness settles as the image fades and the pain in her head dissolves.

"Margaret?"

She opens her eyes. She's on her back on the ground. Kenneth is bending over her, his face framed by a circle of bright blue sky. The four dogs stand around them, posturing high alert.

"Just give me a minute," she says as she sits up. "Sorry. I just need a minute."

Kenneth is sitting back on his heels, trembling. She scrambles to her knees facing him. His eyes are nearly colorless, his face too pale, his breathing shallow and unsteady. She grabs her water bottle. "Here. Drink."

He drinks and sits back staring at her, shaking his head.

She takes his face in her hands. "I'm so sorry. I—"

"I thought you were dying." It comes out a rasped whisper. "I..."

She throws her arms around him, sobbing garbled reassurances that dissolve into soothing, wordless sounds. He slumps forward into her, surrendering to vulnerability. She rocks them both until she feels a surge of energy ripple through him. She pulls back and watches the sea return to his eyes. He leans back in and hugs her.

"It's not your fault," he says as they rise and walk to the water's edge. "It just... It took me back to—"

He doesn't have to finish. She sees what he's seeing as he gazes into the water. A woman is lying on a sculptured floral carpet. Her thick red hair is spread out in waves around her face and shoulders, stark against the subtle shades of peach and soft green etched into the rug. Her eyes are open, her mouth distorted. His beautiful Liza, a sprinkling of pale freckles across her nose.

As the image fades, Margaret waits.

"An aneurism," he says. "My wife. Liza. She died of an aneurism. We were talking. Just standing there talking. And suddenly she was on the floor."

Margaret's heartbeat flutters and then settles.

They walk in silence, the rhythmic swaying of their bodies turning them each inward. He, she suspects, into memories of a day he'd sooner forget; she to worry about their deepening friendship. The dogs are subdued, loping along on either side of the trail, heads down.

"Here's where we get off," Kenneth says as they reach the knoll. "I left my truck at the new job site and trekked up from there." He points down into the valley where a narrow swath cuts through the thick forest to the south.

Panic seizes her. Is this it? Does their relationship end here? She's jolted him back into the trauma of his wife's sudden death. How can he not be on edge in her company?

She's back in Camden, standing in the doorway of her home as two police officers deliver the news. Pain floods her body, numbs her mind. Joe, her beloved husband for such a short time, gone in a blink. Killed by a drunken driver, unlicensed but hellbent on getting to his next bottle.

"I'll be pretty much out straight for the next week or so." Kenneth's voice brings her back, his words confirming her fears. "This job isn't the joy that building your workshop was. I made a big mistake in agreeing to do it, but I'm committed now."

Here it comes, she thinks. *He's easing away from me.* She maintains a neutral smile.

"My daughter wants to have us over for dinner one night. Can I call you on short notice when I have a better idea of the timing?"

She stares for a moment, gathering herself, breathing again. "Sounds lovely. I have a gallery order I need to finish, so I'll be sticking close to the studio, eating at my worktable. A real dinner break will be welcome, no matter how last-minute."

"Mandy will enjoy dazzling you with something fabulous. She's looking forward to meeting you."

A twinge of anxiety as he turns to leave. Then he whirls around and bends for a brief hug. "I never asked if you were all right back there. It must have—"

"I'm fine." She places her hand on his chest to allay his concern. "I'm just sorry you had to be there. There is a price to pay for hanging around with me, I'm afraid."

"I'm not. Afraid." With that, he calls to his dogs and heads down the hill.

She watches him descend and disappear into the trees.

Chapter 2

"I kept it from you. I thought it for the best. Forgive me."

Her mother's whispered words follow her home and up to her bedroom where she drops to her hands and knees. She drags the heavy box out from under the eaves and sits staring at it before removing the lid. She reaches in and takes out item after item, laying them around her on the rug. Near the bottom lies a folded burgundy smock.

She lifts it to her nose. It smells of linseed oil and old paint. She buries her face in it. Him. It smells of him. Of pipe tobacco and coffee beans and male sweat and something she can't quite name.

She is kneeling on this same rug, mesmerized by the sight of him standing at his easel, sunbathed in brightness. Hand held high, gripping a fat bristled brush, he is poised to attack the canvas already thick with paint. His loosely woven smock is flecked with paint spatters of varying hues. His dark eyes are ablaze, and the look of pure concentration on his face has shut out her and all else. He is one with the canvas and the paint and the moment. She bears silent witness to the act of creation danced to the edge.

That was the morning before—the sun-filled, breeze-softened morning—before he shot himself. And she has that morning back again. That shimmering morning, a sense of magic floating just beneath the tick of ordinary time. And then it's gone.

She knows all the objects in this box of her father's things. Nothing new to discover here. No large black sketchbook tied with a strip of sheeting. And yet something has been calling her attention to this box.

"It's Mommy's, Maggie. Not Daddy's."

"Mattie?"

Her twin brother's voice switches from that of the little boy he was when he died to that of the mature male she's come to know in recent weeks. "It's Mommy's box," he says. "It's hidden away in her hidey-hole. 'Shh,' she would say. 'Everyone needs a little secret place, my curious boy.'"

"Her hidey-hole?" Margaret smiles at the little boy word spoken in a grown man's voice.

"In her sewing room, Maggie. In her close-the-door-and-have-a-little-mending-time room. Remember?"

Margaret's mind wanders to the days after Mattie's death, after his terrible fall in the woods, when she would go to that very room and sit in the rocker and wait for the mending her mother spoke of to begin. Five years old and alone for the first time since before she was born. Missing the lost part of herself. Missing the brother who'd floated beside her in the womb from the very beginning. A beginning she vaguely remembered as a scattering of light and a burbling of underwater sounds.

Margaret rises and walks down the hall. The door to the room is closed. Kept closed but for an occasional airing since her mother's lingering death in another room downstairs.

The door creaks as she opens it. The stillness stops her on the threshold, the waiting silence a palpable presence. She lets out the breath she's been holding and steps inside. Tidiness and order make the room seem more spacious than it is.

"A place for everything and everything in its place." She hears her mother's voice, endlessly repeating this mantra against her daughter's need for creative clutter. "Everything has its place, Maggie," she'd insist. Which begged the question for Margaret: "Even me?"

She lifts the lid to the cabinet under a dormered window. The black sewing machine embellished with golden scrolls and flourishes lies on its side in the recessed compartment, gleaming dully. She runs her fingers over the lettering, then closes the lid with a dull thud. She opens the drawers down the sides one by one. Segmented interiors are filled with notions and accessories categorized and labeled. Sewing needles, common pins, scissors. Spools of thread, ribbon, and embroidery floss arranged by color. Buttons and beads. Trims and bindings. All in appropriate wells.

She reaches in and pulls out a coiled measuring tape, yellow and black. Unfurling it, she slips it around her neck, letting the ends hang down in front like a scarf. How often did she see her mother draped thus? How often did she watch her jotting measurements in her little notebook as she created patterns for dresses or pants or a man's wool vested suit? How often as a child did she count out the inches? Sixty every time.

Closing the last drawer, she turns in a slow circle, wondering how a hidey-hole has remained a secret from her for all these years.

"I used to hide in it," Mattie says into the quiet of the room. "But then she put the box inside and I couldn't fit anymore."

Margaret walks to the opposite side of the room.

"Getter colder," her brother teases, reviving the old game they used to play.

Her eyes scan the wall beside the tiny closet in the corner diagonally across from her. She walks to it as her brother chants, "Getting warmer!"

And as she runs her hand down the door casing inside the closet, he laughs, yelling, "Hot. Hot. Hot!"

A sharp sting. A blood drop sprouts on the tip of her finger as she pulls her hand out. A darker splotch of red on white snow flashes and is gone.

"Oh, no! Sorry, Maggie!"

"It's okay, Mattie. It's just a scratch." She sucks the fingertip. "I should have been more careful. I didn't know the closet goes behind this little partition. You helped, Mattie." Again, she's transported back to childhood. Again, he's shivering beside her. So very sensitive. So careful not to hurt others. Such a sweet spirit.

Margaret reaches up and tugs the string hanging from the bare bulb in the closet. Squatting, she pokes her head inside and examines the simple metal latch nearly hidden along the outer door casing. As she flicks it upward, an invisible door pops open to reveal a narrow cubby. She peers inside.

But for the large tin sitting among the cobwebs, the space is just big enough for a very small boy to tuck himself inside, knees to chin. Memories flood her as Margaret pulls out the tin. It's the bread box that once sat on the kitchen counter beside the matching cannister set. She remembers sitting beside her brother, squinting as the morning sun bounced off the box's shiny red surface and danced across the room to play with their flashing spoons. And later, standing alone before it as a teen, flipping open the hinged lid and breathing in that yeasty aroma of freshly baked bread she would always associate with her mother. Once an ordinary household tin, integral part of the prosaic rhythms of dailiness, it is now a secret trove hidden away from sun and spoon and girl child.

She sits on the hard wood of the floor, hands resting on the cool metal, mind roaming inner landscapes in the sepia tones of the past. Her phone rings, barely audible, left in her bag somewhere downstairs. She remains unmoving.

"Open it, Maggie. Let's see what's inside."

"I'm not sure I dare. She thought it best to keep it from me."

"I think there's something in the box for you, Maggie. Something you should know. Why else would she come to you? Why else ask forgiveness?" Her hip protests as she uncurls herself from her cross-legged sit. "Why, indeed?" The box rattles as she sets it on the sewing table. She lifts the lid, and a whoosh of lavender rushes up her nose. The tiny vent holes along the back side are sealed with bubbles of clear glue, keeping the scent in and tiny critters out. A folded cloth covers the contents. She lifts it out, her fingers tracing the nubbly flowers embroidered along the hem of the bureau scarf. Laying it aside, she removes the items beneath it one by one, quieting her mind to simply be with each. A packet of letters tied with string. A black and white photograph with scalloped edges. She and Mattie, toddlers bundled in snowsuits. A tiny box of baby teeth. A bracelet woven of sweetgrass. A velvet ring box with two coiled locks of reddish-brown hair tied in ribbons, one blue, one pink. "Chipmunk colored," she hears her mother say.

She eases out a soft bundle wrapped in tissue paper. As she unwraps the pair of blue knitted caps, her mother's laughing words float back to her. "I was so sure you'd both be boys! I should have listened to Lucinda. But I was so sure."

Smiling at the words and memory of her mother's eyes as she spoke them, Margaret looks down at the last item in the box, the black sketchbook tied with a strip of torn sheeting. Laying the hats aside, she reaches in, breath held. The air thickens around her. Her ears buzz. Her vision narrows. Her mind blurs into a white nothingness.

She exhales, her fingers tingling as she pulls the book to her chest and closes her eyes.

Warmth radiates from its pebbled surface. It spreads into her hands and chest and rises to flush her cheeks. The strip of raw muslin wrapped around the book gives off a faint odor of turpentine, cedar, and pine as an unfamiliar heaviness settles in her body. It weights her in place as she stands at the table. Remembering now that this table belonged to her father's mother. This was Lucinda's table. Lucinda's room. Lucinda's book.

The bookshelves downstairs are stuffed with photo albums and decorative boxes filled with memorabilia from both sides of the family. Each artifact a piece of the family story. So why would her mother hide Lucinda's book?

I kept it from you. I thought it for the best. Forgive me.

Margaret pulls over a chair and sits. Carefully, she works out the knot and unties the cloth binding. As she lays the book open on the table, a sheaf of loose pages slides out. Charcoal sketches and complex ink drawings. Soft watercolors in various stages of completion. Poems with slashes and corrections written in erratic strokes.

She spreads them out, taking them in as a whole while zeroing in on certain aspects. Her gaze stops, focusing on three words faintly scratched beneath a nebulous egg. She looks more closely at the egg and the watery images within. Two babies float, umbilical cords entwined. *Maggie and Mattie,* written beneath.

"She knew us before we came." Mattie's voice echoes in the silence of the room, dancing with the dust motes in the thinning shafts of sunlight.

Margaret moves the drawings aside and flips through the book's pages. An artist's journal—a blending of imagery and written passages—all in her grandmother's hand. Some entries are dated, some are not. There are gaps, long periods of silence followed by a flow of daily entries.

Again, Margaret hears her phone ringing downstairs. She looks around. The room is darkening, shadows spreading into the corners. It's late afternoon, and she hasn't eaten in hours. She scoops up the book, the loose pages, and the binding cloth and leaves the box and its contents on the table.

She starts to close the door behind her as she steps into the hall, but lets it swing back into the room instead.

🌿

At the kitchen table, a steaming cup of tea before her, Margaret opens the journal. On the inside cover the name Lucinda Hamilton Meader is written in a delicate upright script, no slant. Almost childlike, yet radiating quiet strength.

White space sets off a simple prayer on the first page.

> *May I be of service today.*
> *May I never forget that my gifts come through me and are not of me.*
> *May the blessings be.*

Below it is a sketch of a single pine tree at the edge of a pond. A lone heron stands on the far side.

Margaret turns the page.

I've always had the dreams.

She sits back in the chair, tears welling. She breathes in the words again. *I've always had the dreams.* This simple statement reaches into the deepest part of her being and touches a place she's never dared acknowledge. She feels her brother's presence gently urging her back to the page. She wipes her eyes and reads on.

Sometimes they filter in as I sleep and burble up when I wake. Other times the one called the Shepherdess ushers them in.

One time when I was little, She brought the same dream night after night. With a rustling of fabric, She swept into my room, draped in a mourning cloak. She bent low and spread the scene before me with a wave of her shepherd's crook.... I felt the deep rumbling before I saw it. The terrible flash flood. Not of water, but moving just as fast. A dark viscous something. Screaming people running out ahead. Some not fast enough. An overpowering smell stinging my nostrils. Burnt sugar. Beyond burnt....

Then two nights with no dreams at all.

And then it happened.

Margaret knows what her grandmother is describing before she turns the page. She's read about the incident. She takes a breath and opens to the drawing sketched across facing pages: a huge tank at the top of a hill blowing its top and bursting its sides; something brown and thick erupting into the air and flowing like lava down toward the houses below; people running for their lives; one man, his face a mask of agony, lunging forward as the flow overtakes him; nearby buildings collapsing as the tar-like tidal wave knocks them from their foundations.

Margaret scans her grandmother's rendering of this tragedy that she witnessed as a child—a week before it happened. Two million gallons of molasses burst from a holding tank on a hill above Commercial Street in the North End of Boston in January 1919. It killed people, maimed others, swept away horses and carriages, and destroyed buildings in its path. Just recently, Kenneth brought it up in a conversation about the loosening of government regulations around building standards. He pointed out how often we wait for disasters to occur before regulating. He explained that the Great Molasses Flood and the more famous Coconut Grove Fire led to standards and codes unknown before and taken for granted today.

But the details of the event, though horrific, never affected her so deeply as they do in this moment as she looks down at Lucinda's dreamscape. A little girl dreamed this event again and again. A dream so vivid, she could reproduce it in detail as an adult.

I didn't know it was molasses. And I didn't know when or where it would happen. I just knew it would and that I couldn't stop it.

I had such dreams when awake too. I would meet someone and see a scene. Or I'd know the secret they were carrying. Or I would know something was going to happen to them. Usually something bad.

When I was very little, I blurted out what I saw. But I later learned to keep it to myself and tell my parents only when we were alone. Still later, they told me that Dad and his sister Jenny Lynn had the dreams too. They called it "the sight" and said it ran in the family.

Dad taught me to breathe my way through them. And the Shepherdess began to help too. When she brought the dreams, she told me to step outside them and watch them unfold without emotion. And Mother did her best though she didn't have the sight. She listened and soothed me when I was full of questions and confusion.

Margaret looks up, nodding. Lucinda had someone to guide her—someone who didn't hush her and pretend her experiences away. Someone to comfort her. A moment of quiet envy surprises her, and she shakes it off with a shudder.

"I'm glad they were there for you," she tells her grandmother. "I know how much that must have meant."

As she sits with this, the air around her is empty. Handling the journal and running her fingers along the handwritten words hasn't brought even a glimpse of the Lucinda she longs to see. She settles back in her chair and is startled when her phone rings in her bag on the harvest table by the door, reminding her she's ignored it twice already.

She retrieves the bag, but by the time she digs the phone out, the caller has hung up. Since she doesn't recognize the number, she waits to see if they've left a message. Nothing.

She's reminded of the earlier call from Molly Makepeace, and this brings back questions she started to ponder before her walk with Kenneth.

What does she really know about the woman? Does she have family besides the husband who clung to her at the police station when she was returned? Does she have children? Friends? Was she running out of fear or looking for a fresh start?

Her mind wanders back to the search for her. Why such difficulty zeroing in on her? Why had the images been so hazy, the messages jumbled?

"Trying too hard," she says aloud with a sigh and a smile.

Sophia and Grace wriggle up to her, wagging their tails and nudging her from both sides. "You're right. A walk will do a world of good." She throws on her coat, hat, and gloves. As she slips her phone into her pocket, it rings.

She can see the smile behind his voice as Kenneth greets her. "Hi. Sorry for interrupting your work, but Mandy has asked if we can do dinner tomorrow. A necessary shipment has been delayed on my jobsite, so I'll be free. I'm hoping you can make it?"

"I'd like that." She says it without hesitation despite the fact that she has already been sidetracked and is even further from meeting her gallery deadline.

"Great. Pick you up at six tomorrow then."

⚜

As she enters the woods, the girls well ahead of her, the light shifts, making it feel more like dusk than late afternoon. A strong impulse steers her to the left at the first fork in the path. She whistles to the dogs who have gone the other way, and they crash back through the underbrush toward her. The way becomes steeper and rockier the deeper in she goes. The girls stay near, loping along, running ahead and circling back in waves as she climbs.

When she arrives at the clearing with the huge glacial erratic known as Wandering Rock at its center, she stops, surprised. She's gone just beyond the eastern edge of her property into Land Trust territory. She didn't intend coming this far this late in the day. Lost in the placing of each foot on the ground, she had become the walking. Beyond thought. Beyond plan. Beyond the darkening of the day.

She runs to the mammoth rock and places her hands on its cold face. She leans in to press her left cheek against it, listening. Images from Charles Simic's poem "The Stone" filter into her mind. "So perhaps it is not dark inside after all." She closes her eyes, imagining her way in as she recalls the final lines. "The strange writings, the star charts / On the inner walls."

Smiling, she backs away. She turns around and steps into a six-inch snowdrift, yelping in surprise. At her feet, a body lies facedown in the snow.

She flattens herself against the rock as blood reddens the snow, spreading slowly toward her. She closes her eyes and is inside the corpse. Cold. So very cold. Screaming without sound. Reaching without movement. Pleading without words.

A cold wind stings her cheek, and she is standing at the far edge of the clearing looking back across brown and brittle grass toward Wandering Rock.

Sophia and Grace have come close, their dark eyes sharp with concern. She shakes free of the vision and buries her hands in her coat pockets with a shiver. Head down, she hurries toward home, the girls at her sides all the way.

As soup warms for her dinner, Margaret pulls an old cardigan on over the thick sweater she's already wearing. Unable to dispel the deep chill she's carried home with her, she surrenders to the wisdom of layering and ministering with hot liquids. As she gathers up Lucinda's drawings to set them and the journal aside, one drawing slips out and flutters to the table—a sketch of a body splayed on the ground, the head cocked at an unnatural angle. Suddenly she's back in the cavern with Kenneth, reliving the flurry of images she envisioned there. One image is strangely illuminated, drawing it into stark relief against the rest. She watches again as the horse rears and the rider flies backward through the air and lands with a jolting bounce. This time she hears the crack as the neck snaps on impact. This time the scene widens to reveal the field and Wandering Rock just yards away. This time she can see that the rider is a young woman, her blonde hair cascading out from under her helmet and encircling her twisted neck like a delicate ruffle.

Back in the kitchen with the sound of soup bubbling on the stove, she looks at the drawing in her hand. It's the same young woman, her hair curling about her throat. But in the drawing, her face is turned upward, her eyes open, looking into Margaret's. Drawn decades ago, Lucinda captured a question in those eyes.

Lucinda, the grandmother she desperately wishes she had known. The woman through whom she received this gift of seeing and knowing, but who left too soon to teach her its ways. The woman who could have soothed her through the difficult adjustments.

For a moment, anger at her mother flares. Vivien, the mother who knew what her daughter carried inside. The mother who told her to bury it—to hide it and herself from the world. Vivien, the fragile wife and daughter-in-law who hid this journal away, this important piece to the puzzle that was her daughter's life. This connection to the line from which she came. Vivien, the mother who consciously kept her bewildered child in the dark.

"How could you?" she asks aloud.

"How could she not?" a voice answers.

As she turns toward it, she steps inside a memory. Her mother, long dark hair falling forward around her beautiful face, bends over her sobbing father. Maxwell is on the floor, a near empty bottle lying in a puddle of amber liquid beside him. A battered canvas covered in thick splotches of blacks and purples hangs from his easel, a hole punched in the center.

"There, there," Vivien says, lowering to sit beside him on the floor. "Some black coffee and a hot bath and you'll feel yourself again." She takes him in her arms, stroking his head and cooing softly. He folds into her, allowing her to rock his shivering body.

"I can't get them out of my head." He cries. "Can't get them onto my brush."

"Tell me about them," she whispers. "Paint them with words, my love. Help me to see."

Margaret sucks in a breath as the scene shimmers and shifts. She's standing in her father's studio now, looking out. She watches her mother cross the yard, her face an empty white, her arms at her sides. She holds the gun so loosely in her right hand, it looks ready to fall. Her hazel eyes shine as she turns back toward her daughter before stepping into the house.

The scene dissolves.

"I'm sorry, Mother. I didn't understand. I never really tried."

Again, she looks at the sketch. Again, the young woman's eyes ask questions. Eyes she's seen before.

She hears the thud of a car door in the front yard, and the dogs jump up and scramble to the back door. As she tucks the drawing inside the journal and sets it on the china cabinet, there's a tap at the door and a familiar hello as it opens.

In a flurry of doggie greetings, Emily Donne is welcomed in. Her freckled cheeks are flushed from the evening chill, and a fiery burst of spiraling curls bounces around her face as she stoops to receive wet kisses before giving Margaret a quick hug.

"Ned's moving to a higher level of physical therapy at a new rehab," she announces, green eyes shining as she plops into her usual chair at the table. "Oh! You're about to eat. Sorry for dropping in unannounced. I can—"

"There's more than enough for two, and you know you're always welcome." Margaret retrieves two bowls from the cabinet shelf. "You come bearing such good news, the least I can do is feed you."

As she sets out the bowls and spoons, she's reminded of Emily's first visit. It was early summer, and she'd come seeking the woman her uncles Otis and Mert had described as a real puzzler. Filled with curiosity and questions that needed answers, she eventually accepted Margaret's help and a friendship blossomed.

"I've always loved that piece," Emily says, nodding toward the turquoise cabinet with its copper fittings and decorative carvings down the sides. "And those dishes. The colors. They make me think of the desert where bright colors pop against the brown landscape."

"They were my mother's. The dishes and the cabinet," Margaret says as she sets the bowls beside the stove. "From her time in New Mexico."

"Ah. No wonder. And the dolls? Did she make them?"

Margaret stops ladling the soup into the bowls. She turns and looks up at the pair of cloth dolls slumped shoulder to shoulder, feet dangling from the top shelf. Their yarn hair is interwoven with sweetgrass, one headful short and spiky, the other flowing to its knees.

"No. My grandmother made them. My father's mother, Lucinda." Margaret remains motionless, staring up at the dolls, aware of the quiet presence that has entered the room with them. A soft humming fills her mind as an image of gnarled fingers braiding sweetgrass flickers and disappears, leaving behind the familiar scent of the grass. An afterimage hangs in the air for a moment—a luminous egg, two babies floating inside. As it fades, she feels her brother's little body bumping against hers in the warm and watery world.

"They're so sweet. Well-worn and well loved." Emily says.

"Yes." Margaret says no more as she fills their bowls and slices a loaf of sourdough bread.

In keeping with the introspective tone that has settled between them, Emily remains quiet as they eat. Finally, she lowers her spoon and says, "Ned's been working hard for two months now, but he's reached a plateau and he's depressed. I was hoping it would begin to lift by now, but it's deepening."

Margaret slips back to that day in August when she knelt on the ground on the mountain, fear thick in her throat. Ned, part of a rescue squad with the Game Warden Service, was caught in a landslide in a search for lost hikers. In her mind, she could see his battered body amid the debris of a cave-in. He was close to death, and yet she found a way to talk to him. With her voice as a tether, she asked him to rise up and show her his surroundings so she could guide the searchers. She'd always felt a bond with this young man, but in those moments he was more like a son to her than friend. And the fact that he'd met Emily through her and they'd fallen in love, added another level to her desperation.

"I'm really scared." Emily's words bring her back.

A note in her voice reminds Margaret of the night they sat at this same table shortly after they'd met. Emily had written a piece about her dead father and distant mother. As Margaret listened, offering comfort, the dogs announced an arrival. It was Ned. A child was missing in Tilson Woods and he needed her help. On the way to the site, with Emily in the back, Margaret felt the sizzle of connection between the two.

"He's pulling away from me." Emily says, again drawing her back. "He's rejecting my help, and I don't know what to say or do that won't send him further away."

"You're right to be concerned."

Emily straightens in response to this straightforward reply.

Margaret hurries on. "The physical pain is bad enough, but this kind of recovery work takes a tremendous emotional and psychic toll as well. He's always been so vital, so active and healthy. That works both for and against him in this. He may never regain full mobility and strength, and on some level he's beginning to understand that. He has to find the balance between hope and acceptance."

"You've seen something." It's a statement. Not a question.

Margaret looks her in the eyes, knowing truth is always the best path. "I've seen him struggling. Felt his pain and frustration. Sensed him pulling away, as you say. But I've also seen radiant scenes of happiness. Isolated glimpses. Snapshots. All just moments. I can't see the outcome because the future is his to create. And yours."

"But how?"

"It's time for you to ask yourself some deep questions. Your answers will help you navigate whatever is to come."

"What questions?"

"Ah, there's the rub. Life is always about finding the right questions."

Emily is silent for a while. Eyes closed. Hands folded in her lap.

Margaret rises. She gathers their dishes and carries them to the sink. Then she ushers the dogs out the door for a run and returns to the table. She waits for Emily to speak.

"Am I strong enough—is our very new love strong enough—to deal with the really hard stuff? Am I prepared to be in this for the long haul, however long that may be? If he only partially recovers, will he be the Ned

I fell in love with, or will this change him irrevocably? And if I allow him to push me away, will I be able to live with myself?" Leaning forward, elbows on the table, hands folded one on top of the other, she looks to the ceiling.

"Yes." Margaret's voice is soft. "Those kinds of questions."

"Now I'm really scared." Emily rests her chin on her folded hands and looks across at Margaret.

"That's good." Margaret leans in to meet her gaze. "It means you're facing the reality of what's in front of you. It would be so much easier to escape into fantasy or busyness and avoid the hard work that comes with being human. Easier to let him push you away, shed a few tears, and move on with your life." Margaret settles back against her chair. "Avoidance is so much easier. Less scary."

Tears slide down Emily's cheeks and she makes no move to wipe them away.

"How about I pay him a visit tomorrow? Alone." Margaret offers. "And you take some Emily time. Sit with your questions. Write. Meditate. See what comes up."

Emily nods. "That sounds ... good."

"How's your writing coming along? We haven't had a chance to catch up in a while."

Emily straightens, wiping her eyes and looking across the room. Slowly, she begins, easing into an update on her novel in progress. Margaret watches the worry lines along her brow melt as she talks.

And as she listens, an image blooms. Gordon Willoughby, the young man who died in the cave-in in that rescue attempt, appears. He stands as she saw him that day on the threshold between life and death. Wanting to turn into the brilliance just beyond, he chose instead to come back into his ravaged body. But this time, Margaret watches as he bends over Ned's still form and whispers, "Don't waste it. This life you get to live. Don't waste a precious minute."

As Sophia and Grace yelp to come inside, Emily grabs her coat and bag and readies to leave. She hugs Margaret and greets the girls as they scramble in out of the cold. With a quiet thank you, she closes the door behind her.

A burst of fragrance—rosemary, sage, and lemon verbena—greets Margaret as she reaches for her grandmother's journal and sets it on the table. She turns back to the cabinet and takes down the rag dolls. As she holds them to her chest, the subtle scent of sweetgrass seeps inside her, carrying memories so old, they surprise her with their specificity. Swaddled as one, she and Mattie rest against Lucinda's ample breasts, drinking in lullabies as nourishment while their exhausted mother sleeps nearby. Melodies melting one into another. Words indecipherable but laden with love. A tear slipping onto her tiny cheek.

"She knew I wasn't going to stay long." Mattie's voice is so soft. So sweet. So baby small. "She knew I'd leave early and that your life alone would be hard for a long time. And she knew she wouldn't be here to help. So, she held us tight and loved us hard. And she left you her book."

Margaret revisits the cluster of visions from the morning in the cavern. The woman rocking the bundle is Lucinda, cradling not one but two babies. The woman on the bed, her mother, shimmers now as she changes from old to young and to old again. Young: sleeping after childbirth. Old: shivering on her deathbed. Her grandmother nurturing the just born twins, knowing what lies ahead. Her dying mother begging forgiveness.

Wanting time to sit with the book and savor each page, each authentic mark, she feeds the girls and steps outside with them. As they race down to the stream, she lets her mind rest in these newly awakened memories. She wraps the cardigan more tightly around the sweet-smelling dolls she's carried with her and breathes in this precious moment—this moment before.

She settles the dolls in the Morris chair in the corner of the kitchen and sits at the table. A cup of tea and plate of apple slices beside her, she spreads the loose drawings around the journal and opens it to the last page. To her grandmother's final entry.

And so, Maggie Mine, I see for you a life of service to a higher purpose— a hard life at times, punctuated by heartbreak and loss. But I see it as a life steeped in love and highlighted by moments of inexpressible joy. I will not be there for most of it. And so I do my best to infuse your early days with love. I hold you close to my body and immerse you in the warmth of my being and light of my knowing. I sing and read poems to you in readiness for all that is and all that will be. I leave you this journey-book filled with sketches and scribblings to companion you as your version of the gift unfolds. We each have our own, you see. It manifests uniquely for each of us.

Many will fear you because of this gift of Sight my family has passed down to us. They will strike out at you, hurt you, shun you, hate you. But you are a carrier of the Light. No matter what they say or do, remember that. Your Daddy may falter, too heavy his gift. But he prepares a way for you. You carry the best of him. And you will pass it along to daughters and sons of your heart.

The Buddhists say life is 10,000 joys and 10,000 sorrows. In that sense, yours will be a very normal human life. How you choose to live each day of that life, my beloved child, is up to you.

love,

Grandmother Lucinda

Beneath her name she has drawn a heron in flight against an October blue sky. Margaret feels the delicate brush in her own hand, moves her wrist just so to catch the flicker of a feathered wing. She breathes in the momentary peace once done—the work as complete as it will ever be.

heron's pumping wings

echo of my beating heart

coming home to nest

The three lines come to her as one. Five, seven, five. Remembered or freshly given? She can't be sure. She feels no urge to write this haiku down. She knows she won't forget.

Shaking herself more fully alert, she flips to the front of the journal and pages through it, gathering images and impressions as she goes. Drawn to a passage or phrase or mark, she stops from time to time, but moves on. She consciously holds herself aloof, scanning, observing, noting. Guarded on some level she doesn't quite understand. Seeking an overview before reentering at some later time to move more slowly—more deeply.

She settles into a rhythmic monotony of hand and eye. Turning. Scanning. Turning. Scanning. Turning. Stopping.

Her hand hangs in the air above the page. A black-and-white photograph. Glued to the center of adjoining pages and creased down the middle from the many openings and closings of the book, it is highlighted by a narrow brush-width frame of red paint. A candid shot of her father—laughing, dancing, dark eyes alight—his infant son and daughter in his arms. Scattered around the photo are deft studies in charcoal, all of his face caught unawares in darker moments. Black eyes troubled. Brow perplexed. Front teeth pressed into the lower lip. And within the mix, a different face arrests her eye. The face of a round-cheeked boy who looks like her, eyes wide, head cocked with listening. And in the bottom right-hand corner of the busy page, tiny words are inked in black on a patch of white.

Margaret bends closer, squinting to read her grandmother's hand.

too sensitive

too sweet

to bear the knowing of
too much

She closes the book, her hand still on the page, marking it. Not wanting to let it go yet not able to continue looking. She bows her head and allows the feelings to come. An ache in her chest. A pain above her left brow. A thickness in her throat. "Everyone thinks it is the heart, but it is not, it is the throat." ... The words of the poet rise, then stick there. "And it is the throat that will close in around us until / we cry, or laugh, or say yes, or / finally scream no." "Throat," the title poem of a chapbook tucked somewhere in a bookcase in the other room. S. Stephanie, was the local poet who made her lift her head and listen more deeply as she read her works aloud at an artists' gathering.

Her thoughts trail off, the thread lost. The sweet distraction abandoned as sensation breaks through. Insistent. Demanding recognition.

Pain. She slips behind her father's eyes, seeing her child-self seated on a chair. His little model trying so hard to sit straight and be good. For him. He sees the look in her eyes—the wanting to be outside woven through the wanting to please. He sees that she is called by the natural world without, while drawn to the wilder world with him.

And then he knows. In one terrible moment, he knows his little girl is seeing something beyond the room in which she sits. Not the fields outside. Something beyond that, something beyond the sight of him kneeling before her. And he knows he cannot reach her there. Knows not how to help her through this moment of sudden sight. Knows beyond doubt that he's passed it on.

Seated at the table in her darkening kitchen, Margaret bends into her father's agony, forcing herself to feel it fully. A montage of images spreads before her. Her brother Mattie, such a little boy, tumbling into the ravine, bruised and broken on his way down. Her own young body trapped in a root cellar, her desperate cries rising into empty air. A man facedown in a muddy puddle, too drunk to lift his head. A young woman smiling as she walks into water, stones in the pockets of her dress. A series of faces, twisted mouths laughing and jeering. Backs turned, fists clenched, knuckles bloodied.

The line of images stretches to breaking. A curling reel of film flaps wildly on an old-fashioned projector. A blinding light flickers on an empty screen.

Before she can straighten, thinking that it's over, she's inside her brother's head. The crinkling of a candy wrapper, the buzzing of a bee, the slamming of the bathroom door—all of a level, all too much. Exaggerated beyond the ordinary thrum of daily life, simple sounds assault her ears. His ears. His tender ears. And then the voices come, the whisperings, the cries for attention. The ugly words. The vicious taunts. The strident warnings of things to come, things that can't be stopped. Tides that can't be stemmed. Tales that won't end well.

Again, she sinks into the anguish. Knowing now from the inside out what it must have felt like to be her father or her brother or the woman with the stones in her pockets.

She realizes sitting here, her hand still inside her grandmother's book, that for some sensitive souls the gift of too much knowing is beyond unbearable. She understands for the first time her father's devastation at what his children would go through. How responsible he felt. How impotent. The famous Maxwell Meader, revered for the ethereal quality illuminating his paintings, couldn't reconcile it with the shadow side of such light.

And Mattie. Dear, sweet Mattie. Gone at five years old. Too tender for the too loud world. Leaving her to grieve at every birthday since. Her twin. Her other half.

Lucinda knew. Knew it all. And Margaret slips inside Lucinda's breaking heart and sobs. Sobs for her father, her brother, Lucinda, and herself. Tears she thought she'd already shed. Feelings she thought she'd processed long ago.

When the sobbing stops, she reopens the book to the page that started it all. Her father dancing in the center, she and Mattie babies in his arms. She strains to remember being in that happy scene. Tries too hard to breathe in the smell of him, to sense the sway of his body, to hear the music of his laughter, to be in the dance. Nothing comes.

She flips the page and finds a mirror image of herself. Not her child self but her older self. More wrinkled. More fleshy. More … present.

"Lucinda." She breathes the name aloud. "You knew me before I grew to know myself."

Across this future face, more words cover the page.

You are the last of the line, dear Margaret. None remain to guide you. But the Sight will serve you well for all your long and well-lived life. Countless folk will benefit from your wise and prudent care. Some will merely brush your sleeve and be forever changed. Some will run from you, afraid. And some will do you harm. Yours is to remain here and do your quiet work. Trust in the rightness of this. You will love and be loved more deeply than you'll ever be hurt.

No healer ever lived who was not wounded first. And you are a healer, dear Maggie Mine. In these pages, I leave messages of hope. I will teach as best I can how to live this other way of knowing.

Margaret gets up, leaving the book open on the table. Anger at her mother sticks in her throat. As she paces the kitchen, mumbling, Sophia and Grace lift their heads, eyes following her.

Finally the words erupt. "How could you keep this from me all these years? How could you not know this would have helped? Knowing I wasn't an aberration. A freak! Or as the Bible thumpers loved to tell me—an abomination!" She grabs a pot holder and hurls it across the room. It flops against the far wall and slides to the floor without a sound. "Damn!" she shouts as she pounds the table with her fist.

The dogs are up now, nervous, shuffling in place, until she begins to laugh as she drops back into her chair. "A pot holder? Really? Not the dramatic oomph I was looking for." She rubs her shoulder and then reaches out to the girls as they rush forward. "I think it's time to throw a few sticks. What do you say?"

They're at the door before she has her coat on. The cold has deepened as she steps out into it and looks up into an overcast night sky.

Chapter 3

The dogs are already stirring as Margaret awakens. The bedroom is dark, the thick curtains closed against the cold. Usually quick to rise, she snuggles deeper under the covers. *What if I were to just stay here all day?* The thought, so unlike her, makes her laugh. "Because you have promises to keep and you have to face the cold floor sooner or later!"

She grabs her robe, slides her feet into her slippers, and crosses the room. As she sweeps wide the curtains, she gasps. The world is white with several inches of snow and fat flakes swirling in a light wind. She blinks, thinking to dispel the vision. But it's real. An early snow has come in overnight. Not unknown in October in Maine, but not common either. She'd simply not been paying attention to the forecasts or the mild ache in her hip.

She drops a slice of bread in the toaster as she poaches an egg. A rumbling out front has Sophia and Grace racing to the living room at the front of the house, barking. After a couple of passes to the driveway with his plow, John Longfeather toots in farewell and is gone.

"Time to dig out the shovel," she says to the girls as she finishes eating. "Luckily, I didn't drive at all yesterday and the car is still in the barn. Talk about unprepared!"

An hour later, she has shoveled the walkways, front and back, as the snow continues to fall. As she's stamping her booted feet on the mat by the door, her phone rings on the counter across the room by the stove. Stepping into her slippers, she rushes to catch it, ready to explain to Emily that she'll go to visit Ned when the roads are cleared. The phone stops ringing as she picks it up. The screen tells her it was Detective Jay Horner calling, and she waits to see if he's left a message.

She listens as he asks her to call him, and a twinge of guilt niggles. She should have called him yesterday.

He answers on the second ring.

"Hi, Jay. If this is about Molly Makepeace disappearing again, I owe you an apology. She called me yesterday and—"

"Molly Makepeace called you?"

"Yes. She asked if I remembered her and told me she's about to run again. Told me not to find her. Sorry I didn't call you right away but—"

"Molly Makepeace is dead, Margaret."

His words land like a punch. She leans against the counter for support. "Dead? Are you sure?"

"I'm standing in a field looking at her body right now. It's definitely her. ID in her purse, plus I recognize her from before."

"But…" She can't finish her thought. Her mind is grappling with the fact that she sees and feels nothing. No images. No words or phrases. No sense of connection to the woman she spoke to only twenty-four hours ago. That same odd lack of clarity, the same emptiness she experienced last time Molly Makepeace came into her life.

"Where?" She finally verbalizes one of the churning questions that has surfaced.

"She's lying in the snow out by Wandering Rock. Do you know it?"

Margaret lowers into a nearby chair. "Yes. I was just out there yesterday."

"Hate to ask you, but can you—"

"I'll be right there. I assume the roads up there are plowed. I don't have the truck anymore."

"Yep. I'll tell them to let you on up here."

※

All the way to the site, Margaret replays her phone conversation with Molly, then revisits her vision on her walk yesterday. The body lay at her feet, and she slipped inside it briefly with no sense that it could be Molly. She thought of her as the woman thrown from her horse in the earlier vision. So, she didn't make a connection, and she still felt nothing.

As she gets out of her car and heads toward the ribbon of police tape fluttering in the wind, she can see Jay and a woman standing back as several people in protective suits lean over the body. She shivers.

Wrapping her scarf more tightly around her neck, she stops several yards from the group. Jay and the woman are talking quietly. A photographer is taking pictures from various angles. The three suited persons are studying the body and the ground immediately surrounding it, their voices muffled. Several uniformed men and women are fanning out into the woods from the outer edges of the clearing. The snow cover within the clearing is undisturbed except in the vicinity of the body.

She waits, watching and listening. After a while, she closes her eyes, hoping to adopt a more receptive stance. Silence but for the murmur of voices and the distant crunch of boots on snow invites her to deepen her inner gaze. A subtle wetness touches her cheek, and she opens her eyes. Huge flakes swirl in a sudden flurry and dance playfully around the frozen body on the ground. Wandering Rock rises into the whiteness, a hulking figure waiting for a return to peaceful solitude.

"Tracks." A shout dispels the quiet.

A barked order sends several people in the direction of the call, all carefully traveling the periphery and then off into the woods. A sudden image fills Margaret's field of vision. A mound of ragged pelts. A dirt-streaked bearded face. Thick matted curls framing a pair of pain-soaked eyes as blue as her own. The staccato rapping of a frightened heart. A feral grunt.

"Stop!" She is surprised a moment later to realize the word came from her.

Jay runs to her side as she again calls out, alarm rising. "Stop them. Please, stop them!" She's screaming now, caught up in an empathetic response to the old man's terror. Feeling his fear as if it were her own.

"What's wrong?" Jay is bending over her as she crouches, trembling.

"This is not about him, Jay. Please make them leave him alone. It's nothing to do with him."

They're interrupted by a piercing scream. Primal, more animal than human. It rends the air, leaving behind a vibratory signature shivering through her bones. Everyone stops, momentarily frozen, mouths open.

Inside the pause, in the rift in time that follows, Margaret reaches out to him, hoping to calm the hammering of his heart, quiet the thrumming of his blood. Even as she feels the futility, she desperately tries to reach those who are grabbing at his flailing limbs, trying to subdue this untamed spirit. Begging them to let him be.

With a curt command, Jay shocks her back to external reality. She looks up at him and straightens. "They're manhandling him. This"—she points toward the body—"is not about him. I'm sure of it. James is not connected to this in any way. Please make them stop." It takes all her restraint to deliver this calmly.

Jay walks over to a uniformed trooper she doesn't recognize. As they talk, the other man exclaims, "We found a suspect in the woods yards away from a dead body and you want us to let him go? Seriously?"

Jay places his hand on the man's shoulder as he leans in and says something. The man seems to mull this over, then nods and takes out his phone. A minute later, he speaks to Jay and heads off into the woods.

"He got away," Jay assures her as he comes back to her side. "Seems his tracks completely disappear a few yards into the thickest part of the woods. No sign of him at all." At her obvious relief, he adds, "They'll continue searching, but I don't think they'll likely find him."

"Good. Though I can't imagine why he came this close. James steers clear of people."

"James who?"

"James Harchett. Known around here as Odd James. And by some as Odd James Hatchet. A Vietnam vet. He lives in the woods, a hermit who prefers the natural world to that of men. Local lore thrives on 'Odd James' sightings and stories. Lots of stories."

Margaret stops, losing herself in a memory.

Standing in the woods in the farthest corner of her property, she hears an unusual bird call. Puzzling over its source, she looks up to see something large leap from the middle branches of an old pine to the thick limb of a young oak. She wills herself to be still as what appears to be a large animal turns toward her. Through the tangled mass of dark curls, sharp blue eyes stare into her own. She meets his gaze, acknowledging the brief sizzle of connection with the slightest upward turning of her lips and a gentle nod. He stays crouched on the limb, bare-chested and in ragged camouflage cutoffs, his eyes softening as his lean, muscled shoulders relax. And then he's gone, disappearing into the leafy canopy of midsummer's forest without warning.

Did she imagine the shadow of a nod in return to her own? She wonders still as she returns her attention to the snowy field of cold and death.

"Even if he's not involved," Jay says, "he may well be a witness to whatever happened to Molly. They'll want to question him, I'm afraid. Hell, I'd love to question him myself."

Margaret opens her mouth to respond, but changes to a different tack. "So, you're sure it's not suicide, I assume."

"Definitely not. But beyond that, we won't know until the medical examiner is done with her. My guess is hit from behind and strangled with her own scarf. Sometime in the night before the snow started. It then covered her and any tracks or evidence, but we'll protect the ground around her from the elements. Being October, this snow should melt off soon. Weather report calls for rising temps. Then we'll do a more thorough search of the whole field and the surroundings. Would you mind stepping over to the body with me? I'll clear the technicians away and give you some time to—to pick up whatever you can."

As they walk toward the body, the woman she'd noticed earlier approaches. Margaret notes the aura of sadness about her and senses it's not because of the circumstances of this day or the work she does, but something much deeper and more personal. As Jay introduces her as his new partner, Cynthia "Cyn" Green, the woman offers a quick, firm handshake and stiff nod but does not smile. Her olive skin and caramel brown eyes would be a more beautiful combination, Margaret decides, if there were any lightness at play there. Then she chides herself for such a superficial assessment.

"You're the psychic," Cyn states without preamble.

Margaret's jaw tightens as she withholds a taut response to the label.

After a moment of awkwardness, Jay jumps in and says, "Margaret has helped us many times. Usually to find lost or missing persons. As I told you before, I asked her to come here to see if there's anything she can offer that helps us." His tone imparts a mild rebuke.

"I don't know what I can offer," Margaret says. "I've never worked on a case like this, but I'll see what comes up." She turns to Cyn Green. "I don't use the word *psychic* to describe myself or my process. Too many charlatans and grifters have tainted the word. But other than the outlandishness surrounding it, the word does apply."

Cyn nods in response, and Jay follows Margaret along the narrow path leading into the circle of untouched snow around the corpse.

Margaret steps closer, placing her feet carefully in already disturbed patches. Jay and Cyn stop a few feet behind her, and Jay nods when she turns to him before beginning. She closes her eyes and whispers a prayer, asking to be of service to this dead woman and these officers into whose care she has been given. As she opens her eyes and looks down on the frozen body of Molly Makepeace, smaller flakes are falling around her. The woman's upturned face surprises her. In her vision, she was facedown in the snow, but Margaret dismisses the discrepancy. The face, an uncanny blue and mottled red, reflects the final moment of terror—eyes wide, mouth open in an unfinished scream, lips curled back in a grotesque scowl. Snowflakes land lightly and dissolve into the thin layer of hoarfrost along Molly's cheeks, reminding Margaret of freezer-burned meat. There is an odd beauty to the delicate crystals clustered around her open mouth and eyes.

Margaret stands mesmerized as the image of the young rider thrown from her horse flickers across the empty face of the corpse. She sees the question in the eyes of the sketch drawn by her grandmother and wonders if the answers are hers to find.

Behind her, someone clears their throat, moves impatiently. Irritation sizzles, and she nearly snaps out an angry curse. But the moment is gone. The moment of almost knowing something important. Of almost grasping the wisp of insight as it lifted up and away, drifting past the corner of her left eye just above the pale scar and out of reach. Lost. At least for now.

A shadow descends as she turns away from the body and toward the two detectives. Ominous and dark, it threatens to pull her into its depths and hold her there. It tugs at her, weighing her feet and legs down as she tries to move. She struggles to shake it off, looking toward Jay as if for help, and then she realizes its source. His partner, Cyn. It's coming from Cyn. The air around her is thick with a gray mist. It permeates her being and pulses outward as fingers of liquid smoke reaching for something—someone—to grasp. A momentary panic seizes her before she summons the calm reserve that sits always at her center.

Fortified, she turns back to the body and circles it slowly with her mind. Pain jolts her as she rounds to the back of the head, and she drops to a squat. Forearms resting on her thighs, she bends to peer at the woman's head and neck. Gasping in surprise, she claws at her wooly scarf as it's pulled tightly around her neck from behind, choking her. Then as the scarf loosens and cold night air rushes into her burning throat, she screams.

All is quiet for a glorious moment afterwards. Dim stars flicker overhead. Wind stirs the branches of the towering pines. A coyote calls out. Fingers squeeze her windpipe.

Her skull is fractured by a single brutal blow, and she crumples to the ground. Nearly toppling onto the frozen body, Margaret cries out. She catches herself before she disturbs minute particles of evidentiary material. Before she contaminates a crime scene. Before she lives up to all the misgivings of all the law enforcement personnel she's ever dealt with. Before...

Jay pulls her to her feet, soothing her with the familiar sound of his voice, bringing her back into the present. As Cyn Green steps toward her,

Margaret throws out her arm. "No! Please." It's all she can manage as she steadies herself, gathering what she can of the experience before it fades.

Cyn stops, frowning. She looks from Jay to Margaret and back again. It is clear she expects an explanation. Without thinking, Margaret says, "Such sadness. I can't... I—I'm sorry. I need to separate this from you, what's here from what's in you. Sort through... I'm sorry. I can't explain better than that."

Cyn backs farther away, her expression unreadable.

As her focus returns to the body, Margaret realizes she was not leaning over it. There was never any danger of contaminating anything. She physically remained several feet away the whole time.

Again she squats and closes her eyes, feeling her way back into the experience before the... She shakes her head, dismissing thoughts of everything but the task at hand. She adopts a detached stance, a neutral witnessing awareness, and places herself back at the moment of the blow to the head. Pain sizzles as she slips inside the body. Passing through the pain, she listens.

A grunt. The soft whistle of something flung through the air. A muffled thud. A faint shiver in the earth beneath her before her body is rolled roughly onto her back. The dim stars overhead fade as a veil of clouds skims the darkening sky. Thick-gloved hands paw at her chest and sides, fumbling in and out of her pockets as they go. A sound she cannot name and then the unzipping of her purse. The scattering of its contents on the hard ground. A scrabbling through the dry leaves and brittle grass. A curse.

A screech. A thrashing in the woods. Booted feet thudding away. A truck engine rumbling to life well down the entrance road. Exhaust fumes hanging in the crisp October air. A star winking through a break in the racing clouds.

A thick stickiness warms the back of her head. The smell of wet animal fur. A hovering presence. Softness brushing her face, turning her head to the side. A mild pressure on the side of her neck. Cool flakes landing lightly on her cheek. An empty darkness closing in. Silence.

"She was choked with her scarf and then struck from behind." Jay leans down to catch her whispered words. "He threw something away, maybe what he used to hit her. That way." She points off toward her left as she rises. "He was wearing gloves, and he searched her body and dumped out her purse and rummaged around in the contents. He dropped something light into the mix. Then something scared him off. He ran away in heavy boots and drove off in a truck parked down the road."

Something tells her not to mention the rest. To keep it to herself for now. To wait until she has a chance to sit with it. She trusts Jay implicitly, but no one else.

"He?" Jay says. "You sure it was a male?"

"Is that what I said? *He*?" She stops to reassess her impressions. "Yes. The grunt. The curse. Definitely a male voice."

"Just one?"

"Yes. At the moment of death anyway." She says it without hesitation.

Jay continues to question her before releasing her with a promise to meet soon for a proper interview. "I assume you'll write down anything else you recall, as usual," he calls after her as she walks, head down, back toward her car. As she passes Cyn Green, she stops and apologizes for her rudeness.

"Not a problem." Despite the accompanying curt nod, Cyn's brown eyes linger on Margaret's face, then she turns and walks away.

As Margaret climbs in behind the wheel, the smell of her car's interior stops her spiraling thoughts. Recently forced to relinquish her well-seasoned pickup truck, she hadn't intended on buying a car, let alone a new one. But her friend John Longfeather convinced her that the peppy little hybrid would suit her needs, and his brother gave her a more than fair deal. She's decided John was right to pull her out of an old mindset, but the new car smell still surprises her every time she gets inside. A reminder of old habits giving way to change.

She sits without starting the engine, her mind sliding back to the body lying just yards away. And then to thoughts of James Harchett. He frightened off the killer, then visited the body. She is sure of it now. His calloused finger pads pressed against her neck, checking for a pulse. His training as a medic overrode his need to hide away from the world of human cruelty.

The thought of gathered evidence sending the police in his direction with the wrong idea has her tapping her phone. She watches from afar as Jay pulls his phone from his pocket.

"James Harchett was there but he's not the killer. You have to know that. And you have to protect him. I think I can help with that."

Jay looks toward her car and then out into the surrounding woods. "You're sure?"

"Yes."

"Okay. I'll hold off on that line of inquiry until we talk further. Only because I trust you. But I will need to find him and talk to him soon. For now, I'll focus the manpower elsewhere."

She watches him sigh heavily as he slips his phone in his pocket before turning back to Cyn.

⚘

Back at home, she puts a pot of vegetable stew on to heat while she gathers her cold-weather hiking gear. She fills her winter backpack with a smaller pack of foodstuffs, a loaf of bread, and a thermos of the stew. Just outside the back door, she straps a set of snowshoes to her pack and heads down the hill, the girls racing ahead of her.

It's nearly noon by the time she reaches the far corner of her wooded property. She steps into a patch of sunshine brightening the snowy landscape through an opening in the tree cover. She commands the girls to stay at her side as she drinks from her water bottle, the sun warming her face and bare hands. Sweat prickles her chest, back, and underarms.

She looks around. A narrow trail of small tracks crosses the snow in front of her and disappears into the thick brambles to her left. Birds chitter in the trees overhead, and a clump of snow plops from a sunlit evergreen branch. The only other ambient sound underscoring the stillness is the faint trickling of water. It's the natural spring she first discovered as a child, protected by a thick stand of spruce and a jutting expanse of granite ledge sprinkled with sparkling mica chips. Though tempted, she doesn't poke through the tangle of undergrowth to the source.

"James," she says softly. "I hope I'm right in thinking you come here. Please accept this offering and the note inside. I mean you no harm."

She loops a nylon rope over the thick crotch of a maple tree and hangs the smaller backpack from it. She attaches a plastic bag with an index card inside with his initials printed in large letters. With gloved hands, she rubs down the pack with a pine branch and some sage she carried in her pocket and then hoists the bag high, tying the rope off around the trunk of the tree.

⸙

Back at home, she showers away the chill from the rapid cooling of sweat inside her hiking clothes. Then after a quick bite, she's back in the car and heading for the rehab center where Ned Burrows has been upgraded in his physical therapy.

☙

Standing in the hall looking through the windowed door, Margaret watches a painful scene play out for the second time. The first time was weeks ago, and she was seated in her own backyard. This time, she looks on from the hallway as Ned collapses onto the right-hand bar of the parallel walking rails and sinks to the gleaming hardwood floor. He rolls on his back, grimacing, surrendering to a wave of despair. This time, Emily is not there with him, and he does not bark at her and send her away like last time. The vision has changed only in that way. The agony is palpable now.

As she reaches to open the door, she sees a gray-haired woman standing by as if waiting for his frustration to dissipate. As she bends to him, she says, "I think that's enough for today. Good work."

Margaret steps back out of sight as the woman helps him into a wheelchair. The door swings open and Ned is wheeled through, and she greets him as if she's just arrived.

"I thought we'd take a short ride in the sunshine if you're up to it," she says. "First snow of the season, and it's gorgeous out there."

Ned hesitates and she goes on before he can refuse. "I imagine you're feeling a bit antsy cooped up inside on a day like this."

He slumps back in the chair, resigned to go along.

☙

Not far down the road with miles of untouched white fields on either side, he straightens in the passenger seat. "You're right. It's beautiful. Makes me want to strap on my skis. Makes me..."

His words trails off, and she doesn't fill the gap, doesn't urge him on, force him to say what he's not ready to say.

She slows and turns onto a single plowed lane leading through a short stretch of pine woods to Cott's Pond. As they come out into the sunshine again, it bounces off the car's hood and the surrounding snowbanks and glistens on the surface of the water. She stops and rolls down the windows, and they sit listening to the natural world. Wind. Bird calls. The flapping of wings as a lopsided V of Canada geese fly low overhead. She feels Ned relax into the seat beside her. He sighs and leans his head against the cushioned headrest. The scream of an eagle brings him upright, eyes searching the treetops along the distant edge of the pond.

"Thank you," he whispers. "I needed this." He turns to her with a small smile. "I didn't know how much."

They share a thermos of hot chocolate and quiet conversation—simple words about ordinary things—as the sun moves down the afternoon sky. Then Margaret turns the car around in the retreating tracks of the plow and heads back to the center, Ned nodding off beside her.

Exhausted, he settles into an armchair in his room when they return. She gives him a quick hug. "You're on your way back to yourself. I've seen it." She lets these words sink in. "We'll talk further next time."

She turns back as she reaches the door. With his eyes lightly closed and a smile on his handsome face, she notes the hint of color in his cheeks.

As she passes through the lobby on her way out, the gray-haired therapist nods and winks, a broad smile spreading across her pleasant face. Margaret stops. The woman's nametag reads Virginia Felder, DPT. Margaret extends her hand.

"Margaret Meader. Ned's a pretty special young man, Dr. Felder. I'm glad to see him here. You have a wonderful reputation."

"Ginny, please." She shakes Margaret's hand. "He has quite the reputation himself. He's barely arrived and we've been inundated with calls asking after his recovery. Quite the community hero, I hear."

"That and so much more."

Ginny's eyes brighten suddenly. "Margaret Meader. Now I remember. You're the one who helped find him and the others that awful day. He came to us with a very public backstory, with you at its center. I'd love to know more about your methodology."

"I had a connection to the team who found him. That's all."

"I understand your reticence. Sorry. Clinical curiosity is an asset in my work but a drawback in a social context. I didn't mean to pry. Glad to have you on board."

Margaret smiles. "Ned's going to do well with you on his side."

"Between us, we'll get him there."

As she exits the building, a quick snapshot clicks in her mind of this amiable woman lifting Ned's arm in a victory salute. Out the window behind them, the trees are covered in green buds ready to burst.

Chapter 4

Five o'clock. Kenneth is picking her up at six, and she's just arrived home. She lets the dogs out for a quick romp while she calls Jay. They arrange for him to come by in the morning, and she hurries upstairs to change for dinner with Kenneth's daughter.

Settling on a royal-blue tunic and gauzy scarf over a black turtleneck and leggings, she slips a pair of comfortable flats into her oversized purse. Her thick hair gets a quick finger comb before she gathers it up in a silver clip, and she adds lapis lazuli earrings and a dab of pale lipstick before heading downstairs.

Kenneth is his usual punctual self, and she slides her feet into winter boots as he comes through the door. As she grabs her coat, he takes it from her and helps her on with it.

"I've no idea what Mandy has in store for us tonight," he says, "but it's bound to be delicious. I told her you're not a meat eater, so we're safe from any exotic animal experimentations. Beyond that, it'll be an adventure, I'm sure."

A sliver of concern surfaces and then sinks into the depths of let's-not-think-about-it as they head out. A little discomfort is understandable with a first meeting, she reasons. They chat about Kenneth's latest project until he pulls up in front of Mandy's condo.

As Mandy reaches for Margaret's coat in the entryway, a spark of static electricity snaps between them. Eyes wide, they share an awkward laugh at the unexpected zap, but Margaret notes an underlying sizzle of something else—something akin to repulsion coming from the younger woman. Hoping she's mistaken, she follows Mandy through the living room and on into the kitchen.

The appliances and countertops gleam with modernity. Spartan yet well-appointed with every possible convenience—some she can't identify—the kitchen is, to Margaret, both spacious and claustrophobic. A part of her mind marvels at this curious combination she's never experienced before, but she withholds judgement as she adjusts. *Open your mind, Margaret. Embrace the new. That old mindset is fighting to hold on.* But she knows this is not about the kitchen. It's about the woman who inhabits it.

"Amazing," she finally manages to say. "What an incredible work space." She runs her hand over the domed top of an unfamiliar stainless-steel appliance. "And look at these." She indicates a small platter of sushi, nori-wrapped circles of color and texture artfully arranged. "How beautiful. Almost too lovely to eat." As she sits on a stool at the counter beside Kenneth, she notes the slight frown that flashes and disappears on Mandy's face.

As they sample this first course, Mandy peppers Margaret with questions about herself. At first the questions are innocuous enough—how long has she lived in the area, is her family native to Maine, what does she do for work—but gradually they grow more pointed. Was she ever married? Divorced? Does she have children? Why not? Margaret answers succinctly, mostly with a simple yes or no. But this clearly doesn't satisfy Mandy's curiosity. She continues to probe as she turns away to the stove to deep fry their next course, tempura shrimp and vegetables. It feels more like an interrogation than a friendly getting-to-know-you conversation, and Margaret becomes more and more uncomfortable. She tries slipping in easy questions of her own, but Mandy drills back relentlessly with an undertone of hostility. For his part, Kenneth seems oblivious to his daughter's intensity and Margaret's discomfort as he continues to sample the sushi, exclaiming over the flavor combinations his daughter has concocted.

A mingling of enticing aromas fills the space as the sizzling oil makes quick work of the tempura course. With a flourish, Mandy sets out bowls laden with lightly crisped delicacies, along with an array of dipping sauces. "Voila! I've added a touch of my own, Americanizing it a bit. Hope it works for you."

Grinning appreciatively, Margaret and Kenneth respond as one: "Oh, my!" They exchange a look of shared delight and laughter.

"If there's any of your dead people hanging around," Mandy says, "tell them hands off." Her laugh has an unpleasant edge to it.

Margaret takes a beat, looks over at Kenneth, back at Mandy, and decides to make light of it. "Just us. It's all ours." With this, she picks up her chopsticks.

"Just making sure no unwanted guests came riding in on your coattails. Or perhaps there's a way you could dispel them?"

"I'm not quite sure how to respond to that. I do experience things in an unusual way, but I'm neither a medium nor a witch." She manages a laugh.

"Maybe you could tell me how this psychic business of yours works? I admit, I'm curious. I mean, why would you want to tell people things they're not meant to know? Aren't you concerned that your methods are ethically questionable? Morally dubious? Spiritually suspect?"

Margaret sets down her chopsticks and stares at the young woman. She debates leaving the room before responding, but that would widen the chasm already gaping between them. So, she meets the challenge head on. "Excuse me?"

Eyes wide, mouth open slightly, Mandy feigns innocence. She looks for a moment like a sly teenager playing games with Daddy's new woman friend. "I'm sorry. I didn't mean to offend you. But I naturally have questions. I'd hoped you could talk me through them. You have to admit, your story is ... unusual."

Understanding the situation better now, Margaret chooses another tack. "Answering your questions as posed would require a deeper, and maybe harder, conversation than I think we can have over dinner. You clearly have some strong opinions on what you call my 'psychic business,' and I'm not sure what you mean by my 'methods.' Perhaps you could explain what your overall impression is and we can go from there."

She smiles and lifts a tempura mushroom to her mouth. But as soon as she pops it inside and bites down, she gags. It's beef. Batter fried on the outside but raw in the center. Without thought, she spits it out into her hand. Then she rushes to the sink and drops it into the bin underneath. As she washes her hands and rinses her mouth, embarrassment swells.

With as much dignity as she can muster, she returns to her stool, her cheeks burning, and apologizes.

Kenneth leans in to her. "Are you allergic to mushrooms? I didn't know. I'm sorry. Will you be all right. Should we—"

"It wasn't a mushroom." Mandy almost sounds apologetic. Almost. "It's beef. My Americanized version of tempura. A little surprise I thought you'd like."

Margaret lays her hand on Kenneth's. "It's okay. I'm not allergic. I just haven't eaten meat for so many years, my body reacted instinctively. The taste and texture ... I'm sorry. I'm thoroughly embarrassed." Head down, cheeks still burning, she says, "You've gone to such trouble and everything is so lovely." As she looks up, meeting Mandy's eyes, she sees the satisfied gleam of triumph.

"I told you Margaret doesn't eat meat, Mandy." Kenneth doesn't look over at his daughter, his focus still on Margaret.

But Margaret sees the flash of anger in Mandy's pale-green eyes. The flash that doesn't match her tone and words as she claims she didn't hear him. She apologizes profusely until her father turns his attention to soothing and reassuring her that no harm has been done.

For the rest of the meal, Margaret barely tastes her food. She answers more dinner-appropriate questions as simply as possible with the sole aim of getting through the evening and out of there. A heaviness presses in around her, and she struggles to maintain a light tone. Struggles against the desire to call the young woman out—to have it out. Struggles at times to breathe.

She's aware of Kenneth's discomfort as they gather their coats and say their good-byes. She's aware of Mandy's smug resistance to engage in any meaningful way. And she's aware of her own deep disappointment at her remarkable failure to navigate a situation she should have anticipated without the benefit of second sight.

In the car, silence sits between them for several miles. Then Kenneth clears his throat and speaks into the emptiness between them. "Not the evening I'd hoped for. Sorry. Mandy was out of line with her questions. As for the beef, I'm sure she got caught up in planning to wow us and forgot what I'd told her. I don't know what to say."

"You're her father. A father who not only brought a woman friend to dinner, but one with a dubious reputation. She's protective of you. Of course she had questions and concerns. I should have been sensitive to that. I'm sorry."

"Not your place to be sorry. I'm sure she'll do better next time."

At the thought of a next time, Margaret shudders, thankful for the dark interior.

Kenneth turns to another subject. "When I picked you up, you kept the focus on me for the whole trip. And I, like an idiot, let it go. How was your day before your semidisastrous dinner date?"

Margaret's dark mood begins to lift. "And I'm supposed to be the psychic here." She smiles though he can't see her face. "The truth is, a woman died last night. Murdered."

"Oh? Someone close?"

"No. But someone I've encountered before. A few years ago, she went missing after a car accident and I helped find her. Then she called me yesterday, out of the blue. She said she was about to run again and didn't want to be found.

"It shook me. Though it was inadvertent, I had interfered in this woman's life. Mandy's words may have conjured my guilt."

Margaret sits with this, exploring the emerging feelings.

Kenneth reaches over and touches her hand on her lap. "Your instinct is to help. Of course, you would help find a missing person. Especially if she'd been in an accident. You shouldn't feel guilty for that."

"The whole situation was 'off' somehow. And her call yesterday brought it all back. I debated calling Jay—Detective Horner—about her planned disappearance, but I waited. I thought I had time. And then he called this morning to tell me she's been murdered."

"And you're sure it's her?"

"Yes. I saw the body."

"Saw or 'saw'?"

"Both, actually. But in the vision, I didn't know the body was her."

They're both silent, and she loves that he is giving her the space and time she needs. Images dance in the glow of the dashboard lights.

Finally she speaks. "I was on a walk with the girls and ended up at Wandering Rock. Do you know it?"

"I do. It's a good romp out there for Maxie and Gulliver."

She smiles at the thought of them, then continues. "I'd been standing by that massive rock, lost in a fanciful reverie, imagining what it might be like inside—" She stops, realizing how odd this must sound to him. But having come this far into the telling, she resumes. "And then I turned around, and the ground was covered in snow and there was a body lying at my feet. I ..."

She shivers and decides to keep the experience of slipping inside the body to herself.

"The vision didn't last long. When I awoke to real snow this morning, I had other things on my mind and didn't give it a thought. Then Jay called with the news about Molly—Molly Makepeace was her name—and he asked me to come out there. He's the one I worked with on the original case."

Again Kenneth waits in silence.

"That first time around, Molly's mind was like a blank slate, offering nothing to help me connect. I nearly gave up. Then a physical clue—a scarf caught on a branch—led me onward. But even when they found her, I couldn't get a fix on her. The few images that did arise were blurred, like ... like a double exposure. I wrote it off to her head injury. She'd run her car into a telephone pole."

"That would be understandable then."

"But I'm getting the feeling again that it's something else. Beyond the fact of her phone call saying she was about to run. Beyond even the fact of murder. Something here is ... off."

As Kenneth pulls into her yard, she is still caught up in thinking about this. Wondering about the peculiar sense that something's missing. But she releases it, focusing instead on the man beside her.

"I'm sorry I didn't handle tonight well. Mandy is an amazing young woman. I should have anticipated her concerns. I hope I get a chance to set things right with her. And I hope that we, that you and I, can ... " She leaves the sentence hanging, unable to find the words.

Kenneth turns to her. "I want Mandy to get to know you for who you are. I love my daughter, but she doesn't get to choose my friends."

She places her hand on his on the seat between them. "Whatever comes, I'll be more attuned, more present. Less prickly." She gathers up her purse and reaches for the door handle as he jumps out and runs around the car to open the door.

He walks her to the house and bends to brush her left cheek with a light kiss. "Thanks for coming tonight. A potentially uncomfortable scenario under the best of circumstances." He laughs. "Can I call and check in with you tomorrow? Not sure just when, but—"

"Anytime. Anytime is fine." She reaches up and pushes a stray curl from his forehead, then laughs as it falls back down over his brow, catching for a moment on his lashes. She rests her palm on the center of his chest and whispers, "Thank you."

Smiling, she opens the back door and finds her dogs staring up at her, quiet for a change, brown eyes expectant, bodies subdued. A gentle greeting from this exuberant pair seems fitting in light of the evening she's had. She walks with them to the top of the hill, snow crunching under her boots. Knowing the day's events will soon parade in review, she savors a moment of stillness. The girls off in the darkness. The wind still. The earth at rest beneath an early snow.

Chapter 5

Emily takes a breath before entering Ned's room. She hasn't caught up with Margaret to discuss her visit with him the day before, so she's walking in cold. *Positive*, she instructs herself. *Keep it light and let love guide you.* She laughs. *I'm sounding more like Margaret every day.* And so she enters with a genuine smile and hint of laughter in her voice as she sings out a hello.

Sunshine glancing off the waxed floor and the competing scents of a dozen bouquets lining the windowsills greet her. Ned's wheelchair and walker sit side by side in the corner beyond the tidily made bed. The clock on the wall ticks. Otherwise, all is still in the empty room.

"Well, hello." His strained voice startles her, and she turns. Accompanied by a solidly built older man, Ned shuffles in through the door using only a cane, his right leg dragging slightly. Rivulets of sweat trickle down his pale face, his jaw clenched in concentration. She steps out of the way and watches, a mix of emotions churning.

Each step has him wincing, but he doesn't slow or stop until he reaches the armchair under the row of windows on the far side of the room. The man steps in to guide him as he turns awkwardly and eases down into the chair. He closes his eyes, head against the chairback, and breathes heavily for several minutes. As he opens them, his smile spreads. Those pale blue eyes glisten with wetness, triumph and joy and hope written there despite the weight of his exhaustion.

The therapist bends to take his cane and leans it against the wall. "Hell of a workout, Ned. Well done. See you tomorrow, same time."

He is gone, and they are alone, and she is sobbing with happiness.

"That was amazing. I am in awe yet again!"

"Didn't think I had it in me," Ned says. "These guys around here are taskmasters from hell. Now I need about three days' sleep." His voice is becoming more and more breathy. "But they're not going to let that happen."

"No rest for the wicked?" She laughs.

"Just don't expect a repeat performance anytime soon."

"I don't know how you've done what you've done so far. I don't think I could have."

As he closes his eyes, she asks about Margaret's visit. He yawns and answers without opening them again. "Took me out for a ride. Fresh air, nature... Didn't know how much I needed it." His voice trails off.

Emily waits.

"Sun on water. Untouched snow. Eagle on the wing. Margaret and her..." And he's asleep.

Emily sits on the room's only other chair watching him, his face at peace, sun shining on his blonde head. "Thank you," she whispers. But on the tail of gratitude, anger rides in. She sees Ned striding across a beach. Lean. Muscled. Graceful. Ned laughing, head thrown back. Ned holding her, looking down into her eyes, his face open, so unbelievably handsome. Ned loving his work—the work that took him into the woods, up mountains and cliff faces, down into forested valleys, and along Maine rivers and coastal waters. Strong. Fit. Athletic. Comfortable in his body. His skin against hers, his hips... She has to stop herself from going deeper into this wishing away of reality, this yearning for what has been lost, perhaps forever. This journey into *if only*.

She crosses the room and rolls the bedside tray table back to her chair. Silencing her phone, she takes out her laptop. At first the words don't come as she rests her fingers on the keys, the document open, the cursor flashing. But the anger won't let up. It wants to be felt. Acknowledged. She tries to shake it off, but it persists until her fingers are tingling. She closes the file, opens a blank page, and lets her fingers loose. Soon they're flying, her mind on automatic, her anger racing across the white screen. Finally it slows, walking now. Halting from time to time. More and more white space between the words. Ellipses. Hyphens and dashes and symbols. Elaborate font changes until the words are dancing and no longer anger. Until something close to acceptance settles in, and she can hear music in her head accompanying the movement of her fingers. The music becomes her father's songs. The one he called "Emily's Song" and then the others, "For Janet" and "Family Man." The ones encapsulating his regrets, his *if onlys*. If only life had… If only he'd done this or that… If only he'd been stronger or wiser…

Her fingers stop. The music fades, the dance done. The anger diminished if not gone. What remains is a grace note shimmering in her mind. No more words. Just this shimmering note—and a shift to her inner landscape.

She closes the file and reopens her novel in progress. This time, her main character jumps in to meet her, words tumbling from her mouth. Then other characters join in, the dialogue rising and falling, switching from cacophony to symphony and back. And they don't stop talking until the sun has passed beyond the bank of windows in the room.

Concentrating on trying to finesse a minor plot twist, Emily looks up to find the room darkening as sleet tinkles against the windows.

She looks over at Ned still asleep in the chair, snoring lightly. She rises and searches the closet for an extra blanket and lays it gently over him. "No matter how long it takes and no matter how far we have to go, I'm here with you. I love you, Ned Burrows. And if I could do it all for you, I would."

A slight clearing of a throat tells her someone has entered the room. She turns to find the man who'd been with Ned earlier smiling at her. He turns on a lamp as he explains that it's nearly Ned's dinnertime and he has to get him ready to get back in bed. "He's worked hard today and deserves dinner in bed. Sorry to send you out, but—"

"That's okay. I have a class tonight, so I have to be going anyway. Thanks for all you do for him. I'm Emily."

"I figured. He talks about you all the time. I'm Carlton. You got yourself one determined young man there. His progress has been amazing. Even on the most challenging days."

"Can't a man get a little peace and quiet around here?" Ned is grinning when she looks over in surprise.

A satisfying warmth fills her. She decides to take this as a sign that he's turned a corner, breaking up the pattern of two-steps-forward-one-step-back they've been living with. Carlton's wink as she says her good-byes reassures her.

Chapter 6

As soon as the sun is up, Margaret packs a duffel bag with food stores and the thick sweater she knit for Joe when they were first married. Even though one arm was slightly longer than the other, Joe's only complaint had been that it was too warm for any but the coldest days spent outdoors. This is not the first such bag she's packed over the years. But it is the first of Joe's sweaters she's included. It feels right this time, in keeping with the nature of the exchange.

John Longfeather's truck rumbles up the drive. As she swings the bag up into the cab and climbs in, John hands her a travel mug of hot black coffee. "Sesalie's finest."

Turning to thank him, she notices the streak of gray running from his temple, skirting his right ear, and disappearing into the thick ponytail hanging down his back. John has been a close friend ever since the women of his extended family took her in as apprentice to their ways, allowing her to join gatherings usually closed to outsiders and teaching her to honor and appreciate her gift of sight as a blessing. She realizes now that they stood in for the grandmother she could barely remember. And when John met and married Sesalie, a sisterly friendship quickly developed. As their little family grew, Margaret was included as another one of the many aunties.

"Thanks for coming," she says.

"Hope it works."

She nods, choosing not to voice her worries as they drive north. The sun is bright, the temperature rising. Following a warm night, the blanket of early snow has begun sinking in upon itself. When they turn onto the old fire road just beyond her property line, they head into the semidarkness of the woods, climbing steadily. John pulls over to the side where the road veers off to the left, and they get out and head east on foot. When they come to her first posted tree, with the NO HUNTING/TRESPASSING sign boldly marked and an inch-wide strip of purple paint on its trunk, she checks the signage up and down the line on both sides as far as she can see before crossing into her property.

Birds chatter and flit as they hike up steep embankments and down into deep hollows. Finally, they emerge into full sun again and ascend the hill toward the spot where she left the hanging bag and note the day before.

The bag is gone. The ground beneath the overhanging limb is strewn with pine boughs and dotted with patches of dried grass where deer have scratched out bedding spots, warming the earth into ovals of bare ground with the heat of their bodies.

"He's good." John speaks just above a whisper as he loops a rope around the limb and hoists Margaret's duffel up.

"I wonder if—" Before she can finish her thought, she sees it. A curl of birch bark pierced on the point of a sapling near the base of the tree. She walks through the softening snow and carefully removes and uncurls it. A symbol is etched on it with charcoal—four small circles laid out like a string of evenly spaced beads. The first circle is empty, the second is colored in, and the third and fourth repeat the pattern but are crossed out with slashes.

"Time passing," John says as he looks down over her shoulder. "They come in strings of four. So this first empty one is today. The second blacked out one is tonight. The other two, crossed out, are not to be counted."

"So tonight?"

"Seems so. Yes."

She slips the rolled message into a zippered pocket in her jacket and starts back down the hill.

⚘

As John drives away, Margaret lets the dogs out and watches as they leap and prance about in the snow like puppies. A wave of fatigue surprises her. She knows it's not from the trek through the snow that morning, but from the apprehension that has been sizzling just beneath the surface since yesterday.

early snow melting
secrets whispered on the wind
what lies hidden here

The poem comes without preamble, and she tucks this one away in her mind with the other.

The girls race up the hill at her call and follow her in through the back door. She refills their water dishes, puts the kettle on, and prepares lunch. Carrying a tea tray into the living room, she intends to rest in the deep cushioned armchair. The puzzle on the card table in the corner draws her instead, and she pulls over a wooden chair.

But for one in her bedroom, it's the only puzzle in the house now. In early September, in a moment of stunning certainty, she swept most of her puzzles-in-progress into separate bags and gave them away. She dumped the remaining few into a huge bowl, tossing the pieces with her fingers like a colorful salad. When her studio was finished, she placed the bowl there, and the contents became integral to her art works.

As she scans this lone puzzle, her own words come back to her from the day she first met Emily. She had tried to explain why the last piece of one sat off to the side alone—why she had put off setting it in place. She told the girl she was *internalizing an understanding of timing*. And now she recalls how it felt when that moment came and she snugged the piece into place.

Later, when the moment arrived to let go of rooms full of puzzles in various stages of completion, she acted without thought. After years of surrounding herself with them, she cleared them away in minutes.

This new puzzle appeared by the back door in a coffee can a week ago. That evening, feeling the same rightness, she set up the card table and laid out the pieces. Working at it from time to time, she watched portions of the picture emerge. An old stone wall. Grays and blacks and browns. Tumbling rocks. Splotches of blue-green lichen covering pocked dark stone.

"'Something there is that doesn't love a wall,'" she says aloud, her mind traveling back to the classroom. Miss Miranda Welks seated on her desk, stockinged legs dangling and crossed at the ankles, reading Robert Frost one line at a time, savoring the sounds, encouraging her students to follow her lead. Thus they learned to memorize entire poems with ease through the rhythms of call and response.

More pieces: weathered shingles, warped and cracked, on the side of an old shed. A crooked window casing, black beyond the hanging shards of broken glass. A yellow tangle of forsythia blossoms, sunlit at the corner of the shed. Deep shadows crawling across a yard of scraggly grasses and patches of dirt.

As she scans the loose pieces, a smattering of pink surprises her. Here. And here. And...

A child's dress. A sneakered foot. A ruddy cheek. Her hands move quickly, fitting tabs into slots. Her gaze travels the tabletop.

Two children on a rusted seesaw. One in the air, legs dangling. The other crouched in an awkward squat, knees sticking up, feet planted and ready to spring. Margaret's fingers stop as she hears the creak of the seesaw, the laughter, the thud, the crunch of broken bone. The shriek.

She closes her eyes. She is in that backyard, she and her brother Mattie. But there is no seesaw, just a rope swing hanging from a high branch. They're so small, they can sit side by side on the narrow wooden seat, arms stretched—her right and his left—crossing behind their backs as they clutch the ropes and pump their legs and swing ever higher. Lifting off. Laughing. Flying.

Smiling, she opens her eyes, a puzzle piece poised in her left hand. Its shadings of brown and gray match the nearly finished section beneath. Earth tones. Nothing but earth tones. No pink. No dresses or sneakered feet. No ruddy cheeks. No children. Just a quiet scene dressed in muted tones.

Weary, Margaret moves to the armchair, her tea now cold, her food untouched. She leans back, wondering what the experience is trying to tell her. But her mind is blank, and she drifts into sleep.

The ringing phone tugs her out of the depths of a dream, and she rises from the chair before she's fully awake. A trailing wisp of the dream teases her, and she leans forward, reaching to grasp it, but her hand closes around empty air. The silence around her thickens. The phone has gone silent. The sun has shifted to an afternoon slant across the room. The message carried on a dream has disappeared.

She swears under her breath as she searches the room for her cell phone, then heads for the kitchen. As she crosses the threshold, she's startled by the shrill ring from her sweater pocket. Shaking her head and suppressing a laugh, she answers.

"So it's set?" Jay's voice is gruff, bringing her up short although she knows not to take offense. He's dealing with the myriad threads in his investigation and has no time for pleasantries. "Yes. Tonight. Not sure what time. Shall I call you?" His voice is muffled when he speaks. She assumes he's covering the speaker and talking with someone nearby. Finally, he responds. "Should be done here by seven. I'll come by then unless you call before that. Gotta go." As she looks at the now dark phone screen, she mulls the wisdom of her plan. To Jay, it must seem terribly naive of her to suggest it, yet he is giving her the benefit of his understandable doubt. "Nothing more I can do for now," she says aloud, shaking off the dark worry that has surfaced in those few minutes.

Sighing, she retrieves her tea tray and lights the stove under the kettle. She chops the browning apple slices from her luncheon plate, drops them into a pot with leftover oatmeal, and sets it on the stove to warm. As she stirs in a tablespoon of almond butter, she pictures Molly's body in the snow. What was she doing out there? Was she meeting the one who killed her? Did someone unexpected show up? Was the killing planned or spontaneous? How much did James Harchett see? Is the killer still in the area?

Nothing arises. No images. No bursts of insight. No dream fragments.

Before spooning her oatmeal into a bowl, she removes a container of soup stock from the freezer and sets it on the counter to thaw. Her fingertips and palms burn for a moment. As she rubs her hands to warm them, the snowy field again spreads before her. Wandering Rock rises, a dark backdrop to the body gleaming on the ground in the half light of evening. Like a heat mirage on pavement, it lifts and shifts and shivers—doubling and settling back into a singular frozen mass before doubling again. She blinks, trying to clear her vision, but knows even as she does so it is futile.

Ethereal one moment, corporeal the next, the shimmering continues as the pink scarf around her neck flutters like a feather boa in the still air.

Sophia and Grace yelp, and the scene collapses into the rising steam from the teakettle. She rushes to join them at the backdoor, heart quickening. On the crest of the hill not far from the house, a handsome buck stands, looking at her through the window in the door. Regal, with massive spreading antlers, he remains motionless, nose lifted, dark eyes staring into hers.

The girls, quiet now, stand on either side of her. She doesn't move, stilling her breathing. Listening. Questioning with her whole body.

Minutes pass as she and the deer step outside time. She feels it coming seconds before the deer turns with lifted tail and leaps over the rim of the hill. Dropping to one knee between the girls as they shiver with pent-up energy, she lays her head on each golden back and ruffles the hair at their necks. She steps out back, surprised by the lowering of the sky, and releases her dogs with a command to stay close by.

As she speaks, a sudden squall spits fat flakes into her mouth and eyes, momentarily whitening the world and blinding her to her own backyard. Then the wet snow turns to stinging pellets. Sleet tinkles against the windows and exterior of the house behind her and the windowed wall of her studio nearby. She turns to go back inside, but it stops as suddenly as it came. The wind dies and all is silent, as if the earth itself has paused between an in and an out breath.

Listen, stillness speaks
snow is melting quickly now
secrets surfacing

Hanging in the silence, Margaret hears the thrum of a heartbeat and sees the stag suspended midleap above a valley miles away.

☙

At five o'clock, Margaret crosses to the barn with a canvas sack loaded with fresh vegetables, a fat thermos of soup wrapped in a handknit scarf, and a flashlight with extra batteries. She flicks on a panel of lights, flooding the main chamber while leaving the back end in semidarkness. Setting the bag among the bins of potting soil and racks of gardening tools by the backdoor, she surveys the small tack room in which she now stands. She climbs the stairs to the loft above and rummages in an old trunk. As she pulls out the rolled rug, the heavy scent of cedar rises with it. The memory that surfaces stops her midmotion. She and Mattie seated on the rug here in the loft, picture books spread around them, telling each other stories before they could read. She lowers the trunk lid and descends to the tiny room below.

In a whoosh of cedar, she unrolls the rug and spreads it on the floor. Again the memory flutters. She moves some hay bales around and centers the rug between them. Bending, she finger combs the ragged fringe on either end, admiring the beauty of the pattern woven in faded threads of turquoise, ivory, and brown.

Refuge. The word floats in.

Satisfied, she returns to the house, calling the girls inside as she goes.

A half hour later, John Longfeather arrives. She watches through the back window as he stands in the yard looking out across the fields. The setting sun casts a pink glow, merging into purple across the western sky. She sighs at the turning of another year toward shorter days and darker nights.

After a while, John turns and heads to the door, and she steps out to meet him, a backpack slung over her left shoulder. The rumble of the barn door as she rolls it open again sends a small animal scuttling off into the gathering darkness. "I had a visitor earlier today," she tells him as they step inside. "He was standing on the hill where you stood just now. A gorgeous buck. Elegant. He looked like an old sage come to counsel me as he looked right at me through the window."

"Hmm. Sounds like Old Cyrus. Doesn't usually come down this far. But you never know."

"Oh?"

"The stuff of legends. Supposed to be a hundred or more. Of the wild north woods."

"Hmm."

"A sighting down here is thought to be auspicious."

"Hope so."

"Isn't a hunter in Maine wouldn't want to see him. Not to kill him— woe to any who might try—just to lay eyes on him."

Margaret rolls the door back, leaving an opening just wide enough for a person to pass through. The interior smells of old wood, sawdust, and hay, and underneath it all, the redolence of something more earthy still. Raising a finger to her lips, she eases past her car and heads toward the darker recesses where she left the canvas bag and laid the rug earlier. John follows. They both stop a dozen feet from the back wall with its narrow exterior door in the corner.

She senses rather than sees him standing in the shadows under the wooden stairs that lead to the loft. He is barely breathing, his body coiled and ready to spring. Ready to be gone and leave no trace.

Margaret takes two deliberate steps back. "Thank you for coming," she whispers. "We need your help."

Silence. No easing of the tension hanging in the air. No movement. "We know you tried to help her." John's voice is steady. Quiet. Calm. Margaret hears the crunch of footsteps coming toward the barn and quickly speaks into the darkness. "A friend, Detective Horner, is coming. He means you no harm. He needs your help."

The footsteps stop outside. Margaret reaches forward, palm facing downward, and lowers her hand slowly. "Please stay. Please help us."

The air crackles around her as she waits for a response. She smells his fear. Her heartbeat races to catch up with his and then slows, coaxing his along. She hears the release of his breath, senses the slumping of his shoulders.

Still in shadow, he takes a step toward them. "Okay." The word comes out pitched somewhere between a croak and a grunt.

"Margaret?" Jay says softly from the doorway.

She looks to the man hulking in the darkness, asking with her body if he is still okay with this. A slight nod of the shaggy head tells her he is. She turns, inviting Jay to join them.

They sit on bales of hay. Jay speaks first, his voice low, his eyes looking straight into the space between them, his body relaxed. "Thank you for coming, Mr. Harchett. I know you'd rather be deep in the woods and well out of this." He pauses.

James Harchett grunts and leans in closer, nodding toward Jay, Margaret, and John in turn.

Margaret admires the detective's calm but direct approach—his use of long pauses and the easy cadence when he does speak. She's reminded of her instant liking for this sensitive man when they first met, and smiles with what she hopes James reads as reassurance.

"We know you didn't harm the woman in the field," Jay continues. "That you were at the scene shortly after she was ... killed." His voice drops to nearly a whisper on this last word. "We need to know what you saw and heard that night. Whatever you remember. Exactly what you did."

The silence that follows stretches past the point of comfort, and Margaret suppresses the urge to fill the emptiness, to prod him toward some response—sound or word or gesture. Helpful or otherwise. Anything. Worry blossoms into grave concern as the cold seeps in, filling the void between them. As she's about to speak, the hoarse rattle of a voice unaccustomed to conversation crackles in the still air.

"Past help. No pulse. I checked."

Jay waits before asking for more. "Did you see what happened? Or who did it? Did you—"

"Heard a scream. Not fast enough. Too late. Again."

Margaret knows the look in his eyes without seeing it. She knows the glassy stare of someone caught in a distant memory from another time. Molly's death has brought it all back for this man who retreated to the solace of the woods to try to forget. How many lives had he, an army medic, been unable to save? How much blood and death had he witnessed? What toll had he paid for the madness of men who waged wars they never had to fight?

She senses Jay's reluctance to push further and looks to John Longfeather, who nods as if knowing what she intends. With this as confirmation, she rises and moves toward James.

She sits beside him on the hay bale, leaving space between them, offering only her quiet presence.

He smells of animal skins and wet woods and sweat. She folds her hands in her lap and waits, hoping he'll return to this moment. The two men across from them remain still, honoring the wisdom of patience.

"Didn't see the face. Baseball cap, long bill. Dark jacket. Biker boots. Buckles." He lifts his head and nods. "All straps and silver buckles. He searched her—" James stops, lowering his head before resuming. "Searched the body."

Margaret feels the pain of his remembering and the enormous strain to remain detached. She and her companions understand the huge difference between *the body* and *her body* in the retelling.

"Took something. Tossed the handbag. Dropped something. Ran." He pauses, breathing fast.

They hold the silence.

"Ford pickup. Late nineties. Loud. Burning oil. Broken taillight. Right side." His voice cracks as he loses himself in a harsh fit of coughing, and the rush of words ends with, "No way to catch him."

Jay sighs. "Any idea what time it was?"

"Hour before dawn maybe. Before it snowed. Nothing I could do. Had to leave." He lowers his head to his hands, elbows on his knees. A mass of dark curls falls forward, hiding his face as he rocks back and forth.

Margaret aches to put her arm around his shoulders. Nothing she can say or do will ease this man's anguish, and the wrong move may compel him to flee. So, she waits.

"You've been a great help," Jay says, rising. "And I'd like you to stay around. I'm concerned for your safety. Not only did you see the killer, but you were sighted near the crime scene. People are stoked, and I don't want someone going off half-cocked and—"

"No one's gonna find me if I don't want 'em to." James is on his feet. "I gotta go." With a swiftness that startles everyone, he's standing at the back door, caught in a shaft of light from the main area.

Margaret steps toward him without thought. "Wait. Take these." She hefts the canvas bag and backpack she left in the corner. Holding them out to him, she stares into his wary eyes, noting the flecks of violet in the blue depths. "Please. Stay close. Stay safe."

His eyes soften as he nods to each in turn, grabs the bags, and is out the door.

Chapter 7

"*There's a new whack-a-doodle in town,*" Emily's great-uncle Otis says, looking over the top of his newspaper.

"Oh?" she and her mother Janet respond in unison.

"Horning in on the investigation into that poor girl's death up by Wandering Rock." He snaps the paper back up in front of his face.

"And?" Janet smirks at her daughter. "Is that all you're going to tell us?"

Otis lays the paper flat on the table and leans forward on his elbows. "This reporter for the *Gazette* says he has it firsthand from—" He looks down and traces his finger over a section of the paper, searching. "Here it is. From 'Miss Marcella Catriona McCray, certified psychic medium, that the dead woman was attacked and killed with an axe by a creature—part animal, part human—who lives in the woods.'"

"No!"

"Yep. Then the son-of-a-gun goes on to take a potshot at Margaret. Margaret, for god's sake!"

"What do you mean, a potshot?" Emily leans across the table, reaching for the paper.

Otis pulls it closer to his chest. "He says... " Again he searches the article, his head bobbing behind the paper. "Here. And I quote, 'Seems there's a new psychic in town stealing Margaret Meader's thunder right in her own backyard.'"

Otis looks up, shaking his head. "Can you believe that ignorant little snot? Goes on to talk about Margaret's special ways and about her working with the police to find that missing teen a month or so ago. What was her name? Alissa?" He nods. "Alissa Cates. Other stuff too, going way back. Some bits of truth in the middle of a whole lot of fantastical lies."

He slaps the paper with the back of his hand. "Putting Margaret out there on display and making it sound like she and this 'psychic medium' woman are cut from the same cloth. In some sort of competition." He drops both hands to the table, crumpling the paper in his fists. "The *Gazette* used to print honest-to-goodness news. Now it's turning into a rag with the likes of that guy onboard. I'm gonna write a letter to the editor. And how exactly does one become a *certified* medium, anyway? Do you—"

"Oh, God!" Emily rises, looking from her mother to her uncle. "Odd James. The old hermit in Margaret's woods. This will send people out after him. There's no telling what they'll do if they find him. We have to do something." She carries her dishes to the sink. "I'm going over to Margaret's. She'll know what to do."

"Emily—" Janet starts to object, but Otis cuts her off.

"This reporter's made Margaret a target, too, by bringing her into the story. Damn him and that Marcella what's her name." He's out of his chair, dishes clattering as he helps Emily clear the rest of the breakfast things. "I'm going into town and see what's brewing there."

"But—" Janet tries again.

"Let's keep each other posted," Emily calls as she rushes out the door.

⁂

Emily pulls into Margaret's yard and parks behind John Longfeather's pickup and Sam Kingston's camper. She nods in satisfaction at finding both men there. John is a longtime and reliable friend of Margaret's, and Sam, although a famous writer from away, has become close to them all in the short time since he arrived, staying on to write a book about his grandmother with the same gift of sight as Margaret.

The three of them are out back of the house.

She calls as she walks toward them, "Margaret. Have you read the paper about—"

"Yes," Margaret says. Her blue eyes scan the horizon before landing back on Emily. "We've been out posting more no-trespassing signs around the property lines. But I'm afraid that won't stop the determined."

"Where did that McCray woman come from, anyway?" Emily asks. "Have you heard of her before? Will the investigators take her seriously?" Emily's loose curls bounce as she looks from one to the other.

Margaret sighs. "Never heard of her, and it's not the investigators I'm worried about. It's the crazies who are likely to run off half-cocked, chasing down another wild tale about Old James Harchett. Chasing *him* down. God, he doesn't deserve this."

"If I could get my hands on that little shit of a reporter!" Sam spits the words, his Southern accent becoming thicker as his anger rises. "He and the rag that printed this stuff. Totally irresponsible."

"The damage is done, I'm afraid," John says. "Now we have to protect James from the fallout."

"The man has clearly chosen the life of a recluse," Sam goes on. "Why can't people let that be? Do you know what brought him to that? Do you know his story?" Realizing the writer in him has overstepped, he quickly backtracks and apologizes. "Guess I just stepped in the same hole. Sorry. None of my business."

John waves the apology off. "Understandable. James served in Vietnam and tried his best at reentry when he came home. Made several attempts to live at the old home place with his folks and his younger sister. Worked. Tried to adjust. Spent weeks at a time in the woods." John pauses, looking across the hills. "After the parents died and the sister got engaged, he retreated altogether. Can't say I blame him. Easier to know what to expect in the natural world. I like to think he's happy out there. And I'd like to see it stay that way."

They are interrupted by the sound of tires crunching up the dirt drive and the thunk of a car door. All heads turn as a tall young man rounds the corner of the house, a camera bag swinging from his left shoulder and a smartphone clenched in his right hand. His pale face is pocked, and the thick lenses of his rimless glasses accentuate large brown eyes. He strides across the yard, soggy from snowmelt, his focus on Margaret as if the others don't exist.

"Ms. Meader? Margaret Meader?"

Before she can respond, Sam takes three steps toward him, blocking his path. "And who might you be?" he barks. "Not a certain 'reporter'"—he punctuates this word with air quotes—"from the *Gazette* here to stir up more trouble, I hope."

As she watches, Margaret flashes back to her first encounter with Sam. Remembering him rounding that same corner of the house. Her, drying her hair in the sun. Him, coming toward her. Her dogs growling. Fear prickling before she could sort him out. And now, months later, this good and trusted friend is ready to defend her.

The younger man stops, towering over Sam, scowling. "I'm here to talk to Ms. Meader, the psychic. Get her take on the murder up at the Wandering Rock." He looks over Sam's shoulder at Margaret. "Give you a chance to—"

"It's okay, Sam." She walks up beside him and addresses the stranger. "I am Margaret Meader. And you are?"

Visibly flustered by this simple question, the man pats his many pockets and finally digs out a crumpled business card, handing it to her. "Name's Ross Templar. Reporter for the *Gazette*. I'm just trying to get a statement. Just doing my job." His gaze lands everywhere but on Margaret's as he speaks.

"And you want a statement from me because...?"

"Because you work with the lead investigator on the case. It's well-known you're his resident psychic. Pretty accurate too, from what I've been told."

"I have nothing to say. And if I were you, I'd stick to printing facts and information released to you by those in charge of the investigation, not wild accusations and unsubstantiated remarks. The who, what, when, where, and how of it all. Provable, reliable facts. I would say *that's* doing your job."

"I go where I'm led by the information I'm given, Ms. Meader. And the information Marcella McCray gave me led me to you. Or are you afraid of a little psychic rivalry, perhaps?" He smirks, challenging her with raised brows. "If not, why not tell me your version? What do you see when you look into the case?" At this, he leans down, his face inches from hers.

The sun glinting off his thick lenses has his eyes shimmering, multiplying and retracting in a grotesque dance. A disturbing image surfaces, forcing Margaret to step back and look away. Two sets of eyes stare out of the dead woman's body with bursts of spidery red lines—petechia—reminding her of a drawing from her grandmother's journal.

Without a word, she rushes to the house, leaving the back door standing open behind her.

John, Sam, and Emily close in around Templar.

"You call yourself a journalist?" Sam steps closer. "Where's your pride, young man? Sensationalism serves no useful purpose. Stirring up rumor and endangering innocents? You should be ashamed. And if anyone ends up hurt, it's on you."

"I don't know who you are, old man. So back off." Templar starts to turn away.

"Better watch yourself, son." John Longfeather's arresting voice has him turning back.

"Or what? You threatening me, Tonto?"

Emily gasps, and Sam opens and closes his mouth, shocked beyond speech.

"Just cautioning you." John's face offers no clue to what's going on inside, and his voice is so quiet, Templar is forced to lean in to hear his next words. "I'm sure you don't want harm to come to innocent folk because you didn't do your due diligence. Because you didn't think before you put the incendiary remarks of a dubious source into print."

Templar's body stiffens as he glares at John. Then, without a word, he turns and walks away.

John's voice follows him. "Like Sam said, it's on you if anyone gets hurt. Not a good thing to have on your heart."

Inside the house, Margaret grabs her bag and fumbles for her phone, then nearly drops it as she presses Jay's number.

"Jay. Twins. Is Molly a twin?"

"What? I don't know. She has a sister. Mira. Haven't been able to reach her. Why do you think she's a twin?"

"I'm not sure she is. But I keep getting images, like double exposures."

"Let me check. Her husband's here. Not much help, still pretty much in shock, but I'll ask him."

"It's important, or—"

"You wouldn't have called otherwise."

"And I…" She can't finish the thought. Her mind is whirling, trying to process what's niggling to get to the surface but remains submerged. "Never mind. That's all."

"I'll get back to you."

When she rejoins the others in the backyard, they're still discussing the old vet and the danger he's in. Margaret explains to Emily and Sam that she knows James came upon the scene of the murder after the fact, but she keeps the meeting in the barn to herself. When her phone rings, she answers immediately.

"You were right," Jay says. "She has a twin. Mira. Their last name was Clark. Moved away years ago. Close as kids but pretty much parted ways after high school. Rarely spoke after that. Hard family life—lots of baggage."

"Identical?" There's a significant pause on the other end, and Margaret continues, "Are we sure the dead woman is Molly?"

She hears a low whistle before he speaks. "Well, there's a new wrinkle. I'll get back."

Margaret looks at her silent phone and then at her companions. "Molly Makepeace was a twin."

"So that's why you asked if he's sure it's Molly," Sam says. "The plot thickens." The moment it's out of his mouth, he apologizes. "Again, the writer in me is not always appropriate."

"If it is Molly, the fact of a twin may have no significance," she says, thinking out loud.

"But I get the feeling you think otherwise." John is looking at Margaret with questioning eyes.

"It feels important somehow, but I'm not sure why."

John looks off to the tree line on the far hill. "Look. I'm going to drive around a bit. Check the property lines again. Keep an eye out for trespassers. Maybe go up and down the old logging roads. Want to join me, Sam?"

"I'll follow you out to the ridge road and we can split up from there."

"I'll call my cousins. Have them keep their ears out. We'll keep in touch, Margaret," John calls as he leaves.

"I have to move my car out of the way," Emily hollers as she follows them on the run.

When she returns, Margaret asks her to join her for a walk in the woods. She calls the girls, and they descend the hill.

Chapter 8

A half hour into the woods, Margaret and Emily come to a small clearing and stop. Though their walk has taken them through slushy snow in the shade of the trees, the center of the clearing shines green in full sun. The sudden snowstorm came in before the grasses had begun to brown, and the sight of this lush patch glistening with water droplets has Margaret smiling. Across the way just before the trees resume, a red leaf on a small green bush flutters in a gentle wind.

She walks to the bush and squats. Cupping the crimson leaf in her hand, rubbing it lightly with her thumb, she loses herself in a memory. Her mother's voice chanting, "Double doodle, double noodle, double-dee-doodle-dee-doo," and her brother responding, "Double dee, double do, double-dee-doo..." punctuated with giggles. Her own small voice joining his and then falling away in laughter. Two bodies tumbling on the bed against the softness of their mother's belly and breasts. Arms hugging and releasing them. Long fingers tickling lightly. Her laughing voice singing, "Double trouble, double bubbles," and the mattress sagging under the weight of their father jumping on board, sending springs and twins squealing. A woman bouncing into the scene in a purple caftan, her white-blonde hair framing a too-pale face. Disrupting the flow, smashing the memory into a thousand floating fractals. Shards of mirrored glass reflecting identical puzzle pieces hang suspended and then drop without sound, dissolving like melting snow.

Margaret pulls herself back to the present, focusing on the suppleness of the red leaf in her hand, the warmth of the October sun on her back, the sound of Emily clearing her throat. She lets go of the bush and stands, gathering herself before turning back to Emily.

"Sorry, lost myself for a minute."

Emily smiles. "Is that a blood spot bush? I've heard you mention it before but I've never seen one."

"Yes. They're quite rare, and when I do find them, they often trigger memories for me. Take a closer look. Not only is the one leaf red, but its lacy network of veins is slightly different from its green companions. Notice how much more intricate the venation pattern is here."

As Emily bends to examine the leaves, Sophia and Grace lift their heads and point off into the woods. At their sudden alertness, Margaret shields her eyes from the sun and strains to see into the darkness under the trees.

A crackling and snapping of branches precedes the appearance of three men dressed in hunting gear with orange vests and caps. Two carry rifles against their shoulders, pointed at the sky. The third carries a shotgun in the crook of his right arm, aimed casually at the ground. As they step into the clearing, they stop, eyes fixed on the two growling dogs.

"Gentlemen." Margaret nods and walks forward to stand with the girls.

"Ma'am," the tallest of the three says. "Probably shouldn't be out here. There's a dangerous criminal on the loose. Crazy wild thing. Killed a woman. Dogs won't do you no good. Better to stay inside until we find him."

"I thank you for your concern, but this is posted property and—"

"A couple of signs aren't going to stop this creature. He's violent and you—"

"What I'm saying is, guns are not welcome here. I understand your concern. Really. But I'm afraid the whole community has been misinformed. The woman was not killed by a wild creature. Irresponsible reporting has circulated false information. Dangerously false. I pray no one gets hurt as a result."

"But—"

"Wait a minute." The other man with a rifle, short and wiry with a thick beard, steps in front of his companion. "Aren't you Mrs. Meader? The psychic lady."

Margaret stiffens. "I am Margaret Meader. Yes." She smiles, keeping her voice light.

"You saved Bobby Dolloff when his tractor tipped over on him, didn't you? Would have bled to death if it hadn't been for you. That's you, right?"

Margaret's shoulders soften. "I called for help. Yes."

"Well, if you say the stories are bullshit, I believe it. Come on, guys, let's get out of here. Sorry, Mrs. Meader. Sorry as all get out."

As the others turn to leave, the third man remains, staring at Margaret. Slowly he lifts his shotgun onto his shoulder, briefly aiming it in her direction. "If I find out anything different, I'll be back, signs or no signs."

Emily comes to stand beside her when they've gone. "God, Margaret. That was too creepy for words. And that last guy. Damn that reporter. Now I'm even more worried about Odd—sorry—Old James."

Margaret sighs and leads the way into the woods in silence, the dogs running ahead. They walk along the eastern edge of the property, stopping just shy of the crime scene at Wandering Rock and looping back along a different trail. Emily matches Margaret's pace and rhythm without breaking the silence.

About a mile along the winding path, they hear voices up ahead, and Margaret slows, listening. She can't make out words but picks up the back and forth rhythm of two people in conversation. She quickens her pace.

The dialogue at closer range is sharper, more staccato, the voices female. As they round a boulder jutting onto the path, she glimpses two figures in thick parkas and bright leggings disappearing around another rock a few yards ahead. Pale blonde hair cascades from under a woolen hat on the taller of the two. A sizzle of recognition runs the length of Margaret's body, raising a question and then an answer. "Her," she says aloud.

"Who?" Emily asks.

"I don't know yet."

Emily opens her mouth, then closes it and continues following in silence.

The voices cease, and Margaret cocks her head, listening harder. The path descends into a thick stand of young eastern white pines. Pushing aside branches, she slows, pointing out exposed roots and jagged points of embedded rock sticking up along the path as they go.

As they emerge, pine tassels brushing their faces, they nearly run into a petite woman kneeling in the middle of the trail tying her boot. Her companion sits on a rock a few feet ahead, her white-blonde hair falling down around her shoulders, covering her chest. Her eyes are closed. Her hands rest on her knees in what Margaret recognizes as a yogic gesture, a mudra. Palms up, index fingers and thumbs forming circles, the woman hums softly and then mumbles a series of unfamiliar words.

The kneeling woman stands, head bowed, and places her hands in the namaste position in front of her heart. A frisson of disquiet quickens and then slows Margaret's breathing. She remains still, respectful yet curious. Emily shifts her weight from one foot to the other and waits beside her.

The blonde woman's eyes open. They are the lightest shade of gray Margaret has ever seen—nearly colorless. Her skin is translucent. As Margaret stares, she realizes the woman is much older than she'd first thought. In her late fifties, at least. Her face is wrinkled with puffy sacks beneath her eyes and deep creases radiating out from the corners. The air of youthful grace Margaret had noted as she glimpsed her up ahead on the trail is gone as the woman stretches stiffly.

An image surfaces as if from the depths of a still pond, sending out concentric ripples as it breaks through in a frothy burst. It shivers, then settles. A younger version of this face is sketched along the right-hand side of a journal page, hair swirling down the edge and along the bottom of the page. A watercolor wash hints at a vague blondeness. A nest of woven ribbons sits cocked over the right brow like a jaunty fascinator, if not for the dead bird cradled inside. Empty eyes stare from the woman's face. Colorless. Revealing nothing. And out of the dark mouth, spiders and beetles and wasps crawl onto the page.

"Well, if it isn't Margaret Meader herself." The woman stands and stretches out her hand, shattering the image with her words. "I was just talking about you with my assistant, Louisa." She nods toward her companion, who offers a shy smile and looks at the ground.

"I'm afraid you have me at a disadvantage," Margaret says, giving her hand a quick, firm shake.

"Oh, of course. Sorry. I'm a great admirer of your work, but we haven't met. I'm Marcella—the c pronounced as ch—Marcella Catriona McCray." She spreads her arms and bobs a quick curtsy.

Margaret stiffens despite having anticipated the name. "Ah, yes." Unsure of what else to say while keeping her ire in check, she introduces Emily and then calls to the dogs who have been snuffling about in the woods just off the trail.

Marcella laughs. "So, not a cat lady, eh? No feline familiars? No fuel for the name-calling? Margaret of the Witchy Arts, Devil's Whore, and all that?" She grins and drops to pat the dogs, gazing into the eyes of each in turn. "I sense they're helpful to you in your work. Dogs take empathy to a deeper energetic level than most humans, don't they. *Clairempathy* at its finest, right, ladies?" With exaggerated enthusiasm, she ruffles their coats and scratches behind their ears, oblivious to the stiffening and wary posturing of both dogs. Rising, she adds, "I admit to living out the cliché myself. Two cats, Pyewacket and Gillian. My little homage to Kim Novak."

Margaret smiles and nods at the allusion to *Bell, Book, and Candle,* a favorite old film.

Now closer to Margaret and gesticulating broadly, the woman seems larger, her presence overwhelming. Margaret resists the urge to step away from her. But when Marcella advances, her voice booming in the quiet woods, Margaret does step back.

The woman continues, despite Margaret's withdrawal. "I have been so wanting to meet you. I so need someone I can talk to, confide in, maybe even learn from. Someone who speaks the same language." Her eyes widen as if the last thought surprises her. "Someone who knows what it's like— understands the highs and lows of being a sensitive. The burdens. The energy drain. The responsibility pressing down upon my shoulders—*our* shoulders." With this, she turns and plunks herself back down on the rock, shoulders slumping, head bowed. "It's all so exhausting. People just don't get it."

Emotions tumble as Margaret processes her response to this woman and to her sweeping performance. She wants to reconcile her roiling sensation of being played—grandly and theatrically—with her wish to be open to a stranger's need. She searches the wariness, the skepticism, looking for something to hang onto—some sense of authenticity in Marcella's demeanor. Some inkling of empathy in herself and some way to temper the anger she feels at this woman.

"I have to be honest," she finally says. "You stirred up a lot of trouble with that interview about the murder. Your statements may well have put someone in grave danger. It's hard for me to put that aside, so I'm telling you straight out, I'm feeling pretty pissed off right now."

The woman looks up at her. "I heard you're direct." She smiles approvingly, seemingly unfazed by Margaret's anger. "Which interview?"

"Your interview about the murder."

"The one in the paper or the one on TV?"

Emily speaks for the first time. "You mean you said those same things on TV? What were you thinking?"

Margaret looks to the sky, shaking her head. "You talk about responsibility, but you've put false information out there for public consumption. That's the epitome of irresponsibility. You have no idea what you've done."

"So, Templar was right. Said you'd be territorial." Marcella stands, hands on her hips. "There's something dangerous out there." She drops her hands to her sides and lowers her voice. "Come on. Let's work this together. Prove Templar wrong about you and show the world what two feisty psychics—*women* psychics—can do when we put our energies together!"

Margaret looks into the woman's pale eyes and pauses, seeking the right words, but before she can speak, Marcella explodes.

"You really are a tight-assed old has-been. Afraid of losing your status as Queen of the Hill around here? Afraid the newer, younger version will outshine you? Replace you in the limelight? Afraid—"

"Look," Margaret says. "A woman has been murdered, and the only thing I'm interested in is a safe and swift resolution to the case. There is no limelight here. There's a devastated family. There's an anxious community—made more so by your words. And there are facts and physical evidence waiting to be gathered by the proper authorities. Without fanfare. And without limelight."

"I know what I saw. My visions are never wrong, and I'm going to prove it. Somewhere in these woods"—she waves her arms around—"there's proof, and I'm going to use my gifts to break this case wide open. I'm giving you a chance to be a part of that."

"Well then, let my first act be to escort you *out* of these woods. This is private property. You must have missed the signs. The purple paint stripes signal the need for permission to enter." With this, Margaret rouses Sophia and Grace and points down the trail they've just traveled. "Let's go, girls. Let's show Marcella the way out."

Visibly surprised, Marcella snaps at her companion, "How did you not know this? I told you what I wanted."

"I..." The younger woman's look of confusion clearly exposes Marcella's lie. "I thought..."

"I doubt your being here is on Louisa." Emily speaks for the second time. "Where did you park, anyway?"

"At the parking lot back that way." Marcella gives a vague wave of the hand.

"What parking lot?" Emily asks. "These are private woods for miles around."

"Look, whatever your name is, there's a dirt lot off a dirt road a ways back. No posted signs anywhere. So you can get down off your high horse."

"We'll get you started in the right direction," Margaret says. "I assure you there's nothing out here for you to find. The killer took off in a totally different—" She stops herself.

Marcella jumps at this. "Go on."

"If you get any more hunches, run them by the police and not the press. And if that approach doesn't align with your methods, you and I really have nothing further to talk about."

Marcella steps in front of Margaret and starts down the trail, but then stops and whirls around. "Why are you protecting him? The stories are rampant in town about a giant Sasquatch or something living in these woods. Evidently, *your* woods. You protect him, or rather *it*, and call me irresponsible?"

Margaret stares at her. "So. You didn't 'see' the so-called beast murderer in a vision. You heard some tall tales and fit them into your made-up version of the crime? To insinuate yourself into the headlines."

"That's not true," Marcella shouts, her face reddening. "I saw it and then I heard the stories. It killed her. I simply reported it."

"To the press. Sounds like a limelight kind of move to me." Margaret is surprised by the depth of the animosity in her sharp tone. She pulls back before continuing. "Look. It's dangerous to act without certainty when it comes to sharing what you see. Things are usually more complicated than a single image might suggest. Oversimplifying can be dangerous not only to others, but to yourself. You said earlier that you might learn something from me. Let this be that something."

"But—" Marcella stops herself. "Are you suggesting the beast might be connected in some way but not as the killer?" Clear gray eyes search hers.

"And again, you jump to a conclusion. I'm simply saying you should hesitate to trust a solitary image. Even if—*especially* if—it's propped up by rumors and local lore." Margaret's steady gaze meets the questions in the woman's eyes. "It's too easy to get swept up in the energy of the fanciful. Think about it."

Marcella opens her mouth, then closes it as her shoulders soften with a sigh. She turns back to the path.

They walk the rest of the way in silence, the dogs continually running ahead and circling back.

When they reach the dirt lot, the two women climb into a red sports car, and Marcella looks back at Margaret. "I really would like to sit down with you. Talk sometime. Maybe over some of your famous tea?"

"Maybe, first, you can undo some of the damage you've done with your public statements."

"Food for thought," the woman says.

As the car rolls away, sunshine glints off the red paint as strands of blonde hair trapped in the window as it closed flutter in the rising wind.

Margaret turns to Emily. "My famous tea?"

"Guess you're more of a celeb than you thought." Emily laughs, but her tone is serious as she continues. "I have to say it. I don't like her and I don't trust her. She's a fake, isn't she?"

Margaret doesn't answer right away. Instead, she calls the dogs and takes the more direct path toward home. "I'm not sure what to make of her. If genuine, she's certainly of the more flamboyant variety. Far more likely to blurt than reflect. Worrisome under the best of circumstances. Deadly under these."

"I'd love to get Louisa alone and have a chat with her." Emily falls back as the path narrows. "Bet I could learn a lot about her boss with a little girl talk and some carefully crafted questions."

"Ah, the journalist in you is aroused. Maybe that could be arranged as well?"

Chapter 9

Margaret rounds the front corner of her house in time to see a dusty black car pull into the yard. With the glare of the sun on the windshield, she can't see the occupants. *Damn. Too late to pretend I'm not home.*

Relief wells as Jay steps out on the passenger side. It's followed by a wave of sadness as the driver gets out and stands looking at her over the roof of the car.

Jay says, "You remember my partner?"

"Detective Green, yes."

The woman comes around the car and takes Margaret's outstretched hand. "Cyn, please."

The shadow Margaret senses just behind the woman softens and withdraws as their hands meet. In the sun, amber flecks highlight her caramel-brown eyes, beautiful against her flawless olive skin.

Jay clears his throat, and Margaret releases the woman's hand and invites them into the house. As she leads them through to the kitchen in the back, she chides herself for her lapse. How long past social comfort did she hold that handshake? For how long was she caught in the enigma of this woman's past?

As they settle at the kitchen table, pulling their arms out of winter coat sleeves and letting the coats hang over the backs of their chairs, Margaret grinds coffee beans and starts a pot brewing. Her questions remain unspoken as she waits.

She's setting out the creamer and sugar bowl when Jay begins. "It was Mira. Molly's twin sister died in that field. And Molly Makepeace is missing."

"How did you identify her so fast?"

"Her fingerprints are on file. She works in childcare, and prints are part of background checks."

"Did you find Molly's fingerprints on file to rule them out? Since they're twins—"

"Interesting, that. Twins share the same DNA but not the same prints. Seems development of prints in the environment of the womb can vary according to each baby's position and other factors. It's definitely her sister, Mira."

The coffee machine signals, and Margaret fills three mugs and joins them at the table. She scans for any helpful images or stray thoughts, and is stopped in her mental searching by the heavy darkness swirling around Cyn.

The woman is stiff. Unreadable. Her back is straight, not touching the back of the chair. And Margaret struggles to pull her focus away and concentrate on the business at hand. She shifts in her own chair, lifting and lowering her right shoulder, rolling it up and back, trying to work out a building tension there. She hears a baby crying, its initial whimpers intensifying to insistent wails. The front of her blouse feels wet, and she looks down. It's dry, but though she's never been pregnant, she now knows what it feels like to leak breast milk. She looks up to find Cyn and Jay staring at her.

"What is it?" Jay asks. "Did you see something? A lead?"

Quickly rechecking her shirt front, she shakes her head. "Sorry. No."
But Cyn continues to stare. Her eyes are unsettling, the amber highlights
now submerged in darker tones, and they're filled with questions. And
something else, something Margaret can't quite identify.

"Do you think it's a coincidence that Molly decides to disappear just
when her sister comes for a visit?" Even as she says it, Margaret knows she's
reaching.

"I never rule anything out," Jay answers. "Molly's husband says the
sisters have been estranged for years. Then Molly tells you she's going to
disappear on purpose—rather suspicious in and of itself—and her twin
shows up here and is killed. We can't rely on whatever her husband says.
You know what they say, the spouse or a close relative tops the suspect list
in a homicide."

"The spouse and Molly might even be in on this together," Cyn adds.
"Whether intentional or an accident, we may have a case of self-defense or
manslaughter." She shakes her head. "Bizarre. Lots to consider here.
Including the crazy guy in the woods."

Margaret flinches. "The killer was definitely a man. I'm sure of it. I
suppose a woman might have been waiting nearby. As for the 'crazy guy in
the woods,' I'm sure he's only a witness." She keeps her voice even, tamping
down her anger, not wanting to alienate Jay's partner.

Again, her right breast feels wet, and she resists the urge to look down.
"Does either twin have a baby? An infant?"

Cyn answers with a question. "Why do you ask?"

"Just responding to a quick impression, but it may not be about this case.
It may be—" She stops. Something tells her to go no further. "Sorry. May
be unrelated. Happens sometimes."

The baby screams. A door slams. A heaviness settles into both breasts as
silence replaces all sound except the beating of her own heart.

Jay's voice breaks through. "You look as if you've seen—"

She cuts him off. "I can't tell whether or not it's about the twins." Her eyes find Cyn's. Alarm flares there, then disappears. Margaret looks away.

"Before I forget," she says to Jay. "I met Marcella McCray in the woods today. Right after Emily and I met three men with guns. They were hunting for James." As if on cue, distant gunshots ring out from the thickest woods to the north and west.

"Shit!" Jay gets up, grabbing his coat, as does Cyn. "Damned idiots. And when I meet up with that McCray woman..." He doesn't finish as the two head for the front door.

Margaret follows them. "John Longfeather and Sam Kingston were going out to check the property lines this afternoon. We're all worried for James. I hope they didn't run into trouble. Or..." She can't finish the thought.

"I've sent people out as well," Jay says, "but there's a lot of territory to cover. Stay out of the woods for now." He turns back to her as he steps outside. "Think it's time for the signal." His eyes meet Margaret's, and she acknowledges the directive.

"Signal?" Cyn asks as they head for the car.

Margaret doesn't hear his response as they jump in the car and then race down the drive.

She tries calling John and Sam on their cells. Both go to voicemail. As she punches in another number, her phone rings in her hand.

"Margaret?" Annie's voice is breathy. "I heard shots and last I saw you, you were heading into the woods with Emily. Everything all right?"

"I'm fine. I've been home for a while now."

"Normally I wouldn't worry, but with all this craziness around that poor girl's murder, I'm in a dither. That woman who claims to be a psychic medium was just on TV again being even more outrageous."

"Seriously? It wasn't a repeat of her earlier interview?"

"Nope. A different outfit, all purple and flowy, and she appeared to have a vision right there on camera. Hands raised to the heavens, mouth open, eyes sort of glazed and staring, breath shaky. Very dramatic. Then she went limp and reached out for support. The reporter almost dropped her mic when she had to grab for her. Afterwards, she said she'd been given new details to add to her previous cockamamie story. And she said, 'Margaret Meader is holding back. Knows things she's not telling.'"

"What new details did she say she got?"

"Oh, that's the best part. She said she couldn't reveal them yet. Basically said, 'stay tuned for more information,' like a promotional tease. Oh, it was quite the spectacle. Everyone was jabbering about it at the market when I went for groceries."

"So, she didn't correct any statements she made earlier? About the killer being a creature with an axe? Or—"

"Definitely not. Simply promised more to come." Annie's voice rises in alarm, "Oh, no, Margaret! Those gunshots in the woods. Could they... I've been so worried about Old James. Do you think—"

"I don't know. I'm worried too. I met that woman in the woods today and asked her to fix the mess she'd started if she had the chance. Looks like I may have pushed her forward instead."

"You actually met her? Wish I had been a fly on the wall—or I should say in the trees?—for that. How did she behave when she met the genuine article? She's such an obvious fake. All show and no substance."

"I took an instant dislike to her, I have to admit. But I need to step back and assess my response. Both she and the reporter accused me of jealousy or competitiveness. I hope that's not the case, but I have to take a deeper look."

"You're a better person than I am. Always giving the benefit of the doubt. I say she's a charlatan with all the trappings of a carnival psychic. If it looks like a duck and quacks like a duck, you'd better be ready to duck, Margaret!" She laughs at her play on the old adage.

"I'm not a better person, by any means. I guess I'm hesitant because of all the skepticism I've experienced over the years. All those people rolling their eyes and writing me off, questioning my motives. All the ridicule. The suspicion."

"I understand."

"I know you do. Thanks."

"I'd better let you go. Let me know if you hear anything. I'll do the same. I'll be so glad when Molly's killer is caught."

Margaret hesitates, then plunges in. "Because you are my trusted friend, I'm going to tell you something you can't repeat. The dead woman is not Molly Makepeace."

"What? So the newspeople are wrong about that too? What the—"

"The police just found out. And they haven't told the press or next of kin. That's why you can't repeat this." Margaret takes a breath. In this far, she can't stop now. "It's Molly's twin, Mira."

Silence on the other end, then an expulsion of breath. "Oh, my. Mira Clark. I forgot about her. I met her once."

"Really? When?"

"I remember because I'd never met identical twins before. I mean, I've met sisters or siblings who look a lot alike. But Molly and Mira were beyond indistinguishable. It was uncanny. So, it stayed with me. You're the only other twin I've ever known in all my life, can you believe that? And you were fraternal."

Mattie's smiling face comes toward her, then recedes. She opens her mouth to call out to him, but bubbles burst forth instead of words. When the bubbles clear, some popping softly, she sees the Clark twins on a beach, posing for a photograph. Petite, young, and slender. Pink with sunburn. Shoulder-length blonde hair whipping around their pretty faces in the sea breeze. Laughing. Perfect teeth shining. Vibrant. Arm in arm. Athletic. Radiant. Healthy. Their pink bikinis the only difference between them— one polka-dotted, the other striped. The shutter clicks and whirs, and they are gone.

"How did you meet the twins?" she asks Annie once she's sure the imagery is done.

"Jake's company hired a firm to promote a community project. They brought in the twins because one of the campaign slogans was 'double the value, double the impact,' or something like that. They weren't professional models, but they were stunning. It was one of those chance discovery stories, like the actress sitting at a drugstore soda fountain. They were at a horse show. Only one of them won a ribbon, but they were both in all the photos at the winners' circle, and the story of beautiful twin riders made quite a splash. "

Margaret's mind settles on the only time she saw Molly in person, and she finds it hard to imagine that woman in Annie's description.

"Well, anyways," Annie goes on, "Jake invited me to the photo shoot because I was into photography at the time. Afterwards, he was not happy. One of the twins was difficult and mouthy, delaying things and killing the budget." She laughs. "I'd almost forgotten the little poem he made up after the shoot. 'They were monozygotic but one was psychotic! Double the trouble, not double the fun.' I couldn't tell them apart, but I think someone said the troublesome one was Mira."

"Do you mind if I pass this along to Detective Horner? You never know what might be helpful."

"No problem. Happy to help."

"I'm going to see if I can reach him now. See what's going on in the woods."

After ringing off with Annie, Margaret needs time to think, time with her hands in warm water, washing the coffee mugs, allowing her mind to drift.

The sisters were once close, but their temperaments differed and they became estranged. Molly was about to "disappear" for the second time, and Mira shows up dead. Who and where is Molly now? Abused wife? A victim since childhood? On the run or taken?

She tries Jay's cell but hangs up without leaving a message. He'll get back to her when he's able, she assures herself.

She fills two canvas bags with nonperishable food stuffs, a can opener and utensils, a loaf of bread, a pound of sharp cheddar, and jars of peanut butter and jelly. She sets an insulated bag on the counter beside the refrigerator and a thermos next to the coffee machine. In the back pantry, she pulls out a sleeping bag and a lantern with extra batteries.

Her stomach reminds her she hasn't eaten since breakfast, and it's now well past noon. She doesn't want to take the time, but the beginnings of a headache convince her to fix a plate. As she bites into her sandwich, focusing on the taste of warm cheese melting into crisp apple slices, an image floats in. The back of a man's head wearing a black baseball cap, a thinning fringe of dark hair hanging to the collar of a brown leather jacket. He turns to the side, his large nose and the green insignia on the front of his hat revealed briefly before he turns away again. He reaches up to scratch the back of his neck, the pallid skin of his hand a spiderweb of veins. Then he's gone.

She knows better than to pursue the image, and so she continues eating. Receptive but not reaching. And with the last bite, the smell of exhaust sours the tastes in her mouth. A truck races down a hill, fumes billowing out behind in the cold night air. In the dim glow of the single taillight, the license plate is smeared with dirt but the truck is a rusted red. Shadowed in the dashboard light, two heads are clearly outlined in the cab. An owl hoots. A single star twinkles and then disappears. Snowflakes float down and around the still warm body on the ground.

She remains receptive, hoping for more. After several trips to the barn and back, she walks to her studio in the backyard, the snow cover gone now. Work. Work will pass the time if not settle the worry.

Sunlight streams through the wall of windows, warming the space. She smiles up at the opposite wall and Kenneth's grand surprise when he finished construction on the place. A triptych—three framed panels of her original hand-drawn plans—hangs centered at eye level. Above it, his own artistic composition—a giant three-dimensional wooden puzzle, its pieces not quite fit into place, the gaps between them casting shadows as the sun moves across the room, creating a whimsical dance of light and sculpted shapes. The scene, depicted in soft watercolors on the surface of the puzzle and completed by the eye of the beholder, is an enlarged version of one of Margaret's paintings: a great blue heron gliding against an autumnal sky above a peaceful stretch of marshlands. Three simple lines rendered with deft brushstrokes grace the lower portion of the piece.

heron's outstretched wings
carry her in homeward flight
bathed in brilliant blue

She smiles at the memory of Kenneth's face, his obvious nervousness, as he removed her blindfold that day and waited with breath held for her reaction. Her heart swells with affection—she doesn't yet dare call it anything deeper—as she remembers taking in the magnificent piece for the first time. The triptych was more or less expected since he'd said again and again that her plans should be framed one day. And though she hadn't imagined the aesthetic impact of them arranged as a panel of three and framed in stunning shades of red and gold, it was the puzzle that took her breath away. A marriage—the word stops her for a moment, and she breathes it in before indulging further in the joy of the memory—a marriage of their two artforms, three if she considers puzzling an art. Him, the master of anything created in wood. Her, the watercolorist and poet. Blended together in this extraordinary piece. And since receiving it and working in this new studio, her work has taken her to inner depths she's never reached before. Her commissioned galleries are pressuring her for more, one curator describing her newer works as having a mystical quality, another calling them ethereal, as if she's painting with light.

She walks to her worktable by the windows and gazes at the drawing there. She dips a brush in a waterpot, wipes it on the rim, and touches the wet brush to a dimple of dried brown paint on a palette, swishing it around. Lifting the brush, she creates a puddle of brown water in a clean dimple on the same palette. She swirls her brush in the water again, this time in a figure-eight pattern, before touching it to the dimple of dry green paint and creating a new puddle in a new well. She nods, satisfied with the resulting colors, the perfect shades for the cattails and marsh grasses already inked on the paper. With gentle strokes, she works quickly, the colors lightening with each outward sweep of the brush.

Leaving the painted portions to dry before adding an overwash, she creates new puddles, one of blue and one of gray. The heron stands on one leg, waiting. Stillness personified. She takes her time filling in the contours of its feathered body. Softly. Lightly.

Her cell rings as she is changing out the water in the pot, her mind lost in the play of syllable counts—fives and sevens—as words come in groups of three. She quickly jots a line in her journal before answering.

"Margaret, it's John. There are guys in the woods armed with everything from crossbows and traps to guns. The police are running them off or detaining them, but there's a lot of ground to cover. Best to stay clear for now."

Her heart is pounding. "My God! Let's talk when you're safely away."

The sun has lowered and the room has taken on a chill, surprising her now that her focus has shifted from her work. Late. Time to act. She grabs her coat, hat, and gloves. In the yard, she gathers strewn branches, throwing smaller ones for the dogs as she works. She drops a bundle by the fire bowl on the crest of the hill. Breaking several into shorter sticks, she arranges them in a teepee in the center of the bowl. She places a pile of fat wood shavings from a nearby bin under the sticks and stuffs crumpled newspaper in on top. Sparks fly as she scrapes a kitchen match on a rock beneath the bowl, and it flares to life. She touches it to the paper, and soon flames dance as the resins in the fat wood take hold.

She sends the dogs off with a quick command to stay close while she tends the fire, slowly adding large chunks from the woodpile. Once she has a good blaze going, she rakes up clumps of leaves, adding them a handful at a time until the backyard bowl sends the strong autumnal scent into the air. Then, in plain view of the woods on the far hills, she continues raking and adding to the fire.

An hour before sunset, Jay arrives alone. "Cyn's helping the local police process the shooters from the woods," he says as he approaches. "Damned idiots. One of them shot a man in another group in the shoulder. Turned out to be his own brother. The woman responsible should be ashamed."

"Marcella has a lot to answer for, that's for sure," Margaret agrees. "But those men are accountable for their own stupidity. I pray James isn't lying wounded in the woods somewhere. Or worse. "

"Meanwhile, we're no closer to finding the murderer than we were yesterday." Jay slumps into a nearby Adirondack chair, dropping his head to his hands.

Margaret sets her rake down and sits in the chair beside him. "I have a little more information, but then, it came to me in a vision, and I'm sure you're wary of such a source since Marcella came on the scene." She pats his shoulder and smiles, hoping to lighten his mood.

"From you, I'm glad for any scrap." But he doesn't look her way.

First she relays Annie's account of the twins from the past, and then adds her own new details. The green insignia on the man's cap, the dark hair, the brown leather jacket, the large nose and pale skin, veins on the hand. Then she goes on to describe the truck, saving the most telling detail until last.

"There were two heads in that truck as it drove away. And though I want to say one was a woman's, I can't be certain. I can't separate out what I saw from what I think I saw."

Jay raises his head and looks at her. "That's more than a little information, Margaret. Now we have a partial description of him and his truck. And a second person on scene. Could it have been Molly?"

"I honestly can't say." She closes her eyes, straining to recapture the back window of the truck as it sped away. Two heads in shadow. Both wearing hats. One baseball cap and one...

"A watchman's cap. The second person was wearing a knit hat. Either they had a very large head, or thick hair was tucked up under the hat."

Jay rises. "Thanks. I'd better go check on a few things. I'll call later."

She stays seated, looking at the darkening fields and on up into the woods circling the property. The fire crackles.

John's truck rumbles up the drive and soon he is standing beside her chair, staring off into the distance as well.

"Sesalie sent over a pot of her three-alarm chili," he says. "Thought I might join you in a bowl if you don't mind me inviting myself."

"I'd love the company. And Sesalie's chili. How are she and the kids? We're overdue a get-together."

"She's doing good. Worried about Old James, of course. But with her work and the kids, she's pretty busy. Those boys are growing way too fast."

She calls the girls, who greet John and race him to the backdoor. Inside, she puts the kettle on, preheats the oven, and slices a loaf of grainy bread while John gets the chili from his truck. When he returns, she lights a burner under the pot and slides a covered pan into the oven as they talk about everything but what's on their minds and hearts.

Finally John says, "Nothing else we can do for now."

They both fall silent, present yet alert for any sound from the world outside the warm kitchen.

When they're done eating, the dogs lift their heads and get up. As they pace around the table uncharacteristically, Margaret settles them with treats and gentle attention. They finally lie down close to her chair, and she has to step over them to clear the table. As she opens the oven door, a blast of fragrance fills the room. Baked apples, cinnamon, and nuts. When she sets the bubbling apple crisp and two bowls on the table, John feigns reluctance, then laughs and grabs the serving spoon and a bowl and heaps the golden mixture into it.

"Have to walk home after this." He winks and catches her in a broad smile, and they both step briefly into a moment of pure enjoyment without worry.

When they're finished, John accompanies her outside. She keeps the dogs close as she adds wood and leaves to the fire. Turning back toward the house, she looks to the barn and stops. Dangling from a wrought iron hook by the door, something glints in the firelight as it sways and turns in the easy wind. John follows the direction of her gaze and waits for her to turn back to him. When she does, his dark eyes hold hers, the hint of a smile playing on his lips. They walk back to the house without a word.

"Guess it's time to be on my way," John says once they're inside. "You'll be fine?"

Again, his eyes look hard into hers, not letting her avoid the question. She nods and insists he take a container of apple crisp along to his family. She gives him a quick hug. "For Sesalie," she says, and sends him on his way.

She fills a wide-mouthed thermos with leftover chili, wraps the bread in a tea towel, and spoons the remainder of the crisp into a lidded bowl, setting them all into a basket. Humming, hands immersed in warm soapy water, she takes her time washing the dishes.

She tells the dogs to stay put as she shrugs into her heavy coat and trades her shoes for boots. Bringing the basket, she closes the door quietly behind her and walks to the fire bowl. As she stirs the remnants, the flames flare to life and then die back down. Satisfied, she walks to the barn and stops by the door. The rising moon whitens the willow lantern hanging on the hook, which she'd noticed earlier from across the yard.

She steps closer. The mild fragrance of willow woven with sweet grass dances on the night wind. Tightly curled tendrils of bittersweet peek out here and there around the edges. Rising on her tiptoes, she can see a cluster of twigs and stones nested inside the body of the lantern, and something else she can't identify in the dark. Feathers, tiny pine cones, acorn caps, and mica chips dangle on thin strands of grass of varying lengths tacked to the lantern's base. A tiny bell of hammered silver is attached to the central strand. It's clapper, a drilled acorn strung on a slender reed, swings silently.

She'll need daylight for a better look, so she rolls the barn door open and slips inside. Breathing in the quiet of the shuttered barn, she speaks into the darkness.

"I'm glad you came. We've been worried about you. May I join you?"

Chapter 10

He stands in the tack room, the supplies piled against the near wall, his smell mingling with a familiar, older scent. His eyes are just visible in the dim light of the Coleman lantern set on a low shelf. He doesn't speak but nods his shaggy head and steps back.

When Margaret enters the space, he moves to the farthest corner by the backdoor, his body tense, his eyes darting from her to the door and back. As she sets the basket on a hay bale and sits beside it, he relaxes with an expulsion of held breath, but he doesn't move closer.

"I'm so glad you came. I wasn't sure you'd receive the message. Then I wasn't sure if the fire would be visible from where you were. Then..." She stops. "Sorry. I do go on sometimes." She smiles and sees his shoulders relax further as his blue eyes scan her face and the basket beside her. "I'm just so relieved."

He takes two steps toward her, his eyes never leaving hers. "Thank you." His voice comes out in a husky rasp. He clears his throat and repeats the words, and they both smile at the resulting pleasant baritone.

"The craziness out in those woods today is an embarrassment to us all," she says. "This is the least we can do. Please stay for as long as it takes to settle down out there. Please." She holds his gaze, hoping for a sign of acceptance.

He sits on the opposite bale. A smile flickers and is gone. "Do my best. Don't worry. Worry is a poison."

Quietly, she says, "I have a request. I'd like to bring my dogs out to meet you. Once they know you, they won't raise a racket as you come and go. They'll welcome you without a doggy fuss." She smiles. "Would that be all right?"

He nods, his blue eyes alight.

A few minutes later, she reenters the barn, the girls on either side of her. She can feel the electricity inside each golden body as they work at containment. With her voice alone, she guides them toward the stranger, easing their exuberance with a soothing tone. She stops them a few feet from him, and he takes it from there, sliding down onto his knees and extending his hands for them to smell. They are not tentative in their explorations. Their bodies wriggling, tails wagging, tongues tasting, they dance in wild acceptance. He plunks down cross-legged and lets them rub against him, vying for pats and scratchings.

"This is Sophia. And this is Grace. And this, girls, is James." She laughs as they settle on either side of him, a nose resting on each knee. "But I think we've moved beyond a need for formal introductions, or even names."

After a while James smiles, the lines around his eyes crinkling. "I know what they call me out there. Odd James Hatchet."

"Some things about the human community never change, it seems." She sighs. "They have some choice names for me as well. I consider myself in good company."

"Sticks and stones. Long as they leave me be."

"There are a lot more who don't call you that than do. They're the ones I'm counting on until we get this solved. We can trust Jay—Detective Horner—too."

He nods. "If you trust him."

Margaret is touched by his words and the fact that he has settled into conversation. "It's possible he may come by again later. If so, is it all right for me to bring him out here?"

He is silent, but again nods.

"In the meantime, please make yourself comfortable."

Before leaving, she identifies the contents of the various containers she's brought out for him. As she turns to go, she says, "The lantern is beautiful in the moonlight. Such a lovely gift."

The girls rise, nuzzling James before following her. As Margaret turns back toward him, his eyes are glistening. She rolls open the door just wide enough to step through and walks to the crest of the hill. Sending the girls off for a quick run, she covers the fire bowl and sits in one of the Adirondack chairs facing the distant woods. She chuckles as a thought floats in. *What a peaceful prelude to sleep. Moon bathing.* For the first time since morning, she feels an easy calm settling in her solar plexus.

The soft thrumming of a harp has her reaching in her pocket for her phone. "Margaret, it's Jay. How's everything at your place?"

"Lovely and quiet. The fire's gone out. No need to stoke it further. All snuggled in for the night." She smiles at her attempt at code.

"Sounds good. Listen, we're going over to inform Molly's husband in the morning. We've kept it from him long enough. Wouldn't mind getting your take on his reaction. Could you come along?"

She agrees to meet him in town at eight and rings off. Tired now, she remains seated when the girls bound up the hill and stand waiting for her to go inside. Sensing her mood, they lie down on either side of her chair, but do not lower their heads.

She leans back, eyes to the sky as wispy clouds race across the moon and shadows dance across the nightscape. An owl hoots in the distance, reminding her of her earlier vision of the night Mira Clark was murdered. But nothing new comes.

She focuses her attention on Molly's husband, a man she interacted with only briefly before. She can't raise a clear picture of his face, but recalls that he was neither short nor tall, stocky of build, and deeply tanned. He was definitely not the man of her vision with the distinctive spidery veins in his pale hand. Beyond that, she receives nothing, and she relaxes her attention, hoping their meeting in the morning will yield something more useful. She hopes, too, that she will be able to tell if he's involved in Mira's death or is a hapless casualty.

How will he react to the news that his wife is missing and not dead? How would anyone react? How *should* anyone react?

"Okay. Stop. Time for bed. Have to be open and focused in the morning." She gets up and heads inside, the dogs at her heels.

Her dreams are busy and jumbled. She is walking a dirt road at dusk, a rising chorus of peepers singing—the heartbeat of a spring night. A quiet presence floats along beside her. *Mattie?* As she asks, a grumbling disrupts the air, and she knows it's not her brother. Her heart thumping, she turns, ready to confront it, ask what it wants, send it on its way.

Nothing but empty air.

"'Ring a ring a rosies, a pocket full of posies.'" The squealing voices of children carried on the wind. Twin girls on a seesaw. The one on the lower seat suddenly slips off with a laugh; the one in the air crashes to the ground with a thwack and a scream.

A summery scarf snagged on a bush blows in the wind. A wooly scarf twisted around a neck darkens soft flesh. The hiss of spent air. The thud of a bloody rock. A pallid torso covered in tattoos. Spiders and symbols inked across muscled shoulders and down two wiry arms. A blue spiderweb dark against a too-white hand. Hooves kick up clods of dirt and snow. A trophy shines. A tug of war. A blue satin ribbon rumpled in a muddy puddle.

Hoofbeats approach. The ancient stag, elaborate rack etched against a sun-bright sky, leaps a dark ravine. Beneath his graceful body, a tangle of brambles and vines thick with the odor of rot.

A steamy jungle. Fecundity. A constant encroachment. An encampment draped with netting, shrouded in camouflage. The smell of gun oil and sweat. A cloying cloud of blue-gray smoke. Cannabis and cigarettes. Distant gunfire. A flash of blinding light. All hell breaking loose.

An eerie silence. A photograph floating down amidst raining debris, its surface crinkled with spidery cracks. A double exposure.

Walking in the dark. Beside her, slender hooves raise poofs of silent dust. Old Cyrus speaks, his voice deep, redolent of woodlands and waterways. Of all that is untamed. Of time outside of time.

"May you leap beyond the veil of illusion. Dive beneath the surface. See through deceptions sown by those with much to hide."

She turns to him, her questions dissolving as she looks up into clear brown eyes.

"May this day land gently on your heart, Margaret."

He is gone, and she is left longing for more of him. Breathing in the emptiness of absence.

Margaret sits up, residue of the dreams settling in her chest. She goes to the window and stares into the darkness, unsure of what she's looking for. The dreams seemed so real despite their shifting imagery and mystical trappings. Standing barefoot in the dark feels surreal in comparison, yet she knows she's awake. The cool floorboards are solid underfoot, and the blackness around her is the ordinary dark of night. She's aware of Sophia and Grace standing beside her, noses pressed to the windowpanes. Still, she waits for something she can't name. A touchstone to dispel the sense of loss. Something, anything, to alleviate the ache of absence.

She pulls on a sweater, sweats, and a thick pair of socks and heads down the stairs. The girls scramble behind her as she shrugs into her winter coat, dons a hat, and wraps a scarf around her neck. She stops, pulled back into the imagery of the dreams. Swallowing, she loosens the scarf. As she bends to slide her feet into brown rubber boots, silver buckles twinkle against scuffed black leather. She doesn't try to brush the images away.

She yanks open the door and steps into the cold night air. The girls rush past her, stopping by the pair of Adirondack chairs. As Margaret's eyes adjust to the dark, she sees his shadowy bulk seated there and smells the woodsy scent of the tea steaming in the thermos cap on the arm of his chair.

"Mind if I join you?" she asks as she approaches.

He nods.

She indicates the tea as she sits. "I love the smell of eastern hemlock. So soothing. Full of vitamin C, I think."

"Clears my mind. Want some?"

"Thanks, but I'm afraid I can't drink tea in the wee hours or…" She doesn't finish. She can feel him smiling in the dark.

"Did I wake you?"

"No. Dreams."

"Ah."

They sit in easy silence.

Grateful for the companionship, Margaret relaxes into a receptive state. Waiting still, but free of the anxiety of trying too hard. Open. Hopeful. Curious.

Leaning forward, James watches the dogs race down the hill and drink from the stream below, slurping noisily.

Margaret watches him watching them. Her artist's eye traces the craggy profile, the deep-set eyes and thick brows, the chin buried in a thick ruff of beard, the mass of tangled curls plumping out from under a knit hat, bulging around his neck and shoulders like a thick fur collar. She smiles at the curly-haired boy of six or seven chasing a mutt of a dog through a backyard dotted with flowerbeds. Lost in utter joy, his chubby face is lit with laughing. *Rumpus.* The name slips in.

He's on his feet, facing her, hunched forward, tense. "How—"

Both befuddled and startled by his reaction, by the enormity of his physical presence standing over her and his stricken tone, she stares up at him, her heart thudding. Then she realizes what she did. She said it out loud, the dog's name.

"You couldn't know," he says as he drops back into the chair. "You're too young. How...?"

"I'm sorry. I'm not quite sure how to explain. I—"

"You're like your dad." It's not a question. "I remember now. People talked."

"Yes. Runs in my family. Sometimes I blurt things out. I see something and it comes out of my mouth and I stun people and... I'm so sorry."

"Explains a lot."

Sophia and Grace have come on the run and stand watching them, vigilant. James reaches out and pats each cocked head. As he and Margaret settle back in their chairs, the girls lie down in front of them, watchful.

"My mother named him. Rumpus." His raw chuckle sounds like gravel in his throat. "Lived to be fourteen. Died just before ... just before I went away."

Margaret is silent, allowing him space and time to continue or not. Hoping he will.

"Scraggly little runt of a thing." He wipes his sleeve across his mouth.

She smiles. "Dogs are sacred beings in my book. Asking little, giving much."

"Got that right." She can see him nodding his head and working his bearded jaw as if chewing on this and finding sustenance in it. "Had twin goats once too," he adds. "All sharp angles and bleats. Nothing like a dog."

She feels he's working up to something, coming around the back way, warming up to small and not so small talk. And so she waits.

"That woman who died. Can't sleep thinking about her."

"She was a twin." The air around her goes still as he draws in a breath. "They misidentified her because they didn't know. They thought she was Molly Makepeace. Informed her husband and everything. But fingerprints later proved she's Molly's twin sister, Mira. Mira Clark."

"Hmm. Sounds like *mirror*."

"You're right. It does, doesn't it? I hadn't thought of that." She mulls this and then goes on. "I'm going with Detective Horner in the morning when he informs the husband. Molly may not be dead, but she's officially missing."

He lets out a low whistle. "Pretty messed up."

"I really hope you'll stay until things are more settled. I know that's a big ask. But a man shot his own brother in the woods today because of the hysteria over this case. I'm worried about both your safety and your privacy."

"You haven't seen it?"

"Seen what?"

"The outcome of it all."

"No. That's what's troubling me. Something's clouding the issues of the case. The imagery is sketchy. Jumbled." She hesitates, wondering about filling him in completely, then plunges ahead. "I've experienced her before."

She tells him about Molly's earlier disappearance and her recent phone call saying she was about to run again. She describes the ways information usually comes to her and the fuzziness of this case in comparison. As she's concluding her explanations, another name floats into her mind.

This time she stops short of blurting.

"James, another name has come to me. I think this one's for you and not about the case." She strains to be sure this is true, her fingers rubbing the crescent scar over her left brow. "I'm not sure if I should go there."

He turns toward her, his head and ruff of hair silhouetted against the faint light of early morning. "Go."

"Kasha."

He rises and walks away from her, head down, feet planted with care, movements slow and deliberate. He stands on the crest of the hill, his back to her. The dogs lift their heads but remain where they are, bodies alert.

Margaret waits, hoping she's done the right thing. A shooting star streaks across the horizon just above the tree line.

James begins to pace, a few steps toward her and then away. She marvels at the grace of his movements despite the bulk of muscle under layers of clothing. Lost in a haze of pure perception, she notes the silence of each footfall, the earthy odor emanating from him, the sweep of his hand to remove his hat; how he loosens his hair with a shake of his head, thick wild curls bouncing out and around his bearded face like the mane of a lion. This man, somewhere in his seventies, both ancient and ageless, backlit by the blue light of morning, touches the deepest part of her soul.

"Saved my life," he says.

Margaret straightens, pleased to find James seated beside her again.

"Kasha. Kasha Marie Gula. Photojournalist."

Margaret leans toward him but doesn't speak, again giving him space. Another star grazes the treetops and is gone, a short burst this time. They turn toward each other, the words *Did you see that?* hanging unspoken between them. She wonders how it must feel for a man used to being alone to share such a moment. Then she smiles at her own presumption. This man, at one with all the sentient beings around him, is not unused to companionship.

"Embedded with us," he goes on. "Gutsy. Damn good at what she did." He leans forward, elbows on his knees, forehead braced on his clasped hands. "And funny."

Margaret rests her head against the chairback. Birds chirp and flit from the backyard oak to the bushes beyond, heralding the coming of day. Sophia and Grace stir and saunter down the hill. She watches, ready to call them back if they wander too far, but they go no farther than the stream.

"Earned our respect right out of the gate. Always in the thick of it. Camera clicking away. Getting it all down. Every bloody fucking bit. Sorry."

"I didn't think there were women allowed there at that time." As soon as she speaks, Margaret hopes the intrusion of her words doesn't silence him.

"Rare. She was Polish, living in France. Spoke five languages. AP credentials. Knew her way around a camera and anyone who got in her way."

"Sounds remarkable."

He lifts his head and nods. "Like one of the guys ... yet anything but." He sighs and leans back.

"You say she saved your life."

"More ways than one. Owe her. Wish—"

Margaret slows her breath, waiting for more, wishing dawn away.

"Had to be in the thick of it. Right in the bloody fucking thick of it. Had to get the shot. Had to—"

His head is in his hands again, and she reaches out but stops short of touching him.

Dawn lightens the rim of the hills.

"I'm so sorry," she says. "To have brought this all back for you. I—"

"She looked like her."

Margaret waits for more, not sure of his meaning.

"The woman who died. By the rock."

"Ah." She nods, seeing the connections at work.

"Blonde. Pretty in that … that translucent kind of way. Fragile looking but tough to the core."

As he talks, Margaret sees what he's seeing.

She is crouched in a field. Brown grass and stubble. Hunkered down under fire, a scattered group of soldiers around her. Shouts. A blast. The ground shuddering with concussion. Chunks of dirt and rock flying. The whup-whup-whup of distant chopper blades. Too far off. Way too far. An empty helmet upside down on the hillside.

Margaret looks down into a woman's face. Pale skin streaked with dirt. Thick blonde braids matted with blood. Lids fluttering. Light blue eyes rolling back, mostly white as they close. Strong hands, dirt and blood seared into the cracks, clutch her against a blood-stained chest. A camera on the ground half buried in muck and rivulets of blood. The click of a shutter.

She waits as James rocks forward and back in the chair beside her.

"Airlifted her out. Never saw her again."

Margaret sees an array of black-and-white photographs spread across the open pages of a magazine. In one, a group of laughing young men lean against a jeep, the essence of camaraderie. Barely men. Boys. Some not old enough to shave. Another photo, a battlefield. Boys again. Wounded. In shock. Field bandaged. Bodies are strewn at odd angles in a field. A fallen soldier on a hillside, the tortured face of a comrade leaning over him, dazed and bloody. Dog tags in the dirt. The attribution on the glossy page in tiny print reads, *K. M. Gula, 1966–67.*

"She survived," Margaret says aloud.

He sits back in the chair and nods. "Somehow. Wrote a book later. Then … dropped out."

Margaret feels the depth of his grief. She can barely breathe with the weight of it on her chest. Losses too many to name. Frightened boys clutching to life and to him. Deaths and dismemberments. Sights no eyes were meant to see. Sounds no white noise can ever erase. A searing sense of helplessness in the face of it all. Impotence.

A scene from the TV series *M*A*S*H* floats into her mind. The fatherly colonel explains that there are certain rules in war. "Rule number one," he says, "is that young men die. Rule number two is that doctors can't change rule number one."

Nor can medics in the field, she thinks. Especially not medics in the field. Too often, the best they can do is comfort—hold a hand until life leaves, bear silent witness.

Then live with it afterwards. For years, decades, a tortured lifetime.

Sophia and Grace race up the hill barking, slicing the chill morning air with alarm. Margaret leaps up and meets them at the top of the rise, scanning the wooded hills along the horizon. She turns back to James.

But he is gone.

Chapter 11

Margaret finishes off her morning shower with a blast of cold water and then steeps a pot of strong morning tea. Lacking sleep and not at all hungry, she forces herself to eat a bowl of thick oatmeal with chunks of apple. She transfers the remaining oatmeal into a covered glass jar and zips it into a thermal bag, along with a travel mug of leftover tea.

She takes time for a short walk with the dogs to the edge of the woods and back to clear her head. She returns energized and more centered, her earlier concern about meeting Molly's husband unprepared now abated.

On her way to the barn, she feigns a phone conversation, talking loudly as she walks. She rolls the door wide, glances toward the back room, and sets the thermal bag inside on a crate before backing her car out. After she rolls the door closed, she takes a moment to examine the woven lantern in the daylight.

Inside the rounded, tightly woven belly, a nest of grass and leaves holds a cluster of tiny egg-shaped stones. Some white, some gray, some nearly blue. A bundle of silvery sage, lavender stalks, and gray feathers rests among the stones, tied with the stem of a flower. Just above the nest, hanging from the lid, a tiny, winged figure glints and gleams as it turns. She reaches in and cups it in her hand. Shaped by beating, smoothing, and twisting a rectangular piece of metal, the detail is exquisite.

"Oh!" she says aloud, nodding in appreciation. "A dog tag. Oh, James."
She lets the figure go to dangle freely, light as a fairy must surely be.

※

Jay greets her with a curt nod, engrossed in a text message. She climbs into his car, and they head out toward the Makepeace farm. She waits for him to speak.

"This is a new one for me," he says. "Telling someone their loved one is missing instead of dead. No protocol for this."

"And yet you always seem to find your way through."

He smiles for the first time. "Glad I have you on board. I'm hoping you'll pick up on something helpful. But no pressure." This time he laughs.

As they approach the farmhouse, Margaret sits up, scanning the yard and outbuildings. A border collie races out of a shed, barking furiously and running alongside the car, snapping at the tires.

A woman steps out onto the front porch, straining to see inside the car as Jay brakes by the stairs. Short and plump with straight dark hair, she squints at him as he steps out, eyes on the snarling dog.

"Mind calling off the dog, ma'am?"

"Have you found the bastard? You better have found the bastard."

"Sorry, ma'am, no. Is Clarence around?"

"Shut up, Dubbah." The dog skulks away at the sound of her voice. "Haven't you brought him enough grief? What do you want now?"

"Please, ma'am, is he here?"

As Margaret gets out of the car, the woman stares at her, a flurry of expressions playing across her round face. The last is one of recognition. "What the hell is she doing here?" she screams. "What you doin' bringing her here?" Stabbing a thick finger in the air, she takes a step forward. "You get right on back in that car, bitch." Turning on Jay, she yells, "Get her and your damn self out of here." Her face red, her body heaving, she stomps back inside and slams the door.

Jay looks over at Margaret. "I think we just met old Ma Makepeace. Heard she's pretty feisty. First time I've seen her in action."

"Between her and Cujo here, I'd say we're not exactly welcome."

"Detective?"

They look up to see Clarence Makepeace leaning out an upstairs window.

"Come in. Be right down," he says, and disappears from sight.

Inside the kitchen, Mrs. Makepeace nowhere in sight, Clarence fidgets and looks from Jay to Margaret and back. "Have you caught 'em? Was it that wild old bastard in the woods?"

Jay steps forward and urges Clarence to sit in a nearby chair as Margaret observes him closely. The man is clearly in distress. Though in his early fifties, he looks much older. His bloodshot eyes are underscored with sunken hollows like two thumbprints the color of a bruise. His sallow skin stretches like tanned leather over wide cheekbones. He rubs his hands up and down the thighs of his oil-stained pants, but cannot hide the tremors. Margaret wonders if it's grief, guilt, or drink that has ravaged him so.

Jay's voice is gentle as he leans in once Clarence is seated. "It wasn't Molly, Clarence. It was her sister. It was Mira." As the man's eyes widen and his mouth drops open, Jay hurries on. "Molly is missing. We don't know where she is and we don't know if she's involved in any way, but the body in the field is not her."

Clarence stands, his chair crashing to the floor behind him. "What the fuck? What th—"

"We're certain. Fingerprint analysis proves it was Mira. We didn't know Molly had a twin, and we understand how you could have misidentified her in your shock and grief."

Margaret, focused on his physical and verbal reactions, catches the subtle twitch of his mouth, the furtive look toward the window. So subtle are both, in fact, that she takes a moment to examine her impressions. A jolt and sudden nausea rising in her throat confirm it—something is amiss. Something just beneath the surface is at work as Clarence Makepeace reacts to this news. She walks to the sink and looks out the window.

Jay continues. "I'm sorry you had to go through this, Mr. Makepeace, but we still have to figure out where your wife is. We need your help, your full cooperation. Even if it seems unimportant or trivial, or just a feeling about what might have happened to her, we need to know."

"What are you saying? That I know something about all this?" Clarence stares at Jay. "How would I know anything about her sister's death? We've barely seen her in years. And if I knew where Molly was, I'd go and get her myself rather than wait for you to get around to it."

The old woman comes into the kitchen. "What's going on in here? What have you done to upset my boy?"

"I can handle this, Ma." Clarence says quietly.

"Did they catch 'em? Who was it? What—"

"It's not Molly, Ma."

The woman stares at her son and then at Jay and Margaret. "What th—"

"They fucked up. It's Mira."

"Her sister?" She steps forward. Her face changes. "Then where's Molly?"

Margaret notes the look that crossed the older woman's face then disappeared before she could name it. Something else mixed in with the surprise at this piece of news. Fear? Was it fear?

"That's what we're trying to figure out, Mrs. Makepeace," Jay says quietly, trying to calm things with his tone.

"Time for you to leave." Clarence leans down and rights the fallen chair. "You've done what you came out here for, and now I'll thank you to leave." He drops into the chair, lowering his head as if suddenly depleted.

Jay stands silent, looking down on him. "Okay, we'll leave. But first I'd like to look around the property. With your permission, of course."

"No!" Mrs. Makepeace shouts at the same time Clarence nods in the affirmative.

"It's okay, Ma. Can't do no harm." He slumps, his body deflating.

"But—" The old woman stops herself. She stares at Margaret, who is watching her closely. "What you lookin' at? Get out."

As they descend the front-porch steps, Margaret glances back. Ma Makepeace is watching through the screen door. As they reach the bottom, the hinges squeak and the door bangs behind them. Ma has clearly stepped out onto the porch to watch them as they head for the barn and the cluster of outbuildings.

Chickens peck and scratch in the dirt, scattering in spurts as they walk among them toward the coop. A kick to the chest has her reeling backward. Struggling for breath, she bends at the waist. Jay rushes to her side. She drops to her knees, clutching her belly, and stifles the scream clawing to come up. Jay squats beside her, one hand on her back, the other supporting her forehead.

"Something happened here. Sudden and dark." She looks up into Jay's worried eyes. "Maybe recent. Maybe not. I—"

She is grabbed by her coat collar and yanked upright. The broad flat of a hand smacks her between the shoulder blades, pushing her each step of the way toward the doorway of the coop. As she crosses the worn threshold into the dark interior, she is slammed to the ground, her cheek cracking against the hardpacked earthen floor. A kick to the head sends shards of pain through her brain.

"Margaret. Margaret." She can hear the urgency in Jay's tone but can't summon her voice or open her eyes. She feels his hand on hers and squeezes. Then she's sitting up. Still on the ground outside, she's staring into his relieved face.

"Sorry," she says, surprised at the meekness of her voice.

"Just tell me you're all right."

"I am." She attempts a smile and knows she's fallen short. "Something brutal happened here." As she explains her experience, Jay shakes his head, looking from the chicken coop to the house and back to her. He helps her to her feet and asks if she can go inside the coop with him.

She knows it's important and asks only that he go in ahead of her. The imprint of the hand still radiates on her back. Breathing deeply, she steps in after him.

It takes a minute to adjust to the darkness, though some light filters in through the dirty windows set high in one wall and through the low openings for the chickens to come and go. She is aware of Jay's watchfulness as she circles the coop, exploring the roosting perches and nesting boxes. An egg nestled in the straw of one of the boxes stirs a memory. As she reaches in to cup it, she discovers another buried beneath it. It's cool as she expected, and she holds it up toward the windows.

Hand-blown glass, it's lighter than the ceramic versions her mother slipped into the boxes at home to encourage the hens to lay where she wanted them to and not wherever they pleased. "Everything in its place," she'd say.

She and Mattie are running in early morning sunshine, their mother's voice trailing after them. "Careful. Eggs should be scrambled in the skillet, not on the way in from the coop." And the two are giggling, remembering the day Mattie stuffed the top of his overalls with eggs and then tripped in the yard and lay in an eggy mess. With echoes of her brother's laughter dancing in her mind, she places this hand-blown beauty back in the straw beside its companion, resisting the urge to slip both into her pocket.

A baby cries. A woman screams. She lifts her head, listening.

"Okay?"

It takes a moment to separate Jay's voice from the imagery. "Yes," she finally says, her voice hoarse. She clears her throat. "Yes. Sorry."

She looks up to find his worried eyes questioning her again.

"There's a lot coming at me here. I'm not sure what any of it means, but it's relevant. Right now it's like a connect-the-dots puzzle with more than a few missing dots and no numbers to guide me."

"Do you need more time or shall we go?"

"I—"

A fist to the stomach. An angry snarl. "Do as you're told, bitch! Or you'll end up like your sister." A splat of wet tobacco on the floor. The splintering of wood as the door is knocked off one hinge. Sunlight winks through the crack at the top.

They leave and walk the property, checking out the empty barn and the smaller buildings. Cows graze in the fields, and gardens stretch for acres. And above the rot of composting vegetation, the air is saturated with unrelenting misery. All is quiet. Except for a baby crying somewhere.

As they head toward the back of the house, Margaret catches movement in an upstairs window and looks up to see a curtain fall back into place. She shivers.

"This was never a happy home. Ever. The darkness is palpable. If the place could talk, it would tell a tale of tragedy—of multiple tragedies." She stops talking, feeling more disturbed with each word she speaks.

"I feel it too. And I'm about as sensitive as a chain saw," Jay says.

"Au contraire, my friend. Your intuition serves you well. Perhaps sensitivity runs along a continuum from a gut feeling or a little voice that tells you to check out that innocent-seeming witness, all the way up to full-blown kick-ass clairvoyance." She laughs, needing to lighten the heaviness bearing down on her.

As they drive away, the dog races out from behind a tree, snapping and snarling. It dives in and out, biting at the wheels.

"Hold on," Jay shouts. "I'm going to have to outrun the little bastard. Don't want to kill it and give this family any more grief." He steps on the gas, leaving the yapping dog in the rearview.

Once back on the road, he asks for her final impressions of Clarence and his mother.

"They both seemed genuinely surprised it wasn't Molly. But the mother seemed frightened by that. Maybe Clarence as well."

Thoughts form as she speaks, and she lets them through without editing. "They're both hiding something, perhaps many somethings. That chicken coop was ground zero for something harrowing. I'm certain it was recent."

A new thought comes, and with it a brief picture. It's the clearest image she's seen of the missing woman. She's standing at an upstairs window, looking out at the rain. Her hand is on the shade, having pulled it halfway up. Someone else is in the room. Molly drops her hand and turns toward the door. A key rattles in the lock.

"They may have isolated Molly, cut her off from her sister." She looks over at Jay as he pulls up to a stop sign. "Or she may..." She shakes her head. "I need more. I need to go upstairs in that house. We both do."

"Techs did a preliminary search when the body was found. We planned to go in deeper later. Right now I have to drop you back at your car. I have a meeting I can't miss, but I'll see what I can arrange. Of course, they have a right not to let you in on a search."

Chapter 12

Rounding an end cap in the grocery store, heading for the canning supplies, Margaret nearly crashes into an unattended shopping cart. As she moves it aside, Marcella McCray approaches from the other end of the aisle and calls to her.

"Didn't see that one coming, eh?" She laughs. "Is the great Margaret Meader slipping?"

"That, and I'm apparently guilty of withholding information." Margaret immediately regrets engaging with the woman and starts to push her cart past her.

Marcella blocks her path. "Look. I thought about what you said, but I'm not convinced the creepy guy in the woods didn't do it. I think people should be informed. For their own safety."

"Ah, yes, a public service announcement. How altruistic of you." As the words come out, Margaret is surprised at how good it feels to let fly with a little snark of her own. Surprised that she feels no shame. Surprised that her innate civility has given her a pass.

Marcella looks surprised as well. For a moment, Margaret witnesses the truth behind the mask. A little girl of five or six, so fair that Margaret can see right through her to the ducks bobbing on the pond behind her. A click of a shutter and it's gone.

She focuses on the chunk of turquoise hanging from a silver chain around Marcella's neck. It rests in the subtle valley just above the ruffled neckline of her gauzy purple dress. Dramatic. Bold. Genuine?

Marcella, hands on hips and sounding like a little girl in spite of the pulsing energy she is giving off, rounds on her. "Your high opinion of me doesn't matter. I know what I've seen. I know what I know. And no one is going to silence my voice. Especially not another woman."

A group of women at the end of the aisle turn toward them as Marcella's voice rises. They do not move or look away when Margaret glances toward them.

She turns back to Marcella. "This is not about silencing anyone and you know it." She keeps her voice level, her body language casual. "It's about doing no harm. An ethical principle. A useful mantra that you might adopt."

Marcella is quiet. Looking into Margaret's eyes, she appears to be considering this. At the clearing of a throat, she turns and straightens at the sight of their small audience.

"Just imagine the good we can do pooling our psychic energies," she says loudly. Lower, she adds, "You'd have the perfect platform to correct any harm you think I've done." Again, she raises the volume. "And we could share our visions and solve this thing once and for all. In service to the public and the greater good." And a whispered, "And, yes, a moment in the limelight wouldn't hurt either of us or our kind."

The women have stopped pretending they're shopping and have moved closer. Margaret looks straight at them, nodding with a slight smile. Just a casual acknowledgment of neighbors in the market.

"I appreciate the offer," she says quietly to Marcella, "but I don't think that would work out well for either of us. If you truly want to talk sometime, I'm open to that, but I'll pass on any public collaboration."

"I'm not trying to steal your thunder."

"I have no thunder to steal."

"But—"

"Really, this is not a competition. Don't try to make it one."

"Is that a threat?" Again, Marcella's voice is raised, and she looks around defiantly, making sure she's been heard.

Margaret stares at her, considering her next words. "I see what you're doing. And I'll not be manipulated. Good day, Ms. McCray," she says as she wheels her cart around her. One of Annie's favorite expressions rings in her ears—*When you see crazy coming, cross the street.* Smiling, she again nods to the other women in the aisle.

To shed the irritation sizzling in her chest, she takes her time gathering canning supplies and a few groceries and then strolls to the checkout. Erica, the quiet teenager running the cash register, smiles shyly as she scans each item. Margaret sees her in cap and gown delivering the valedictory on a sunny spring day.

"A senior this year, right?" The girl nods and briefly meets her eyes. "What's your favorite subject?"

"Biology. I'm going to be a marine biologist." The shyness disappears as she describes her course of study, her face bright and animated, her voice assured.

"Sounds like the perfect plan for a girl who swims with seals." Margaret laughs as she hefts her purchases into the cart and a new image comes. She turns back to Erica. "Oh, I envy you. A lifetime of studying what you love. Priceless."

Smiling good-bye, she catches the dour expression on Deborah Cowell, the person next in line. With her finger raised to admonish the girl for ignoring her, she glares at Margaret.

"You forgot the lemons," Margaret says, meeting the woman's stare. "A shame to get home without that key ingredient." She winks at Erica as Deborah wheels her squealing cart around and sputters off toward produce.

In the parking lot, Margaret runs into Emily, who catches her up on Ned's remarkable progress in rehab. They agree to meet for a lengthier visit, and Emily turns to leave.

"One more thing," Margaret calls.

Emily turns back to her.

"Louisa, Marchella's assistant. Do you think..."

"Already on it." Emily grins. "I bumped into her at the office supply store. Turns out she has questions about the MFA program I'm in, and we're meeting for coffee later today."

"I don't want to interfere with a potential friendship."

"Not to worry. I intend to find out what I can about her role in Marcella's act, but that doesn't preclude our becoming friends. I'll fill you in later."

Chapter 13

Checking the time, Emily hurries to change before meeting Louisa. Afterward, she'll be seeing Ned. With a half hour before she has to leave, she begins an online search for information on Marcella Catriona McCray and her young assistant. Skipping the news items about Marcella's recent statements to the press, she jumps to her website.

The home page is alight with bright colors and bold text, with bouncing gifs and flashing lights along the margins. In the dark pupil of a huge gray eye, shifting photos of Marcella slip in and out of focus. Wind-blown and artfully disheveled, her long blonde hair flutters around her air-brushed face. Her pale skin shimmers in a wash of lavender lighting. Intermittent blasts of white light burst from her signature turquoise pendant.

Labeled buttons at the bottom of the screen blink intermittently. *About. Special Services. Videos. Testimonials. Private Readings. Blog.* She clicks on *Videos,* and a link appears to a video-sharing site called Psychics & Seers. The link takes her to an array of video options, three of which are underscored with Marcella's name. Emily scans the first two. One is a grainy, poorly shot promo for a psychic fair featuring Marcella and someone named Cassandra. The second, shot on a smartphone, shows Marcella using her favorite divination tool, the Mystical Tarot Deck. And the third is a professionally produced episode of a talk show on the Psychics

& Seers Network. Emily watches for a few minutes as Marcella and the host discuss psychic phenomena. Not hearing anything of interest, she fast forwards but hits pause seconds later. She resumes watching at regular speed.

Marcella is slumped forward in her chair, then she rises and dances across the stage, her arms floating gracefully around her. She drops to the floor in front of an old woman seated in the audience. Marcella's body, face, and demeanor shift subtly, becoming childlike. Looking up into the woman's surprised face, she says in a tiny voice, "Grandy?" The woman dissolves into shuddering sobs.

"Don't be sad, Grandy. Don't cry." She rises to her knees, reaching for but not quite touching the distraught woman. "I'm happy. I'm dancing. And I'll be here waiting."

There is a collective intake of breath in the audience as the woman slides to the floor, weeping. "Penny. My beautiful Penny."

At this, Marcella gets up, becoming her woman self again. She stands over the kneeling grandmother. "Yes. Your Penny wants you to know she's all right—happy, in fact—and will be waiting for you when your transition comes."

Done, Marcella returns to her seat and accepts a glass of water from Louisa, before discussing with the host her extreme fatigue and subsequent lethargy following a "channeling session" like this.

Emily fast forwards again, looking for more shots of Louisa. Finding none, she returns to the homepage and clicks over to read the testimonials and then the dropdown list of special services. Looking up at the clock, she regrets not having set aside more time to explore, and saves the blog and other featured sections for later.

‡

As Emily seats herself at a corner table in the Spotted Zebra Café, she realizes it's the same table she and her friend Jacquie occupied after Jacquie's assault a few months earlier. She has a sudden idea that makes her smile. As soon as she gets to Ned's rehab center, she'll check to see how soon she can take him out to dinner at his childhood friend's restaurant, Jaqueline. Still smiling, she looks up to see Louisa scanning the tables. She waves and then watches Louisa wend her way through the crowded café.

Petite, Louisa is dressed in a blue tunic and scarf that match her denim-colored eyes, navy leggings and hiking boots. Her black pixie cut perfectly frames her heart-shaped face. Her lipstick is so subtle, it gives the impression she's wearing none. A heavy-looking laptop bag slung over her right shoulder bumps several chairs as she passes.

As Emily offers her hand in greeting, Louisa's acceptance is tentative. As at their meeting in the woods, the young woman lowers her head and speaks so softly, Emily has to lean in. "I probably shouldn't have come. If Marcella finds out, she—"

"I'm really glad you did come." Emily cuts her off. "You're going to love this place, and if you're supposed to be on the clock for Marcella, consider this a working lunch."

"No. It's my day off. I just…"

"Surely your life and time is your own. Sit down. Check out this menu. All organic. All delicious." Emily sits back down and resolves to keep the conversation comfortably light.

After they've ordered, she asks Louisa about herself. Where she's from. What kind of writing she's interested in, both as a writer and a reader. What her dreams are, personally and professionally. She stays away from anything Marcella related, hoping Louisa will bring that in on her own, but content to save that for another time.

By the time their coffee and warm quinoa-honey-&-almond bowls arrive, they are deep in conversation with Louisa loosening into laughter.

"I worked three jobs through school and came out with a pile of debt and a BA that wasn't going to land me anything that paid better. When Marcella's ad popped up, I couldn't resist the beginning salary and the thought of working just one job. But now that I'm doing it..." She stops and looks away without finishing the thought.

Emily waits, hoping for more. She doesn't push. She knows better. Margaret has taught her well the art of maintaining a listening silence.

"It fascinated me at first. I'd never been around anyone quite like Marcella." Louisa looks off into the distance, smiling at a memory. "Never a dull moment, as they say." With a light laugh, she returns her gaze to Emily.

"And psychic phenomena? Was that an area of interest for you before your work with Marcella?"

Louisa looks down at her bowl, back at Emily, then down again. The shifting focus takes only a second or two, but combined with a fleeting look of alarm, it deepens Emily's curiosity.

Louisa clears her throat before answering. "I found it curious, as I think most people do." She hastens to add, "I'm a writer, and it seemed like an interesting topic when I read the job description. I'd never imagined working in the field, but I was open to a new experience."

"And has it been satisfying?"

Louisa's gaze slides to the right as she considers the question. "Yes and no."

Emily leans forward and rests her folded arms on the table, waiting for her to go on.

Louisa sips her coffee, her blue eyes searching Emily's face over the rim of her mug. "It's like..."

Emily encourages her with a nod and a smile. Louisa puts down her mug. There's a subtle shift in her eyes, the closing of a shutter, a darkening of the moment.

"It's like any job, I guess," she says. "It has its pros and cons. You know what it's like, I'm sure. When you worked at the gallery in Boston, it must have been both interesting and tedious at the same time."

Emily is surprised by this reference to her past, and she knows it shows on her face.

Louisa rushes to explain. "I looked you up. Habit. Research, an integral tool to my work. My writing. I can't help myself."

Emily laughs in recognition of a sister, deciding in that moment to let go of trying to tease information out of her.

As their server tops off their mugs, they resume discussing the pros and cons of the low-residency MFA program Emily is enrolled in. Though Louisa is based farther north in the Lewiston-Auburn area, Emily describes her newly formed writers group for those enrolled in the program.

After thanking her, Louisa says, "I hear the sci-fi author Samuel Kingston is living in the area. Have you heard of him? His book *Skylark 99* is amazing. Rumor has it he's writing a memoir about a psychic relative. Do you know anything about it?"

"I can neither confirm nor deny the rumors." Emily laughs, then makes a decision. "As a matter of fact, I've met him. He's offered to read some of my book and tell me what he thinks. I must admit, I'm a bit intimidated at the thought of showing my work to someone like him, but excited at the same time. We haven't worked it all out since I've been... My life has been ... chaotic for a while now. My boyfriend was—"

"Ned," Louisa says softly, shifting in her chair and looking past Emily's left shoulder. Quickly, she adds, "I read about that too. I'm so sorry. How's he doing?"

"Recovering slowly but surely." Emily is surprised as emotion rises in her throat and tears threaten. When, she wonders, will she stop being blindsided by the terrible flashes of memory?

Louisa reaches across the table and squeezes her hand. "He's going to be all right. Different but fine. You both will be. I'm sure of it."

Emily looks at her, into those denim-blue eyes, aware of something between them she can't quite define. Something having to do with Margaret. She can imagine Margaret speaking those same words in the same knowing tone. Unlike the plastic platitudes empty of substance she's been offered in the past months, Louisa's words slip like a comforter around her shoulders.

"Different but fine," she repeats aloud. "Hmm."

Both are silent as they sip their coffee. Neither finishes her food.

"Do you mind if I ask you a question?" Emily asks, unable to hold herself back. "I watched a video on Marcella's website—the one with the grandmother she called Grandy. And—"

Louisa stiffens, frowning as she sets her mug down and reaches for her bag. "I can't talk about that."

Emily plows ahead, a niggling concern for the younger woman eclipsing her earlier resolve to move gently. "How does she treat you? Is she difficult as a boss, or was she having an off day when we met in the woods?"

Louisa straightens, adopting a defensive tone. "She's a passionate person. She's easily excited but quick to apologize when she flares. She values my work—says so all the time—and she pays me very well."

Emily searches her eyes, her face, her body language for more—and she is certain there is more. Louisa looks away and rummages in her bag. She pulls out her wallet and ignores Emily's offer to pay the check. Emily reaches across the table and stays her hand, forcing her to look up.

"I didn't mean to upset you. I'm sorry." She searches for a word to describe this need, this instinct to protect a woman only a few years younger than she. When the word comes, it surprises her. *Maternal.* "I got the impression she was hard on you, but I realize your work relationship is none of my business. Again, I'm sorry."

Louisa sits back. "I appreciate your concern. I take it she's not at all like your friend Margaret. Having psychic abilities in common clearly doesn't mean two people are alike in any other way. The truth is, Marcella *is* difficult. Demanding and hard to please. I never seem to get it right. To do enough. I hold on because the money is good and I... What's Margaret like? I wonder if she could... if she might... I'd love to talk to her. Without Marcella around."

"I think she'd love to chat with you. I'm happy to give you her contact info." Noting the return of Louisa's shield of shyness, Emily quickly changes tack. "Would you like me to arrange a visit?"

Louisa sighs in obvious relief. "That would be great."

"It's set then. I'll call you later with details."

As she gathers up her bag and rises, Louisa stops, a strange look on her face. "Is Margaret a twin?"

"Yes. She had a twin brother."

"Had?"

"He died when they were little."

"Oh. I thought... I'm sorry."

"What made you ask?"

"I saw— I mean, um..." She looks off as if trying to recall something but, oddly, it feels like an act to Emily. As she ponders this, Louisa continues. "I must have read it somewhere. I just wondered if there were two with the sight. I thought it would be interesting if—"

"She doesn't really talk about him. It's a difficult subject."

Louisa continues looking across the room. Finally, she hefts her bag on her shoulder and meets Emily's eyes. "I can't imagine losing someone so close. Especially as a child. Does she have any other siblings?"

"No. She grew up alone."

A range of emotions flickers across Louisa's face before a mask of neutrality slips into place. "Sad. I'd better be off. Talk soon."

Emily watches her cross the busy room and exit the café. Her curiosity piqued, she pulls out her phone, eager to arrange a meeting with Margaret sooner rather than later.

Chapter 14

Margaret parks in the side yard to unload the groceries. Her stomach tightens as she glances toward the barn, sensing the emptiness within. James has slipped away. She has to let go of worrying. Somehow.

She fumbles with the grocery sacks as Sophia and Grace greet her inside the door and rush past her for a run. Swept off balance, she stumbles toward the ringing kitchen phone. It stops just as she reaches it. She dumps her purchases on the counter and fishes her cell phone out of her coat pocket as it begins to chime. An unknown number; she lets it go to voicemail.

As she shrugs out of her coat, she's drawn to the pair of dolls on her mother's cabinet. With their long legs dangling from the shelf and their soft bodies leaning into each other, their crooked smiles coax her into a reluctant smile of her own. *Okay. What? What are you thinking? What would you say if you could talk?*

Tears bubble out through the coarse fabric and slip down cloth faces, startling her. A baby cries. She looks around. Another joins in. Heart-wrenching wails rise, filling the kitchen, the house, her world. She covers her ears, trying to breathe the sounds away, but the cries pierce flesh and bone and swirl inside her head.

"Stop!" she yells.

And they do. Her own voice echoes in the empty air. In the quiet that follows, a chorus of tiny voices filters in. Barely audible at first, it builds as more and more voices join. The sound is sweet yet earnest, empty of childlike mirth. "One little, two little, three little Indians..." She stares at the dolls. The words resonate, not because they're from a familiar children's ditty, but because of some deeper recollection. "What in the—"

"And two hundred and six more." The words sting, a targeted taunt that reverberates, swirling round and round before fading back into the silence of the empty room. Tears again slip down the rounded cheeks of the dolls.

"Two hundred and nine," a lone voice sounding very much like Mattie's says as the number shimmers in the air and then dissolves into mist.

She reaches for her grandmother's journal on the shelf below the dolls. Opening to a random page, she writes out the words she's just heard on a sliver of white space at the bottom. *One little, two little, three little Indians ... And two hundred and six more. ... Two hundred and nine.* Again, she feels the sting of rebuke.

As her cell rings, she starts to close the journal but stops. In the upper left-hand corner of a page filled with colorful drawings sits a large teardrop rendered in charcoal. Within the drop, three small heads are lined up. Thick dark hair hangs down around three sturdy sets of shoulders. Three sets of dark eyes glisten, wet with long-held tears. A jagged X is slashed across each tightly closed mouth. A pair of scissors, open and ready, hangs above the three heads. Beneath the teardrop in Lucinda's now familiar script: *And then there were none.*

Drawn to the hushed mouths, Margaret's field of vision narrows as a memory surfaces. Her mother's long-ago words, spoken quietly but traveling to the deepest levels of her being: *Best to put it behind us, Maggie. Best to forget about it. Best to forget all about it.* A clenching in her chest hunches her forward, folding in upon herself, sending her back into that terrible moment. Bruised and barely alive, she lies tucked into a fetal ball on her bed. Nine years old, bullied and battered and left locked in a root cellar for three days by a group of kids bigger and older ... and no one to stand for her afterwards. With her mother's words, the door closed and that had been that. And she'd kept her mouth shut in the years following, keeping it all under wraps, ever working to bury the fact of it and the resulting outrage. Assaulted, then silenced.

Something tells her these darkly drawn children in her grandmother's journal stand for countless generations suspended in a silence denser and more debilitating than her own. A silence so pervasive, they can't even imagine words that might set them free.

Margaret's phone chimes, announcing a voice message. She ignores it. She sits staring at the page and the words she's written there, knowing this is deeply important yet not knowing how or why.

Nothing surfaces. Finally she asks aloud, "Is this related to Mira's murder or something else entirely? Can you give me more?"

The ticking of the clock followed by the barking of the dogs outside offers nothing but a reminder that time is passing and the girls need food and attention.

She heads for the backdoor, opening her voicemail as she goes. "I'm looking for Margaret Meader." The trademark vocal rhythms of a newscaster washed free of regional identifiers bleats into the quiet before she can lower the volume. "This is Caitlin Hammond with the Channel Eight News Team. I need a comment before I go back on air. It's urgent Ms. Meader. Please call. I'm sure you'll want to tell your side in this unfolding story."

When she opens the door, Sophia and Grace rush in, carrying the cold with them. Energized bodies bump against her thighs and cold noses nuzzle her curled fingers as they work their magic and pull her into the immediacy of the moment. As thoughts of the murdered and the missing and the six o'clock news report evaporate, she bends to snuggle. The dogs press against her, slathering her with wet kisses, and the world is righted and her mind begins to clear.

Her phone rings again, and she knows she must answer in spite of a darker wish to toss it and all its "smartness" into the trash.

"Margaret?" The note of concern in Sesalie's voice surprises her until she realizes she answered without saying a word and the resulting silence lasted many seconds too long.

"Yes. Sorry," she said. "I have yet to master the art of multitasking, and you caught me with my mind lagging about three steps behind. Oh, and thanks for the chili you sent over with John. Wish I could master your knack. How are you?"

"I'm fine. Better than you must be with all this craziness around you. That's why I've called, actually. The women are meeting tonight—the grandmothers and aunties and cousins. A little impromptu potluck with guaranteed laughter. Baubo will be the guest of honor, if you know what I mean."

Sesalie's laughter finishes the work begun by Sophia and Grace. Shoulders relaxed and belly softened, Margaret takes in the deepest breath she's known in too long a while.

"Annie's coming," Sesalie finishes on a hopeful note, "so you can ride over together."

"I'd love to. What time?" She accepts this lifeline without debate and breathes out a grateful prayer.

As she hangs up, the phone rings again. Seeing Emily's name on the screen, she smiles as she answers, and within a few minutes she has arranged a lunch for the next day with her young friend and Marcella McCray's assistant.

Humming, she sets about making a squash and apple soup and two loaves of spiced pumpkin bread. The girls snuffle around the baseboards and corners of the kitchen before settling beneath the table with contented sighs. Soon the kitchen is redolent with warmth and the heady scents of autumn in the oven.

Grounded in the comfort of kitchen busyness, she answers her next phone call—it is Annie this time—without salutation. "Yes. I'd love to ride to Sesalie's with you."

Her cheerful words are met with silence followed by a stuttered apology. "I … um, I didn't call for that. I mean I intended to, but … I'm calling about the news story that's on right now. Or maybe it's over by now. I'm not sure. It's about you and—"

"Slow down. It's not even six o'clock yet and—"

"Channel Eight News. It's their teaser about the six o'clock newscast. They're going to talk about you and Jay and the investigation."

As Annie takes an audible breath, Margaret asks for a moment and hurries to her little-used television in the sitting room. She flicks it on, and when she lands on channel eight, an afternoon talk show has resumed with two vaguely familiar celebrities arguing the pros and cons of Botox to stay forever young. Margaret shuts it off.

"What did it say exactly?" she asks Annie as she returns to the kitchen.

"That there will be a special report on the use of a team of psychics, one a local woman, by Detective Jay Horner in solving the case of the 'Woman of Wandering Rock.' That's what they've named her, the Woman of Wandering Rock. And you are the 'local woman.'"

"Well, I guess it was inevitable. When the police found Alissa Cates, the case created a minor blip about all things psychic. Up until then, I'd managed to fly under the radar. But since Marcella McCray inserted herself into this latest matter, the blip got reactivated, bleeping out on all frequencies. I'm afraid my anonymity has been blown. And I'm sure I'm mixing all sorts of metaphors here."

"But what will you do? They'll be all over you, making it up as they go along. Digging around in your backyard. What in the world will you do?"

"Well." She inhales deeply. "I'm going to start by going to Sesalie's tonight and bathing in the balm of a circle of very wise and funny women."

"But—"

"But nothing. We're going to get our butts into my car and leave the worries and what-if's behind for the evening. I'll pick you up at five thirty."

She knows it is with great reluctance and much tongue holding that Annie disconnects without protest. She loves her friend for that—her most talkative friend by far.

She swipes to her voicemail page and listens again to Caitlin Hammond's message. Finger paused over the return button, she debates making the call, then turns the phone off and slips it into her pocket.

"Nothing good can come of this," she says aloud. There is no way to tell another side to a story that someone started with an agenda. No explanation or refusal to comment will disabuse another person who's set on starting something with their misconceptions. She knows that. She's lived that. She sighs.

The kitchen timer buzzes, and she heads to the stove. A blast of pumpkin and spice whooshes up in her face as she opens the oven door. She sticks a toothpick in the center of each loaf and, satisfied, sets them on the cooling rack on the counter. She gives the soup a stir and a taste and lowers the flame. She ladles some into a squat thermos and sets that next to the pumpkin breads, worrying that James won't return under cover of darkness and then stay put in the barn.

With a sudden volley of sharp barks, Sophia and Grace scramble out from under the table and race to the back door.

Hushing them and holding her breath, she peeks through the curtained window in the door but sees no one. She cracks the door open. Nothing. As she opens the door wider to step out, she's blinded by a camera flash.

Ross Templar, reporter for the *Gazette*, is in her face. "Would you like to comment on the story Channel Eight is about to air about your involvement in previous and current investigations of Detective Horner's into—"

Margaret grabs the camera from his hand, surprising him. Turning her back to him, she deletes the photo and then flips to the "recently deleted" page, deleting it there as well. Whirling back around, she says, "I'll thank you to leave my property, Mr. Templar." Keeping her voice level and her shaking under tight control, she adds, "I have nothing to say to you."

He reaches for the camera but she holds back, staring into his eyes. "And I'll thank you not to invade my privacy again, by ambush or otherwise. If you'd started off with a modicum of civility, we might have had a conversation. But since you chose—"

"Your funeral," he says, grabbing the camera from her, his knuckles bumping her chest as he does so.

"Is that a threat, Mr. Templar?"

"Nope. Just doing a little fortune telling of my own. A story is blowing wide open, and you're at the center. Choosing not to get ahead of it may well mean the demise of your relationship with the good detective *and* your good reputation. Just sayin'… But if you—"

"Good-bye, Mr. Templar." She closes the door and directs her dogs to resume barking, hoping it will remind the irksome man that she is not alone out here. She relaxes at the roar of a car engine and then the spit of gravel under his tires as he leaves.

"Well, here we go, girls. I just made a bad situation worse. The snowball's rolling down a giant hill and there's nothing I can do to stop it. Time for the healing company of the women."

Chapter 15

Sesalie welcomes Margaret and Annie into the mud room. Their arms full, bearing food and a gift basket, they lean in for awkward hugs. Sesalie relieves them of some of their bags and waits while they exchange boots for slippers before leading them into the kitchen.

As the smoky fragrance of sweetgrass and sage greets her, Margaret stops, Annie nearly bumping into her from behind. She closes her eyes, taking in the warmth of herb-infused air, the crackling fire in the open hearth, and laughter coming from the other room. Breathing in the comfort of the familiar—women's voices rising and falling in easy conversation, underscored by the heavy aroma of mulled cider simmering on the stove and the smell of seasoned apple wood burning on the grate—she allows her body to settle, to open.

She heads for the long wooden table against the kitchen wall laden with hefty pots and assorted dishes. Platters of fruit and goat cheese, slices of pears and apples drizzled with honey, vegetable dishes, a squat bean pot on a trivet, bowls of saltwater taffy and handmade chocolates. Salads and sauces and dips. She plugs in her Crock-Pot of soup and sets it next to another filled with a savory lentil and root vegetable stew. As she places a loaf of pumpkin bread on a cutting board, Sesalie's sister Sylvia plunks down a platter heaped with bubbly pillows of fry bread fresh from the pan.

As the smell wafts into the other rooms, she listens for the collective inhale and satisfied sigh and is not disappointed. In moments, the kitchen fills with smiling women, each stopping to hug Margaret and Annie as they head for the stacks of plates and bowls and dig into the feast. Smiling, she drinks in the spirit of potluck.

"Margaret. It's been too long." The quiet voice and light touch to her back has her turning with a smile. Sesalie's mother's upturned face is alight with happiness.

"Aiyana." She bends to hug the diminutive woman. "Too long, indeed. It's good to see you looking so well."

Aiyana takes Margaret's hands in both of hers and places them on her heart. "Thanks to you."

Margaret receives her words with a gracious bow, acknowledging the need for humble acceptance when gratitude is offered. Looking down at this woman with the bright eyes and shining spirit, she is transported back to the time when those eyes were dull, the spirit nearly gone from that vibrant body. Aiyana's health had suddenly declined, and the medical community had dismissed the family when they sought answers.

When John told her of their struggle, she had a vision immediately. She saw the heart defect in minute detail. Her anger surfaces again as she remembers how the specialist—that condescending god-in-a-white-coat—called them ignorant Indians and tried to send them away. And how proud she was when they stood their ground, strong in their faith in Margaret's truth and in their love for their beloved Aiyana, and got him to do the tests that ultimately saved her life.

She leans in and hugs the woman again, surprising her. As she pulls back laughing, Sylvia turns away from the food table with a brimming plate, bumping into them. "Better dig in before it's gone."

The two women join the others carrying full plates out to the closed-in porch, where place settings are laid out on another long table. Its surface is pocked and scarred from years of daily use. As she sits and runs her hand along the wood, golden in the candlelight, Margaret sees John, her dear friend, bent over the table. As he sands it and then rubs it with oil, Sesalie looks on, her long hair swaying as she rocks a baby on her hip, her love for her husband shining in her dark eyes.

"What you seeing, girl?"

The old woman's deep voice pulls her back into the moment, and she meets the twinkling eyes of Sesalie's eldest aunt.

"Love in action," she says to the woman whose name suddenly comes back to her. Auntie Ha-Ha—named by John and Sesalie's youngest when he couldn't yet say *Hasaleen.*

"Ah, yes. John's handiwork in their first year." She looks intently at Margaret, her brown eyes sunken in rolls of leathery skin. "How are you, Margaret?"

"I am well. Now. Here." She sighs heavily.

"It's been long. You have been missed."

"And you as well. I get lost in the outside world sometimes and forget how much I need this. You. All of you."

"And you remember just in time." She waves a gnarled hand in a sweeping motion. "Eat. Breathe. Listen to all there is." As laughter lifts and floats to them from the other end of the table, the old woman adds, "And laugh."

Sesalie sets down her bowl and a plate of fry bread and sits at the head of the table, between Margaret and Hasaleen, as Annie settles in next to the elder. The four of them slip into companionable silence amid the ring of utensils against crockery and the murmur of voices up and down the table.

❦

After clearing their dishes, the group reassembles with desserts and the family stories begin. Even the smallest stories are met with deep listening. The storyteller has the floor.

This is the first pass, and all present know it. The circle stories and the more ancient ones, of the beginnings of all there is, are told by the elders and will come later. In another room. It is tradition.

Melody, her abdomen round with her second child, has everyone laughing, dessert forks dropping on plates, as she spins a graphic tale of her three-year-old's latest escapades. Sandra brings them to tears with her remembrance of her sister's last hours. Angel makes an announcement that has them grinning with pride: she has passed the bar exam. Her sister Kalie breaks the unwritten rules by shouting, "Blew them away with her score!"

As Margaret listens to the women share these snippets of lives lived in community—the big and small moments alike—an image arises of a tapestry, its myriad threads shimmering in the middle of the table. Some sections have faded with age, others are bright with newly dyed cottons and wools. Some are woven of silk and flecked with silver and gold. Some are plain and coarse and of the earth. All interwoven and ongoing.

Then come the more colorful stories told by women only in the company of women. Tales of marital mishaps and misunderstandings, but never mean-spirited. Just funny human tales of life lived in relationships, gender to gender, woman to woman, generation to generation. Some on the steamy side produce belly laughs and tears of giddiness. And before long someone, someone old, says, "Baubo is here." The laughter erupts more loudly than before.

"Sesalie," Auntie Dawn calls out. "Read your little goddess poem, your Baubo poem."

Everyone prods until she agrees. In preamble, she explains that while taking a women's studies course at the university, the professor assigned a written piece about a goddess from Greek mythology. She chose the little-known goddess Baubo because she was the most obscure.

"She's the goddess of mirth who came to coax the earth mother, Demeter, out of her despair when her daughter was kidnapped by the god of the underworld. With her naked dancing antics, Baubo made Demeter laugh, bringing sun and life back to a shriveling earth. Her medicine engenders deep breathing."

"Okay, so on with the poem," her aunt pleads.

Sesalie stands and clears her throat. Her long blue-black hair shines in the soft light of wall sconces and candles. A single streak of silver runs from crown to the feathered tips at her waist. Anticipation sizzles in the pause before she begins. All lean in.

> On the rim
> of the blue light of morning
> it comes.
> Laughter.
> Rolling,
> rumbling,
>   reaching into my sleep.
> Deep and rich,
> redolent of earthy matters.
> From the belly.
>
> That kind of deep.
>
> Out of the silence steeped in sadness—

laced with grief,
rife with loss—
she comes.

Dancing.

Laughing.

Clearing the air of static
still sizzling from the thundering night.

Her naked belly puckered,
seared with faint remnants of wondrous stretchings.
Her grinning face wrinkled—
crow-crinkled around indigo eyes of knowing.
Her jiggling breasts—free of restraints—
reveling.

Her bare feet beating out a sacred rhythm
on the bottom of an upturned tub.
Her luscious mouth spilling stories
meant for women's ears alone—
wild tales dripping with juice
and full with bawdy bits—
cracking the crusted husk
encasing a long dried well.

I awaken,
rubbing what I'd always thought to be
my too-round belly.
Laughing.
Remembering.

Inhaling like I never knew I could.

Silence sings in the air around the table. Smiles settle on every face. No one moves as they inhale the words and images offered in the honeyed voice of a shy sister.

Auntie Dawn breaks the silence. "And that, dear ladies, is little Baubo, who sees with her nipples and speaks with her vulva."

This sends the women back into laughter. Baubo laughter—from the belly, redolent of earthy matters.

Her sides aching, tears running down her face, Margaret raises her mug. "To Baubo. To Sesalie. To Dawn."

In response, everyone raises her mug or glass in salute.

In the collective catch of the breath that follows, a quiet voice speaks from the armchair in the far corner of the room. "And…"

All eyes turn to Sesalie's grandmother, Winowa, the oldest woman in the house. As she lifts a frail arm, her glass shaking in her hand, she nods to each woman of her family and then to the two guests. Her rheumy eyes rest briefly on Margaret before she resumes.

"…to all our woman stories, songs, and poems. Our Sister stories. To honoring the First Mother who birthed us and sacrificed herself to nourish us. To giving voice to all the stories since, the big ones and the little ones. Especially the little ones."

A coughing spell stops her, and those closest lean in to place their hands upon her. When the coughing stops, she closes her eyes and rests her head against the back of the chair.

Then her hand goes up again. "To weaving them into the work of our hands and hearts. To keeping them alive. To passing them down and around. For our children and our children's children. May they never be taken from us again. May the lost ones never be forgotten." Her hand lowers gradually, and then she thrusts it upward as she speaks the final words. "To never forgetting."

"To never forgetting," the women respond.

In the ringing silence after, images float and dance above the table as Margaret settles into a receptive haze. A baby crying. And another. And another. Women walking, their fingertips brushing the soft heads of the tall grasses. On into the woods they walk, honoring the ash and the curling bark of the birch, touching them as they pass, every movement saturated with reverence. Beside a brook they walk as it winds through the thickening forest. Each step landing softly but with purpose. Each face beautiful in its uniqueness. Each body its own. Moving as one. All grace. All fluidity. All of a single intention.

Margaret straightens, pulled by a distant murmuring.

"Shh, she's dreaming." The voice is far away yet near at hand. Familiar.

"Let her be. Let her dream the dreams."

At this, Margaret senses a drawing back around her.

Walking again, her long skirt swirling around her legs. The brook gurgling to her right. A corridor of pines flanking her on the left. The swishing of skirts before and behind her. Quiet breathing, the many as one, stirring the air. A subtle force like gravity pulling her toward ... something. She surrenders to the gentle tug.

The brook flows downward, quickening as it spills over rocks and boulders. She stops atop a moss-covered ledge overlooking a waterfall. White foam froths and bubbles two hundred feet below. Mist rises, glistening with tiny rainbows.

She leaps from the ledge, grace in flight. Her hands stretched out before her, she breaks the surface, the icy water shocking her into a heightened state of awareness. Down and down she goes into the churning depths. Her lungs burn, and she wonders if this is death. With the question comes a slowing and a floating, her hair drifting around her.

Expecting darkness, she is suspended in liquid light. Soft music somewhere near. All strings—cello, viola, harp.

Bony fingers rip her away from the warm, the soft, the sounds. A wailing. A tearing of fabric. Hands holding her down. The gleam of shears. Hanks of hair falling. A jab to the tongue. An injection filling her with words she does not want.

She pops to the surface, lungs bursting. Before she can get her bearings, she is swept along a flume of raging water. Bruised and battered, she calls out for help. The only response is the cry of an eagle high overhead.

As she's pulled under again and again, a fork in the river ahead has her frantic. She grabs for the branch of a downed tree, hooks her elbow around the thickest part, and swings up as the wild current screams by. Straddling the limb, she squeezes her thighs against its rough bark and inches along the trunk to the shore. Atop a hill, she collapses in a grassy patch of sun and breathes in its heat.

Below her, two rivers stretch beyond the fork. One drops abruptly onto jagged rocks. The other gentles over the course of a mile, flowing languidly toward the ocean.

The bloated face of a woman obliterates the sun. Her chest heaves and rattles under a smock covered in afterbirth. She smells of stale cigarettes and dirty diapers.

Margaret stares at the oddly familiar face, the tangle of greasy black hair, the spittle as curses fly.

"This ain't got nothin' to do with you, bitch. Mind your own damn business."

The woman lunges, and Margaret falls backward. She opens her eyes with a start.

The room is quiet. The women around the table are holding space for her, allowing her the time she needs to come back to them and into the present.

From her armchair in the far corner, Sesalie's grandmother smiles. "Welcome back. We'll wait while you right yourself."

Sylvia sets a tall glass of water in front of her. Annie places her hand on top of Margaret's. Margaret acknowledges these acts with a smile and a nod to the room in general, but she is not yet ready to speak.

Hasaleen stands and pushes back her chair. "Your gift can be hard. We know. Recovery can take time. We're going to move into the weaving room now. It's time to make stories into art. Join us when you're ready. And if you choose to keep this story to yourself, we will understand."

Unable to move, Margaret is aware of the scraping of chairs, the rattle of dishware, the voices kept low on her behalf as the women move away. Annie remains seated beside her, and Sesalie helps her grandmother to her feet. Supporting Winowa by the elbow, she steadies her as they shuffle past Margaret to the door. The old woman turns at the threshold, surprising her granddaughter and throwing her off stride.

"Dreams are stories the ancestors send," Winowa says to Margaret. "They know you are a vessel for receiving them, a receptacle for keeping them safe and using them for good."

Margaret watches as the two women turn and cross the threshold, their movements a study in opposites. As she watches, an image superimposes itself on their retreating figures, a woman and a child.

The plump woman in the heavy full-length coat tugs the child along behind her. The child, bent at the waist and turned toward Margaret, struggles to escape the iron grip, her eyes beseeching, her screaming mouth mute. As they fade, a baby cries. Then another. She covers her ears and bends forward, elbows on her thighs as the chorus of wailing infants builds again.

The gentle weight of a hand on her back relieves her shivering, reminds her she is not alone. The hollow sense of abandonment lifts, although its shadow remains. The babies stop crying, one after another, and in the silence that follows she can breathe again.

The rhythmic clack, clack, clack of Sesalie's loom draws her attention toward the other room. She rises, knowing she must go there and sit beside that beautiful instrument and watch Sesalie's gifted hands. Watch the shuttle carrying the thread through the shed. Observe the dance of warp and weft. The vertical and the horizontal, weaving a pattern with a steady constant motion. Becoming something new. Something useful. Something infused with the spirit of the maker. Interweaving the sacred and the mundane.

⚜

As she and Annie sit on cushions on the floor beside the loom, the women shift to make more space for them. All hands are busy. Wooden knitting needles click as wiggling strands of yarn snake out of holes in specially designed bowls. Balls of yarn turn and bounce inside the bowls as the knitters work. Tiny beads tinkle and shine in sorting trays as three of the younger women slip them onto the tips of fine needles and string them into colorful patterns on dangling strands of wire. The woody smell of dampened ash rises as several aunts fashion gathering baskets with practiced hands.

Annie pulls a ball of yellow yarn out of a quilted bag and sets to work creating a simple chain with a crochet hook. Margaret looks down at her own hands, folded in her lap. Right now, she is here to listen and be in the experience. To absorb the energy of this circle of makers. To rest her mind and hands and heart.

She closes her eyes, opening to sound. The slap of the reed pushing woven threads into place, the clack as the warp is raised, the whoosh of the shuttle traveling through the shed, the nearly inaudible whistle of the trailing thread filling the weave. Vibration travels across the floor and up through her body. She feels the distinctive spirals that mark Sesalie's work forming, senses the mystery in the handwoven symbols along the selvage edge. Sesalie's signature.

She opens her eyes, grateful to be welcomed here, honored that these women call her friend. The stab of guilt that follows is familiar. She carries this guilt always for the deeds and beliefs of her forebears. And she sends up a prayer asking, not for the first time, to be shown the way to become an instrument of healing and reconciliation. To tend in some small way the wounds inflicted upon generations of the First Peoples, those living on these lands for thousands of years.

As the older women—Aiyana, Aunties June and Hasaleen and Dawn, and Grandmother Winowa— begin the Creation and Sister stories, Margaret's mind settles into full presence. The teller is the only voice of the moment; and each moment is the container for the story. The freedom to tell what needs to be told in all its truth, its beauty, and its messiness is the power of the story circle.

As she listens, the image of the tapestry reappears. This time, she focuses on the ancient beginnings where the edges are frayed. Where the colors are nearly uniform, faded to the same soft hues. Where the weft has been worn almost away, warp threads now visible. As the stories unfold, the colors brighten as patterns and images reemerge.

She sees the First Mother, the Three Sisters, the Great-Grandmothers going back to the beginnings of their line. The Wisdom Keepers. The Light

Carriers. The Story Minders. The Dancing Women. All spiraling outward from a nebulous center. Hand in hand in hand. Stately, strong, and whole.

"May we never forget."

Grandmother Winowa concludes with the familiar words. All repeat them and begin a chant Margaret first heard when she was a lonely girl overwhelmed by her burgeoning abilities.

"And so, Margaret."

Surprised to hear her name, Margaret sits upright, opening her eyes.

Smiling at her startled response, Winowa continues, "What have you seen tonight? If you're ready to share."

Returning the smile with a nod, Margaret takes a moment, then begins. "As you were talking earlier tonight, I heard babies crying. Not for the first time. I've been hearing them off and on for a while now." She pauses, revisiting the cries. When they stop, she continues, describing her vision of walking with the women, diving into the waterfall, riding the wild river that divided into two, and meeting the cursing woman.

"I feel I know her from somewhere," she adds, "and she was trying to frighten me away from something. Something important."

"Anything else?"

"Yes. When you and Sesalie were walking from the other room, I saw a woman in a heavy coat pulling a little girl along. The child was trying to reach out to me. As they disappeared, I heard the babies again." She leans forward, hugging herself, rocking, tears slipping down her face.

She feels rather than hears Grandmother Winowa's breath slowing. Her own follows the elder's lead. When Winowa speaks, her careful words sink into a quiet place at her center.

"Let's walk back through your story. Listen as I repeat what you told us."

Floating again in liquid light, Margaret closes her eyes and reexperiences the power of each image as Winowa recounts her vision.

"I heard an eagle," she says. "I'd forgotten that. I cried out for help when I was in the rapids. She was too high up and could only call to me." As the sound of the answering cry fades, tears come again.

"Lie down in the center of the room and rest," Winowa instructs. When Margaret complies, an uncomfortable heaviness settles into her body. Deeper than tired, she searches for the word to describe this sense of depletion.

All is quiet as she floats in a purple mist, her heart slowing, her breath deepening. A child laughs. A baby gurgles and coos. A woman hums a soft lullaby. Margaret smiles, her body resting in the peace of the moment.

A hand closes around her smaller one. She is walking beside someone who towers above her, someone whose stride is much longer than hers and whose steps are hurried. She struggles to keep up. The hand tightens around hers, tugging her along. She stumbles and goes down, skinning her knees.

"No more crying, you. It's your own damn fault. Stop dragging your feet and keep up." She's yanked upright.

She recognizes that voice. The same harsh voice she heard above the roar of the river. And somewhere else. She tries to pull away, leaning back and twisting at the waist. She sees a woman seated in a chair and tries calling to her, but no sound comes. An eagle screams high overhead. Strong hands grab her, sharp fingers digging into her flesh. Crying out, she sits up, heart racing.

"It's all right." Winowa's voice is warm. "We're here with you. Breathe."

Though no one touches her, she feels the presence of each woman in the room. Her heartbeat slows and her breathing becomes easier. She opens her eyes. Winowa is seated in an overstuffed chair by a set of French doors.

Behind her, through the glass, Margaret sees the twinkle of solar lights dotting the backyard. A fanciful image floats in. Winowa, a mystical figure, sits on a throne in an enchanted garden.

"Better now?" the old woman asks.

"Yes. This time I was the child. Pulled. Yanked." She pauses. "Taken."

As she looks into Winowa's eyes, she sees the child, legs dangling over the woman's coat sleeve, the sheen of bloodied knees gleaming under a waning moon.

"You may be carrying my story, Margaret." Winowa's voice drops to a whisper. A tear ripples down her wrinkled face. Her dark eyes clear as she looks off into a distance no one else can see.

"I was taken from my mother. Put in foster care. This, after my older sister and brother were sent far away. They called it boarding school. Wasn't." She stops. "Lila never came back. Her story is lost."

Everyone breathes as one. Every face is suffused with sadness.

"Will came back when he was grown. Full of shame. Anger. Said he was not an Indian anymore. Said he was nothing." She looks into Margaret's eyes. "Killed himself. Deep in the woods."

Hasaleen begins the chant, and one by one the other women take it up. Margaret and Annie lower their heads, barely breathing, until it fades into a single mournful tone. When it stops abruptly, all hands take up their work again, and the rhythmic clack and whoosh of the loom fills the emptiness with the sound of life being danced.

Margaret hopes Winowa will take up the thread of her story again—the story of being taken, wrenched away from home and hearth and everything she'd ever known. But the old woman's eyes are closed, her head resting against the cushions, the garden lights twinkling behind her. As Sylvia covers her with a knitted shawl, she begins to snore softly.

"They said foster families would save us." Auntie Hasaleen speaks as she threads a strip of black ash, a weaver, through the stakes along the sides of the basket she's fashioning. The room is quiet as she packs the weavers more tightly together. "Save us from our nature. From being Indian."

A deeper hush settles in the room. Margaret can barely breathe. Despite the stoic expressions she's so used to seeing on the faces around her, pain sits behind every pair of eyes staring off into the middle distance.

Then, as if in response to some silent cue, all eyes lower back to the work of their hands.

"There was a young woman—one of us by birth—who helped take the children away." Winowa has awakened and looks at Margaret as she speaks. "With Social Services. Called herself Miss Rivers. Daughter of Esther and Jason. Esther and Jason Two Rivers."

Margaret steps back into her dream. She's looking down at the place where the single waterway becomes two—the fork. Two rivers. And again she sees the screaming woman and recognizes that angry face.

A simple melody separates from the sounds of the rushing waters. It grows louder and more distinct as words take shape and lift into the air.

One little, two little, three little Indians...

⁂

As Margaret and Annie step outside, the warm wind surprises them. On the ride home, Margaret can feel her friend's struggle to stifle the many questions crackling in the air between them.

She sighs and sits up straighter at the wheel. "Thank you."

"For what?"

"For being you. For giving me time and space to process. But maybe it's time to let loose. So, ask. Share your impressions and insights."

Annie plunges in. "For what it's worth, I was shaken to the core tonight. I was aware of the 'boarding schools' that were anything but schools and of the 'foster care' travesty, but only recently did I begin to hear the detailed stories of women and families I know.

"A few weeks ago, I attended an educational program that travels the state in the spirit of healing. For days afterwards, I could think of nothing else. It wasn't a lecture. It was an experience. An opportunity to put ourselves—our actual physical selves—into the historical events in the area we now call Maine. Tonight brought that experience home in an even deeper way."

When Margaret stops in Annie's drive, Annie opens the door and gathers her things, and Margaret again notes the warmth of the wind.

Annie leans back in. "I'll email some material I've researched. It may be helpful. I don't know how or why. But you never know."

As her headlights bounce up and down along her own driveway, Margaret notices that the lingering patches of snow in the shaded spots around her yard have melted away. And as she dims the lights before making the turn toward the barn, she breathes in relief, spotting the silhouette of a shaggy head in the Adirondack chair on the crest of the back hill. She pulls into the barn, and before rolling the door closed, she leaves a basket with leftovers from the night's feast inside on a nearby crate.

Sophia and Grace tumble out as she unlocks the backdoor to the house. They race past her to the man in the chair, tails wagging. He leans forward, patting and scratching their wriggling bodies, and then sends them off down the hill with a flick of the hand.

Margaret sets her bags inside the house and walks over to sit beside him. "I'm glad you're back. I—" She stops herself, realizing this man is used to a life free of constraints on his comings and goings.

"Appreciate the concern. But don't worry yourself."

She rests against the solidity of the chair back. "Warm tonight. Feels good. And with the snow gone, there's one less thing to worry about."

"Uh-huh. No tracks."

The girls scamper up to them and vie for attention. Margaret marvels, not for the first time, at their ability to ground her in the moment—the only moment she can ever be sure of. "Okay, girls, time to go in." She hefts her tired body out of the chair. "Good night," she says to James. "There's a basket for you just inside the barn door."

"You do too much."

"You'd do the same. Besides, it's all leftovers from a potluck. The many delights of many hands. Some of the best cooks in the state. Be a sin to miss out."

Heading for the house, she stops, taking in a brief image even as it disappears on the warm breeze. She turns back to him. "We're meant to walk this path together for a time. The details are fuzzy, but the fact of it is clear. Reciprocity, I'm told. Good night."

She hears the intake of breath and unspoken question as she opens the door. She pauses, listening. Silence crackles in the freshening breeze, and when she turns back, his chair is empty.

Chapter 16

The dream is lovely—until it's not.

Kenneth pulls away suddenly. No more soft lips on hers, no more firm chest pressed against her breasts, no more floating in the beauty of the moment. The look on his handsome face is one of revulsion. He spits the words at her as he turns away.

Too deeply submerged, she can't rise out of this world of monstrous floating shapes and garbled sounds. Kicking furiously, she sweeps her arms overhead, scooping her hands through the water, aiming for the wavering patch of light above. But the murky waters darken as she sinks even farther. Eyes stinging, she tries swimming laterally, but the downward plunge continues.

Midstruggle, a thought slides in, and she goes limp, surrendering. As if caught in the suction of a spiraling bathtub drain, she is pulled, rear first, down into a gurgling tunnel. Trying to orient herself, she twists and turns as she's pulled through the pulsing darkness. Her lungs burning, she exhales in a rush of bubbles and then clamps her mouth shut, trying not to breathe in. In a gush of dark water, she is spit from a culvert and lands hard on a beach, tumbling onto her hands and knees. The wet sand smells of low tide and seaweed. Spluttering and coughing, she retches salt water and grit and collapses onto her belly.

Kenneth's words, carried on the harsh wind, whip around her head. *I can't be with you. You're too strange. Scary, even.*

Margaret sits up, sweating in the cold room, his final words echoing in the semidarkness. *My daughter saw what I didn't want to. I can't do this.* Sophia and Grace are standing beside the bed, bodies still. As she reassures them that she's fine, she wonders. Was this a vision, a metaphorical glimpse into the real-life loss of him? Or was it simply a nightmare, her subconscious working through an underlying fear?

As she heads for the shower, she says aloud, "Sometimes a cigar is just a cigar and a dream is just a dream." She laughs. "It's not working, is it, girls?"

As she towels off and puts on her robe, she pulls her phone out of the pocket. No messages, text or voice mail. She sighs and heads for the kitchen.

§

Her phone rings as she's washing the breakfast dishes. She smiles as she greets Emily.

"Louisa and I will be over at eleven thirty if that still works for you. We're bringing lunch from the Spotted Zebra. All your favorites."

She takes a beat before answering, banishing the residue from the dream. "I look forward to seeing you both," she says as her mind clears. "I'll have the teapot ready and the kettle on."

After setting the table and readying the kitchen for their lunch, she heads for her studio, hoping to lose herself in work. As she crosses the yard, she looks to the barn. Empty again. *I'll do my best to not worry, James,* she promises.

As she flicks on the studio lights, a catch in her breath awakens the pain. There it all is, Kenneth's grand surprise. The beautiful triptych centered on the back wall, three panels framed in red and gold. The wooden puzzle, its pieces almost but not quite touching, casting shadows. The wall of floor-to-ceiling windows, his brilliant design. The building itself, the work of his hands. And no word from him in—

She walks to the sink and fills her water jar, then sets out a dimpled tray on her worktable. *Don't think. Don't go there. It was only a dream.* She dips her brush in the water and begins. The task at hand is to recreate the heron she can clearly see in her mind—a gorgeous bird at rest, head curled beneath its wing. But a slip of her wrist sends a splotch of muddy wetness spreading across the thick paper. Frustrated, she lays it aside to dry, hoping to salvage it later.

She rummages in a drawer, pulling out a handful of fat tubes. She unrolls a sheet of freezer paper and rips it from its box along the serrated edge, enjoying a sense of release. She tapes it to the floor, kneels, and squirts out blobs of paint onto the shiny whiteness. Red. Yellow. White. Blue. Green. She runs her fingers through the colors, crisscrossing the page. Then she flattens both hands and moves her palms, fingers spread, in widening circles. Rising up on her knees, she flicks globs of paint onto the page, then grabs a tube of black and squirts a thin line that spirals from the center to the edges. Sitting back on her heels, she opens and closes her fists, a colorful, viscous mess squishing through her fingers.

She wipes her hands on a rag and crosses to a basket of dried flowers on a shelf. She plucks out two hydrangea heads, airy clouds of ivory and mauve, and sprinkles the flowerets onto the wet paint. To these she adds a scattering of lavender buds. A sense of completion settles as she sits cross-legged on the other side of it, the bottom now the top. Viewed from this angle, a pattern emerges in the array of petals and buds. A face. Kenneth's face. Another hitch in the rhythm of her heart.

The knock on the door surprises her.

Damn. There's no way she can ignore the visitor, who can lean forward and see her seated here. She surrenders and crosses to the door.

She can see Marcella through the window. Margaret takes a moment to breathe, tension reigniting in her body. She dashes off a text to Emily, warning of this surprise visitor, promising to let her know when she's gone. Centering herself, she opens the door.

"Hope you don't mind drop-in company," the woman chirps as she sweeps past Margaret without invitation.

Margaret turns but remains where she is. She watches as her guest twirls, taking in the room, her batik tunic flaring out around her in a swish of turquoise and purples and blues. Layers of chunky beads and her signature turquoise pendant sway and bounce against her chest as she stops abruptly beneath the triptych and puzzle. Margaret is grateful for the sudden stillness that allows her to adjust to the almost frightening energy this woman carries. Reminding herself to take it in in small doses—sips, not gulps—she readies herself for the next wave.

"Wow!" Marcella proclaims her love of the work and the space before turning back to Margaret. Her voice drops and her demeanor shifts as she looks into Margaret's eyes. "Truth is, I didn't call first because I figured you'd tell me not to come and I really want to talk to you."

Margaret crosses to her. "Actually, I am in the middle of something." Noting Marcella's glance at the paint and flower mess on the floor, she softens. "As a friend in art school used to say, 'Sometimes you have to paint shit to get to where you want to be.'"

Marcella smiles. "An apt metaphor for what's going on between us right now."

Margaret nods. "I also have a luncheon meeting, so I only have a few minutes." She motions to the table and chairs, alight now as the sun breaks through the morning's clouds.

As they sit, Marcella begins. "I'd really like to pick your brain and coordinate our efforts in solving the case of the woman of wandering rock."

"First, I won't call her that. Second, you've been very clear about your animosity toward me, and I've responded in kind. So why wou—"

"Oh, I *do* like your bluntness, Margaret. May I call you Margaret?" She goes on without waiting for an answer. "I don't think we have to love or even like each other to work this case together. But imagine for a moment the power of our combined energies."

"I don't thin—"

"If you're mad about what I said on the news, we can—"

"I don't know what you said on the news. And I don't think I want to. That's not the—"

"Look." Marcella raises her hands in a gesture of surrender. "I tend to go big and speak before I think sometimes. But my intentions are good. We could be a team. I think you're the genuine article, and I know I am. I was born with a veil—in the caul, as my grandmother would say. I've had the visions all my life. You know what that's like, and we're both women."

"Tell me something." Margaret holds Marcella's gaze with her own. "Do you understand the harm your public statements have caused? A man shot his own brother in the woods in the frenzied aftermath of your allegations. I asked you to walk them back publicly, and you not only didn't do that, you evidently added more incendiary comments. So I—"

"Damn it!" Marcella pounds the table as she stands. She crosses to the windows, her back to Margaret. "I know what I saw. I stand in my truth. You're protecting a dangerous man, or whatever that thing is in the woods. And you can't handle it that I'm telling the truth about it and about you. Exposing your deceit. People need to know so they can help catch him before he rapes again."

"What?" Margaret is on her feet. "Rapes?" Enraged, she glares at the woman's rigid back. "You've put *that* out there? That *lie*? You can't—"

"I can and I did!" Marcella whirls around, screaming now. "He raped and killed her. I'm just not sure in what order or why you're protecting him."

Margaret's mind shuts down as she slips into the tunnel vision of anger, everything narrowing, tinged with red.

"Go!" The word explodes. "Now!" She jabs a finger at the door.

Marcella hurries past her, fear and something else in her gray eyes. She stops at the door and opens her mouth.

"Now." Margaret commands. This time in a whisper.

As the door closes, Margaret steadies herself, one hand on the table and the other on her chest. She lowers to the chair, eyes focused out the window on a large bird in flight. Words float in, strung along the tail of a melody. *And we follow the heron home.* The red haze of anger softens into the pink of a pale sunset. The image of a quiet stretch of river, marsh grasses bending low, slows her thudding heart.

Listening with her inner ear to the song that has come to calm her, she texts Emily and walks to her easel. Dabbing her most delicate brush in a shallow well of black, she begins sketching on a new piece of thick paper. Quickly, the lines take shape into the bird that stands waiting in her mind— the heron at rest.

Chapter 17

Margaret shuts down her phone and calls out a greeting as Emily and Louisa hang up their coats on their way into the warm kitchen. As she pours the water slowly over the fragrant leaves in the teapot, her guests, cheeks pink from the chilly turn to the day, breathe in deeply.

Emily sets a brown carton beside each plate as Margaret transfers the warm chickpea salad they brought from its larger carton into a bowl and places it in the middle of the table. The dogs yelp from outside, and she takes her time at the door gentling them. Emily bends to pat each soft head as they inch toward her. She reintroduces them to Louisa, who relaxes into the experience of them.

Sending the dogs to settle in the corner with treats, Margaret watches Louisa as she sits. A fey creature, her artist's eye decides, taking in the large blue eyes, the short dark hair with just enough curl to wisp around her pretty face, and the diminutive frame. She envisions the girl (for it's hard to think of her as a woman) dancing in the woods before stopping in for a visit.

"Margaret?" Emily's voice breaks through the pleasant daydream.

"Sorry." She notes the shy smile on Louisa's face as she resurfaces. "Distracted there for a minute."

Emily laughs. "That's okay, I'm used to your moments away. I just asked if we might add some of your signature pickles to the feast?"

As Margaret opens the cupboard, a wee face peeks around the door and winks. *Two of a kind are not always twins.* A giggling voice tingles in her ear before the image disappears. Musing over the odd expression, she grabs a jar of pickles and sets it on the table with a small fork.

As they eat, Emily tells Margaret of her plans to take Ned to Jacquie's restaurant and to introduce Louisa to Sam Kingston. Margaret realizes her twinge of concern must show on her face when Emily rushes to qualify her intention.

"I'll run it by Sam, of course. He's been pretty much the recluse since renting that beach cottage in York to write his book about his grandmother. But he's offered to mentor me, and I think he'd be open to having Louisa join us. No harm in asking. Right?"

Margaret again feels the twinge but lets it go and looks to Louisa. "What sort of writing do you do?"

At first hesitant, Louisa is soon animated as she responds to Margaret's gentle questioning. She tells of receiving her first diary when she was nine from her grandmother, who frequently sent Louisa three-page letters written in longhand. She smiles as she describes those detailed letters, perfect samplings of the power of specificity. Letters filled with allusions to great works of art, literature, and poetry. She explains how her grandmother footnoted each reference with a challenge for her granddaughter to look to the source and read, read, read. The smile fades. She stops and sits back in her chair, her expression a study in deep sadness.

Margaret pours fresh cups of tea, and in the steam rising from the pot, she sees a shimmering face. Same blue eyes, same heart-shaped face, but shoulder-length white hair. Then she's given a long view of the woman seated at a desk, pen in hand, looking out a window. Fog floating in the yard beyond filters into her kitchen as the vision dissolves.

"Alzheimer's," Louisa says, answering Margaret's unspoken question. "She's still here, and yet she's not. But I still write to her every day, and whenever I'm home I read my letters to her. I don't know if any of it gets in, but I..." She sits as if in a dream state, unable to finish her thought out loud.

The words come as Margaret speaks them. "Oh, it gets in. All of it. How can it not? You are her..." She smiles as she delivers her next words. "Her Pixie Lou. The sound of your voice—your familiar, beloved voice—goes straight to her heart. No fog. No filters. Carried on love, your words are received as pure sensation. I have no doubt."

Folding her arms around herself, Louisa leans forward. Eyes fixed on Margaret, she lets her tears flow.

With the gift of quiet companionship, Margaret and Emily honor her grieving. Nodding in affirmation, Margaret encourages her without words to feel her grief fully for as long as she needs. Emily's green eyes fill with tears as well, and Margaret reaches across the table to cover her hand. A fleeting series of images reminds her of the many reasons Louisa's story resonates with Emily. As she sits in silence with them both, a maternal warmth fills her, followed by a profound sadness—a regret for the daughters and sons she could never have.

"Sorry," Louisa manages at last, wiping her face.

"No." Margaret's sharp tone clearly surprises her companions and causes the dogs to lift their heads. "Don't ever apologize for having emotions. You are suffering a tremendous loss. It's ongoing. It's heartbreaking. You *must* express those feelings. Please consider us and this kitchen safe containers for expressing your grief. Please."

Again, the tears come. And again, they sit in silence, hands touching around the table.

Louisa sits forward and wipes her eyes. "Nana has her lucid spells. But those brighter episodes in the midst of a sea of emptiness are infrequent now." She chokes on this final word, then rights herself and manages a smile. "Nana would use the word *glin* to describe them."

"What is your nana's name?" Emily asks softly.

"Claire. Nana Claire."

"And a *glin?*" Margaret asks, not wanting to lose the thread she sees trailing after this old word from Nana Claire's past.

"Nana's father was a lobsterman. She said that he would tell her stories of his life on the sea in his thick Yankee accent. How there were times when the boat would get socked in with fog so dense, you couldn't see the man standing next to you. When that happened, they could do nothing but sit there and wait for even a momentary lifting of the mist. He called it, *Awaiting a glin.*" Her lower lip quivers, then she continues. "That's me now. Awaiting a glin. And when it comes, I fill it with as much conversation as I can before the veil drops back into place."

Margaret wipes her own eyes. "An apt image. A poignant phrase. You, my dear girl, are indeed a poet. Thank you for sharing this."

Louisa straightens, looking everywhere but at either of them, clearly uncomfortable with this acknowledgement. She rises, bumping the table leg, and begins gathering their dishes and take-out cartons.

Rather than stop her, Margaret crosses to the stove and relights the burner under the kettle as Emily pitches in with clearing the table. "I hope you have room for Indian pudding."

As she turns from the stove, Louisa is standing at the sink, her hand under the running water, her face raised toward the upper corner of the window, mouth slightly open. She is a study in absolute stillness, and Margaret is aware of the great distance between them. Louisa is not here in the kitchen and she is not lost in thought. Her entire being is elsewhere. Recognition stirs. Margaret doesn't know exactly where the young woman is, but she knows how it feels to be there.

Then the moment is gone. Louisa is washing the dishes, eyes on her work, a smile on her lips.

Margaret is left wondering. Did she slip into a vision so swiftly that time stopped and then resumed before she could adjust? Or, ...

"Where do you keep these now that they're open?" Emily asks, holding up the pickle jar.

With that, all is normal again. The kettle whistles, and she pours hot water over fresh herbs in the teapot. Breathing in the familiar fragrance, she grounds herself before turning back to the table.

Over steaming bowls of the pudding, smelling of cinnamon and molasses with dollops of vanilla ice cream melting into the tops, they resume the light chatter of the first minutes of their lunch. Margaret waits patiently for Louisa to find her way into the territory she's come to explore. Her questions are general at first, and Margaret answers with as much specificity as they allow. Then they become more focused. *Have you seen things all your life? Did you ever wish it away? Were you born in the caul?*

"What's a caul?" Emily asks.

Margaret answers. "Some people believe those born with a piece of the amniotic sac around their bodies or their heads have psychic abilities or supernatural powers. It's also known as being *born with the veil.*" She turns back to Louisa. "No, I wasn't, and I couldn't prove or disprove that belief one way or the other."

"Marcella says she was a 'caul bearer' and that her grandmother predicted it. She says it means she was marked for something special and is immune to drowning."

Margaret simply nods and says, "Hmm."

"Were you scared? When you started having visions?"

"They were a natural part of who I was, and my brother was my only companion until..." She looks down at her hands then back up. "It wasn't until I discovered that other kids didn't see and hear things like I did that I got a bit scared. My mother shushed me when I talked about my visions, and I came to believe there was something wrong with me and that she was ashamed of me. When I lost my temper with some kids and said things I shouldn't have, that scared me even more. I thought I'd caused bad things to happen by foreseeing them."

"So your mother and father didn't help you?"

"My father died when I was little, and my mother..." Margaret looks away. "It frightened her. I know now that she was frightened *for* me, not *of* me. And with good reason. She..." Margaret looks back at Louisa. "You don't need to hear my whole life story." She lifts her cup to her mouth, looking over the rim at Louisa as she takes a sip. What she sees in those denim eyes settles a question that has been niggling. One that she's repeatedly pushed aside until now.

Louisa plunges back in. "You're a twin, right? The brother you mentioned was your twin?"

"Yes."

"Was he like you?"

"He had his own sensitivities, his own way of knowing things and an extraordinary auditory sense." She looks off, following the tail of a memory. *Did you hear that, Maggie? That gunshot?* And then came the actual shot. *After* Mattie had heard it. Well after.

She shakes herself free of that thread and continues, "I don't know how similar or different our modes of experiencing the world were. We were only five when he—"

"Died. When he died, right?" Louisa finishes for her, and then keeps talking when Margaret nods. "Such a sweet and beautiful little boy."

Margaret looks up at her.

"I imagine," Louisa adds.

"Yes." Margaret sees his laughing face just before he turns and runs away, teasing her to follow.

"And you didn't foresee it?" Louisa looks up and away, brows knit as if pondering something.

"No. I've rarely seen what's coming for me or mine. My own life seems strangely out of bounds." As she speaks, an image of Kenneth, his back to her, flashes and is gone. In its wake, a sliver of hope follows. Perhaps a dream really is just a dream. Then she's back in the woods running with her brother.

Louisa is silent, then returns to her questioning. "Were ... *are* your visions like night dreams—scattered images, fractured and hard to understand? Or are they sequential and easy to decipher, like watching a movie? Or both?"

Pulled back from her romp in the woods with Mattie, Margaret is momentarily thrown by this turn in the questioning. To get her bearings and ground herself, she focuses on the tiny chip in the cup Louisa is holding.

"They're varied. Some are dream-like. Others tell a story, beginning to end. Others are a mix or something totally new. A snapshot out of context. A voice speaking in my ear. Puzzle pieces arranging and rearranging themselves. I see those often. As I said, they're varied."

"Before I met Margaret," Emily muses, "my uncle referred to her as a real puzzler." She smiles at Margaret. "Turned out that fit in more ways than one."

"Are they always correct?" Louisa asks. "Your visions."

"Afraid not. I've misinterpreted them at times, and a few have turned out to be just plain wrong. Fortunately, that's never happened in serious matters. In life and death matters or emergencies."

"How did you learn to handle them, if not from your parents? To not get tangled up in them? Not let others use you?" Her questions come in rapid fire, the urgency in her voice beyond mere curiosity. "How did you not let them interfere with living your life? The day to day. Your work. Did you have a mentor, somebody to guide you? Some way of—"

"Have *yours* been with you all your life?" Margaret's voice is soft, low, her gaze fixed on her guest.

Louisa stares at her, mouth open, body rigid.

"It's all right. I understand." Margaret lets the maternal stirrings rise and guide her. "It's you and not Marcella, isn't it."

"No. I mean, yes. But I'm not... I mean, Marcella is certified and everything. She gets hits. Names and initials and bits of information that help people. And I assist her." She slumps forward, elbows on the table, head in her hands. "She ... I—"

"It's all right, Louisa. Let's leave her aside for now. Let's talk about *you*. Let's figure out what *you* need and how we might help."

Louisa lifts her head and looks at both of them. "She'll be so angry if she finds out that you know. That I'm even talking with you." She looks away, avoiding Margaret's eyes. Her voice when she resumes is just above a whisper. "Besides, I signed a paper. A legal paper."

"You mean like a nondisclosure agreement?" Margaret tries to control her anger, but it comes through in her voice's unintended sharpness.

Louisa flinches, flushing with embarrassment. She lowers her head again, shoulders hunched.

"Oh, sweetheart. I'm sorry. I didn't mean to snap at you. It's Marcella that—"

"I needed the job." She looks up. "I wanted it. It felt good to use what I knew for good. Marcella had an established practice, and I was happy to remain in the background. So I agreed to keep it all secret and let her have the credit. I wasn't trying to be dishonest or—"

"Of course you weren't. But it was unfair of her to ask that of you. We can have Erin Irvine, a lawyer I know, take a look at the paper you signed. I suspect it's not legally binding. In the meantime, what you say here stays here. Between you and Emily and me. And the girls," she says as the dogs raise their heads. "And the kitchen table, of course." She smiles. "You can talk to us."

"I don't know what to say." Her cheeks are wet again, but she seems unaware of the tears this time.

"You see things, know things, feel things in ways most others don't. Say it out loud. You don't have to ever say it again. You can choose to be quietly psychic and use whatever word you want to describe your abilities. But I invite you to talk about it all, out loud, right now, right here." Margaret and Emily exchange smiles as Louisa hesitates. "But only if that feels right."

"Yes." She looks each woman in the eyes. "My visions—" She stops, looks to Margaret, and begins again. "This *other way of knowing* has been with me all my life. Even before I could talk and had no words for it. It was part of me. Integral to who I am. A secret, a hidden-from-the-world part of me." She laughs. "Guess I'm on a roll."

Laughing with her, Emily raises her cup in a toast. "Rolling is good. *Laissez les bons temps—ou mots—rouler!* Let the good times, or words, roll! Let them roll right off your tongue."

Louisa lets go into laughter again. "Outwardly, I was a solitary only child. But in truth, I always had a circle of playmates surrounding me. Some would call them imaginary friends. But I know better.

"Two were twins." She grins, clearly seeing them. "Identical in every way, right down to their signature color, yellow. Because of them and because I was shown things in my dreams that would happen later on, I thought life came in duplicates as often as not. I felt comfortable with twins in my inner and outer worlds because they seemed more in keeping with the natural order of things. The twin calves on my uncle's farm. The three sets of twins in my grade school. Even the twin chimneys on my grandmother's house, every odd feature exactly the same. Nana called these embellishments her bricklayer's flights of fancy, and she loved them." She laughs again. "And now you. Born a twin."

Buoyant, arms spread wide, she says, "It feels so good to say this." With her back arched and her whole being lit from within, she sings it out again.

Margaret applauds. "Ah, the blessing of a safe container. Whether or not you ever tell another soul, your body has been freed of the constraints of a secret held too tightly and too long."

Louisa reaches across the table for her hand. "Thank you." Then she grasps Emily's with her other hand. "Thank you both. I feel so much lighter."

"Just don't float away. You're only a bit of a thing as it is," Margaret says, laughing. Then she becomes serious. "You asked if I had a mentor. There is a group of wise and wonderful women who took me under their collective wing when I was young, and they nourished me through the learning times. They gave me support and tools and rituals. They helped me accept and adjust to my natural way of being in the world. They were my surrogate mothers and grandmothers, sisters and aunts. They loved me and grounded me and helped me make sense of what came to me. They taught me the joy of being witnessed."

"How beautiful." Louisa draws her hands back and places them over her heart. "How grateful you must be."

"I am indeed. And the best way for me to repay them is to offer you the same. There is no manual that comes with our particular set of needs. We'll be flying by the seat of our pants, but I'm willing if you are."

Louisa is silent as she meets Margaret's eyes, and a single tear slides down her face. She swallows, and the struggle to compose herself enough to speak plays out on her face. Finally she finds her voice. "You would do that?"

"You are a gift, my opportunity to pay forward what I have been given."

"I can't believe this is true. That you would... But don't pinch me. If this is a dream, I don't want to wake up."

Margaret's heart clenches as she's carried back to the sting of the dream that awakened her. Kenneth pulling away, revulsion on his face, hate on his lips. Kenneth who hasn't called. Kenneth with the daughter who—

She pulls herself back to the present. Back to Louisa who is now looking at her with an odd expression. A frisson of connection passes between them.

"Yes," she says in response to Louisa's unspoken acknowledgment. "New love can throw you for a loop at any age. Even what looked like love."

The empathy in Louisa's eyes touches her more deeply than any comforting word or gesture could. A flicker of embarrassment is banished by a swell of gratitude for this sweet young woman.

As she acknowledges this, a scene unfolds before her. Louisa stands at a lectern reading from a book with a bright cover and a title she can't quite make out. Like a camera pulling back for the wide shot, the scene opens out into a large room with floor-to-ceiling bookshelves and rows of folding chairs filled with people. The mesmerized audience leans in, listening. Then comes the applause as Louisa closes the book. And before it all disappears, a close shot of the inside page—the dedication.

To my mother who read to me and named me for this.
To Nana Claire who encouraged and reminded me.
To Margaret who opened me to my truest self.

Chapter 18

After Emily and Louisa leave, Margaret turns on her phone to find twelve missed calls and three voice-mail messages. Only one of the missed calls is a number she recognizes, Annie's. The voice mails are from Caitlin Hammond from Channel Eight News, Detective Jay Horner, and an unknown number. At the latter, a shiver ripples through her body and is gone. Jay's message is for her to call him, but her attempt goes straight to his voice mail. She leaves a brief message and then listens to Caitlin's voice mail.

"I'm really hoping to speak with you, Ms. Meader. Off the record if you like. I think you're being unfairly portrayed, and I'm not comfortable letting the claims made against you stand. I'm hearing more positive than negative about you from your neighbors. Please call me at your earliest convenience. Time really is of the essence in this."

Margaret pulls on her coat and thrusts her phone in the pocket as she heads out back, Sophia and Grace at her heels. She stands for a moment at the top of the hill, her mind churning. Images tumble until they become a soft blur, the crackle of static their soundtrack. Prompted by a need to move, she descends and leaps the stream. The dogs run out ahead as she starts up the opposite hill toward the woods, but a volley of gunshots stops her. The girls circle back to stand on either side of her, bodies rigid, noses raised, open nostrils scenting. Grace leans against her left leg, her rugged body shivering. A hunting dog by birth, but one who's known the sting of a bullet.

Margaret lifts her head toward the left as three more shots ring out. Grace slips forward, crossing Margaret's body with her own—protective in spite of her own distress—as Sophia steps crosswise in front of them both. The shots have definitely come from her woods and close by. Alarm for James's safety has her running toward them.

"Margaret!" Jay's voice is carried to her on the wind. "Stop." His sharp command brings her up short and back into herself.

She turns and walks back to the stream, head down. He descends from the house and meets her there, and they climb back up together.

"I understand the impulse," he says, "but you can't safely go up there right now. Even though it's your own land. That friggin' story on the news last night has the crazies in an uproar again. That thoughtless bitch— Sorry. That piece of work from away has created a nightmare for law enforcement. And Old James is in even more danger than before. I hope he's staying put in the barn."

When Margaret offers no reassurances, Jay swears. "Fuck. Seriously? He's not up there?"

"He's in and out. I understand his need to be outdoors, his anxiety at being cooped up. I'm trying not to worry."

"But with this latest accusation—"

"I know. But he doesn't know about that." She touches Jay's arm, stopping him. "I'll watch for his return and fill him in."

Jay nods reluctantly, resigned to leave this to her.

They begin walking again, and she continues. "The whole thing sickens me. Marcella actually came here this morning. I hadn't seen the news last night, and I couldn't believe it when she blurted out the word rape. *Rape?* I couldn't see straight. Then I kicked her out." She revisits the moment in her studio. Her disbelief. The slide into the tunnel vision of rage, everything narrowing, backlit in red. Neck throbbing, blood pounding in her ears, at her temples, in her chest. Shaking herself free of it, she stops again. "Not my wisest moment. I've now cut off any chance at reasoning with her. I—"

"That's not on you. She seems to have a hair across her ass when it comes to you. It's jealousy, pure and simple. She's after attention, trying to make a name for herself at your expense. Friggin' narcissist. Sorry."

"Stop apologizing. She is, indeed, a piece of work."

They stand atop the hill as the girls sniff and rummage in the grass and hang close. "I have a warrant," Jay says, "to search the Makepeace house and grounds again."

"Great. I—"

He raises his hand to stop her. "But it doesn't include permission for you to join me. Caitlin Hammond's piece put us in a serious bind. Now I have some higher-ups clamoring for me to cut my connections with you as they pressure me to get this solved.

"Damned idiots. Willing to take credit when you help us out. Finding the lost. Finding bodies. Rescuing children. Saving Ned. But now that there's a little heat on the subject, they go all weak-kneed at anything extrasensory. Public perception. Negative PR. Yadda, yadda, yadda. Damn it!"

The girls stop snuffling in the dried grass and raise their heads, dark eyes watching intently as Jay paces. Nostrils flare as he stops to unearth a half-buried tennis ball with his toe. When he kicks it toward the barn, their bodies do not move. Not a twitch of a muscle. Just motionless observance in stoic silence.

Margaret watches too, and when she sees him look at the dogs, sheepish regret dawning on his weary face, she smiles. "Sticks are always welcome in lieu of an actual olive branch."

He grins and bends for a sturdy branch, snapping it in two across his knee. Calling their names, he tosses the sticks in a high arc over their heads and down the hill, and the girls take off.

After a few minutes of toss and retrieve, he drops into an Adirondack chair and leans back, eyes to the sky. "I'd really like to get you over to that farmhouse."

Margaret stands beside him, watching the dogs splashing in the stream below. "How much do you know about Ma Makepeace?"

"First name Lydia. Maiden name Rivers. Used to work for the state. She's lived with her son for a couple of decades now."

When Margaret doesn't say anything, he looks up at her. "Any particular reason you ask?"

"She knows something. She's afraid of something and wants me out of the picture. I'm sure of it. She's connected to Mira's death and Molly's disappearance in ways that are not clear yet. Her past may be key to figuring it all out.

"Did you know that as a social worker, she was responsible for removing Native children from their homes? Placing them in foster care or up for adoption? Her own people. All legal and aboveboard, of course. Her family name is actually Two Rivers. Sesalie Longfeather's grandmother mentioned her."

"And you think this is relevant to our case?"

"I do. I just don't know how yet."

"Time to do a little digging, I guess." Pressing on the wooden arms of the chair, he pushes himself up with a groan. "I'll see about getting you out to that house with me. I have a favor or two to call in."

Margaret stops him as he's about to turn and go. "Caitlin Hammond left a message. She wants to talk to me."

He sighs. "She's been on my ass too. The only thing I was willing to share was that there was no rape. And I gave her a piece of my mind for putting that out there. If you decide to talk with her, be careful. She's really good at ferreting out information you never intended to give." He turns toward the side yard, heading to his car. "Talk soon," he calls over his shoulder. "Damn that McCray woman," he adds, more to himself than to her.

Margaret's phone chimes. Annie. She answers.

"I've just emailed you the research I promised. I'm still looking for more, but this is enough to make you mad. Really mad. I look around the world, and it's all still rampant. These ongoing attempts at genocide and this 'othering.' Sorry. Here I go off on a rant. I'm just so disappointed in people. The lack of empathy. The absence of a sense of connection." She stops. "Sorry."

"No need to apologize. I'll check out what you sent. Let's talk later. Thanks."

She slips the phone back into her pocket, then takes it out. She pulls up Caitlin Hammond's voice message, listens again, and then dials and leaves a message.

Chapter 19

Margaret looks up from her computer, a mild headache gnawing at the edges of awareness. The back of her neck crackles as she turns her head from side to side to loosen the tension there. Annie was right. The research material has stirred her to a new level of anger.

She'd thought she knew a lot about the dark side of America's history. By turns, she'd felt deep empathy and flaming outrage as she learned about the treatment of indigenous peoples around the country and specifically in Maine. But reading page after page of the material Annie compiled has her seething.

First, the Christian Doctrine of Discovery. Declared by Pope Alexander VI in 1493, it was used to justify colonization and seizure of land. It allowed Europeans to take "discovered lands" and lay claim to them because the people residing on them were not Christians. Then in the 1800s, the essence of the doctrine became part of American law. The US Supreme Court ruled that those of European descent could own land while indigenous peoples could only occupy it.

Between 1616 and 1619, the Great Dying occurred when diseases introduced by Europeans reduced Native populations by 90 percent. Later, the government gave blankets purposely infected with smallpox to Indians, disguised as gifts. Throughout history, treaties, which were sacred agreements to Native peoples, were broken.

Then came the Indian Boarding School era from 1860 to 1978. Colonel Richard Henry Pratt, an army officer, founded the first Indian boarding school based on principles used to assimilate Apache prisoners of war. Children were taken from their homes and sent to off-reservation boarding schools. The "schooling" was forced assimilation. In Pratt's own words, the purpose was to "Kill the Indian in him and save the man." In a speech in 1833, he said, "I believe in immersing the Indians in our civilization and when we get them under, holding them there until they are thoroughly soaked. ... All part of 'civilizing the savage.'"

Children were forced to give up all Native ways, including their language. Their hair, believed by them to be a part of their spirit, was cut off. They were cut off. Torn from everything they'd ever known.

Head throbbing, Margaret starts to close the document she's just opened when a string of highlighted words flashes like a cursor, stopping her.

One little, two little, three little Indians—and 206 more—

Stunned, she stares at the words. As they settle back into the document, no longer highlighted, she slows her breathing and focuses. The document is a press release entitled "Adoptions of Indian Children Increase." Dated April 14, 1966, it was from the US Department of the Interior, Indian Affairs, and began:

> One little, two little, three little Indians are brightening the homes and lives of 172 American families, mostly non-Indians, who have taken the Indian waifs as their own.
>
> A total of 209 Indian children have been adopted during the past seven years through the Indian Adoption Project, a

cooperative effort of the Department of the Interior's Bureau of
Indian Affairs and Child Welfare League of America.

Adoption and foster-care placement took up the role of boarding
schools. Families deemed unfit because welfare services didn't accept their
"family as a village" ways of childrearing were coerced or forced to give up
their children.

Though this removal of children was finally outlawed with the Indian
Child Welfare Act in 1978, its requirements were frequently ignored.

When her phone rings, Margaret looks at the screen and takes the call.

As she hangs up, she wonders if she hasn't made a grave mistake in
agreeing to an interview. Caitlin Hammond's words play on a loop in her
mind. "You step into the arena of the public's right to know when you work
with the police. Wouldn't you rather explain things in your own words and
not those of Marcella McCray?"

It isn't for her own sake that she's agreed to a phone interview in an
hour. It is for James, and Jay, and the dead woman and her missing sister.
In the meantime, she returns to her laptop to review the previous day's news
story. A quick search finds the piece on several sites.

It's disconcerting to see herself included in two brief videos and a
montage of photos taken from a distance as she shopped, walked her fields
with the dogs, or stood conversing with Jay Horner and his partner, Cynthia
Green, at Wandering Rock. Of course, the media would have access to some
crime-scene shots. She doesn't like it, but accepts the inevitability of them.
But those taken as she went about her daily routine or in private moments
on her own property shake her deeply.

Marcella is as Annie had described her: dressed in a flamboyant purple
caftan and laden with necklaces, including the turquoise pendant, and
ornate dangling earrings. She has adopted an air of mystery for her

interview, looking into the camera, chin tucked, gray eyes wide, then looking away and back again. When she speaks, she leans in and delivers her prepared speech in a hushed tone, as if the words were coming to her in the moment—through her and not from her—and meant for each viewer's ears alone.

Margaret sits. "You gotta give it to her, she's good," she says aloud. "An Oscar-worthy performance."

But it is the woman's final words that have her reeling. Cocking her head as if listening to the unseen, Marcella lets out a whimpering cry of surprise and gasps. "He brutally raped her and strangled her. A beautiful life snuffed out in one violent act of depravity." She straightens, and her voice hardens. "The animal must be stopped. And Margaret Meader must be called to account for protecting…" She falters, eyes wild. "For protecting the beast of the woods. Her woods."

Margaret rubs her chest, trying to ease the ache there. She watches the woman feign exhaustion, and the camera pan to an empty field, the glacial erratic silhouetted against a darkening sky.

She is shaking with rage. Such a vile accusation against a man she's come to care for. A man who seeks only what Wendell Berry calls "the peace of wild things." A man who served his country and fellow soldiers well. The man who tried to save Mira from the true beast, the killer.

At midafternoon with clouds moving in, she calls the dogs to join her in the backyard. She rakes scattered leaves into a pile by the fire bowl and gathers twigs and branches. Soon, streams of fragrant smoke lift and float toward the woods, hanging at times over the landscape in the heavy air. Little by little, she feeds sticks and leaves to the crackling flames, keeping the fire small but lively. As she works, she prays her message reaches him.

Satisfied at last, she stands at the crest of the hill, watching Sophia and Grace chase each other in widening circles below. Then she bends to smother the fire.

Tightening her coat around her against the deepening chill, she turns toward the house. "Come on, girls," she calls. "Time to face the music," she adds under her breath.

⚜

The kettle whistles softly and then builds to a screaming crescendo as she rushes down the stairs too late to catch it. It sputters as she lifts it off the burner, splattering her hand with pinpricks of pain. Startled, she yelps and nearly drops the kettle. She sets it on an empty burner and focuses on three conscious breaths.

Okay, Margaret. Pay attention to what's going on inside. Acknowledge the anxiety. Breathe through it. Calm and easy does it.

The phone rings, bringing her back to the task at hand. She looks at the clock. Caitlin Hammond is seven minutes early. A surge of anxiety pressures her to rush, but she catches herself this time. Slowly, she pours the steaming water over the herb basket in the small teapot as the phone continues to ring. She breathes in the fragrance of the calming blend and reaches for her phone.

"Fucking bitch! Murdering rapist's bitch. You're going to p—"

She hangs up, hand shaking, the harsh voice triggering a memory. Dazed from being run off the road, she's slumped in the cab of her truck. A meaty hand grasps her by the hair. That same hand yanks her toward him, smacking her head against the window frame. Another hand prods her between the shoulder blades, pushing her down the stairs and into darkness. Damp earth against her bruised cheek. Nausea rising. The frenzied clucking of the chickens and the mad flapping of wings. Shards of a broken glass scattered in the dirt, ripping the skin of her forehead, just above the eye.

"Mind your own business, bitch."

Her hand still on the handle of the teapot, her phone on the floor, she looks around as fat raindrops splat against the kitchen window. A decorative basket filled with porcelain eggs and sweetgrass sits on the counter, a gift from a friend. Along the length of one egg, a jagged crack glistens golden in the overhead light.

The Japanese word she seeks escapes her. She loves the artform but can't think of the word as her mind fills with a swirling mist. She waits for the mist to lift and smiles. Awaiting a glin, she tells herself. And there it is, the word. *Kintsugi.* Golden joinery. The art of mending broken pottery with gold. The underlying belief: the cracks are part of an object's history. Absently, she touches the crescent scar above her brow as the phone rings.

She sets the teapot and a mug on the kitchen table before picking up the phone. This time she checks the caller ID. "Hello, Ms. Hammond. Could you give me just a minute, please?"

She takes her time settling into her chair, pouring the tea from pot to mug, and stirring in a scant teaspoon of honey. Bending forward, she inhales the fragrant steam, then sits back and unmutes the call.

"You said I step into the arena of the public's right to know when I work with the police, and that's true to a degree. Neither I nor they have ever tried to hide my involvement, limited as it is. But I never discuss details I might know of a case. Any specific information must come from the police.

"I've agreed to talk with you because a disturbing lie is floating around in the community. As the police have already told you, there was no rape. And I think it's your responsibility as a reputable journalist to say so on air."

Silence on the other end. She takes another sip of tea and waits.

"Okay." Caitlin's voice is matter of fact, back to business. "So, as a psychic, how exactly do you work with the police? How do you get your information? Where does it come from?"

Margaret sips again before responding. "It's not easy to explain. I don't know if I can dispel skepticism in just a few words. But I'll try.

"Images and details come to me. I don't know from where. Sometimes they arrive as prescient warnings. Sometimes they show me events happening in real time. Sometimes they reveal things that happened in the past. Over the years, I've learned to trust them. So, when I can, I offer my impressions as suggestions. In the spirit of helping. Otherwise, they would serve no purpose.

"That's the extent of my involvement in this or any investigation or search. The police do the tedious investigative footwork. They gather the facts and evidence. They follow strict procedural and evidentiary protocols. I can only point them in a direction, if you will, with as much specificity as possible. They decide if it's a direction worth following."

"You recently helped find a missing girl. Isn't that right?"

"I passed along my impressions of a location, and the police found her."

"And you assisted Search & Rescue in finding some lost hikers and rescue workers in the mountains two months ago. In a cave-in."

Margaret stares at the steam still rising from her mug, the sound of chopper blades loud in her ears, her inner eye fixed on the soft blur they made as the helicopter rose up out of the trees and carried Ned and Gordon Willoughby to the hospital.

"Miss Meader?" Caitlin's voice breaks through. "Are you there?"

Margaret clears her throat. "Yes. Sorry. Yes, I helped to locate them. That's all. But I'd like to get back to the reason I agreed to this interview. Your broadcast last evening."

"Okay. ... What would you like to say about it?" But for the brief pause, Caitlin reveals nothing of her reaction to this turn. Grounded in professionalism, her tone is both direct and encouraging.

Margaret smiles, aware of how easy it would be to drop her guard and tell this woman anything. And how disappointing it would be to find her words plastered across a chyron on the six o'clock news. So, with her shields firmly in place, she responds. "A young woman was murdered and that's tragedy enough. She was murdered but *not* raped. That's the conclusion of the medical examiner. Based on science, a postmortem examination, it's indisputable.

"And now someone—someone who was falsely accused of involvement in the first place—is in great danger because that accusation has been bandied about. And you know what they say about unringing a bell." She stops, tamping down the rising anger crackling in her voice. "Did you know people are out in the woods shooting at each other in pursuit of this manufactured bogeyman?" She pauses. "Did you know one man actually shot his own brother out there? You may not have manufactured the accusation, but you were used to put it out there. It is my hope you will do what you can to counter that lie. On air. Immediately."

"Tell me about this someone you say has been falsely accused."

"Sorry. I'm not going to add any fuel to that story."

"Off the record? Will you agree to answer a few questions?"

Margaret hesitates. "Depends on the questions."

"I know there's a ... I guess you'd call him a hermit who lives in the woods. Odd James Hatchet, they call him. If not the murderer, it seems he's somehow connected to the case. Do you know him? Do you know where to find him?"

"Off the record, I know *of* him. Most everyone around here does. But I would never use that vile nickname. I know a thing or two about unkind labels." She lets that sit, then resumes. "And even if I thought he could be found, I would honor his privacy and leave him be. I can guarantee you, off the record, that he is no murderer."

"Marcella McCray said—"

"Frankly, and we're still off the record, I wouldn't take anything Ms. McCray says seriously. I think she heard the local tall tales about him and inserted him into her outlandish narrative for dramatic effect. The perfect target—the recluse, the mystery man, the *other*. Drama seems to be her specialty. Havoc the result. In my humble opinion, of course. And off the record."

"And why wouldn't people say the same about you?"

Margaret smiles. "They do."

"And that doesn't bother you?"

"Nothing I can do about it. I can't be attached to outcomes. I can only live in my truth and offer what I can. What people do with that is up to them."

"And why should I take seriously anything you say? How can I be sure this isn't a case of jealousy between battling psychics?"

Margaret is taken aback, but only temporarily. She laughs and answers. "You can't, I guess. You'll have to trust your instincts. You have Detective Horner's assurance that there was no rape. That's all I'm asking of you, that you set the record straight and do your best to quell the frenzied search for an innocent man."

Caitlin is quiet. Margaret can hear a rustling of papers as she sips her tea and waits, her heartbeat quickening.

"So, if he isn't the murderer, who is? What can you tell me about that?"

"Truthfully? I don't know who it was. And I don't know what the police know either. I only know with certainty that it's not James Harchett."

"How can you be so sure about him?"

Debating her answer, Margaret sets down her mug and leans back in her chair. As she does so, Caitlin's face appears before her. Behind it, there's a shelf filled with books and awards and a single framed photograph of a younger Caitlin with a handsome man and a dark-haired boy. All laughing. All frozen in a moment of happiness. But the man's face fades as Caitlin ages and the boy becomes a teen, the laughter gone.

The scene dissolves, and she's standing before a gravestone with an urn of white geraniums in front. The epitaph etched beneath the family name reads: *Integrity his watchword. Honor his choice. Ever in service to truth.*

Margaret is carried back to an incident of a decade ago. Everett Hammond, journalist for the *Times,* was killed while investigating a domestic-terrorist cell in upstate New York. His wife, a news anchor moving steadily up the ranks at a major network, left New York City and moved with her son to Maine. She disappeared from public view for two years before joining the news team on channel eight and rising quickly to local celebrity status, a household name.

Margaret's mistrust dissolves with the scene. She can trust this woman, the widow who chose to honor her husband's memory with the words on that stone. Integrity. Honor. Truth.

"Off the record," she says.

"Of course." Caitlin's voice is quiet, nearly a whisper.

" I know because I saw him come to help her. After she was already dead. He was a medic in Vietnam. He would never take a life, only do his best to save them. And as he knelt beside her, there was such tenderness, such reverence in his manner, that a quiet peace settled over the scene. As if her soul had been freed to slip softly away."

"When you say you saw him…"

It takes a moment for Margaret to register her meaning. "With my sight. My second sight."

"And you always trust it?"

"In this case, absolutely. I heard the anguish in his cry when he knew he was too late to save her. I felt his pain."

"And you don't know where he is?"

"No. And I'm worried sick about his safety. He lives apart by choice. I can't imagine all he's seen in his life. The deaths he must have witnessed. The horrific wounds. The screams as young men died. The acts of cruelty all around him. Steeped for months at a time in the obscenity of war." She stops, realizing she's rambling and could slip and say something she shouldn't. She has stayed on this side of the line of truth. Hasn't lied outright and doesn't want to.

There is silence on the other end of the phone but for the sound of Caitlin's breathing and again the rustle of papers.

"They're out hunting him like an animal," Margaret continues, "the words *rapist* and *murderer* sour in their throats. You have to stop them. Put an end to the madness."

"It may be too late." Caitlin's voice is low. "You're right about unringing the bell. But you're also right that I owe him this. I aired Marcella's words. Time to air some of my own."

"Thank you."

"No. Thank *you.* He's lucky to have you on his side. The journalist in me would love to seek him out and write his story. My younger self might well have followed through on that impulse, but you've made me see the harm that would do. And even though I think people would benefit greatly by hearing his story, I am not the naïve intrepid girl reporter of my youth."

Margaret smiles.

"The same goes for your story, Ms. Meader. People could benefit greatly from it. There are lots of strong opinions floating around about you here.

There are those who would lay down their lives for you, and those who would—"

"Line up to curse my grave or help to put me in it!" Margaret laughs. "Again, I can't control what others think or say. There will always be those who fear my ... otherness. And there will always be those who will not let that go."

"Nevertheless," Caitlin says, "from what I've been told, your unique way of knowing things has done a lot of good around here. I remember the case of those two women whose bodies were recovered a few years ago. But I don't recall hearing anything about you and your connection at the time. I hear you've found lost children, saved lives, and given comfort. Frankly, I feel sorry for those who can't appreciate that. It would be so nice if they could let the origins of your second sight remain a fascinating mystery and let it be."

Margaret doesn't respond. Images swirl behind her eyes. A baby cries, and then another as a turkey vulture circles in an overcast sky.

"I appreciate you agreeing to this interview," Caitlin continues. "I'd love to talk more soon if you're willing. For now, I have to pull this together for the six o'clock. It will be a simple statement about the false allegation. And I'll do a longer segment at eleven.

"Thank you again. I appreciate your authenticity and your... I can't quite put my finger on the right word, but it'll come to me."

"Congratulations to your son on the award and scholarship. You must be so proud."

Margaret straightens with a jolt. The words came out without warning. No filter.

"Wh—"

"I'm sorry. I—"

"I'm not aware of any awards in the offing. But I am proud of my son." The woman's voice is crisp, a degree sharper than moments earlier. "I'm coming up on deadline. I'll get back to you."

Leaning forward, elbows on the table, Margaret rests her forehead on her hands and curses. All that rapport built as the comfort level improved, and she's blown it. Credibility shot. "Damn," she says into the air. And then she begins to worry.

Chapter 20

The kitchen has darkened with the coming of the rains. Margaret turns on the overhead light, then turns it off again and takes her rain gear off the hook by the backdoor. The girls are on their feet and ready as she slips on thick socks and slides her feet into her boots.

She half runs down the hill and splashes through the stream, delighting her companions. She looks up to the tree line. The woods are calling her. The leaves of yellow and gold, russet and orange, muted by the rain and the gray sky, beckon.

"Damn it," she says aloud. "I'm not going to let them stop me. Stay close, ladies." And she's off up the hill.

A half mile into the dim woods, her shoulders soften and her jaw releases the tension locked there. The patter of rain on the leaves overhead and carpeting the ground underfoot lulls her into a quiet space—an absence of thought. The smell of pine and wet wood comforts her, opening her senses. The sudden drips from overhanging branches surprise her. She lifts her face and smiles, then blinks as a cold drop lands on her cheek. Her body settles into the rhythms of the forest as she walks on. Her footfalls sink into softness, cushioned by layers of pine needles and organic matter breaking down and releasing nutrients back into the black earth. As her heartbeat matches the thrum of the universe, her spirit meets the moment.

A crackling in the bushes stops her. She stands motionless as Sophia and Grace freeze, pointing to a spot just ahead where the branches still shiver. Something small and four-legged skitters away along the shrub layer, and Margaret laughs and moves on. The rain is coming harder now, though it is slowed and softened as it passes through the canopy overhead.

When she comes to the glacier-chiseled rock at the bend in the path, she stops again. The day is waning, and from here the trail steepens. She decides to sit awhile before heading back.

The Goddess Seat. She tries to remember when she gave it that name, then lets the question go. Like an undulating chaise longue—although a hard one—with a pine branch flared above it like a royal fan, it invites her to take a seat now as it did back then.

The memory comes without effort.

She's thirteen. Used to finding solace in nature, she is on her daily trek when she comes upon a fallen tree. It's a young one, a part of the forest her mother calls the *understory*. When she tugs at it and moves it to the side, she discovers this rock behind the bushes the tree took down when it fell.

She lies back in the seat, looking up into an umbrella of green. She imagines herself a goddess among her beloved forest beings. Gaia. Earth goddess. A stand of young trees encircles her perch—more understory. She turns the word over in her mind, loving it as it spins outward and upward, sprouting multiple meanings and myriad images.

The screech of a jay has her sitting up. She looks around, back to herself, not the teen of a moment before, but a woman clad in rainwear sitting on a rock in what has become a soft mist. A large crow lands in an ancient pine, making the branch bend and sway. It looks down as if scanning her for identifying features, as crows are apt to do.

"You know me. We wander these woods together often enough."

The crow cocks its head and lifts off, cawing loudly. It circles above her, coming closer than is usual for crows. Margaret marvels at the iridescent sheen of water on its wings as, with a loud flapping and accompanying squawk, it lands on a sapling an arm's length away.

Her artist's eye takes in the shape of the head, the beak, the body. The blue black of its feathers. The glistening brown bead of its eye, not the blue or gray of a younger bird.

"So you're an elder like me," she says quietly.

It turns toward her, studying her with a fierce concentration. Then it gives a throaty squawk.

"And what do you have to say for yourself?" Margaret continues, as if the fact that it has stayed just feet away means she's passed inspection.

She opens her mouth to go on but stops. She sits upright listening, her body sensing something. A presence bigger than a bird on a branch and close at hand. She turns in the seat and dangles her legs over the side, scanning her surroundings. But all she hears is the usual buzz and hum of the woods as a wet October afternoon turns toward evening.

She looks back at the crow. Gazing into that glistening eye, she has a sense their time together isn't over yet. She leans her hooded head back against the stone. As she does, she is certain they are being watched, she and the crow. Another presence, perhaps more spirit than corporeal, waits just out of reach. Another...

The crow lets loose a series of hoarse caws and rattles. In the deep quiet that follows, the skin at the back of her neck prickles. Twigs crackle very near. The heavy odor of musk and black earth. A snort. A wave of moist heat in the air around her.

She turns.

He stands four feet away, clear brown eyes fixed upon her. Raindrops glisten on his shaggy coat; beads of moisture brighten the moss-like velvet along his antlers. The brown and green of him blends in with the young pines and brush around him.

"Old Cyrus." She breathes the name. She wants to go to him, stand face to face with the ancient stag, but remains where she is. Tears come, surprising her. With rain sliding down his unreadable face, slipping into the corners of his eyes and running in rivulets down his jowls, she fancies he is moved as well. Enveloped in wetness, she dissolves, one with it all. The woods, the rain, the crow, the stag.

Words float back to her from a dream. The dream in which the stag counseled her to see through the *deceptions sown by those with much to hide.*

The crow flaps and leaps to sit upon her shoulder. She is aware of the impossible weight of it and of the smell of lilacs on its breath. Lilacs, those purple clumps of fragrance that flourish for but a moment in spring and then are gone. Long gone now. A memory on the wind.

As her hood slides back, she feels a tap, the crow's beak at her ear. Its words echo as they travel round and round inside.

Assumptions hang like clouds obscuring mountains. Freshen your perspective. Objects in the rearview are closer than they appear. Trust not your ears. Trust only in this other way of knowing.

A raindrop splats on the tip of her nose, startling her back into the here and now. Sophia and Grace are barking in the distance, the sound coming closer. The crow is gone. The old stag is retreating, sauntering away. As he turns back toward her, her heart quiets, and she loses herself in the liquid warmth of his eyes.

Her dogs burst through the trees beyond the path. The stag leaps and is gone with a flash of its tail. A rumble of thunder precedes a burst of heavy rain. It beats down through the trees, soaking her uncovered head. Closing her eyes, she raises her face to it, letting the shocking cold wash over and through her. As it penetrates skin and bone and brain, it loosens and lifts a dark thought, carrying it to the surface. A thought that rested in a remote corner of her mind, waiting for her to go deeper. A thought she'd purposely left to lie.

Chapter 21

The six o'clock news begins with a tease: "Local woman close to the case speaks to allegations of rape in the murder of the Woman of Wandering Rock." Then a commercial blasts across the small television screen with an irritating jingle and flashing figures. Margaret adjusts the volume and waits.

When the newscast resumes, two talking heads summarize the headlines and the weather forecaster offers a brief look at the days ahead. Rain through the night, another chance later in the week, but sun and clouds most days with temperatures warming as the week goes on. Then another screeching commercial fills the screen.

Irked at her own impatience, Margaret scrolls through her missed calls while she was out. Two voice mails, Jay and Annie. She starts to click over to listen when Caitlin's voice pulls her back to the television.

"It's time to set the record straight regarding the murder investigation underway at Wandering Rock. First, the victim was not raped. I repeat, there was no rape. Second, there is no 'team of psychics' working with the police as reported earlier.

"It is my responsibility as a journalist to fact-check statements made on air in the course of my reporting. And so I have investigated further. A young woman whose identity is yet to be released was found murdered at a site known locally as Wandering Rock."

As she speaks, footage of crime-scene investigators at work the morning of the discovery plays on a continuous loop. Shot from various angles like the opening scene of a movie, the glacial erratic rises up out of the snow-covered field against an overcast sky as fat flakes fall.

"Little is known about the victim or the motive for her murder. The police have confirmed it was indeed murder, but there was no rape.

"Authorities also assure this reporter that the claim by Marcella McCray that a 'team of psychics' is helping with the investigation is false. They did disclose that they occasionally work with a local woman known for her psychic abilities, or 'second sight,' as one neighbor calls it. The use of psychics is not uncommon in the field of law enforcement, but few departments openly admit to such practices. The lead investigator, Detective Horner, did not hesitate to express his appreciation for and confidence in this particular woman's help.

"The author of *The Role of Psychics in Criminal Investigation,* Peter Townsend, PhD, joins us now."

A photo of a book cover fills the screen and a headshot of the author is displayed in the upper right-hand corner, then a male voice speaks over a crackling phone line. In his photo, Peter Townsend looks professorial in a tweed jacket, bow tie, and wire-rimmed glasses. His speech patterns denote a serious and somewhat aloof persona.

"Though there is much skepticism within the law enforcement community where facts and admissible evidence are crucial to solving cases, many agencies—more than one might think—are using psychics these days," he begins. "Having interviewed hundreds of detectives in many different police departments while researching my book, *The Role of Psychics in Criminal Investigation,* I can say unequivocally that reliance on the input of clairvoyants is widespread nationwide. At least occasionally."

Caitlin asks if this isn't legally problematic.

Dr. Townsend's tone takes on a hint of annoyance as he responds. "Though information gleaned from such sources is not admissible in court, Ms. Hammond, you'd be surprised at how often it leads to solving crimes and gaining convictions. Of course, the police must diligently gather physical evidence, corroborate leads, maintain chains of evidence, et cetera. The case must be made with good old-fashioned detective work, and outcomes result from lines of inquiry separate from anything sourced through psychics. The psychic points the way and often provides useful details. The police must find their own path. But the fact remains, those who have used psychics generally swear by them. Most, with a little persuasion, will tell stories of how psychically derived material has blasted many a case wide open. Cold cases as well as ongoing ones."

As Caitlin prepares to end the call, Dr. Townsend adds a final comment. "Only the most reliable and well-vetted psychics are taken seriously, of course. They are rarely the flamboyant types. If they appear to be peddling quackery or are motivated by a need for attention and publicity, they'll be shown the door. There are ample documented accounts of encounters with those types. But the usual suspects, if you'll pardon the expression, are quite normal. Ordinary and humble as a rule. They don't flaunt their abilities. In fact, most avoid attention.

"There are exceptions, of course, and I cite two such cases in my book. Both were quite theatrical while displaying a high level of accuracy. You might well enjoy reading about them."

As he takes a breath, Caitlin wraps up the interview. "Thank you, Dr. Townsend, for that perfect segue into our next segment. After this commercial break, a few words about the woman one neighbor describes this way."

A clip follows of a wiry man, a tuft of white chest hair curling out of the unbuttoned Henley he wears under a woolen black-and-red-checked shirt.

In an accent heavy with images of salt spray and crashing waves, he strokes his beard as he talks. "She's a right puzzler. Darnedest thing. Looks normal as can be. But if she gives you advice, you better take it."

Another round of commercials blares. Margaret reaches for the remote to turn off the set, but curiosity niggles. She lowers the volume instead. As she waits, she crosses to the card table and surveys the unfinished puzzle. The crumbling stone wall, the old shed, the cocked window casing with glass shards gleaming in the sun, the burst of yellow, forsythia dancing. And a shadow blossoming from behind the little building.

She shivers, senses on high alert. The shadow grows, billowing out into the open, covering the wall, the bright bush, the shed. A diaphanous shroud.

She steps into a swirling mist, hands out in front, feeling her way forward like a child in a game of blind man's bluff. But this is no game. Nor does it conjure Louisa's poetic turn of phrase. This is not about awaiting a glin. This is dark. Dank. Dangerous.

The pleasant clucking of chickens accompanies the thinning of the fog. Feathers fluffed, nine hens plump themselves onto nests of freshly laid straw. A weak beam of sunlight filters through the barred window high above the row of nesting boxes. A faint rainbow flickers on the opposite wall, cast by a tiny heart-shaped crystal hanging between the bars. As a light wind teases it, the rainbow splits into multiples, twinkling and dancing, before settling back to its solitary self. Fainter yet still recognizable, its afterimage lingers as the coop darkens.

A sudden smack between her shoulder blades and she's on the floor, the sting of chicken shit in her nose, the taste of blood in her mouth. A kick to her rib cage and—

"Margaret Meader grew up here in Maine not far from Wandering Rock." Caitlin Hammond's words pull her back to her living room. "Many locals who remember her father, the famous painter, Maxwell Meader, believe she inherited her psychic abilities from him. Whether called second sight, extrasensory perception, or clairvoyance, the phenomenon is widely known if not widely understood. Ms. Meader refers to her own experience of it as 'this other way of knowing.'

"She has helped the police on many occasions in the past, most recently in locating a kidnapped thirteen-year-old girl, and she admits to working with them on this murder case.

"While most people in this small community describe her as down-to-earth, unassuming, and kind, others use less complimentary terms. There are those who laugh at the notion of clairvoyance and others who fear it. And while many swear by Ms. Meader's intuitive abilities, others say they don't believe in them.

"In the words of mythologist and Jungian psychologist Judith Harper, 'Such is the paradox, the blessing and the curse, of Cassandra's Gift.' In Greek mythology, Cassandra was given the gift of prophecy, then the curse of never being believed.

"When I spoke with Ms. Meader this afternoon, she was quick to point out that she does not know who murdered the woman at Wandering Rock or why. But she reiterated three points made by the police.

"Fact. The victim was a young woman. Fact. Her death has been officially designated a murder. Fact. There was no rape.

"She is also concerned that unsubstantiated gossip has linked an elderly hermit in the area to this murder. She is adamant that he had nothing to do with it, and it is this reporter's conclusion, based on extensive research and numerous interviews since, that she's right. This man is not, I repeat *not*, a suspect in this case and should be left alone."

The piece switches to a clip of the Chief of Police, Richard Baker, speaking in front of the town hall. His thick moustache covers his mouth, but he enunciates so his words are clear.

"Unfounded rumors have folks up in arms around here. Literally. One man actually shot and seriously wounded his own brother. Running willy-nilly through the woods with loaded guns is not the way to catch a killer. And we believe the perpetrator is no longer in the area anyway. Careful investigative work by professionals will do the job and do it right. So, stay home. Let us handle this. And let me add for any who don't get my meaning, if you foul up our case by messing where you don't belong, there'll be hell to pay."

Caitlin reappears, the wind whipping her blonde curls around her face. She smooths her hair back and pulls up her hood, blinking against the sting of icy rain. "The police remain tight-lipped about the status of the investigation beyond the facts I've listed. It is important to note the suggestion by the Chief that the killer is no longer in the area. This is the first we've heard of this, and we'll keep you informed as we find out more.

"This is Caitlin Hammond for Channel Eight News, ever in pursuit of the latest. More at eleven."

Margaret clicks off the set. "And now it begins."

She returns to the card table, scanning the puzzle and the scattering of pieces around it. The shadow is gone now. The stone wall, shed, and forsythia are the same as when she first fit the pieces together. She runs her fingertips over the partial picture and then over the loose pieces, picking up one here and there and snugging it into place. Her mind wanders as she works. *Woolgathering,* as her mother called it.

A lovely memory surfaces. She's sitting on the floor cutting out paper dolls as her mother works a puzzle at this same card table in this same spot. Mattie is in a corner with his little cars, immersed in a silent race around an imaginary track.

"Ah! The final edge piece."

Margaret looks up, warmed by the smile of satisfaction on her mother's beautiful face, the worry lines gone, her dark eyes alight. She exchanges a look with her brother, who has also looked up from his play, ever attuned to Mommy's voice. Peace in the room. Peace in the house. Peace in her heart.

She and Mattie stand on either side of Mommy, who has completed the rectangle that will frame the puzzle, giving anchor to the next stage of filling in the picture. She has put the box cover away, adding an element of challenge. But Margaret knows what it will look like without it.

A desert scene at sunrise. An adobe house with turquoise door and window frames. A kiva ladder leans against one wall. Under a window, three large clay pots squat in a row, descending in size. Sparkling with embedded mica dust as the morning light touches them, they are filled with succulents. The gray of the ghost plants blends into the muted, ashy tones of their blue-green neighbors and on into the frosty foliage and purple flowers of the desert sage. Rosettes of agave and the fleshy points of aloe add texture and height to each potted arrangement. To the right of the house, two horses—one white, the other brown—stand, heads hanging over the upper rail of a corral. Smoke rises from the roof of the house, and for a moment the scent of piñon wood hangs in the living room. Mattie whinnies softly and trots back to his cars in the corner.

Margaret turns to find her father standing in the doorway, eyes glistening. She can't read his mind but she can read his heart. Deep love for his family. Deep concern for his children. Deep regret. Caught in the grim knowledge he's passed it along.

"It's okay, Daddy," she says. "I'm finding my way. Using it for good. Mattie helps. And now Lucinda…"

A sudden flash whitens the room, and she is alone again. Seconds later, the crack of thunder pierces her sternum. Her heart slams her ribcage as rain hammers the roof.

She's standing coatless at Wandering Rock, snow falling around her. The world has shifted into slow motion. She turns and presses her cheek into the stone, listening.

Voices. Quiet at first, louder now. Arguing. One voice pleading, the other dominant, unyielding. The harsher one grows faint. Footsteps crunch the frosty earth and fade away.

Soft crying. Deep disappointment. Resignation.

A blow to the back of the head. Searing pain as warm liquid spreads, oozing down her scalp, soaking her hair.

Sensation expands from the inside of her head. Pushing. Pressing. Wanting out.

She scrabbles at the frozen ground, gaining no purchase. Her palms flatten, pushing against the brittle grass as she tries to rise. She lifts her head, and hot coals blister the base of her skull. Her body rises in spite of the pain. Because of the pain. Knowing on some level, it's this or—

Choking. Gagging. Her fingers clutch at the scarf tightening around her throat, pulling her up onto her knees, bending her back against rough fabric, a metal zipper, a hard chest. Clawing at the scarf now. Fighting for air. Panic. Eyes fluttering. Fingers loosening. A lightness in her head, a burst of fireworks behind her eyes. Spiderwebs splintering outward. Red. Blood red.

The scarf loosens just enough for one quick breath. The cold night air smells of snow and wet wool and childhood. A snatch of song: *Here comes Susie Snowflake...* A quick cinch of the scarf. Shoulders twist sharply. The back of her head smacks the ground.

A blue-black void, then pinpricks of light shimmering above in a velvet sky. *Star light, star bright.* Intricate harmonies at play. *First star I see tonight.*

Swimming in the womb waters. *I wish I may, I wish I might.* Two hearts in sync, rolling as one in a slow somersault.

A sudden suction. A jarring dissonance.

Heartbeat erratic now. Desperately seeking entrainment with the other but not quite catching up. Half a beat behind. Perpetual arrhythmia, ever at odds. Ever reaching but not touching.

The crackle of disconnect and she's lying on the hard earth. The jangle of metal. The glint of dull silver, a boot buckle caught in the beam of a flashlight. A riffling through her things—the contents of her purse scattered on the ground, the quiet clink of something dropped among them. Heavy flakes covering them and the spider web on the hand. Beautiful crystals landing on her cheeks and in her eyes, blurring the faces of the stars. The crunch of booted feet across the clearing. A soft hum she can't place. Distant. Smooth. Familiar. Then the roar of an engine and the stench of exhaust. Silence.

The softer smell of woods and water. Calloused fingers listening at her throat. The warmth of a tear landing on her lip. The taste of salt. Woodsmoke on the wind.

The ringing phone pulls her away. She doesn't reach to answer, wanting instead to breathe in the lingering details. Hold onto them.

Chapter 22

Suddenly hungry, Margaret warms leftover potato leek soup for supper and butters a thick slice of sourdough bread. Though she rarely uses butter on her bread or more than a touch of honey in her tea, she drizzles two teaspoons from Jenny Hogan's hives into her steaming cup. On returning from the woods, she'd found two jars of the golden nectar on her back doorstep. Jenny's way of saying, "Here for you."

Here's some sweet tea, dear.

The words, spoken in another voice, come back to her on the heels of this thought. Again she hears Melissa Carroll's Southern drawl and the clink of ice in the tall glass. Her beautiful black neighbor moved into the empty house next door in Camden, Maine, with all the bustle and efficiency of a traveling circus. Bigger than life and generous as all get-out—Melissa's words—she'd taken up residence in Margaret's heart. And on that terrible day when the police came to inform her of Joe's death, Melissa was there for her. Had come running. All hugs and warmth and sweet, sweet tea.

As Margaret ladles out the soup, the phone rings. When she sees the name, she sets her bowl on the table and picks up.

"You were out in the woods today." It's a statement, not a question, Jay's voice pitched with concern.

"Did a little bird tell on me? I'm supposed to be the psychic here." She tries for lightness but fails. "Sorry. I figured I'd be alone in all that wetness."

"Please tell me you understand the potential for danger out there. Especially now that—"

"That I showed up on the news tonight."

"Well, that too. All safe and sound there?"

"Yes. But I worry about James. You know some people will still think he's the murderer and a rapist. Some will never hear the retraction, or they'll choose not to believe it."

"I'll swing by later. In the meantime, I want to fill you in on what we know about Mira Clark."

"I went back to that night. The killer dropped Molly's driver's license among the items he spilled from Mira's purse. That's one of the sounds I didn't identify before. Sorry."

"Thought as much. Damn him. Mira lived in Cambridge. Ran a daycare center there. Pretty exclusive, I guess. Lots of muckety-muck parents and a long waiting list. I had no idea daycare was so competitive until my partner filled me in. Lucky for us my mother took care of ours when they were little. Anyway, extensive background checks are run on anyone in that kind of work. Thus, her prints in the system.

"Nothing controversial in her social-media accounts. Nothing to suggest she might have been anyone's target. Lots of friends. Numerous awards. Lots of good works. Great online reviews. No relationship issues showing up. We'll keep digging, but so far nothing jumps out to point us in any specific direction. Just the estrangement with her missing sister, and we only have Clarence and his mother's word for that. We're releasing her name tomorrow. Then we'll have the press all over us.

"As for Ma Makepeace—Lydia Rivers Makepeace—she was, as you said, a social worker in northern Maine. Not well liked in her own community. When she retired and came down to live with her son due to some health issues, they began taking in boarders for added income. Mostly young women, college students. Still gathering info on that."

"When will you search the house?"

"Tomorrow, eight a.m. You free?"

"Really?"

"Yep. You're in."

"I'll walk over to Annie's and have her drive me to the farm stand at the crossroads. Less chance of press following me."

"Sounds good."

After Jay disconnects, she holds the silent phone in her hand, her mind traveling south to Boston and then north and into the past.

She eats her still-warm soup and then calls Annie to set up the drive the next morning. After that, she scrolls through the voice mails she's let go for the last few hours. There are several numbers she doesn't know but suspects are from reporters. But the name and number she's been holding her breath for isn't among them.

She sighs as she reheats her tea, adding yet another drizzle of honey. How many days now? Reluctantly, she counts back. She last spoke with Kenneth the night they went to Mandy's for dinner. The disastrous dinner. Four days ago. Not a long time in the grand scheme, but there was a request—more or less a promise—to call her the next day.

And then the dream. His words come back with an accompanying shiver: *I can't be with you. You're too strange. Scary, even.* And the final words, the parting shot. *My daughter saw what I didn't want to. I can't do this.*

She knows it wasn't a vision because of the setting, the dreamscape, but she can't convince herself the dream sprang from an underlying fear and is not a premonition. "Oh, Kenneth," she says to the quiet kitchen as tears she's been holding back slide down her face. The girls raise their heads, dark gazes fixed on her. When she does nothing to reassure them, they get up and come to sit beside her, eyes never leaving her.

"I don't think he's coming back, girls. Better now than further along, I guess." She wipes her face with both hands. "Lovely while it lasted."

Taking no comfort in her own words, she clears the table. Her bowl slips from her hand and shatters in the sink. "Damn." She bends forward, looking down at the shards glistening under the overhead light. "Damn. Damn. Damn." The final *damn* a whisper.

She summons the dogs with a gesture and heads out the back door without coat or boots. The warmth of the wind surprises her as she walks to the crest of the hill. She lifts her face to the clearing sky, shoulders back, heart raised. Sensing movement off to her right, she turns.

"You okay?" James asks. He's hanging back, just a dark mass against a darker backdrop. She knows he's giving her space, concerned but not wanting to invade her private moment. Not moved to try to fix whatever is going on with her. Someone who understands the essence of presence.

She smiles in gratitude, knowing his eyes, used to the dark, can see her. Knowing he understands more than she can possibly articulate. The tears come again, balancing the energy of loss with the cleansing of release.

Finally she speaks. "I will be. Thanks. This too shall pass." She lets out a soft laugh.

As he nods and moves to leave, she stops him. "Can you sit for a while?" She indicates the pair of Adirondack chairs. "I've been worrying about you again. Tried not to, but so much for trying." She sits.

"I'm good. But I get it." Though gruff, his voice is soothing, reassuring.

"I think the danger to you may soon be gone. There was an interview, and the reporter, without identifying you, made it clear that you had nothing to do with the murder. She also clarified that the woman was not raped—"

He bolts forward, ready to spring.

She puts out her hand, palm downward. "The suggestion was put out there by a thoughtless attention seeker with an agenda. But both the police and a reputable journalist put truth to that lie today. Word will circulate."

He leans back in his chair, silent.

"Even so," she continues, "I'm afraid the spotlight has been turned on me and my involvement in the investigation. The press and curious gawkers may be hanging around here by early morning. Maybe even now. Good thing it's dark. Some have already been taking photos of me and my dogs. I'm afraid it's no longer safe here. I'm sorry. I—"

"Will you be all right?"

This stops her, stops the thoughts competing for attention, stops her stream of words, stops the anger roiling inside her on his behalf. Tears prickle yet again. His selfless concern when he is the one still in danger touches her deepest self.

"I'll be fine. This is not the first time, nor will it be the last, that I've drawn unwanted attention. Stirred controversy. I'm that strange woman with the witchy ways, after all." The lightness of her tone lifts her spirits. Just a little, but enough for now.

"And I'm Odd James Hatchet, creature of the woods." His voice is a growl. "Quite a pair, we two," he finishes with a guttural laugh.

She laughs as well. "That we are."

They sit in silence again. The male presence feels natural, comfortable. The heft of him, the density of his body beside her in the dark, reminds her of all the times she and Joe sat here of an evening, her mother slowly dying in the house behind them. His easy way of making her laugh in spite of everything. Her beautiful man of few words and gentle ways. His hand in hers. The slight squeeze that said, *I'm here.* No words necessary between them.

Kenneth with the sea-green eyes and wild curls, so near to her in the car, his husky voice close to her ear, asking the question she took for a promise. *Can I call and check in with you tomorrow? Not sure just when, but—*

Margaret sits up, shaking the image away. Four days ago. Three days with no word. Then the dream. The nightmare. The silence grown too long to be explained away.

James pulls himself out of his chair, sensing perhaps that she is lost in someone else's story. Lost perhaps in a story of his own, he begins to pace, long graceful strides back and forth along the crest of the hill, pulling her back to the here and now and the man who smells of wild haunts, earth, and woods. A man who lives at the intersection of the natural observable world and the mystery spread out beneath it.

As he passes her for the fifth or sixth time, a shadow just behind and to the right materializes into a young woman. Laughing, she catches up to him, her long braids flying as she turns suddenly, and then she walks backward ahead of him, chattering away, slipping from time to time into a language Margaret cannot understand, then laughing again as she finds her way back to the English he understands. Her body language flirtatious in an unselfconscious way. Him relaxing with each step. Smiling, shyly at first. Then laughing as he lifts her in the air and twirls them both around. Kids, the war a million miles away for a moment.

Then it's gone. The sound of their laughter. The sight of two young bodies of light dancing in silhouette against the darkness. The feeling of being fully in the only moment they know they'll ever have.

As it all fades into the dark of her backyard, a single image appears, gleaming as if lit from within. A face framed by thick shoulder-length white hair. Crow's feet spreading from the corners of pale-blue inquisitive eyes. A wistful expression—a sadness—on the thin face. An open-collared blouse. Narrow shoulders. A camera hanging from a strap resting against her chest. He stops by her chair. "You sure you're going to be all right?"

"I'm sure." She looks up at his dark shape. She can't see his face and hopes he can't see hers. It takes all her will to remain seated, to not stand and lay her head against his chest, breathe in the smell of him, put her arms around his neck. Pull strength from his solid body. Instead, she says, "Be safe."

"That's my plan."

"When things die down, maybe you could—"

"Count on it."

Sophia and Grace run to him as he turns toward the barn. He bends and pats them, then kneels and buries his head in each furry neck before rising and walking away. Margaret stays seated, listening for the quiet rumble of the barn door rolling back into place. She knows he'll leave sometime during the night, and the thought deepens her sadness, accentuates her sense of aloneness. She surrenders to a rare moment of self-pity before hefting herself up and heading back to the house.

Chapter 23

After a dreamless sleep, Margaret awakens early, eats a light breakfast, and gives the girls a quick run. Back upstairs in her bedroom, she stands carefully back from the window and looks out. Two news vans and three cars are parked along the road below her drive. A handful of men and women drinking from takeout cups stand around chatting, cameras and sound equipment lying idle but near at hand. She sighs, only surprised they didn't come earlier.

She cleans the kitchen and fills a small thermos with tea. Unable to quiet her mind enough to get anything else done, she fills the girls' water bowls, grabs her backpack, and leaves by the back door. She crosses to the barn but stops outside the door, unwilling to face its emptiness just yet. She turns to the lantern hanging from the hook, and her heart lifts.

Nestled inside, a bird-like figure rests. Made of twigs and moss and found feathers, its tiny beak is raised toward her, its head cocked, and the black seed of an eye looks into hers. She wonders in that moment as she meets its gaze how hands so large and thick as James's could fashion such a delicate thing.

She carries the image with her as she walks along the stream toward the section of woods leading to Annie's house. Annie greets her in the yard, stretching her long arms wide for a welcome hug. "How's it looking over at your house?"

"They're camped at the end of the drive. Thanks for driving me out."

"Gives me an excuse to go over to Carrie's Yarn Barn. I need her help figuring out the new sweater pattern I'm tackling. And she called to say she just got in a new shipment of silks and wools. When I pick you up later, I'll have no money left, but I'll be well supplied for the Women's Holiday Art Sale in December."

Though they're early, Jay is waiting at the farm stand at the crossroads. Not yet open for the day, the three-sided structure is festooned with cornstalks, assorted gourds, and pumpkins. An orange tarp hangs over the opening, adding to the autumnal theme.

With a promise to pick her up when she's ready, Annie leaves as Margaret climbs into Jay's unmarked car. Understanding her need for silent concentration, he shifts the car into gear and heads for the Makepeace farm.

The dog barks furiously as they pull up to the house, followed closely by a police van and Cyn Green's dark sedan. Lydia "Ma" Makepeace pushes the screen door open with such force, it slams against the outside wall as she steps out, screaming at the dog. And then at them.

Jay strides up onto the porch and holds out the necessary papers for their search of the premises. This does little to calm the woman. Instead, she loses herself in a creative flurry of curses, flailing her arms at him. The scene reminds Margaret of the contorted face on the riverbank, snarling at her to mind her own damn business. She straightens in her seat, stronger in her resolve to see this through. The dark sense of something about to surface heightens her awareness.

She gets out of the car, hesitating before looking at the coop where a heavier darkness sits. As she turns back to the house, the magnetic pull of the upstairs window draws her gaze and then her body. She is on the porch with Jay before she realizes she's moved, and Lydia Makepeace is apoplectic at the sight of her. She lunges, and Jay steps between them.

"Your daughter-in-law is missing, Mrs. Makepeace," he says. "This is necessary to our investigation into her disappearance and her sister's death. I'm sorry that it feels intrusive, but we must be thorough. I'm sure you'll be happy to have this resolved."

"That bit—" She catches herself. Pointing a shaking finger at Margaret, she shouts, "That woman is not welcome here. She's got no right to search my home. I don't want her touching my things. I—"

"She won't be, I assure you. She's here to simply observe."

"But—"

"I assure you. She will touch nothing." He nods at Margaret.

She looks the woman in the eyes, noting the cloudiness of the right one as a rush of information distracts her. A cataract. Diabetes, dangerously uncontrolled. With this knowledge comes a softening in her body, a lightening of her tone. "I honor your privacy, Mrs. Makepeace. I just want to help find Molly for you. I will not touch anything in your home. I promise."

Lydia opens her mouth, but suddenly deflated, she leads the way to the kitchen and drops into a chair without a word. Several officers and Cyn Green follow behind them.

"We won't take any more time than we have to," Jay says in a soothing tone. He nods at an officer to stay with the woman.

He and Margaret pass the stairway to the second floor as they walk into the living room, and Margaret suppresses the urge to go up—to run up and fling open the door at the top of the stairs. Instead, she follows Jay and adopts a receptive stance. Stopping at the fireplace, she surveys the room. Bland. Neutral. Nothing pulls her attention.

It is clean and nearly bare. There are no homey touches, no family photos, knickknacks, or personal items. No books or reading glasses. No baskets of knitting. The furnishings are practical, plain, and functional. Nothing invites a sit-down as nothing implies comfort.

The gray couch is modern with a low back and clean lines. Two straight wooden chairs sit against one wall with an empty side table between them. A bulky brown recliner dominates the space, its seat cushion deeply dimpled from long use. With a clean ashtray on a metal stand beside it, it faces an oversized flat-screen TV on the opposite wall. The large windows, two on each of the exterior walls, are hung with faded floral drapes in tones muted even before they aged.

Cold. A room misnamed if ever there was one. No signs of living here.

As they move through the back rooms, they find the same spotlessness. Margaret stifles a yawn, her body's way of saying *you've missed nothing here.* The tour provides a baseline impression. All is simple, clean, and cold. Anything significant would stand out against such a backdrop.

Jay points up the narrow wooden staircase rising from the pantry behind the kitchen, inviting Margaret to lead the way. She takes a moment to prepare, knowing something awaits above. When she reaches a closed door at the top and grasps the knob, a tingling in her fingers sizzles up her arms and into her chest. She pushes the door open and steps into a dark hallway.

The stench of dirty diapers hits her, and the wail of a baby in distress has her rushing toward an open doorway midway down the hall. When she reaches it, the room stands empty and silent. Dust motes swirl in the shafts of sunlight slanting in from the two windows. The walls are primed, ready for fresh paint, the floor newly sanded.

She walks to the middle of the room, her footsteps echoing in the empty space. Sadness overwhelms her as a quiet humming pulls her attention to a corner of the room. The words of a lullaby are lost in waves of soft weeping.

The rhythmic creak of a wooden rocker underscores the tableau of mother and child, one pale and drawn, the other red-faced and writhing.

Margaret turns away. The room is now furnished. A twin bed with a sun-faded but clean quilt, white with yellow flowers. A painted bureau, red with six stacked drawers. An outdated crib, its bars too wide apart to meet modern standards. An antique changing table with bathinette beneath. And the offending diaper pail. The windows, painted shut, are hung with yellow curtains and room darkening shades. The ceiling is painted blue with crude renderings of white clouds floating overhead, and a rusty stain fanning out along the seam where ceiling and white wall meet in the corner.

She turns back to the rocker. Empty now. A sense of dread unsettles her.

Jay enters the room. His leather-soled shoes ring hollow on the hardwood floor as he crosses to her without speaking. Her vision is blurred as she stares up at him, and she doesn't attempt to wipe away the tears. They're integral to the experience, not to be dismissed or denied.

"I need to see more," she says.

"The other doors along this hallway are locked. And judging from the telltale holes from old hardware, this one used to be too. Locked from the outside. All of them."

She weighs his words and nods, seeing how this makes sense with what is beginning to emerge.

"Can we get inside them?"

"I've sent someone to get keys. In the meantime, we could go through to the main hallway and check the bedrooms at the front of the house."

Though it's an old farmhouse, crossing from the back to the front hallway feels to Margaret like going from the servants' quarters into the family's domain. As that thought surfaces, a petite woman scurries past them, head lowered, shoulders rounded, full-length apron smeared with fireplace ash swishing. Surprised, Margaret stops, and Jay nearly bumps into her. But true to form, he asks no questions of her.

Margaret heads straight for the front bedroom, her heart thudding as she opens the door. It's the master bedroom. The double bed with an iron slat headboard is centered between the windows, matching wooden nightstands flanking it. Each item is evenly spaced, as if someone carefully measured before arranging the furniture. Unable to resist, she kneels and looks under the bed. Not a dust kitten in sight. The tops of the two standing dressers and the vanity shine, and the room smells of lemon wax and vinegar. The matching bedspread and curtains are brown, and the cases on the exposed bed pillows are crisply ironed. Jay opens the closet door. Typical of those in old houses, it's shallow but long. The hangers are evenly spaced an inch apart. The clothes hanging there are basic. Folded blankets are piled on the shelf above, and a row of shoes is lined up on the floor.

Margaret looks at Jay but neither speaks. He pulls out dresser drawers one by one, their contents arranged neatly, unremarkable. Lots of white cotton, plaid, and denim. Everything, including underwear, ironed. In the middle drawer, Jay pulls a shirt box out from under a pile of folded T-shirts. He opens it and looks at Margaret.

Nestled in a soft heap of expensive lingerie is a hinged velvet box. He flips it open to find a gold cross on a thin chain, a plain gold ring, a silver charm bracelet with a single zodiac charm, and a dried rose with a yellowed sprig of baby's breath tied together by a string.

Margaret's hand pulses with the need to touch the items—to pick them up and hold each one in her palm. Despite her promise, she reaches for the gold band, and Jay doesn't object. Revulsion shivers through her as heat radiates from the ring. She wants to drop it but lets it rest in her palm and waits. Anger swells until a seething hatred has her closing her hand into a fist. She opens it and drops the ring back into the box. She touches the tiny cross and feels nothing. But when she picks up the bracelet by its charm—Gemini—sensations ripple through her. She stands before a mirror, and the face looking back is her own and yet not quite hers. Morphing into Mira, the smile changes from amusement to alarm as she stares back. Margaret's hand is suddenly inflamed, and she looks down to see the symbol of the Twins scorched into her palm like a brand. A myriad of emotions pass swiftly through her as she lets the bracelet slip back into the box.

The once red rose, though brittle, holds together as she lifts it to her nose. A whoosh of scent rises as she steps into a summer garden in full bloom. The figure of a man approaches as she stands barefoot in the cool grass at dusk. Her heart quickens as he looks toward her, his face like a pale light moving through darkness. She feels the heat of him before he reaches her. She extends her arms, and he walks into them. Her heart beats against his chest, his body all wire and sinew. He lifts a hand to cup her cheek, the black spiderweb stark against his pale skin as the moon emerges from behind a cloud.

"Are you certain?" His voice is husky, his breath hot.

"There is no other choice." Her mind is clear, consumed with a certainty of purpose. Then she surrenders to the immediacy of his presence and her desire for him.

Margaret snaps back into the present as Jay's partner enters the room saying, "I think you should come and see this."

Cyn leads them down the hall to one of the previously locked rooms and stands back for them to look inside. The room is filled with baby furniture, with paraphernalia piled high. They can only take a couple of steps inside, Jay first. Cribs, mattresses, bumper pads, high chairs, dressing tables, diaper pails, bottles, breast pumps, boxes of diapers, and clear plastic bags of baby clothes and receiving blankets are all packed tightly together.

As she surveys the contents, the crying begins anew. One baby, then two, then more join until a heartbreaking chorus of screaming infants fills the room. Overwhelmed, she covers her ears, but nothing will shut out the sound of their terrible need. Hungry for the breast. For the taste of mother's milk. For that one familiar heartbeat, the soundtrack of the womb. A dark pain she's felt before blooms in her chest, and she turns back to Cyn, who has remained in the hallway. When she'd come to get them, her face a neutral mask, darkness had surged and roiled beneath that unreadable exterior. Margaret felt it, but distracted by the knowledge that something lay waiting down the hall, she'd rushed past it.

She now understands the shadow hovering over this woman, the shadow she saw at their first meeting. This woman has lost a child. And she's kept the most devastating loss a woman can experience in check, subordinating it to the required demeanor of the professional woman in a male-dominated career. Strong. Aloof. Dispassionate.

On the verge now, Cyn stands shaking in the dim hallway. Ready at last to break the carefully constructed facade. Ready to let the pieces fall where they may, to allow herself to be broken. Openly, unabashedly broken.

Without asking permission, Margaret moves close to her and whispers, "Let go, go into it. Allow yourself to be with it. All of it."

Eyes wide, amber flecks shimmering in their caramel-brown depths, Cyn stares at her. Margaret waits, ready to receive whatever Detective Cynthia Green needs to release. Ready to serve as a safe container, a caring companion.

Fat tears form and run down Cyn's beautiful face. "I can't. Not here." Her eyes plead for Margaret's help in keeping this between them. A portrait of anguish, she reaches out and grips Margaret's arm.

Jay's phone rings, and he takes the call. Margaret reaches for Cyn, gripping her upper arms with both hands. Slowly, she breathes. In through the nose and out through the mouth with a sigh. In through the nose and out through the mouth. More and more slowly with each cycle. Cyn follows her lead, and soon the woman's muscles relax, her trembling lessening.

"Focus on the work at hand," Margaret whispers. "Breathe into the knowledge that release is underway. The burden you've carried alone for so long is lifting. There is a safe place and time for dealing with these feelings. It waits just up ahead. When this day's job is done, I will go there with you if you'll have me. And it will help. I promise. It will help."

She feels the warmth of renewed energy run through Cyn's body followed by a long exhale. The trembling stops, and she straightens, wiping her face with both hands. As Jay joins them in the hall, she blows her nose and mutters, "Damned allergies."

Jay glances at Margaret with a knowing look. "Yeah. My brother's down for the count with them this time of year."

Margaret steps back into the room, a voice pulling her there. *You agreed. She'll have a better life than you could ever provide. It's time.* The crying begins again. A young woman stands beside an empty crib, rubbing her rounded belly. Weeping.

She hears Jay and Cyn talking as they walk down the hall to the next locked door. The tinkling of a music box pulls her out to follow them.

In the next room, frigid air presses heavily around her. A chill slithers through her and settles in her back behind her heart. No crying babies here. No weeping mother. Just silence and the smell of death.

A full-sized bed, its head against the far wall, sticks out into the room. A mattress is rolled up at the end of the bed, its cover of gray pillow ticking pulling her back into a memory. Her grandmother's bed, stripped, the mattress bare, the same gray ticking tufted with loops of thick white thread. She climbs up onto it, sinking into softness that still smells of Lucinda. Rosemary. Lavender. Sage.

The cold yanks her back into the sterile room in the Makepeace house. The only other piece of furniture in the room is a straight-back chair with a caned seat. It's placed by the window along the same wall—a window not just painted shut, but nailed as well. The only covering, a roll-up shade, is drawn halfway.

As Margaret moves toward the bed, an odd sensation in her abdomen stops her. Perplexed, she focuses her awareness there, trying to put a name to it. Her breath catches as a sharp pain slices through her midsection. She bends forward, clutching her stomach as it intensifies.

Breathe. Breathe, damn it. Do what I tell you! The voice is harsh, carrying no comfort or concern. A staccato series of commands. *Don't push, damn it. Not until I tell you!* A slap to the back of the head. *This baby better not die on us or you'll wish you had.*

Though the voice is familiar, it's not Lydia's. Margaret straightens. Outside the pain now, she hears the young mother's screams, then the awful silence that follows. Empty yet full.

Feeling faint, she sits on the bed and lowers her head, weakness spreading through her—a strange lightness. Woozy, her head spins and her body goes limp. A whoosh of warm stickiness flows onto the sheets. A metallic taste in her mouth, part iron, part copper. Then the salty sweet smell of blood.

Jay and Cyn are standing on either side of her as her senses clear. She rises, her strength renewed, her mind sharp. "This was a place of punishment. An isolation chamber. Solitary confinement. "

She looks from one to the other and swallows. "A birthing mother died here." She sees the shock and renewed pain in Cyn's eyes but plows forward, compelled to right this terrible wrong. "This was recent. Not some event from the history of the house. I'm sure of it. I don't know about the baby."

"A home birth gone bad?" Jay asks. "Molly? I don't want to sound sexist or ageist or whatever, but aren't both women of this house well past child bear—"

"Yes. This was a young woman. Not Molly." Margaret sees the woman clearly for the first time. Late teens, maybe twenty. Native American. Rubbing her swollen belly, the girl paces from window to door and back. Dark hair plaited in a thick braid down her back, she wears an open bathrobe with a thin slip underneath. She is humming, her face calm, her gaze inward.

"It was far more sinister than that. Who else lives, or lived, in this house besides Molly, Clarence, and Lydia?"

Jay answers. "They've taken in boarders over the years, but they gave the impression it's been a while. Guess we'd better look into that." As he speaks, Cyn is tapping away on her phone, her face taut. Margaret is aware of the internal struggle the woman is barely controlling.

She turns away, unable to witness without helping, and notices something. Tiny marks on the wall by the window draw her across the room. They become clearer—brightening as if magnified—as she approaches. Pulsing now, what was all but invisible stands out. She bends to read the string of penciled words running down along the frame, clearly meant to look like part of it.

I am Theresa. They may take my Sarah away, but I will always be her Mother. May she one day know who she is: Sarah, Daughter of Theresa— Granddaughter of Helen—Great Granddaughter of Frances—and so on back through the mother line. Sarah, my Morning Star.

Margaret drops into the chair, unable to hold back the tears. Jay and Cyn honor her with a moment of silent waiting. She gets up and steps away from the window, giving them space to see what she's found.

Squinting and bending close, neither of them have the benefit of the illumination and pulsing that aided her in deciphering the minute symbols. So, she reads them aloud for them. Quietly. Slowly. Reverently. Cyn sucks in a breath and crosses her hands over her heart. Eyes welling, she shakes her head.

Jay takes out his phone and photographs the string of words in close-up, then the entire window and frame. Quietly, he asks the women to move to the side as he walks back to the doorway. As he photographs the room, the chair, and the bed, Margaret ushers Cyn to the corner at the front of the room, arm around her shoulders, breathing with her. Cyn doesn't resist. She seems barely aware of her surroundings, but Margaret knows presence matters. Being with is enough.

Jay looks to Margaret when he's finished. His eyes transmit his understanding of the situation. "I'm going downstairs. I have some questions that need answers. Join me when you're through up here."

Margaret feels his battle to keep the anger seething inside at bay. And underlying it, his deep compassion at the sight of his partner in distress. Aware of his desire to reach out and comfort, she reassures him with her body that his inclination is acknowledged and appreciated. With her eyes, she tells him she'll wait with Cyn until the time is right. With that, he goes.

As soon as they are alone, Cyn speaks. "My baby lived for forty-nine days. My beautiful Sarah May. Forty-nine precious days." Her voice is a monotone. Her eyes are fixed on the window across the room as rain tinkles against the panes.

Margaret breathes with her, feeling no need to fill the empty air with useless words. A shiver runs through Cyn, traveling along Margaret's sheltering arm and down into her heart center. As if awakening, Cyn turns to meet her eyes. "The defect was discovered too late."

Margaret hears the rapid thrum of a tiny heartbeat. Healthy. Rhythmic. Steady. And as she listens, smiling without realizing it, her own heart catches. She cocks her head, listening more deeply. And there it is. That minute interruption, and the accompanying squish of liquid swirling and floating in a subterranean world. The black-and-white image she's given looks like a squirt of ink released into an aquarium.

"I'm sorry, Cynthia." She sends these soft sounds in on a whispered breath. "It's the worst thing that can happen to a woman. The very worst thing. And it happened to you. No words can ease that kind of pain. None except your own as you speak of it. Acknowledge it. Tell your story. The story of your precious Sarah May. When you're ready."

She has a moment of concern that she's said too much. Gone on one sentence too long. Proving with her words that there are indeed no words. As she admonishes herself, Cyn pulls away and turns to her.

"Thank you. You're the first one who's acknowledged how terrible it was. Is. It *is* the worst thing that can happen. And it happened. And nothing will ever change that or make it all better."

She crosses to the window and raises the shade fully as the rain beats harder on the glass. "If one more person tells me that time heals all wounds, or that things will get easier, I'm going to lose it. With every passing moment, my body cries out for her. With every passing moment, I wish I had died instead. If I could talk to the young woman who died in this room, to Theresa, I would tell her, better you than your baby girl. As awful as that may sound for me to say."

She traces her finger down the window frame, as if underlining the words written there. "You said you don't know about the baby, the little Sarah born in this room. I pray that she lived. *Is* living. Safe and well somewhere."

Margaret stifles a gasp. The sudden image startles her, and she quickly masks her alarm at what she sees. Cyn need not be told. At least not now. But Jay must be told, and soon.

With great effort, she projects an outward calm as she gauges Cyn's level of composure, her readiness to leave the room.

"I feel certain now that the baby lived."

Cyn turns to her, eyes glistening with hope. "We must search for her at once." She starts for the door, but Margaret reaches for her arm, stopping her.

"Are you okay to let Jay question them at his own pace? Can you—"

"I know my job. I'm fine." She pats Margaret's hand as she brushes it away, a wall going up between them, the intimacy of the moments before lost for now. "But we're going to find out about that baby."

Sensing that Jay is still a long way from getting answers, she tells Cyn to go on without her. "I need to finish going through these rooms before I join you."

Cyn nods, her professional persona back in place as she hurries away.

Left alone, Margaret turns back to the room. She hears Theresa's soft moans. Slipping inside her, the fierce desire to hold the screaming child, held away from her in unfeeling arms, is overwhelming.

Get this cleaned up. We got to get her out of here. I'll deal with the kid for now. She now recognizes the receding voice as she watches Lydia Makepeace struggle to roll the body up in sheets bloody with afterbirth and death.

The baby is crying again, this time from down the hall. Margaret follows the sound.

The door to the room is closed. It's one of two that haven't been opened yet. She reaches for the handle, afraid it's still locked and she'll have to take the time to get the key. But it turns in her hand, and the door swings open.

Assailed by a blinding light, she turns away, eyes shut. Opening them slowly, she eases back around. The sun has burst from behind racing storm clouds and exploded into the long room through three large windows. Curtainless, they gleam wetly, tiny rainbows shimmering in the rivulets running down the glass. Watery patterns of shadow and light dance across walls freshly painted the color of sand. The wide floorboards smell of beeswax and lemon. The empty room invites her into its silence. No crying. No death rattle. No sound at all.

She removes her shoes and walks to the middle window, her socks sliding easily across the polished wood. She looks to the trees beyond the chicken coop, sunshine dazzling on dripping leaves of orange and yellow and gold. The blueberry barrens on the rocky hills beyond the farm are red now, and her soul stirs for a quiet walk up the rugged terrain to sit awhile and let the answers come. A fluttering behind her prickles the skin on her arms and the back of her neck. She turns from the window, knowing she'll find no one there. But the air around her is electric with the energy of a presence.

She closes her eyes again and focuses on her breathing. In. Out. In. Waiting for … something. Not knowing what. Breathing. Settling. Listening.

They're in the baby business. With Hank and others. But not Mira. Never Mira.

The air softens. All is quiet again. She turns back to the window as a cloud passes over the sun, shrouding the chicken coop in darkness. *The walls were closing in. She's flown the coop.* A frisson leaves behind a stinging sense of déjà vu. She now knows more than she can yet articulate. And she trusts the knowing.

She starts across the room, but stops in the center as the long room shifts. Three cribs now surround her, two on the windowed wall, one beside the door. A changing table and chair accompany each, creating separate rectangular spaces. Clipboards hang on the ends of the cribs. Each one lists birth date, height, weight, and gender. Beneath these stats, there's a feeding schedule and notes written in a neat hand. Each sheet is identified with a number. There are no names.

Margaret picks up one clipboard. In the notes section, the letters *A. F.* are followed by a colon and a number. The initials tremble as she realizes what they stand for: *Adoptive Family.* The word *Family* is in quotation marks. She inhales, knowing this is not necessarily a reference to a nuclear family with two parents and children.

A commotion downstairs startles her back into the empty room. Her mind still processing what she's seen, she slips on her shoes and starts down the hall toward the back stairs. She stops for a quick look in the last unopened room. It's tiny with matching headboards leaning against the wall and metal bedframe rails stacked along the mopboards. Rolled mattresses and folded blankets are piled atop two bureaus, and a desk is wedged in the corner. Though she hears a burst of shared laughter, the room offers no emotional or sensory clues of consequence. She closes the door and rushes down the back stairs to the pantry.

Chapter 24

Lydia is shouting in the kitchen, and Margaret hangs back in the pantry before entering. Jay's voice underscores the old woman's curses in a pleasant monotone. His steadiness and calm infuriate the woman further. She slams her pudgy fists on the table, screaming at him to leave her house and leave her alone as Margaret steps onto the threshold.

"I'm afraid I can't do that, Mrs. Makepeace." Jay's voice is firm but still pleasant. "I need answers to my questions. I need the truth, and what you've told me doesn't match up with what we know to be true."

"You got no right." She quiets a bit. "Got no right to even be here. What you're asking ain't none of your business. I have my rights. I can take in boarders." Her voice is rising again. "No law against that. Damn friggin' taxes going up every damn day. And me taking in boarders has got nothing to do with Molly takin' off or her damn sister showin' up dead. I say, good riddance to the both of 'em." Her eyes widen as she realizes she's gone too far. She looks away from him, her face crumbling as she plops down in her chair.

Jay says nothing. The air is thick, her words hanging between them. Lydia squirms, fidgeting with the salt shaker on the table and knocking it over. She sweeps the spilled granules into one hand and rushes to the sink to wipe them away.

"I need something to eat. You're discombobulating me. Got my sugar all out of whack. You need to go." Leaning against the sink, she turns back to him.

Jay nods. "Fix yourself something to eat and try to relax, Mrs. Makepeace. I'll leave someone here with you to make sure you're all right since you're feeling off. We'll do what we need to do outside, then we'll talk more when you're feeling better."

Outside the house, he tells Margaret that Cyn has taken Clarence into the living room for questioning. "The techs found blood on that rolled-up mattress and more in the floorboards. We can make them think we suspect it's Molly's and get mother or son to give us more to go on. But all we really have is a possible death in childbirth of a mother and child—"

"The baby is alive. And in danger."

He doesn't ask. He knows how she knows. So he waits.

"These people are in the baby-selling business. Illegal adoptions, I'd say. With someone named Hank and unknown others. Mira was not involved. I'm sure of that as well."

She describes the room with the three cribs, indicating the presence of several babies at one time. She falters as she speaks of the clipboards. The stats. Babies and adoptive families identified only as numbers, no names. Her worst fears about the word *families*. A wave of revulsion steals her voice as the full impact of what this might mean sets in.

Jay's face grows increasingly grim with each revelation, and he sighs heavily before asking, "Any idea where they keep records cross-referencing numbers with names? Any sense of where the missing baby might be?" Though his tone is hopeful, his face betrays his true expectations.

As she shakes her head, a sudden knowing lands on her heart. "I don't know about the baby, but Molly kept records in a metal lockbox. At least at one time."

"Did she escape or was she taken? Did she go from one abuser to another? Did the killer mistake Mira for Molly? Is she hiding out somewhere, alone and afraid? She was clearly an unwilling participant in all this and—"

"I'm not convinced she's an innocent." Margaret speaks her niggling thoughts out loud.

As she speaks, she sees Louisa walking barefoot toward her through a snow-covered field, carrying a baby. She places the baby in Margaret's arms. Peace rests on the infant's round cheeks, long lashes, and puckered bottom lip. Her belly expands and contracts with each easy breath. Dark hair wisps out from under her pink knit cap. A music box tinkles a lullaby. The child wriggles, stirring, her tiny mouth suckling in sleep. After a deep quivering breath, she settles.

Louisa walks away and slips inside an old-growth forest. Her inner eye follows as Louisa dances alone under towering sugar maples, spruce, and cedar, with an understory of yellow birch and beech. Nimbly, she scrambles over downed trees thick with moss, slowly giving themselves back to the earth. A fairy child dressed in green, at one with the virgin wood, she disappears over a ridge.

When the vision ends, Jay is waiting. "Can you elaborate about Molly?"

"When I'm more certain. But don't assume innocence as you proceed."

His phone rings, and he takes the call, turning away and lowering his voice. As he talks, she looks across the yard to the chicken coop.

Without a word to Jay, she walks toward it, her movements slow, her body heavy. Sunlight filters through a developing mist, casting prismatic rainbows all around her. Near the coop, she stops. A scene she's experienced already plays out before her, but this time she's an observer.

A tall man follows a girl along the path. He pushes her from behind, hand between her shoulder blades, and she stumbles toward the doorway and across the threshold. He knocks her to her knees and raises his boot to kick her.

Margaret is standing inside now, watching, tasting blood in her mouth.

The girl rolls over, drawing in her knees and hugging her very pregnant belly. Her face is hidden by the long dark hair spread out around her head. He spits a wad of tobacco and growls a warning. "Do as you're told, bitch! Or you'll end up like your sister."

Margaret wants to throw herself between assailant and victim, but he turns and strides out the door, slamming it with his fist, knocking it off its hinge. She stares at the tattoo spreading down his forearm and onto his fisted hand.

The girl is gone now, the spot empty but for something shining beneath the straw. She picks it up. A heart-shaped crystal and a broken silver chain.

Jay is waiting outside.

"The killer's name is Hank," she says. "He's the one with the spiderweb tattoo. He's been here, on the grounds and in the coop, at least. A violent bastard, he beat Theresa and did something to her sister. It's still confusing, but he's definitely the one." Rage has her shaking.

"Time to see what Cyn has for us and have a go at Clarence myself." As they return to the house, chickens scattering in their path, she doubles her pace to keep up. "Don't hesitate to interrupt me if you need to," he says as he opens the screen door.

Cyn has let Clarence go to the kitchen with his mother. "He insists they haven't had any boarders in a long while," she says. "He said college students have taken rooms with them for a semester at a time, but they don't keep names and addresses once 'the girls' have gone. I didn't ask about Theresa. Thought it best to have Margaret here for that."

As they enter the kitchen, Clarence is pacing. "'Bout done yet? You got Ma all worked up with your questions and the mess you're making traipsing all over." His voice is sharp but his eyes are on the floor.

"Who's Hank?" Jay asks, catching them both off guard.

Margaret notes the quick exchange between mother and son—the fear in their eyes, Lydia's hard swallow. Clarence sits, his right leg twitching.

Jay repeats the question.

"Hank?' Clarence leans back in his chair, trying for nonchalance and falling well short of the mark. "Only Hank I know is Hank Dawson down the hardware store. What about him?"

"You in business with Hank down at the hardware store, Mr. Makepeace?"

Clarence looks away from Jay's steady gaze. His attempt at casually sipping his coffee turns out to be a mistake as his hand visibly shakes. He sets the mug down too hard, and his mother throws him a look.

"I'm a farmer," he says. "I do business with Hank at the hardware store pretty regular. Everybody does."

"Does Hank at the hardware store have any tattoos?"

This question rattles both residents of the Makepeace household. Lydia looks ready to cry or run from the room, and Clarence struggles to still his twitching leg as he runs his hand through his thinning hair. "What the fuck kind of question is that? I'm not in the business of checking out people's tattoos. Half the guys I know have 'em. Women too these days."

"But you are in the business of renting out rooms to young women?"

"Whoa. What's that supposed to mean? Ma and Molly help the students by renting them rooms and the money helps us. Everybody wins. No law against it. What's that got to do with hardware? Or tattoos?"

"And yet you say you have no names or information about your boarders." Jay's voice is quiet.

"I threw them out." Lydia's earlier defiance has returned. In response to Jay's look of surprise, she adds, "The *papers*. I threw out the papers. The girls left at the end of their terms. No reason to keep their info."

Cyn speaks for the first time. "And you don't remember the names of the girls who lived here with you? Under your roof? At your table?"

Lydia's voice takes on a pouty tone. "They were just boarders. Why would I remember? All those cutesy nicknames, one sounding just like another—"

"What about Theresa?" Cyn's tone is sharp, cutting to the quick.

Lydia's mouth snaps shut. Her gaze darts from her son to the doorway and back.

Margaret can see her mind working, calculating her next move, weighing her options, searching for words.

Finally, the woman settles on feigning ignorance. "Doesn't ring a bell. Nope. Don't recall a Theresa."

"And all the baby cribs and paraphernalia?" Jay takes up the questioning again. "What's that about?"

Silence. Mother and son don't make eye contact with each other or anyone in the room. Jay lets the silence continue. Margaret smiles inwardly. Jay knows what he's doing. Patience is the name of the game. One or the other at the table will feel compelled to fill that silence with something. Anything. Eventually.

"What business is it of yours what I collect?" Lydia is the first to plunge into the void. "There's a lot of folks in need in this world. I used to be a social worker and I know firsthand about that need. So I collect useful items."

Damn, she's good, Margaret thinks, knowing Jay and Cyn must feel the same disappointment. It's actually a good cover story told by a woman used to coming up with them. A collector of useful items. A Samaritan.

"So," Jay says, "you're a retired social worker. Once a part of child protective services. And what do you do now, besides take in boarders?" He is matter-of-fact, casual, leaning against the counter.

"Take care of the place. Cook and clean. Help keep the farm going. This and that."

"So you're not running any kind of business on the premises?"

"We're a farm."

"Any other business? Off the books, maybe?"

"Nope." Her face is set in a smug stare.

"And no idea what might have happened to your daughter-in-law? Where she might be?"

"Not a clue. But then, that's your department, ain't it? And here you are wasting time and harassing an old woman and grieving husband."

"So, am I to understand that you didn't get along with your daughter-in-law?"

"I never said that. We got along fine."

"Then what did you mean when you said 'good riddance to both of them' a while ago? Meaning Molly and her 'damn'—as you put it—sister."

"I was discombobulated. You got me all upset. I meant the damn *situation*. Molly going off missing at the same time her sister's found dead. I was angry. I'm entitled to be angry with what we're going through. What Clarence is going through."

"Calm down, Ma." His voice is quiet, hollow. "Just stop and take a breath."

"Well, he's asking all these stupid questions like I did something or we did something. We're the victims here. And—"

"Ma!" Slamming both hands on the table, he rises out of his chair, leaning toward her. "Shut it."

The kitchen rings with the violence in his words.

Margaret watches Lydia dissolve, biting her lip and then bowing her head as her body folds in upon itself. Empathy wells for this unpleasant woman, for Margaret knows they're watching a long-standing dynamic play out. Lydia, the momma bear, all protective of her son, soundly rebuked for her effort. As she watches, a scene spreads before her.

Lydia on hands and knees in the room above scrubbing the hardwood floor. As she runs her brush through a puddle of water pink with blood, she cries quietly. The body of a girl rolled in a tangle of sheets lies on the bed beyond, and Margaret's heart swells with the poignancy of it.

"Sit down, Mr. Makepeace." Jay's sharp command brings her back to the kitchen. "Please." His voice softens a degree.

"This has gone on long enough!" Clarence shouts, his tanned face reddening. "We're a family. Things get complicated. You show me a mother who doesn't have issues with her daughter-in-law now and then. That doesn't mean we're not worried. Not afraid for Molly." He looks from Jay to Cyn to Margaret, where his gaze lingers before snapping back to Jay. "Angry too." He drops back into his chair. "And now you're all up in our faces like we *did* something to her."

Jay doesn't speak as he walks around the table to stand behind Lydia. "We need your cooperation here." He stares across at Clarence. "Your *full* cooperation. And we're not getting it. We need to know about Hank. And we need to know about the business you've been running out of this house. And it will be best for you both if it comes from you."

Clarence stares at his now folded hands on the table. When he looks up, his dark eyes flare. "Go piss up a rope."

Margaret knew before he spoke that he wouldn't cooperate, but she didn't expect the defiant snarl. Her attention keys onto Lydia's intake of breath and the sight of the woman making herself smaller in her chair, her eyes focused on her clenched hands. The brassy woman has crumbled.

Margaret looks to Cyn and directs her with her eyes to Lydia's distress. Cyn nods.

Jay watches this exchange, his face unreadable. Finally, he walks to the kitchen doorway and turns back to the couple at the table. "Suit yourselves. We will find our answers, and more's the pity for you that you're refusing this chance to cooperate. That will be taken into consideration once the facts are known. Meanwhile, if you rethink your stance, here's my card." He walks back to the table and drops it in front of Clarence. "My team will finish up shortly, and then we'll be leaving the premises."

Footsteps clomp down the back stairs, punctuating his parting words as if on cue.

Signaling with a nod, he waits for Cyn and Margaret to leave the room ahead of him. Once they're on the porch, he turns and goes back inside alone. His words of apology to Lydia are clear through the open screen door. He reassures her that they've been as careful as possible not to mess up her tidy house, a sincere compliment in his tone. Then he directs his final words to Clarence.

"See that you keep that temper in check, Mr. Makepeace. Displaying signs of a violent nature while this investigation is underway will not serve you well. We will be back. Count on it."

As the team gathers at their vehicles, Margaret's attention is drawn once again to the chicken coop. The occasional gust of wind carries the sound of chickens clucking in the yard and the odor of damp earth and fertile rot from the compost heap beyond them in the field. She cocks her head, concentrating, reaching for something subtle just beyond her grasp.

Cyn comes up behind her. The pull of her silent grief is irresistible, and Margaret turns, suppressing the desire to embrace her here in the dooryard. She drops into her own breathing, mindfully creating a cocoon around them.

Cyn looks at the ground, her breathing fast and shallow. "May I... Would it be possible, when I'm off duty, can we meet somewhere?"

"Yes." Margaret's reply is immediate. "Would you care to come to my house for dinner tonight?"

Cyn hesitates. "I don't want to put you to any trouble."

"No trouble. We'll have something simple. I have to make myself dinner anyway. And it will be just the two of us and the dogs."

Cyn exhales. "Thanks. I'm off at six."

Again, Margaret holds back the hug her body wants to give. "Six thirty then. Fair warning, the press will be hanging around at the bottom of the drive. I hope that doesn't change your mind."

"Not a problem. I'll be there. Thanks." She offers a rare wide smile, her beautiful face alight despite the gathering clouds overhead.

⚘

Annie is unusually quiet when Margaret climbs into her car after waving Jay off. They ride a few miles until her concern gets the better of her.

"What's wrong?"

"Nothing." Annie's response is too quick.

"Annie? Something is definitely wrong. What's the matter?"

Annie pulls over to the side of the road. "Oh, damn them. They have me all riled up inside. I didn't want to tell you, but I'm so mad I can't see straight."

"Who? What?"

"A gaggle of customers at the Yarn Barn. They were loudly carrying on about that poor murdered girl as if they were eyewitnesses to the deed. But when they said James Harchett killed her and violated the body, and no one would be safe until he was locked up or, better yet, killed, I lost it. I told them off. Then I charged them to go out and spread the truth for a change.

"Poor Carrie. It wasn't my intention to go a few rounds with her paying customers. And there she was, helping me with this tricky pattern."

"More people should stand up against harmful gossip. Brava!"

"Well, that wasn't the end. One of them brought you into it. Said 'You're as crazy as that cuckoo bird you hang out with.' Then she called you Mad Margaret, Psychic to the Suckers, and accused you of leading the police on wild goose chases. She ended with, 'Or rather, cuckoo chases.'

"I was seeing red about then. But I sucked in my breath and drew myself up and said, 'You should be so lucky to have such a friend. And if you're ever in need of Margaret's wise counsel, I assure you she'll be far more gracious to you than you've just been to her.' Or something like that. And I grabbed my purchases and my work-in-progress and marched out the door."

Margaret tries to keep the laughter in, but it spills out. "Oh, Annie. I can see you now, impressive as hell when you draw yourself up to your full-goddess height and let loose on the unwary. What would I do without you?"

Annie feigns offense as Margaret continues to laugh, but she can't maintain it. She lets loose herself. "Oh, I was a sight to behold, I tell you. I think the poor dear was one of the Kennedy cousins. So, the tale is making its way back to the compound as we speak. Oh, it just made me so mad!"

But the anger is clearly gone, replaced by amusement mixed with pride at a job well done. "I'll have to go back for a dozen skeins of that expensive new yarn Carrie was about to unpack. Make up for creating a scene in her shop. I hate that I left her in the lurch when I made my grand exit."

"Carrie will handle any blowback with finesse and impeccable grace. Takes after her mother in that way."

"You're right." Annie laughs again. "Wish I had such people skills. Maybe when I grow up?"

"You lived up to your warrior goddess name today. She Who Sets Things Straight."

As she pulls back onto the road, Annie resumes her usual animated chatter. Margaret silently thanks her friend for not pressing her about the visit to the farm.

Chapter 25

The walk home from Annie's allows the natural world to do its magic, and soon Margaret feels enough distance to process the morning. The girls burst out when she opens the door. Taking only a moment to vie for pats, they race down the hill. She watches with amusement and then calls them to stay close to home.

Her stomach reminds her it's past lunchtime, and she warms a helping of kale and white bean soup from the freezer and makes a sandwich.

As she eats, she checks her phone for messages and sighs. Five days ago he said he would call her in the morning. Under other circumstances, would she feel such disappointment? This relationship, whatever it is, is new, and the disastrous dinner with his daughter has set them off in a new direction. And the nightmare has unsettled her.

She wishes the memory away, but his words linger like an afterimage. She tells herself to allow the feelings to come in, to accept the outcome, but her mind and body resist.

The phone rings in her hand. Sesalie. She answers smiling.

"Margaret, Grandmother Winowa tells me her dying time has come." Her voice is steady, but Margaret feels the undercurrent of sadness. "There is time for gatherings and prayers. Three days at least. She asks if you will come tomorrow night for a prayer circle."

"Of course. I am so sorry, Sesalie."

After setting a time, she hangs up. As she places her phone on the table, it rings again. She nearly lets it go to voice mail, but she sees that it's Sam Kingston and picks up.

"Hey there." His voice crackles with excitement. "Sorry I haven't checked in in a while. I've been happily—and sometimes sadly—immersed in Clementine's story. It's the best first draft I've written in years, and you had to be my first call."

As she congratulates him, her spirits begin to lift. Grandmothers have been a definite theme of late, and the story of Sam's grandmother is a happy one. Intuition tells her to pay attention to the connections that are showing up. Her grandmother's journal, drawings, and words. Winowa's stories from her wisdom tradition and her own life. Clementine's impact on Sam's life. His decision to write a book about her and her gift, and his subsequent request for Margaret's help.

Her thoughts swirl in a montage of imagery. Louisa's grandmother, Claire, lost in the cobwebs of dementia. Baby Sarah's grandmother and great-grandmother, robbed of their granddaughter.

She pulls herself away from these painful thoughts, concentrating on Sam's words as a lifeline, trying to find the sweet on the other side. And finding it in his next request.

"I want you to see it before my editor gets her hands on it. The truth of it is subject to your approval."

She exhales with a relief she doesn't fully understand. "How's tomorrow morning?"

"Can you come out to the beach house?"

The thought of the ocean air on a day that is promising bright sunshine coupled with the company of this good friend makes her smile. "Sounds perfect."

He tells her he'll send a copy for her to scan beforehand, and they set the time for nine thirty.

Before putting her phone away, another image flashes, and she makes a call. She leaves a message for Louisa and then lets everything else go.

⁂

An hour into the woods, a distant gunshot stops her. The girls circle back and stand at attention beside her. As the quiet sounds of the forest resume around them, her heartbeat returns to normal. She allows herself a brief indulgence, tuning into the concern she always carries for James. Then a cartoonish figure blossoms, and she laughs outright as a lumbering buffoon thrashes through the undergrowth while his prey—the elusive Odd James Hatchet—sits on a limb watching from above.

Head down, eyes on the path, she resumes walking, letting go of conscious thought. The rhythm of her swinging arms and swaying body take her deeper as she circles up to the terraced waterfalls. The air is cold beneath the thickening tree cover and feels good against the sweat on her cheeks. She sits on the rim of the basin beneath the falls and closes her eyes.

Listening to the tumbling water, she is lulled. Two horses gallop across a grassy field, kicking up wet clods of dirt as they leap hedges, stone walls, and streams. The polo shirts and breeches on both riders are spattered with mud. Blonde curls bounce from under riding helmets, one gray, the other black. Their dirt-stained faces are frozen in grim concentration. Blood trickles from the corner of one mouth.

Leaning low, torsos grazing manes, both riders press their heels to the flanks of their mounts as they approach a narrow gate. At the last moment, one horse rams the side of the other, forcing the rider to pull up and away just shy of the gate. Her horse rears, sending her tumbling backward, hitting the ground hard.

A gunshot startles Margaret back to the woods. She's on her feet searching the trees. She waits, her body rigid. Another shot rings out. Far enough away to be of no danger to her or the girls, but in her woods nonetheless.

"Damn!" Her peace shattered, she motions the dogs down the path to home.

※

The kitchen smells of cornbread and three-bean chili as the sun inches toward the tree line. Margaret steps out the backdoor to enjoy the vivid sky as flat clouds float along the tree tops. The leaves, orange and russet and gold, are backlit for a moment before fading to black against the skyline. She exhales. Used to years of aloneness, she thinks of Joe with a tinge of sweet remembrance followed by a pang of longing, sharp and to the heart. She looks to the barn. Her temporary guest, now gone, has reminded her of the missing piece in her life and the silence emanating from Kenneth.

No. She stops herself from going there. Kenneth made no promises. And the stirrings of connection she'd imagined between them? Just that, imaginings. Figments.

The crackle of tires on gravel and the low hum of an engine has her turning back to the house. The distinct sounds coming in tandem elicit a vague sense of déjà vu. She stops outside the backdoor trying to recapture the moment of having heard this before, a moment she knows is significant. But she is trying too hard and lets it go. She hurries through the house to greet Cyn at the front door.

The awkwardness between them is to be expected, Margaret reasons. She leads Cyn into the kitchen, the hearth fire of her home. As she pours her a cup of chamomile and lavender tea with a hint of peppermint, she offers an opening.

"This was a hard day. I can't imagine how difficult it must have been for you."

She sits opposite Cyn, who finally meets her eyes. "I thought I might lose it. More than once."

Margaret says nothing, allowing the quiet to settle around them. Allowing her guest to lead the way into silence or conversation or both.

"She was beautiful," Cyn says. "I know all mothers think that of their babies, but it doesn't change the fact. If I could just have one of those days back, those forty-nine days she graced our lives." She closes her eyes, and Margaret knows she's with her beautiful baby girl, holding her close, cooing soft syllables in a language all their own.

Cyn opens her eyes as if awakening. Her smile disappears as the reality of the now registers. She lifts her mug with both hands and blows on the tea before taking a sip. "This is perfect. Just what I needed."

Margaret smiles.

Cyn leans forward. "There's a baby out there. Another little Sarah." She straightens, setting down her mug with a thunk. "We have to find her."

"Yes. We must and we will."

"Will we?" She looks at Margaret, hope and a question in her eyes. Not just the question she's asked, but a deeper questioning of this other way of knowing she's clearly never encountered before.

"Yes. We'll find her. But beyond that, I have no details. Just how I know we'll find her is hard to explain. I've learned to live on trust."

Cyn sinks back in her chair, tears slipping down her cheeks. "The thought of that orphaned child out there somewhere. Sold to—"

Margaret reaches across the table and pats her hand. "I know. I also know she's all right. In this moment at least, she's all right, and forces are at work to help us find her."

These words surprise her, but she follows her own advice and trusts they have been given to her for a reason.

Cyn sips more tea and sighs.

"You have a partner?"

Cyn looks up, eyes wary. "Yes. Tammi. We've been together six years."

"How is Tammi doing with the loss?"

"She's—She's a puddle. She calls me her rock, so..."

"So, it's hard to let go and be a puddle too." It's a statement, not a question, and Cyn seems to get that immediately.

"Well, her rock is crumbling, and I can't let her see that. I have to—"

"Follow that thought to its completion. You have to what, exactly?"

"I have to keep it together. For her sake. What will she do if I come apart?"

"What will happen to both of you if you don't?"

Cyn looks puzzled, her brow wrinkled. "What will happen to us if I *don't* come apart? We'll push ahead. Get on with it. Get over it."

"Do you talk about Sarah?"

"No! It's too hard. She can't handle even saying her name out loud. I told you, she's a puddle. I have to protect her."

"And who's protecting you?"

Cyn's lip quivers, and her eyes well with fresh tears as she stares at Margaret.

"You carried this baby for nine months inside you. You gave birth to this precious girl child and named her Sarah. You nursed her and held her, and she opened your heart wider than you had imagined possible. You and

Tammi loved this baby together. Dreamed her together. And then she died."

Cyn sucks in her breath, hand to her chest. She bends forward, her head nearly resting on the table, and her body rocks back and forth as the wracking, wrenching sobs take hold. Margaret says nothing, witnessing this anguish only a woman who has lost a child can know.

After a while, the rocking slows and the sobs become shivering, breathy sounds, more heartbreaking than the wailing. Margaret remains still, offering no box of tissues or words of comfort. They would only signal an ending to the open display of feeling.

As Cyn sits up, arms wrapped around her middle, her face haggard and cheeks wet, her body spent, she stares straight ahead, her chin still quivering. Margaret resists the impulse to turn away from this raw portrait of grief.

"My baby." Her voice is a whisper. "My baby is gone. She died. I'll never hold her again. Never smell that baby smell, touch that rose-petal cheek, listen to her breathing. The sound of her suckling, her sigh of contentment."

Margaret nods, acknowledging this hard truth.

They sit in silence, the clock ticking.

Margaret's voice is gentle. "And who will care for you in this time of sorrow?"

"Tammi." It's almost a question.

"Why would you deny her the chance to tend you? To cleanse your wounded self with her watery ways, this puddle you love so much. Why would you not let her ease her own grief by being included in yours? This happened to both of you."

"Oh, my." Silence settles around her as the clock ticks and Margaret waits. When she speaks again, her face is serene. "Thank you."

Margaret smiles and doesn't move. She lets more silence sit between them, knowing it doesn't need to be filled. Finally, when the silence has flattened the intensity of the emotions they both feel and the timing feels right, she speaks.

"Hungry?"

At the unexpected question, Cyn cocks her head as if taking an inner inventory. She smiles. "Famished."

Over steaming bowls of chili and hunks of buttered cornbread, they continue the process of getting to know each other, staying away from talk of the case or the Makepeace family.

Margaret is fascinated to learn that Cyn holds a degree in piano performance from the Boston Conservatory at Berklee.

"I had just finished up when I was in a car accident. Broke my wrist and bones in my left hand, and fractured my right ulna. A police officer stayed with me, calming me, while they cut me out of the wreckage. As I recuperated, she became a friend and then a mentor. Eventually, I found myself on this new career path. Since I'm detail-oriented and good at finding patterns in random data, I ended up on the detective track and I never looked back."

"Are you still able to play?"

"I am. Not up to my former level, but yes." She looks down at her folded hands on the table. "I haven't in a long time." She stretches her left hand out before her, splaying crooked fingers, her wrist cocked slightly outward. "Maybe I should dust off the keyboard and see what comes out."

"Might do a lot of good." Margaret knows there is no *might* about it. She sees a younger Cyn—Cynthia—seated at a grand piano in a simple black gown with a sparkling brooch at her waist in the back. Long fingers poised over the keys, already lost in a melody she alone can hear, she leans in and a hush settles over the audience. A young woman with straight blonde hair is seated in the second row, open-hearted and radiant with love.

Cyn's voice dispels the image. "I'll have to keep it light. No old voices allowed. No critics."

"Sounds perfect." Margaret clears their dishes and sets out two bowls of pumpkin custard. She adds a dollop of whipped cream and a sprinkling of fresh nutmeg.

"Tammi had the piano tuned just before…" She stares across the room. "I think I'll play something for her when I get home, surprise her. Then maybe we can talk."

When they've finished their dessert, Margaret says, "You must be exhausted after this day, so I won't feel insulted if you go."

Cyn gets her coat and gives Margaret a hug. Quickly, she pulls away as her phone rings.

"That was Jay," she says, pocketing the phone. "They found Mira's car at Logan. Great way to stash it—one among hundreds in a long-term lot at the airport. They're also following some leads on who Hank might be."

As she says this, a composite image forms for Margaret—the product of several glimpses from earlier visions. She tells Cyn she'll have a sketch drawn by morning.

"Also," Cyn continues as if not interrupted, a rhythm building between them, "they're searching missing-persons databases for young women named Theresa."

"She has a sister too." Again, Margaret hears the shared laughter in an upstairs bedroom at the Makepeace house. "Anita!" The name comes in a burst of light. "Theresa and Anita."

"Is she missing, too?"

"No. They're both dead." The sudden realization stings.

"My god. What are we dealing with here?"

"Two murders and a preventable death and..." She doesn't need to finish. They both know what other crime they've uncovered.

Cyn has her phone out, texting Jay with this latest. When her phone dings a response, she tells Margaret the police are going out to the Makepeace farm at first light for an extended search of the grounds.

"But tonight," she adds, "I'm going home to Tammi. Start fresh in the morning. We'll keep you informed."

Margaret accompanies her through the house to the front door. All is quiet at the end of the driveway as Cyn gets into her car. A new thought filters in, and Margaret decides to hold on to it. Let Cyn have the time she and her partner need to begin their shared grieving. As the car eases down the driveway, the sense of déjà vu returns.

She's back at Wandering Rock in the snow. Footsteps recede. The truck engine growls to life. Two heads visible by the dashboard light bounce in the cab as the truck rumbles down the road, tires crunching. A single brake light flashes as the truck stops halfway down the hill. The passenger door creaks open, slams shut, and the truck moves forward a few yards.

The soft hum of an engine. Headlight beams bounce out of a side road and then illuminate the truck as a car pulls up behind it. A single head in the cab. A thin fringe of dark hair sticks out from under a baseball cap, meeting the upturned collar of a brown leather jacket. As both vehicles pull away, a baby cries. The plaintive sound hangs in the chill air.

She reaches for her phone and calls Jay. "Two things," she says when he picks up. "One. Mira's car was parked just down the hill that night, in the side road. Hank drove the truck and Molly drove the car away. Sorry I didn't catch that before."

"And two?" Jay asks.

"The compost heap. When you search the farm tomorrow, start there."

Chapter 26

After she hangs up with Jay, Margaret throws on a coat, steps into her boots. Leaving her phone on the harvest table by the door, she steps out into a brisk wind. The dogs nearly trip her as they rush past in their excitement to race each other down the hill. She lets them go and crosses to her studio. Light floods the space as she hits the wall switch, and she dials the dimmer switch back, creating the effect of candlelight. She quickly changes from coat to a long cardigan with deep pockets and a cable knit scarf that wraps twice around her neck. Not bothering with the heat, she goes straight to her worktable and takes up her sketch pad and charcoal pencil.

She perches on a stool, the pencil held loosely in her left hand. Easing into a hazy state of awareness, she begins, barely looking at the page.

With sweeping strokes, she sketches the outline of a head and neck. With smaller strokes, she fills in details. The forehead is wide, the eyebrows thick, eyes spaced evenly and unremarkable. The large nose is crooked, a knot below the bridge, the blunt tip pointing slightly to the left. Broad cheeks and a square chin are covered in thick stubble. Wisps of dark hair cropped close along the forehead run down into patchy sideburns. Longer strands along the back of the neck curl up at the jacket collar. A wide swath down the right side of the neck is rippled with scar tissue.

She leans back, analyzing the sketch while maintaining a soft gaze and receptive mind. After adding some shading with the side of the pencil, she nods, satisfied. Then, in the lower left corner of the page, she draws a black baseball cap and shades the insignia on the front and the underside to the bill with a green marker. In the lower right corner, she draws an arm and hand. Using a black pen with a fine point, she adds an elongated spider with a tiny hourglass on its back to the fleshy part of the forearm. It sits at the center of an intricate web that runs down into the hand and spreads out to the knuckles above the fingers and thumb.

On a sudden impulse, she draws the palm side of the same hand, sketching a tiny rosebud on the heel of it, with thorns and three leaves on its stem. As soon as she's done, she finds herself standing in Molly's bedroom again, holding the dried rose from the jewelry box. Then she steps into a garden, the night air heavy with the scent of roses. As she lifts her arms to him, she sees the same rose inked just above her own palm.

She shivers, wrapping her sweater closer around her. A deep cold has settled into the room with its high ceiling and wall of glass. A cold she didn't register until now—the perfect backdrop for the revulsion she feels as the vision dissolves. She deftly adds another smaller hand below the male's and then rolls up the sketch. Exchanging sweater and scarf for her coat, she steps outside. The girls are hanging near and run ahead of her to the house.

She spreads the sketch on the kitchen table, weighting it on each corner with salt and pepper shakers and two tins of herbs. She photographs it with her phone and then moves around the table to photograph it from the opposite side, the image upside down. She texts the first photo to Jay, deciding not to send it to Cyn until the morning, so as not to disturb her.

She puts on the kettle, still feeling chilled, and prepares the teapot, adding a touch of valerian to the chamomile and lavender in the basket. Setting the pot on the table by her mug, she sits opposite her usual chair to study the sketch upside down. As she softens her gaze and lets go of what she already knows about the man, she allows the drawing to become a nebulous array of lines on paper.

Smoke rises from a stove pipe on the roof of a rustic cabin. A wide front porch runs the width of the building with a green door in the center flanked by two large windows. A rusted red pickup sits in the muddy dooryard, its right rear tire flat. As rain beats down, bouncing off hood and cab, the dirt smeared on the license plate slowly washes away, revealing the signature chickadee, pine cone, and tassel of Maine's general issue plate. The yard is thick with yellow birch and beech trees. Towering overhead, sugar maples, spruce, and cedar dwarf the cabin and truck.

Movement behind the cabin pulls Margaret's attention. For a moment, she sees nothing but standing trees and a massive downed trunk. Movement again and she's looking straight into the eyes of the buck. Old Cyrus blending in with the greens and browns of the forest, lowering his head, eyes still on hers. *Now you're seeing through deceptions sown by those with much to hide.* He raises and lowers his head. Then, shaking off the rainwater streaking down his face, he turns and is gone.

The screaming kettle startles her back into the kitchen just as her phone rings. A part of her longs to return to the woods and the rain and the stag, but she walks to the stove and removes the kettle. She answers the call with a quiet hello, still in a hazy state of mind.

"Everything okay?" The voice is soft, hesitant, and it takes her a moment to place it.

"Oh, Louisa. Sorry. Mind wandering." She laughs to make light of her lapse. "Thanks for returning my call."

"Are you sure everything's okay? I feel a disturbance..."

Her voice trails off, and Margaret understands her reluctance to go further.

"You're right to ask. The truth is, I was just coming out of a vision state. Yanked out, actually, by a wailing kettle. I trust you recognize the feeling it left me with."

"I do."

There's an element of wonder in the girl's voice. Margaret understands it. Unused to being able to share her experiences with others like herself, it must feel both odd and wonderful to interact with someone who speaks the same language.

"Would you like me to call at a better time?" she asks.

"No. This is perfect. Turns out we'll both be at Sam's beach house tomorrow. While he's working with Emily, I'm wondering if you and I could explore something together."

"I'd love to."

Margaret shares only a general idea of what she has in mind, hoping this will open Louisa to receiving information without being influenced by Margaret's suspicions.

"This is really important, isn't it?"

"Yes. I'll fill you in further tomorrow. In the meantime, trust whatever floats in, no matter how trivial it may seem."

After hanging up, Margaret scans her email. She considers opening Sam's book attachment, but a wave of fatigue convinces her to leave it for the morning when she'll be fresh. Instead, she shuts off the lights and takes her tea and her grandmother's journal up to her room.

The windows rattle as the wind increases, and she closes the drapes. Hurriedly, she slips into a thermal shirt and leggings, swirling a knit shawl over her shoulders before climbing into bed. With pillows propped against the headboard, she opens Lucinda's journal on her lap. Holding the mug with both hands, she sips as she explores the two pages splayed before her.

The house in which she sits, with its barn and former chicken coop, is beautifully rendered in four squares, two on each page. The images are soft, only a hint of color suggesting each of the four seasons. Margaret admires the sparse details, how subtlety allows the mind to fill in the completed picture. Three colored leaves represent autumn—one orange, one russet, one gold—and she is transported to the woods surrounding the house.

Among the trees she sees him, dressed in animal skins, lichen, and moss. Behind him, Old Cyrus is just visible, antlers branching wide. All elegance and grace, the stag lowers his head over the man's right shoulder. Two pair of eyes—one a startling blue, the other a glossy brown—flash with alarm. A moment later, both man and deer are gone. The autumnal scene floats on the page, now empty of presence.

Margaret sits upright with a start, nearly spilling her tea. She sets her mug on the nightstand, her heart thumping. Tightening the shawl around her, she stares at the pages spread open on her lap. A dream? A vision? A warning?

She sets the journal beside her and turns off the light. Chilled, she wriggles down into the bed, knees to her chest, comforter up to her neck.

⚜

She awakens in a tangle of shawl, sheet, and blanket, the comforter at the foot of the bed in a heap and Lucinda's journal on the floor. The dream still resonates in her body, but the only remnant she can grasp is a disturbing sense of dread. With the drapes drawn, she can't tell if its morning. Disoriented, she stumbles to the window, the floorboards icy beneath her bare feet.

Bright sunshine has her blinking to adjust, but the fact of it eases her discomfort. The girls are at the top of the stairs waiting, anxiety evident in their twitching bodies and worried eyes. As she motions them ahead of her, she sees Sam's grandmother descending another set of stairs. A little boy, eyes glistening with tears, waits at the bottom, clutching a ragged stuffed dog. The old woman scoops him up in her arms, the little dog pressed between her ample breasts and the boy's narrow chest. Lips close to his ear, she repeats a soothing phrase over and over, and the boy nestles into her. Margaret cannot hear the words, only the rhythmic repetition of sound. Like the little boy's, her body softens.

The vision dissolves as she enters the kitchen and checks the clock. Nearly six thirty, later than she'd hoped. She steps outside to branches, leaves, and tree limbs strewn about the backyard, but the sun is warm for October. She leaves her coat hanging open as she crosses to the barn to pull the car over closer to the house in the sun.

Back at the kitchen table with her breakfast, she opens her laptop and scrolls to Sam's attachment. With the working title, *Oh, My Darling*, the memoir begins with a dedication.

To Clementine,
"If we were to remember every sorrow, we'd crumble beneath the weight
of them.
Our hearts hold what we think we cannot bear until we're ready.
Ready to look.
Ready to have a good long cry.
Ready to see the sweet on the other side of sorrow."
Dear Grandmother Clementine,
I am now ready to look and have that good long cry.
I'm ready to put the sweet I've discovered on the other side of grief into
words.
Ready now to tell your story.

Margaret wipes her eyes, remembering her first vision of Clementine. Remembering the empathy she felt for the woman who was mistreated by those who sought her out. Those who asked for answers they weren't ready to hear. And she remembers her first unsettling meeting with Sam, the stranger who showed up in her backyard cloaked in a secrecy that hung on him like a borrowed coat. She remembers her repulsion and subsequent discovery that he was a famous writer trying for anonymity, overplaying the gruff exterior of the loner. She remembers, too, how he came to her rescue when she was driven off the road by a group of young men who'd been fed malicious stories about her all their lives. Smiling, she recalls the evolution of their friendship.

Interested in all things extrasensory, he requested her help in writing the story of his grandmother's second sight. With hesitation, she agreed. For Clementine's sake at first, and later for his. The subsequent journey awakened her memories, good and bad, of growing up with an intuitive ability many feared and few understood. In exploring Clementine's struggles and delights, she gained insights into her own. And now, having fallen asleep early and arisen late, she has only a few hours to peruse the initial draft of this awaited book.

⁂

The smell of salt and seaweed announces the ocean before it comes into view. Sam meets her in the sandy drive as she pulls up to the gray shingled cottage. The wind off the water is sharp, and the bear hug he wraps around her is welcome. Standing in wait a few feet behind him, Sam's Rhodesian ridgeback, CJ, watches them. Margaret approaches him casually and stops a foot away, understanding his aloof nature. He steps toward her, allowing a gentle pat to his head, and then turns and runs ahead of them to the front porch.

Inside, they settle at the table in a tidy kitchen sparsely outfitted with the bare necessities. The appliances are plain, the counters empty, but the table is piled with books and papers, a mug holding a cluster of identical pens—black ink with ultra-fine points—an index card file, and a laptop. A space has been cleared in front of the chair he offers to Margaret, and she pulls out her own laptop and sets it there. Beside them, a bay window looks out on the water. Beneath it, a metal cart holds a printer, reams of paper, more books, and a router.

Using a chapter outline he's drawn up for her, Sam summarizes the book. He gives her a sheet of highlighted sections for her special attention. His reverence for his grandmother coupled with his quest to fully experience the mystery of her gift carries them into deep conversation, and two hours roll by.

As Sam talks, Margaret catches glimpses of Clementine in his face and his gestures. She feels his grandmother's presence at the table, out the window, in the sunshine, in the water. She shares sudden insights and useful details that surface, and he jots them down. Underscored by the rhythmic roar of the waves as the tide comes in, the session feels like a cosmic dance.

With a low growl, CJ leaps up from his spot in the corner and rushes to the door, pulling them back into the cottage and the present.

"The girls must be here." Sam turns to the clock on the microwave with a look of surprise. "And don't worry, I won't let them know I called them *girls*."

"Smart, though they'll always be girls to us." She laughs, but underneath the levity she acknowledges a mild disappointment at the interruption. She gathers up the notes he's given her and puts them and her laptop in her bag.

"I saw Clementine this morning," she says as Sam starts to clear the clutter. "I nearly forgot. You were standing at the bottom of the stairs, holding a scraggly little dog."

"Hushpuppy." He turns to the window, his voice dreamlike. "She recited a little poem over and over whenever the memories came. Whenever I found myself in the backseat again and my parents in the front. The lights flashing, sirens screaming." He pauses, immersed. "A man carried me. Plopped me in the backseat of another car. I still remember the sour smell lingering in my nose."

"I'm sorry to bring you back to it."

"No, don't be. I can feel her holding me, Hushpuppy squished between us. I can smell her. Hear her voice again. And the words to that little poem, saturated in unconditional love." He turns back to her. "Thank you."

"She's thanking you, her beloved grandson, for writing this love story."

Sam bends to CJ, who has come to sit beside him, silent but alert. He runs his hands along the dog's sides from head to hindquarters, then ushers him into another room, closing the door as Emily and Louisa come up on the front porch. Margaret opens the door, inviting them in.

As Sam returns to the kitchen, Emily throws her arms around Margaret. "Ned's coming home. He's being released tomorrow."

At the eruption of well-wishes, she qualifies her statement. "He's actually going to be at his folks' house for a while before going it on his own." She takes the seat offered by Sam. "A physical therapist will be coming in every day." The brief shadow that crosses her smiling face belies her upbeat tone.

As she and Sam question her about Ned's progress, Margaret notes the anxiety sizzling beneath Emily's enthusiasm. She'll offer a quiet talk alone later.

The fondness she feels for Emily and for Ned, whom she's known for several years, has her identifying with Sesalie's family of aunts. And she likes the feeling.

This has her asking after Uncle Otis, and Emily beams. "He's great. In fact, Kenneth has asked him to consult on a job."

Margaret's chest tightens.

"Uncle Otis will be designing the gardens for an oceanside museum complex Kenneth's designing farther up the coast." Emily continues. "He's over the moon about it. Tell Kenneth when you see him how much he's appreciated."

Margaret manages not to hesitate in her response. Then, she suggests a walk on the beach to Louisa. Emily looks relieved at the prospect of not sharing a fragile new draft with too many eyes, and Sam promises some time with both writers after they're done.

⚜

The sun is hot, and they remove their shoes and coats and leave them on the porch. As they walk toward the lighthouse a mile away, Margaret enjoys the mixed sensations of cold wind and warm sand. They walk without talking for a while, establishing an easy rhythm.

"I saw her," Louisa says at last. "The baby you spoke of."

Margaret doesn't respond. She just keeps walking, eyes on the lighthouse on its rocky island in the distance, ears attuned to the rhythm of the waves and the cry of the gulls dipping and diving overhead.

"And?" she says at last.

Louisa slows. Margaret matches her pace then stops, turning to face the incoming waves. Louisa stands beside her, looking out.

"She was lying in a makeshift bed—a wooden crate lined with rumpled blankets—whimpering. Someone picked her up and pressed a bottle to her lips. Her little eyes, looking up at the hand holding the bottle, were clouded. She seemed listless and empty somehow. The hand, just a hand, detached."

Margaret knows what Louisa is feeling. The terrible helplessness of seeing. The pain of witnessing disturbing or discomforting realities. She gentles her voice when she speaks. "Her mother died in childbirth. We need to find her."

Louisa turns to her, looking very much like a lost child herself. Empathy washes all else away. "How?"

"Let me tell you what I know. Then let's work together. You are integral to this story, I am sure."

They begin to walk again, and Margaret fills her in on the discovery of the birthing room, Theresa's death, and the taking of the child. She describes the writing along the window frame, naming the women of Sarah's line.

Louisa stops. When she speaks, her voice is barely audible. "Sadie. They're calling her Sadie, not Sarah."

Margaret turns the name over in her mind, wondering if it's indeed the same child. Then she lands on the fact of it as certainty. "Sadie." She repeats the name aloud.

Louisa nods, her eyes brightening. Margaret can see confidence filling her. Determination. Intention.

They resume walking, leaving the soft dry sand for the firmer wetness nearer the crashing waves. Silence hanging between them, they enter a mutual space of expanding consciousness. There are no words here. Just a swirling mist like so much sea spray beyond the limits of language.

Images surface. An ancient virginal forest. Standing trees that have never known the rumble of a logging rig, the bite of the axe, the scream of the saw. Louisa walks ahead, more graceful at skirting the coarse woody debris, the roots and rocks and hollow mounds characteristic of old-growth forests. They hike through thickening trees and a lush understory. Margaret struggles at times to climb up and over downed trunks nearly as wide around as she is tall. But they keep thrusting onward, focused on a pulse point always just ahead.

Louisa picks up the pace. Margaret lets her lead, content to follow several feet behind, watching her leap over crumbling stumps and tightrope across a recent blowdown.

The ground underfoot becomes wet as they approach a pond, seepage swamps spreading out along its shore. Louisa examines a rack on the bank holding two battered canoes. A single board stained by a skim of green moss dangles from it. Louisa beckons Margaret to bend for a closer look at the nearly obliterated lettering. *Proctor Wilderness Reserve.*

A shot rings out, sharp in the quiet wood. They skirt the pond until the way becomes tangled with creeping vines and prickly branches. Then Louisa leads them away from the water until the path becomes easier, and they step out onto a rutted dirt trail.

A clearing opens onto a compound, a semicircle of cabins and lean-tos. A tripod of narrow logs with a blood-soaked chain hanging from its apex stands beside a trio of tanning racks. The after odor of death hangs above them, and they move quickly on. The close air vibrates with the resonance of the rifle shot. An image shimmers of a young buck, eyes wild at the moment of impact, collapsing into a mossy hollow. The woods are silent in the aftermath. Life stops for a breathless moment, reverence dwelling there.

Three miles they walk. Then seven. Then ten. The trail all but disappears. Two barely visible ruts run parallel at times and become invisible at others. Under the colorful canopy of sugar maples and yellow birch, they pick their way past groves of gnarled white cedars, the slow, patient growers aging by degrees. They climb over sunken logs—nurse logs—and Margaret imagines the microbial processes at work. She can almost hear life feeding life as the mosses retain moisture and the lichen and fungi do the work of decomposition. Together, they aid in the release of nutrients for the tiny seedlings sprouting along their sides.

The quickening of her pulse pulls her out of her imaginings. They're drawing near.

Louisa pushes aside a fallen limb thick with leafy branches that obscure the way ahead. And there it stands. Up a slight rise and just ahead of them. An interruption in the untouched natural world. A cabin, smoke drifting from the stove pipe in the roof, a woodpile by the porch, a truck in the yard, right rear tire flat.

Without waiting for Margaret to catch up, Louisa runs onto the porch. Margaret's call of warning catches in her throat as she watches her companion lean in, ear to the front door. Then she is standing beside her, listening too.

"We missed the meet. The deal's off for sure." A female voice Margaret recognizes.

"The kid's not looking good. Do something." A male. A voice she's heard though not in person.

"What do you want me to do?"

"It's not worth anything to us like this. Fix it."

"I don't know what else to do."

"Then we got to get rid of it."

Louisa rushes inside. She lifts the baby from its crate and walks out of the cabin. Cradling the child to her chest, she returns to the woods. Unhurried. Humming.

Margaret is startled by the sudden sting of salt water swirling around her bare feet. Beside her, Louisa gasps, and they look at each other in surprise.

"Henry." Louisa blurts the name, fully in the present now. Noting Margaret's look of confusion, she explains. "Hank's name is Henry. Henry Whitfield. And the baby—"

"Is in danger. I know." Margaret pulls out her phone and texts Jay and Cyn with what she knows, promising more to come.

"Nana Claire lived until she was two in a tiny town on the edge of that wilderness reserve. Then the family moved to the coast. I've never been there, but I knew the way somehow."

"I saw the cabin last night in a vision just before you returned my call. No coincidence, I suspect. I had sketched Hank's face, then traveled there. I had no idea where I was, but I recognized the truck in the yard. I had also seen you with the baby earlier, when I was at the Makepeace farm. You carried the baby to me and then went off into the same old-growth forest."

Louisa considers this as they begin walking again. "So, that's why you wanted me along."

"You are clearly an integral piece in the puzzle we're working. The murder at Wandering Rock and the missing woman and baby. It's all tied together."

"Can you fill me in on what you know about it?"

Margaret starts to speak but listens to an inner prompting instead. "What if I share a few facts and leave them with you? That way, any biases, wrong assumptions, or misguided conclusions I've drawn won't get in the way of your clear vision."

"Then we'll see what comes to me on my own."

Margaret smiles at her ready response.

As they come to the point of land reaching out toward the lighthouse, they sit on a stone bench, and Margaret gives her the essential facts of the murder—the who, the when, the where, and the fact of the missing sister.

"Twins." Louisa mulls this. "What Marcella would give to know these facts. But don't worry," she hurries on. "I've quit my job and wouldn't tell her anyway."

"How'd she take it?"

"Had a fit. Screamed. Carried on. Tried to make me feel guilty. Told me I was selfish. Then she said I couldn't quit because I was fired." She shakes her head and sighs. "It was hard."

"How did you feel afterwards?"

Louisa pauses, then grins. "Relieved."

She's smiling, but Margaret understands the flicker of fear in her eyes. Although no longer under the burden of deceit Marcella exacted from her, Louisa is now out of a good-paying job, and her former boss is not someone you want as an enemy.

A quick scene unfolds. Louisa is seated at a desk, an airy bouquet of flowers beside a state-of-the-art desktop computer. Behind her is a bookcase filled with reference books and binders. Two open books are laid out beside her keyboard, and she smiles as she types. A name plate edged in silver reads *Louisa May Perkins, Research Assistant*.

"I'm sure you'll find something far more satisfying. Soon. You're well out of Marcella's grasp."

"And what about you? She's out to cause trouble for you. She's terribly jealous." Louisa looks out to the lighthouse and sighs.

"Don't worry about me. She's not the first and won't be the last. It's time for you to focus on you and your writing, Louisa May." She smiles when Louisa reacts with a wince.

"My mother's way of encouraging me to be a reader. Little did she know I'd want to be a writer as well."

"Speaking of which, it's time we headed back to Sam's. It seems life is taking up where your mother left off."

Laughing, they head back to the cottage.

Before she leaves them to their work, she and Sam arrange a meeting in two weeks, giving him time to step away from the book and her a chance to dive in.

⚜

On her way home, a text comes in from Jay. Her car's audio system reads it aloud in the robotic voice she's still getting used to. *Sending law enforcement in by plane. More info later. Not over the phone.*

Margaret says a silent prayer for the baby's safe rescue, unsettled by the return of the dread she felt earlier. As she nears home, the dread deepens. The end of her driveway is partially blocked by a dark sedan with a news van in front of it. A handful of reporters are clustered nearby, and they raise cameras and phones as she slows to turn in.

"Damn." She breathes to calm herself as she noses forward. A cameraman steps in front of her while reporters shout questions she can't hear. She eases farther forward and gives a gentle toot to the horn, but the man doesn't move aside.

Rolling down her window, she forces a smile. The young woman nearest her sticks a phone in her face. "What can you tell us about your role in the investigation into the murder of the Woman at Wandering Rock, Mrs. Meader? What—"

"You'll have to ask the appropriate authorities about the investigation. I can't speak to that. Now, I'd appreciate you allowing me to enter my driveway, please."

Another phone is thrust into the open window. "How do you respond to Marcella McCray's assertions that you've given the police false information in order to garner attention? That you're covering for a dangerous pervert who lives in the woods? That you're a charlatan?"

Looking up into the pocked face of Ross Templar, his glasses sliding down from the bridge of his nose as he yells for all to hear, she stifles an angry retort. "I won't dignify that with an answer, Mr. Templar."

She forces a pleasant smile and courteous nod as she presses the button to close the window. She accelerates gently, and the cameraman reluctantly moves out of the way but keeps his camera aimed at her as she rolls by. Her body shaking, she holds herself together until she can no longer see them in the rearview. She passes the house and parks in the barn, then walks to the backroom. In the soothing darkness, she sits on a bale of hay, working hard to remember how to breathe.

When she is calmer, she crosses to the house and lets the dogs out, tossing her bag inside before following them down the hill and up toward the woods. Once inside the cool depths, she slows, taking in the peace of this place bright with color—the last burst of life before the leaves begin falling in earnest. She takes the trail just inside the tree line that she hasn't used in a while, following the curve of the ridge above her house. The girls weave in and out of the trees, running into the sunny fields to the left and back into the dark woods. As she picks up their reliable rhythms, the heaviness from her encounter with Templar and the press lifts.

Just doing their jobs, she reminds herself, and her respect for the necessary work of legitimate journalists has her wishing she'd been more accommodating to the others. Less prickle, more pleasantry in the future, she promises herself.

Cheeks flushed, she jogs back down the hill toward home, the girls crisscrossing in front of her until they reach the stream. There they stop to drink, splashing themselves and her in the process. Laughing, she heads up to the backyard.

After placing rice and the beans she's soaked overnight into a CrockPot, she drops an apple and a bag of sunflower seeds into a basket, along with some dog biscuits and a thermos of tea. Then she heads for her studio.

She sits at her worktable looking out the window, watching the play of shadow and light as the sun disappears and reappears amid fast-moving clouds. Pen in hand, notebook open, she waits.

For a while, nothing comes. Then a nebulous image arises, underscored by a series of notes from a solitary flute, silence ringing between them. Then a drumbeat, quiet and low. Tha-thump ... tha-thump ... tha-thump. A heartbeat. And another. And another. And another. Overlapping. Intersecting. Synchronizing.

Three figures emerge from a sweet-scented mist hanging over a meadow. A girl child. A young woman. An elder. The latter is one she knows well.

Then the words come. Her fingers tighten around the pen, and she begins to write. The three figures float, ethereal yet each a weighty presence. When the words cease, she takes up her drawing pencil. As she steps into time outside of time, the tableau spreads before her, and her hand races to catch up. The three figures become a tiny circle of belonging, dancing hand in hand in hand in the shadow of three standing stones—the grandmothers. Secluded, surrounded by a thick pine grove. Together with the ancient maple and the tiny bloodspot bush, they hold sacred space.

She is carried back. John Longfeather's grandmothers and aunts are blessing her again with their teachings and guidance. Again she witnesses spirits of the grandmothers of his line gathering up her brother's broken body and singing him home. She is overwhelmed once more with gratitude for their tender care. And now, Sesalie's grandmother, Winowa, is about to take her leave, and Margaret can hear their singing as she creates this tribute with the help of the unseen.

Without thought, she takes out her paints and touches her dampened brush to the thick paper, stroke by careful stroke. She breathes in a deep satisfaction as the paper drinks in the subtle colors. When she looks up at the clock, three hours have passed. Time for a break.

She and the girls stand at the crest of the hill. The sun hangs low, the clouds flattening along the horizon, and a lone heron wings its way across the October sky. She picks up two sticks and tosses them for Sophia and Grace, losing herself in the joy of play.

Back in the studio, she takes up her calligraphy pen and writes three lines beneath the now dry painting. Taking out a piece of ivory parchment paper, she pens the longer poem that came to her earlier. She remains purposely aloof as she works, not allowing the words to register. Not allowing the impact of the piece to affect the steadiness of her hand. Not allowing sadness in.

Leaving both sheets to sit, she returns to the house and adds corn and finishing herbs to the CrockPot. Then she heads upstairs to shower and change, unmuting her phone as she goes. Three missed calls. Annie. Sesalie. Kenneth.

Her heart kicks up. She stares at the screen. She checks for voice mail. Two messages: Annie and Sesalie.

Chapter 27

Sesalie stands in the doorway backlit by wall sconces set low. She is wearing a simple dress of her own design, an A-line with a square neck and long sleeves. Against an ivory background, female figures the color of sand dance along a six-inch border at the hem. The alpaca and mohair shawl draped around her shoulders is hand-dyed to a subtle peach, the work of her sister Sylvia. Her blue-black hair is pulled back in a knot at the nape, and strings of seed beads hang feather-like from her ears. They shimmer as she bends forward, hugging Margaret.

Margaret can see past her to her mother, Aiyana, standing alone. Gently, she turns Sesalie, and they move as one across the kitchen and enfold Aiyana in a silent embrace. As they draw apart, Aiyana extends her hand and leads the way to the enclosed porch.

Solar lights border the backyard, and they descend the steps and walk toward the circle of chairs. In the center, the firepit has been laid with kindling and fat wood. The quiet humming of women's voices brings her to the verge of tears. Some are already seated, wrapped in fringed blankets. Empty chairs hold folded blankets, each unique in its design.

On the near side of the circle, Winowa rests against the plump cushions of a chaise. A single streak of silver runs through her black hair from the center part down and across her left shoulder. She is wrapped against the evening air in several blankets. Margaret feels the crackle of energy pulsing from her—the life force vibrant still.

Aiyana leads them around to the granite slab embedded in the ground at the easternmost spot. As Margaret waits her turn to step onto this threshold to the circle, she remembers the day it was placed here. A chunk of Deer Isle granite, it is a lovely mix of lavender and gray with flecks of black mica and quartz. A gift from an uncle who worked the northern quarries.

Sesalie enters the circle ahead of her, and Margaret steps onto the stone. A subtle vibration travels up her body as she makes a silent request to enter. It's time to face what awaits, the truth of Winowa's transition. So, she breathes herself into the present, allowing the sadness to enter the circle with her.

Aiyana and Sesalie take the chairs on either side of Winowa, leaving the empty seat across the fire for her—the seat between the aunts, Hasaleen and Dawn.

As she unfolds her blanket and sits, the eldest of the youngsters among them strikes a wooden match to the tinder beneath the firewood. All go silent as the flame takes and the blaze flares in earnest. Then the chanting begins. Margaret listens hard until the syllables become familiar and she is able to join the women's voices. Her body settles into the chair, and her heart entrains to the rhythm set by words both intimate and beyond her conscious understanding. Soon there is only sound. Surrounding her. Opening her. Pulling her inward.

Somewhere along this spiraling journey, the drumming starts. Soft woman-made mallets bounce off hides stretched across rims of ash and maple and birch, bringing forth the song of the drum. The communal heartbeat.

Two more of the older girls feed chunks of wood to the growing fire. They sit on the ground, tasked with tending the blaze, and Margaret watches them. Each face unique, carrying its own beauty. Each body its own being. Each movement individual yet in sync with her sisters'. Each woman and child at one with the timeless dance of the embodied feminine.

Winowa sets the rhythm. Melody rocks back and forth, stroking her round belly. The little fire tenders sway from side to side in the grass at Winowa's feet. The circle of life in all its fullness is playing out here in this backyard. Sacred space sits like a bowl—a container for ritual as old as memory.

Suddenly, the women fall silent. The fire crackles and snaps. The drums are laid to rest against chair legs. Autumn crickets and night beings take up the abandoned song, echoing in a deeper register the first sounds in early spring. The wheel ever turning.

Across the circle from Margaret, Winowa's face shimmers above the fingers of flame. A tone, singular yet layered, rises from her throat, and when it stops, even the crickets go silent. The women lift their faces to the still-leafy branches overhead as stars begin to dot the night sky through gaps in the canopy. A breeze rises out of the stillness, freshens, and dies.

An owl hoots. The smell of woodsmoke and apples drifts in from the east. The scent of sweetgrass and sage wafts from the firepit. And Margaret falls backward into a pile of leaves, arms spread, laughing.

A boy bends over her and grabs her hand. He pulls her up to standing, his handsome face winking with mischief. Just as she finds her balance, he tags her. "You're it!" His face broadens into a grin as he runs away.

This brother, like Mattie only in how he runs away, is eight or nine with shaggy black hair and eyes that dance with humor. And she is chasing him, laughing as she trips on her flapping shoe lace and lands on hands and knees. Looking back, he stops and waits for her to scramble to her feet, then the taunting grin reappears as he takes off.

"Will," she calls after him, her hand extended. But an arm encircles her waist and holds her back.

She struggles, flailing and twisting until a handkerchief is placed over her mouth. A sharp odor stings her nostrils. She wakes up on a bus, surrounded by girls looking mutely ahead. The landscape rushing past the window is strange. The woman in the back scowls when she turns around, and the rest of the women scattered among the seats aren't smiling. And she's shocked to find she's wet herself.

A whirring sound. A man's voice speaking words she's never heard before. She's standing in the front row of a group with taller boys and girls behind her. She's in the same clothes, now soiled, that she was wearing when the hands pulled her away from her brother and everything she knew. Her hair needs Grandmother's fingers to untangle the knots. And her body smells. She tries to hide by becoming small.

The talking man's voice rumbles with strange rhythms. Another man is bent forward, his head behind a box on a three-legged stand. The box is making the whirring sound. The voice orders the group to be still. Words separate themselves out and dangle in the air beside her ear. Words she'll come to know by heart. Savage. Dirty. Indian.

A kaleidoscope of imagery. Scissors snip and clumps of hair fall, taking her spirit with them. Scratchy clothes chafe her body. A smack to the mouth as she slips, speaking words her mother gave her. Straight lines. Rigid rows. Pointless tedium. A deep longing for the lost circle. Spirals on her slate. Chalk crushed underfoot. So much dust.

A swirl of color and a rush of sound. A shift.

Eyes the color of sky. A freckled nose. A yellow beard. Fields of grass riffling in a warm wind. A turning wheel creaks at the top of a metal tower beyond a red barn. Sheets flap on a clothesline. Laughter like music. Happiness wrapped in white. The shadow on the heart shrinking.

Three little girls chase fireflies under a crescent moon. A man falls to the ground, the three piling on top of him. Two look just like him, the third is the image of the woman crossing the yard. The man calls out, "Lila. Save me from the tickle monsters." A small boy emerges from the shadow of her skirts and runs to them. She slows so he can be first to leap onto the wriggling pile.

As the images fade, the family dissolves into laughter. The father, grunting as the boy bounces on his chest, exclaims, "My giggly growing boy!" and calls him by name. The woman gathers her girls on her lap, naming them with a kiss on the nose, one by one.

Margaret opens her eyes. Winowa is looking at her across the fire, expectant. Inviting her to share what she has seen.

The circle waits, and so she stands, dropping the blanket from her shoulders. Slowly, she walks the inner circle, stopping in front of Winowa. Sesalie touches a smudge stick to the fire and circles Margaret, the smoke following, hanging in the air round them both. When she sits, Margaret begins.

"I've seen your sister. I've seen Lila." As she speaks, Winowa's eyes melt into indigo pools. "Lost to you so long ago, dissolving into the mists where stolen children live, she found her way out. At first, her life was hard. I will not tell you otherwise. But later she found joy. Her adopted name was Johnson. Her married name was Davis. And she made a life with a laughing man who loved her well. Together, they had three daughters and a son."

The women hold a collective breath in the beat before she goes on.

"Esther." She pauses, letting the name hang in the air, smoke from the fire curling around it. Then she goes on. "Anne. Winowa. And Will.

"Her native tongue may have been taken away by a school that was no school—meant not to educate but to assimilate—but she remembered. She gave her children the only things she carried from her past. The family names.

"Lila GreyHawk is with us here tonight."

The drumming begins anew.

Winowa looks off into the night, and only Margaret hears the voices she hears beyond the hooting of the owl in the tallest pine. The ancestors murmur words she cannot understand. And in their midst, a younger male speaks softly, his meaning clear. *I am whole again.*

As Margaret returns to her seat, a baby whimpers. The soft sound builds in intensity until it is screaming. She has a sudden urge to leave, to run toward it, but before she can act on the impulse, the crying stops. Silence rings in its absence until the owl hoots again, asking its eternal question.

Winowa speaks, surprising her and everyone else, judging from their faces in the firelight. Her voice is strong, reaching across the flames and up into the night sky. "A child calls out to me. The present-day embodiment of all our stolen children. A girl child. When she is found and returned to her mother's people, the healing will begin in earnest, rippling forward and back through time."

The women look to one another and then back to Winowa, expectation of more on their faces.

The old woman pushes herself more upright on the chaise. "Margaret knows of the child, and someone here knows of her family. The ancestors have spoken. Owl has called it so."

She is seized by a coughing fit, the sound both loose and thick. But she waves away her daughter and granddaughter as they lean in to tend her, resting her head on the back of the chair until her breathing returns to normal. Her voice, when she speaks, is strong again.

"These are good signs. The circle is coming 'round again. Righting itself. I am grateful I have lived to see this turning."

Margaret slumps back in her chair, suddenly spent. Peace settles in her chest. No more sense of unease. No more sense of urgency to go. All is well, and she knows it.

⚜

The fire dies slowly as the drumming, chanting, and closing stories wind down. Although she loves the storytelling part of any ceremony, Margaret's mind is pulled from the circle by another story playing out to the north, involving those she'll never meet but for whom she'll always feel grateful. Those nameless, faceless instruments of justice righting itself.

Sesalie closes the circle with a prayer of thanksgiving, and Margaret accepts the invitation to stay for the sharing of food. She waits for the right time and slips into Winowa's room.

"I wanted to say good night and to thank you." She keeps her voice steady, but she knows the old woman can feel the depth of her sorrow.

"Thank you, dear daughter. It was important that you be here tonight for more reasons than I knew when I asked for you. Such is often the way." She stops, struggling to catch her breath. As Margaret waits, she focuses on the sound of each rattling inhale. Each exhale. Each humming moment in the spaces between. "The child," Winowa says at last. "She'll be all right? You'll see she's reunited with her family?"

"I'll do everything I can."

"The ancestors will guide you." She takes a shuddering breath. "And the young one will help."

"I will listen for their counsel. And, yes, Louisa will help."

Winowa smiles, her wrinkles deepening, her breath quieting. Margaret kisses her forehead and turns to leave.

"Bring me the news. I will remain to hear it spoken."

Margaret nods, letting the tears come as the old woman's eyes flutter and close. She leans down, listening. Satisfied there is still time, she places her gift—rolled and tied with a ribbon—on the mantlepiece, and leaves.

John's truck rolls into the driveway as she reaches her car. They hug, and she offers condolences, knowing his deep love for Winowa. When he asks, she tells him James has gone back to the woods. John sighs but nods in understanding. He reassures her that James will keep low and out of sight. Then he urges her to do the same.

"I see the circus at the foot of your drive when I go by. Call me if anyone gets out of hand." He bends for another hug before opening her car door for her.

She takes a moment to get her phone out of the console.

No messages.

Chapter 28

There are no vehicles at the end of her driveway, and she relaxes. As she pulls around toward the barn, a shadow slips past the stand of lilacs trees. A shiver follows, putting her on high alert. She stops, clicking the headlights up to high. This is not James. Her body's response tells her so. She lowers the beams and backs up.

She hops out by the house and unlocks the kitchen door, letting the girls out. They rush past her, growling. She follows, her body alert, her hand on the pepper spray in her bag. The dogs sniff the ground around the lilac trees and then head out back of the barn. She rolls open the barn door and turns on the exterior lights, flooding the yard as the girls lope back around the corner. Subdued, they come to her and hang close.

"Must have been a visiting critter, eh, girls," she says to calm herself. But she's certain it was more likely the two-legged variety. The dogs hop in the back seat of her car for the short ride into the barn. Before heading for the house, she walks with them to the lilac bushes, and they rush to a spot near the barn's foundation, noses to the ground. She bends to examine what they've found and sucks in her breath. Crushed cigarette butts.

She runs to the house. At the door, she signals for the girls to take a quick run to release the crackling energy radiating from their bodies. She waits for them there, her hand on the knob.

A flash of memory has her back in the cab of her old truck. Sharp pain in her head. The click of a lighter. A flickering flame near the gas tank. A shotgun blast. Her heart hammers the inside of her rib cage.

A wet nose in the cup of her hand, a sturdy pair of bodies pressed against her outer thighs, and she's back. Safe. Home.

As she turns to go in, she nearly steps on the brown bag on the doorstep. Her heartbeat kicks up again as she nudges it with her foot. Its contents are soft and give way as her boot leaves a toe print in the bag. She grabs a stick, although the girls are showing no interest in the bag beyond an initial sniff. Still, she holds her breath as she pokes it open.

A puzzle with a note. *Thought you would like this one. Hilda.* She laughs but hurries inside, nonetheless.

Leaving the outside lights on, front and back, her phone in her sweater pocket, she goes through the house, checking the locks on all doors and windows. She swears as her tea steeps, angry that she's been pushed to this edge of fear. In her own home.

Her phone rings, and as she reaches for it, she knows what he'll say before she answers. The baby has been found, her abductors have not.

Jay expresses both relief and frustration as he delivers the news. Law enforcement flew into the Proctor Wilderness Reserve, landing on the pond near the reserve's campsite. Following Louisa's directions, they accessed the illegal private cabin and found the child. Alone. Unfed. Dehydrated. She was flown to Maine Medical, and her prospects for recovery are positive.

The couple left on foot with backpacks and camping gear, disappearing into a thickening forest with a canopy too dense for an air search.

Meanwhile, Jay explains, background checks on Henry "Hank" Whitfield revealed he lived off the grid with a survivalist community for ten years. When he surfaced, he was arrested for minor drug offenses and was investigated but not charged with trafficking.

When Jay turns to the other subject she's been waiting for—the search at the farm—she again knows what he'll say before he says it.

"We found remains. Just beyond the compost pile. Two bodies, female. We've locked the place down and have both Lydia and Clarence in custody."

Her silence is matched on the other end of the line. Then comes the ripple of laughter. She's on the threshold of the upstairs bedroom in the Makepeace house. Two young women sit on one of the beds. One is reciting Lewis Carroll's "Jabberwocky," her tone dramatic, her gestures wild. The other giggles until both collapse in a spasm of shared laughter.

"Theresa and her sister, Anita," she says.

"We think so. I'll keep you updated."

Jay hangs up, and Margaret is left with an afterimage of the sisters, matching heart-shaped crystals at their necks.

Still in her hand, her phone rings.

"They found her. Did Jay call you?" Cyn's voice is buoyant and edging toward a sharpness uncomfortable to the ear.

"Yes. We just hung up."

"I wish I'd been there. To see her. The reality of her."

Margaret waits, knowing there's more.

"I nearly volunteered to care for her. Just for now, of course. Until this is sorted out and her family is found." Her voice drops. "But I knew they wouldn't let me."

"A lovely gesture, and you would have been wonderful for her, but I can see why it wouldn't be allowed. You're a lead investigator on the case. There would be issues."

"Yes. But I had to tell someone. ... You. I had to tell you. Had to say it out loud. I know she'll be in good hands. They've called in Jane-Susan Miller. She's the best."

Margaret smiles. "She's a treasure. Any child placed in her care is indeed lucky. I'm sure she'll keep you in the loop. It's really the best possible option."

"You're right. I had to hear you say that. Thanks. I better get back at it and see that the right somebodies pay for this."

Margaret is about to click off when Cyn adds, "By the way, Tammi and I talked into the night. It was ... deep. Beyond anything I could have wished for. I've never felt closer to her. Thank you."

Before Margaret can respond, she's gone, the line silent. And yet the connection to this reserved young woman sizzles still.

She carries her tea into the living room. Inhaling the fragrant steam before each sip, she settles back in her favorite chair and lets her mind empty. When the tea is gone, she retrieves the brown bag from the kitchen and dumps the puzzle pieces out on the coffee table.

She smiles at the array of colors intermingled with a mass of terracotta red. Her fingers go to work sorting, flipping pieces over to their right sides, grouping them by color. Her mind rests in the familiar rhythms as sections of the puzzle come together, and she savors the satisfaction of fitting pieces into place. Her practiced fingers fly as the picture reveals itself.

She laughs. Pottery from her friend the potter. Whole pieces and shards. Cups and bowls and pitchers, tall and slender, round and squat. And a scattering of broken bits. Some glazed. Some biscuit, fired but unglazed.

Earthenware. Practical. Useful. And in its midst, a shining multicolored bowl. The design, an intricate puzzle in itself, whose interconnected pieces span the color spectrum. Brighter than the rest, this puzzle within a puzzle dazzles.

Smiling, Margaret imagines the joy Hilda must have felt in finding this. Gift and gift giver perfectly aligned. She reaches for her phone as the clock chimes. Two a.m. She looks at the clock to confirm what she knows but doesn't want to know is true. She drops the phone back into her pocket, shaking her head. "Guess I'll wait on the thank-you call."

The dogs raise their heads, going from deep sleep to wide alert, and she meets their questioning eyes with another laugh. Reluctantly, she leads the way to the back door and lets them out for a last romp. As she stands in the doorway, a shiver reawakens her earlier wariness. When the girls return, taking their time to shuffle in the brittle grass, she decides to leave the back light on.

Before going up to bed, she closes all the curtains with lights still burning in both living room and kitchen. Dark memories surface, and she lets them come, not wanting them to seek expression in her dreams. Her truck crashing into the tree. Testosterone-heavy angst from young males brought up on lies; contorted faces and a single flame threatening her life. And before that, fire destroying her shed and all it held.

A younger face slips into view. At least one boy was snatched from hatred's grasp. As her studio rose out of the ashes, the boy who set the fire was enfolded into the spirit of that rising phoenix and shown another way. Thanks in great part to Kenneth.

Pain grips her anew. Like the memories, she lets the tears come. Out the back window, the studio is a dark shape in a fuller darkness. Her sadness mixes with a sudden sweetness. From that loss came renewal on so many levels. Kenneth was an integral part of that journey. Perhaps that was meant to be enough—his only role as their paths intersected for a while. With that, the pain softens. She ascends the stairs, closes the drapes, and crawls into bed.

Chapter 29

As she sets four loaves of bread to rise in a warm corner of her kitchen, tires crunch in the drive. Since calling Emily after breakfast with an invitation to stop by, she's lost track of time. She wipes the dusting of flour from the board and lifts the kettle to pour water into the waiting teapot when a loud knock surprises her. She goes to the door to see why Emily hasn't come in with her usual quick tap and hello.

Through the curtain she can see that it's not Emily. It's Marcella McCray, and a flash of anger sets her on edge. As she debates opening the door, Marcella calls out to her.

"I know you're home. I need to talk." After a pause, she adds, "Please."

Margaret opens the door and steps outside, blocking the entrance and making it clear she has no intention of inviting the woman in.

Marcella's white-blonde hair is tucked up inside a slouchy knit hat, purple with strands of silver yarn sparkling in the morning sun. She wears a purple and gray quilted jacket, a calf-length gray wool skirt, and purple leather boots with rows of matching fringe above the ankles. Red splotches dot her pale cheeks, and she blows on her hands.

"Could we talk inside? It's fricken' freezing out here."

"Then let's make this short. I'm expecting company." Margaret doesn't move from the doorway.

"Look. You took Louisa and—"

"Took?" Margaret's voice sharpens, cutting her off before she can go on.

"I groomed that girl." Marcella jumps right back in. "Spent my precious time training her. A good assistant is created, you know. And now you want to reap the benefit of my hard work?" She claps her palms to her chest, looking stricken. "You're not interested in the girl, you just want to get back at me. It's not right, and it's not fair to her."

Margaret weighs her next words before speaking. The empty air crackles between them. Squinting, she stares into eyes the color of mist over the ocean on a sunless morning. In them, she sees a fragile little girl hovering at the periphery. Abandoned and afraid.

Margaret's body softens, her heart opening a crack as pity turns toward compassion.

"Marcella." Her voice is quiet, kind. "Louisa is her own person, free to think for herself. She was your employee. Now she's moving on. You'll miss her for the good employee she was, and finding a replacement will not be easy, but that's how life works."

"She never would have left if you hadn't turned her against me. But she signed an agreement." Her voice rises. "I'll sue her and I'll sue you."

The dogs begin to bark on the other side of the door behind Margaret, and she does nothing to stop them.

Instead, she leans closer to Marcella, her tone hardening. "She did your work for you, Marcella. That's the truth of it. I don't know if you really have the gifts you claim. Perhaps you're just very good at reading people and gathering background information readily available online. But I do know you depended on Louisa's gift and used it to keep your customers coming back. It's only natural you wouldn't want to lose that. But neither you nor I nor anyone else can take away her agency."

Marcella lifts her chin. "I'm a gifted psychic with a track record. My clients adore me. And they did so long before I hired that little ingrate. She has a smidgeon of extrasensory perception, I'll grant you that, but I'm the one with the visions. I've mentored her. She had no intention of leaving until you came along."

She turns as if to go, but stops and swirls back around. Her voice is soft when she speaks again. "I didn't come here to fight with you. I came to renew my offer to collaborate. To see if you and I, and maybe even Louisa, could work together. My grief over losing Louisa overtook me for a minute there." She looks down at her feet, avoiding Margaret's eyes. "I'd like to help clear your boyfriend." She stops and corrects herself. "Your *friend* in the woods. I can't explain my impression that she was raped and won't apologize for wanting to warn the public, but I want to work with you. I even brought a peace offering. And I'd like to share my latest vision."

Margaret doesn't respond. She waits for Marcella to look up and then plumbs the depths of her eyes for deception. She is surprised by the aura of genuine concern.

"Tell me about this vision," she says at last.

"I really am freezing here. Can we…" She indicates the door.

Margaret relents. She calms the dogs and lets them scamper by for a run as she lets the woman enter.

Marcella stamps her feet, making a production out of wiping her boots on the mat and removing her jacket. As she pulls off the hat, her hair falls around her shoulders, strands crackling with static electricity and lifting off around her crown like a halo.

Margaret offers her a seat but no tea. "If you have something for the police, you should be telling them."

"Yeah, right! They won't give me the time of day thanks to— They'll listen to you."

"What did you see?"

Marcella opens her mouth and then closes it. She sits back in her chair, looking as if she's reconsidering. "You have to assure me you won't take credit for this and shut me out of the loop."

Margaret rises. "I don't have the time or inclination to play games. Tell me what you saw. Otherwise, there's the door."

"Okay." She waits for Margaret to sit back down. "I saw a man having sex with the woman who died. Consensual sex. She called him *babe*. And it wasn't your... It wasn't the guy in the woods. They were in a motel near the ocean."

Margaret is surprised. The scene feels plausible except for the mistaken identity of the woman as the one later murdered. "You need to tell the police."

"They won't listen to me. But now that I've cleared the old man, let's put our heads together. Maybe bring in Louisa. Then we can tell the police together."

"It's because of you that his name needed clearing. You accused him, on camera and with your trademark theatrical flair, of murder and rape."

"But—"

"There was no earlier vision that led you to say those things. You heard some gossip and fit it into a false narrative. You created a hell of a story that could cost a man his life. Do you understand that he's still in danger? Once the juicy lie gets started, the truth hasn't a chance."

"It wasn't a lie. I believed it to be true. I misjudged. But I—"

"Stop. Just stop. As long as you make excuses and fail to acknowledge your part in misleading the police and the public, you won't be trusted or believed."

"You don't believe I saw the couple in the motel? How else would I know the details? The motel. The ocean. The 'babe'?"

"Look. The police can verify your story, and that's what matters. I hope it's true and useful to them. I want nothing more than to have this solved."

"That's it? Sending me on my way after I share this with you? Trust you."

"If you receive more, let the police know. But no more stunts with the press. Please."

"Jesus, Margaret. Talk about patronizing. You are—" Again, she stops herself. She takes a breath and raises her hands palms outward in a gesture of surrender. "I give up." She heads for the coat rack.

As she fumbles into her jacket and plops her hat on her head, she sighs. "Here." She pulls a wrapped package from her pocket. "A little gift I brought as a peace offering. Take it anyways. Maybe they'll prove helpful with the case." She opens the door and bends to bestow exaggerated hugs on the girls as they meet her just outside. As she straightens and turns back to Margaret, her eyes are a startling silver. "Maybe they're the tool you need, a throwback to your younger days at school on the green."

When she's gone, Margaret sets the package on the kitchen table and fills the girls' water bowls. As she checks the breads and re-covers them, the door opens with a quick tap and hollered hello.

Emily wipes her feet as she hangs up her coat, then swoops in for a hug. "What's this?" she asks as she taps the package on the table.

"Would you believe a gift from Marcella? You just missed her."

"Sometimes I have impeccable timing." She laughs.

Margaret picks up the package to move it out of the way. An electrical charge surges up her arm, and she nearly drops it. As she notes the heft of it in her hand, a series of images tumbles. The final one remains as she closes her eyes. She blinks, waiting for it to disappear, but it hangs in the air behind her closed lids.

A face. One she's seen before but can't quite place. It's a woman's face framed by thick dark hair. Sadness clouds the hazel eyes. As the image fades, a music box tinkles, the melody distorted as it slowly winds down.

She opens her eyes. Emily is watching, having waited patiently for her to come back.

She unwraps the gift and holds up a colorful box for Emily to see. Pinks and purples swirl across the cover. Raised letters embellished with silver stars spell out the words: *The Mystical Tarot.* And in smaller script, *created by Marcella Catriona McCray.*

Margaret sits, wanting to set the gift aside but unable to put it down. She lifts the cover and slides out the stack of cards, larger and heavier than a traditional deck. They pulsate as she passes them back and forth between her hands. Her heartbeat and breathing increase, and her chest cavity comes alive with a twitchy energy. Uncomfortable but curious, she shuffles the thick cards, awkwardly at first, until a humming settles in her chest.

"Are you all right?"

Emily's voice surprises her. She looks across the table to find concern in her friend's green eyes.

"Sorry." She sets the deck on the table. "I've never used tarot cards, but… " She stops. "That's not exactly true. Back in art school, a friend once roped me into playing fortune teller at a fundraiser."

She's back in Cambridge on the grassy square on campus known as the Green. Yards of sheer fabric hang from the wooden frame of her booth creating an enclosed room. Dressed in flowing robes and a turban, a sequin glued to her forehead, she sits inside at a small table covered in fringed satin. In front of her, a crystal ball is perched on a wooden stand. She shuffles a borrowed deck, soft and pliable from wear. A small boy sits across from her, the hollowness in his dark brown eyes accentuated by the buzz cut and large ears. A jagged scar runs down his pale scalp from crown to temple. His mother stands behind him, an unspoken plea in her eyes.

The cards flutter, a soft blur in her hands. Following a guidance she cannot name, she stops and lays out three cards. The Star. The Ten of Cups. The Sun.

She smiles. "Oh, my! What happy cards we have here." The boy's face brightens, a flush coloring his cheeks as she goes on. "What a lucky boy you are. This one is the All Better card." She points to the Star. "The Healing card," she says to his mother.

Though they've given her no names, she adds, "Dr. Pritchard is doing a happy dance, saying, 'Good job, Richie. You get the best fighter award. Soon you'll be playing soccer again.'"

As the mother grabs the back of her son's chair, tears glistening, Margaret continues. "The Ten of Cups is the happiness card. The big celebration card. And the Sun shines brightly into the future." A new image comes. "Daddy is doing the happy dance too and will be home soon."

The next three readings are filled with easy answers to light-hearted questions. When a young man enters and holds out his hand to her, a thickness settles in her chest. She stifles a cough. Not for the first time in her life, she shakes the hand of cancer. The first two cards she lays out confirm this. But as she turns over the last one, light glimmers from its otherwise dark surface. She leans in, holding his eyes with hers. She waits to be sure of his full attention, then delivers it straight. "You need to stop smoking."

He pulls back. "What the—"

"Now." Emotions stream across his face in tandem with bodily reactions. Anger. Confusion. Fear. Back to anger. As he rises, she says, "See a doctor. Quick action will make all the difference."

"Damn quack! I'm reporting you to whoever's in charge here." Turning to leave, he's caught for a moment in the layers of fabric hanging in the doorway. He bats at them with both hands, cursing, then disappears.

A middle-aged woman walks head down against a stiff wind toward a rocky ledge above the ocean. She carries a silver urn. Margaret closes her eyes against the scene.

A voice startles her.

"And?" Emily repeats.

It takes her a few seconds to orient herself and pick up the thread of what she was saying before the memory took hold.

"And I should never dismiss something out of hand. I've always thought of tarot cards as theatrical trappings for hokey sideshow psychics. But I just received a reminder in the form of a memory that life is a never-ending journey of self-discovery. We uncover unconscious biases at every turn *if* we're willing to look."

"What did you see when you picked up the box?"

Margaret reaches for the deck. "A face." She reshuffles, again enjoying the feel of the cards in her hands. Smooth. Glossy. Each one thicker than a playing card but thinner than a puzzle piece, and just as satisfying to the touch. Slipping back into the pleasure of this tactile experience, she forgets she is not alone. Forgets she's talking with Emily. Forgets...

As she fans the cards out on the table, facedown, the image of the dark-haired woman appears again. She runs her index finger along the spread cards. One just past the center radiates a subtle heat. She pulls it out. The Queen of Cups.

She recalls from her past dalliance with the tarot that the four suits are cups, wands, swords, and pentacles or discs. They are a part of the fifty-six minor arcana cards in a deck of seventy-eight. Like regular playing cards, they are numbered from ace through king. This queen is like a watercolor painting, some of the lines of her body and gown mere suggestions in diluted blues and greens. The overflowing chalice she holds is spilling its contents into the waves lapping at her feet. Her unreadable face is streaked with tears but smiling slightly. Her silver hair cascades around shoulders and breasts, and her free hand cradles her belly.

A mother. The thought comes without effort.

She sweeps her finger over the spread again. One card gives off both heat and light, and she pulls it out. The Empress. This card is one of the twenty-two major arcana cards, specially named and numbered from zero to twenty-one. They carry much symbolism for students of the Tarot.

This Empress card depicts a full-bodied female in a sumptuous gown, flaming waves of hair to her knees. She is surrounded by symbols of fecundity, her lips full, her breasts ample. Both a sun and crescent moon hang above her.

The third card she pulls is the Ace of Cups. Another overflowing chalice, a pair of doves balanced on its rim.

The woman's face in her accompanying vision is clearer now. She stands at a window. Two little girls play in the yard below, laughing. Her features dissolve into a portrait of grief. A baby cries.

Margaret scoops up the cards and shuffles them again. A card flips out of the deck and lands faceup. The Death card. She knows this card is often metaphorical—foreshadowing the death or end of something. But this one is literal. She slips it back in the deck and continues shuffling. She lays out three more cards, numbered cards of the minor arcana with simple illustrations. Sorrow drips from the watery image of the Five of Cups. Following that, the Ace of Cups, appearing for the second time, carries a sense of new beginnings. The final card, the Four of Wands with its flowery arch, solidifies this. The baby cries. A music box tinkles. Silence settles into a circle.

She gathers the cards and sets them aside, done with the need to handle them.

Emily rises and goes to the stove to relight the fire under the kettle. She leans against the counter as it heats, watching Margaret as she puts the deck into its box and folds the wrapping paper.

"Marcella, of all people," Margaret says, shaking her head. "What is the saying? Never look a gift horse in the mouth? My prejudices about her and the tarot have risen up to bite me."

She smiles as Emily fills the teapot with steaming water, happy her young friend is completely at home in her kitchen. She remembers the awkwardness of their first meeting, the day Emily came by on the pretext of gathering wild flowers. She recalls their first shared cup of tea and the things she told Emily. And the one thing she withheld.

The image of Emily's aunt Lily May Tyler appears and fades as Emily carries the pot and two mugs to the table.

"So, how are you?" Margaret asks. "And don't pretend you're not concerned about Ned's return home."

As she stirs honey into her tea, Emily says, "I'm so mixed up." She looks up and smiles. "But he is coming home. And he's getting better every day."

"And yet?"

"And yet the future is still a question mark. He'll be at his parents' house and…" Her chin quivers, and she lets go into the tears. "We still don't know how complete his recovery will be. We don't know if he'll be able to keep his job, the work he loves so much." She pulls a wad of tissues out of her bag and blows her nose. "It kills me to see the pain in his eyes even as he jokes and pretends he's fine. I love him so much."

"What's the worst thing that could happen?"

Emily looks up at her, surprised. "I don't want to think about that."

"Indulge me. What if we explore this together?"

Emily looks away. "He could be permanently disabled." Her voice trembles. "He might never be able to climb again. Not rescue anyone again. Not spend his days working in the woods or rafting on the rivers. All the things he loves. All the things he was built to do."

Margaret waits for the rest.

"He might never be able to father children."

There it is. "What else?"

"Isn't that enough?" Emily's voice rises, anger barely held in check.

"In the spirit of exploring everything that's sitting on your heart."

The anger shifts. "Maybe love isn't enough. Maybe I'll be useless to him in the face of such uncertainty. Maybe I'll screw it up, say the wrong things. Do the wrong things. Maybe it's best that his parents will be the ones looking after him for now. Maybe…"

"And maybe you'll do just fine. Maybe now that you've spelled out the fears that have been roiling beneath the surface, you can see them for what they are. Remnants of the brain's negativity bias. Our tendency to dwell on negative experiences or thoughts, to spin them out and scan for more. Our primitive survival mechanism at work."

Emily doesn't respond, but the look on her face tells Margaret she's thinking about this.

Margaret continues. "Sometimes just letting all the *what ifs* out in the open diminishes their power to incapacitate us. Sometimes not."

"Is there something you're not telling me? Have you seen something?"

"No. I haven't seen anything. But I have absolute faith in you and Ned to navigate this. Together."

Emily slumps back in the chair. "I feel okay most of the time. Then the doubts creep in and accumulate."

"Sunlight and oxygen expose the uglies—the doubts and worries and worst-case scenarios. More importantly, sunlight and oxygen nourish hope. "

Emily gazes up and to the left. After a while, she smiles. Margaret knows she could easily step inside this pleasant reverie, but she steps back and sips her tea, letting the moment rest.

As Emily, more relaxed now, returns her focus to her mug, Margaret asks if she has talked with Ned's parents about the recovery plan.

"Yes. They say I'm welcome there as often and as long as I wish. Anytime day or night." Her smile doesn't quite make it to her eyes.

"But?"

"But I want alone time. I want it to be just the two of us. Not at a rehab center or in his teenage room at his parents' house."

"That I can see." Margaret catches herself, laughing. "I mean, get. I definitely get it."

Emily laughs for the first time.

Margaret goes on. "And now that you've said it out loud, that you want alone time with the man you love, make it happen. There's no reason you can't. Right?"

Emily sits up straighter, tucking a clump of red curls behind her ear. "You're right!" Her face is bright with resolve.

As Margaret gets up to return the teapot to the stove, Emily surprises her with a change of subject.

"Uncle Otis asked me to pick up the garlic bulbs you saved for him. He's a bit late with his planting because he's been engrossed in his work on Kenneth's project. Happily, I might add. He's so animated when he brings the subject up, which is often, and he's looking healthier than ever. Please tell Kenneth what a gift it's been."

Standing at the stove, Margaret is grateful Emily can't see her distress at the mention of his name. Kenneth, the man with whom she'd love to share some alone time. If only...

"Too bad about his brother's stroke," Emily adds. "When do you think he'll be back?"

Lost in spiraling thoughts and images, it takes Margaret a moment to register Emily's words. She crosses back to the table and sits. "His brother?"

"You didn't know? Surely he—"

"The truth is, I haven't spoken to him in several days." *Shoe's on the other foot,* she thinks. Their roles are reversed, with her on the seeking end, vulnerable and needing support. She finds it uncomfortable as hell. And humbling.

"I didn't know about his brother," she admits. "I didn't know he *had* a brother. I didn't even know about his project with Otis until you mentioned it at Sam's. Truth is, something's happened between us and I'm not sure how to address it."

Emily reaches across the table and rests her hand on Margaret's. Her look of concern and the slight cock of her head encourage Margaret to open further. She describes the disquieting dinner with Kenneth's daughter and him saying he'd call her the next day as they parted. She leaves out the dream and ends by saying, "That was eight days ago."

"And he hasn't called?"

"I missed a call from him yesterday. No message."

"Did you call him back?"

Margaret winces, embarrassed. "I didn't dare."

Emily's brows lift.

"A nightmare I had unsettled me."

"A premonition?"

"I don't know. It could have been my unacknowledged fears rising up in the dream state." She laughs. "My own words to you coming back at me."

"So, what will you do now? What will give you peace about it?"

The very words she would have offered, the role reversal complete. She smiles. "I'm going to do a little self-reflection and then I'm going to call him."

"And I'm going to pick up Ned and take him to my place before I take him home." She comes around the table and hugs Margaret. "And I leave you to reconnect with Kenneth. I'm sure your fears are just that, no substance underneath." She turns away and then swirls back around for another hug. "You deserve happy!"

Chapter 30

Margaret carefully works out what she'll say, takes a breath, and presses Kenneth's number. After three rings, his voice-mail greeting comes on, and the relief she feels doesn't surprise her. Adopting a casual tone, she says, "Sorry I missed your call yesterday. I just heard about your brother. I'm so sorry. I'm here if there's anything I can do or you just want to talk."

As she disconnects, the phone rings in her hand. She has a moment of panic before seeing it's Caitlin Hammond of Channel Eight News. With but a brief hesitation, she answers.

"Margaret, Caitlin Hammond here. I'm wondering if you have a comment on the arrest of Clarence and Lydia Makepeace in connection with the murder? Or the unsubstantiated rumor about bodies being found at the farm?"

"Sorry. I'm not the one to ask."

"I figured you'd say that, but a girl has to try, right?" Her tone is upbeat and friendly, much different than it was at the end of their last conversation. Again, she feels embarrassment at having gone too far by commenting on the woman's son.

Caitlin clears her throat. "Actually, I wanted to apologize." She pauses. "My son, Jacob, just received an award for an essay he wrote. With it came acceptance to a six-week summer program at the Deep Ecology for our

Times Center in New Mexico with a full scholarship. It's an incredible honor. Only three students in the United States are accepted every two years. I had no idea he had applied for it. None. He wanted to surprise me if he won."

"How wonderful."

"But you knew. The last time we talked, you predicted something and I—I was rude. And for that I apologize."

"Thank you." A comfortable warmth spreads through Margaret. Affirmation. Always a balm. "Tell me more."

"Considering Jacob's sensibilities, it's the perfect forum. Though he's only fourteen, fifteen next summer, he's been studying the works of Joanna Macy and others in the field for a couple of years now. He's explored Buddhist and indigenous teachings, and he's discovered a spiritual side to himself that feels almost uncanny to me. Proof to me that we each have our own path to follow when we come into this life."

Margaret smiles as images swirl. The cry of an eagle pierces the air as it circles in a dark sky above a stretch of desert. In the distance, a mountain range looms, its nearest cliffs dotted with shadows and dark holes—entrances to dwellings older than recorded time. Seated cross-legged on a blanket, back straight, colorful wheels of light spinning along his spine, a young man travels without moving. Empty past hunger, he journeys through realms she can only hope to reach one day. A vision settles upon him as his quest nears completion, changing him on a cellular level until compassion becomes his other name. He rises, reconnected to something ancient and wordless.

"He and those like him are bringing us back to life," she says.

She hears the intake of breath on the other end of the line, and Caitlin's thank you comes in a whisper.

"I see a series of prizes in his future," Margaret continues. "Prestigious ones at that. Your Everett must be smiling."

"And now you've made me cry. I'm a journalist. I'm supposed to keep my emotions in check and I'm blubbering like a…"

"Like a human being? A mother? Good." Margaret laughs, further softening the moment.

"Thank you."

"Look." She follows an intuitive urging. "There are some things I'd like to share, but I have to ask you to keep it to yourself while you pursue corroborative sourcing."

"I can do that. Marcella's on-air blurt cost me in self-respect. I should have slapped that down immediately."

Margaret makes a decision on the fly. "This murder case may be linked to an illegal adoption operation. Maybe even worse than adoptions." She waits before going on, letting Caitlin process this revelation.

"The murder at Wandering Rock may be connected, but the victim wasn't part of the operation. I'm afraid if a certain unsavory print reporter gets wind of this, the criminals will go underground. I'm hoping you can counter that, but I need you to promise not to publish until the police okay it. This will turn out to be a huge story worthy of your investigative skills."

Caitlin sighs but agrees.

"A baby girl was kidnapped. She's been recovered, but the perpetrators have yet to be caught and her extended family has yet to be identified."

"This squares with information I was given by another source that I thought was unrelated to the murder. How sure are you about the connection?"

"Very. But my certainty is not based on concrete or admissible evidence. It mostly comes from what I've seen in visions. So—"

"So, I have to find the provable facts some other way."

"Yes. I can only give you what I know. Also, this baby is Native American. Perhaps she's the only one, but the harm done historically to our indigenous neighbors continues, even if it's one more. At least one of the people involved used to work as a legal agent of the government in carrying out child-separation practices and knows the ins and outs of adoption processes."

"You've got my investigative blood up. And boiling."

"I can't think of a better reporter to expose the operation for what it is. Again, I'm not suggesting this ring targets Native children. This baby happens to be my personal focus right now."

"Tell me what you know, and I'm on it."

Margaret fills Caitlin in as much as she can without giving sensitive information about the case. When she hangs up, she calls Jay and leaves a brief message telling him what she's done. Though nearly certain he won't mind, she breathes a simple prayer.

Looking to her now silent phone with a sigh, she turns to chopping vegetables for a vegetarian lasagna she promised for the Senior Center Supper. When done, she double-checks the phone ringer. She knows it is on and that the phone hasn't rung, but she can't help herself. After a quick message check, she rolls out chilled dough for a pie.

⁂

With the four loaves of bread and a squash pie cooling on wire racks and the lasagna bubbling in the oven, she leaves the cleanup for later and takes the girls out back. Bright sunshine has dispelled the earlier chill, though the wind has picked up. Enjoying the crunch of leaves underfoot, she rakes up a quick pile. Sophia and Grace leap in and out of it like puppies, stirring up the earthy scent of autumns past. Stray leaves cling to their shaggy coats, flying off as they race to the barn and back, carrying her back in time.

She's running. The mound of leaves her father has raked up is as tall as he is. She hears her brother gaining on her from behind. Just as she flings herself forward, her father reaches out and grabs her in his arms, somehow managing to catch Mattie in the same moment. He cradles them to his chest as he flies up into the bright blue air, twists, and lands on his back in the crackling cushion of beech and oak and maple leaves. Buried there with his strong arms around her and his heart beating against her ear, she breathes in the smells of him and the leaves and her brother's freshly washed hair. Mad Maxwell Meader, icon and eccentric genius to the world of art, gentle laughing giant to his twins.

Calling the dogs to her, she returns to the house to turn the oven down before heading for her studio.

※

She's squinting, straining to see as she applies the fine lines of the bird's wing. She looks up to see the room has darkened. She looks out the windows at the gathering of clouds. She can barely make out shapes in the familiar landscape. She puts down her brush and turns on the lights, surprised she's created six new pieces: six haiku and six exquisite watercolors.

One is of a man with a rugged frame and shaggy hair pulled back into a ponytail, curling wisps escaping. He stands back to, his face turned away. Another departure for her. Her illustrations are usually of the natural world, like the Japanese art form they accompany. Trees, shells, landscapes, animals, mostly birds. Seldom people.

She sits on her stool smiling. Painted in the midst of a creative burst, inspired by the memory of the leaf pile, this homage to her father pleases her. Satisfied with this day's work, she puts her paints away and heads for the house.

A familiar truck rumbles up the drive. Her neighbor Hilda Hanson hops out and meets her at the door. She's here to pick up the food for the seniors' supper and is running late.

"Everything's ready," Margaret says. "I just have to pack it up. I completely lost track of time in the studio."

"I know how that goes. Last week I missed a meeting. And I'm the chairperson! I stepped outside of time at the drafting board. The resulting designs were some of my best, but the committee didn't appreciate that."

Laughing, Hilda chooses to wait outside with the dogs while Margaret packs the food.

When Margaret returns, Hilda picks up the thread again. "We must get together soon. I miss our talks—our mutual meanderings."

The word stings, carrying her back to the woods on the day she first met Kenneth. They'd stumbled into each other and he had apologized. "Guess I lost myself in my mental meanderings," he'd said. And she remembers how perfectly his words described her own state at the moment of impact.

As Hilda thanks her for the donation and climbs up into her truck, she brushes the memory away

"A fair return for the gift you left at my backdoor," she manages. "That puzzle was a gem!"

"Couldn't resist." And with a wave, she's off.

Back inside the house, Margaret searches for her phone and finds four voice mails waiting. Jay agrees with her decision to share with Caitlin and promises to call with updates. Annie asks her to call when she has a minute. A reporter from the Portland paper asks for a comment. And... She hesitates before accessing the last message. With a deep breath, she hits play.

"Phone tag again," Kenneth says. "Thanks for the offer of an ear. My brother is struggling to come back from the stroke, but he's made progress. I've sent Mandy off to get some rest. She and Charlie are as close as two people can be, and she's taking it pretty hard."

Margaret checks the time of the call. An hour ago. Hoping he's still alone with his brother, she calls back.

His voice is bright. Happy to hear from her? She gives in to hope and asks if it's a good time.

"I was about to read to him, but talking sounds good. I'll be with him for the long haul." He stops to clear his throat. "Reading aloud is something we used to do as kids. We took turns, seeing who could outdo the other with dramatic voices and creepy sound effects." His laugh is short and thick. Again, he clears his throat.

Margaret's heart reaches out to him. Briefly, she hears the echo of two sisters laughing. Caught up in the fun of a good story, one reading, the other listening, their laughter wrapped in love. She swallows the emotion that rises.

"I'd love to have been a fly on the wall," she says, "for the Kenneth and Charlie show."

This time his burst of laughter lasts, bright and whole-hearted. "We were a pair," he says. "That's for sure."

"And will be again," she says without censoring herself. She knows the truth of it without a shadow. "You knew instinctively that rekindling this familiar way of being together, of connecting as only siblings can, is the way through this. The wisdom of it takes my breath away."

He does not respond, and she pulls back into herself, sure she's crossed a line she should have known was there. She closes her mouth around the words she wants to say.

"Well, here she is," he says. "The one who's supposed to be resting." His intonation makes it a playful question.

It's clear Mandy has come into the room, and it stings. Mandy, the protective daughter who wants her out of his life. The nightmare resurfaces.

She adopts a light tone. "I'll let you go then. We can talk later?" She intended a statement but couldn't help turning it into a question. But was she asking too much?

She nearly hangs up before he can answer, yet holds on to a fluttering image in the corner of her eye—hope, the thing with feathers. Then her inner critic rears its ugly countenance: *No fool like an old fool.* Resistance flares and she tells it to shut up. Then she panics. Did she say that out loud?

"Yes." Kenneth's voice is perhaps a bit too loud. "Sounds good." And then he's gone.

She dissects the words and tone. To someone listening to his side of the conversation, it would be innocuous enough, telling them nothing about the conversation or who was on the other end. Would he tell Mandy?

Stop it, Margaret. A softer version of the inner voice springs from the protective space in which it originated.

The girls are restless, reminding her it's past their dinnertime. And hers. As she fills their dishes, the aroma of the small batch of lasagna she left warming in the oven has her stomach growling.

While she eats, she checks the day's headlines on her phone, hoping to push Kenneth from her mind. As the bold type flashes on the screen, the lasagna burns her throat.

Identities of Two Female Bodies Remain a Mystery.

Again, she hears the two sisters laughing in the room off the narrow hallway in the Makepeace house. Again, she travels to the empty room down the hall, the one with words spilling down along the window frame.

Theresa and Anita. Daughters of Helen, daughter of Frances. Baby Sarah snatched away. Renamed. Her identity stolen. Her heritage lost.

"Not if I can help it," she says aloud as she sets her dish aside and calls Sesalie. The call goes to voice mail. She leaves a message and lets the girls out for their after-dinner run. The second they hit the yard, they circle back to the door, barking and growling, agitated. She throws on her coat and rushes outside. They lead her toward the barn, keeping close in front of her. Protective. Wary. Then they're standing their ground between her and some unseen danger, barking viciously, spittle flying, bodies taut and ready to spring.

Footsteps thud away beyond the barn. A car engine rumbles to life down the road. Tires chirp. The dogs canvas the yard, noses to the ground, then circle farther afield and rummage in the leaf pile. Grace drops a stick in front of her and sits, waiting for her to throw it. Sophia follows suit. It takes a moment for Margaret to notice, her mind and eyes still focused on the far side of the barn. Heart still thumping.

She grabs both sticks and lets them fly.

When her phone rings in her coat pocket, she's relieved to see it's Sesalie. She asks after Winowa, and is pleased to hear the old woman is eating dinner with the family after sleeping comfortably for most of the day.

She asks Sesalie to tell her grandmother that the stolen baby has been found. Then she asks for Sesalie's help in locating that baby's family. She gives her the first names of the two sisters and their mother and grandmother, explaining that she has no surname to offer.

"You said Theresa and Anita *were* sisters."

Margaret hesitates, but only for a moment. "Theresa died in childbirth and the baby was taken. Her sister Anita died sometime before that. I'm not sure how or why. Their mother, Helen, doesn't know any of this. And I don't know if Frances is still living. I just know they're the baby's maternal line. You'll have to keep the details other than the names to yourself for now."

"I see." Sesalie's voice is thick. Her next words come slowly. "I'll find out what I can."

As Margaret hangs up, the phone rings yet again. It's Louisa this time.

"The lost baby, Sadie. I mean, Sarah." Her words are rushed, and Margaret presses the phone closer to her ear to better understand them. "I got a last name. I was washing dishes not thinking about anything in particular and an image floated in. You know how it is. I saw you and the dogs in your backyard. Then you were speaking into your phone and I saw the baby. Then I heard a woman weeping and saw a man surrounded by an ethereal light, like an angel. That's something I've never seen or expected to see, but that's the word that comes to mind. And then the name *Gabriel* was whispered in my ear. It's Sarah's family name, I'm sure of it."

Warmth spreads through Margaret, and with it, the rightness of the name is clear. Gabriel. As she thanks Louisa and prepares to ring off, the young woman stops her. "Is everything all right over there? Are *you* all right?"

"I'm fine."

"Just before I called, I sensed something. Someone there. Or something. I don't know how to express it."

"Not to worry. The dogs were spooked by something earlier. Maybe that's what you felt. But all's fine now. Sometimes you tap into an insignificant ripple of information, though it's always wise to check. You were right to ask."

"If you're sure. But be careful. Take care." She's quiet, then adds, "Keep the dogs close. Just in case."

Margaret nearly shrugs off the warning but stops herself. How many times has she given such a warning, only to have others dismiss it and her? Chastising herself, she says, "I will. I promise."

She smiles, pleased to have someone with whom she can share this way of knowing. Pleased by the certainty that, given time, they will develop an easy shorthand for communicating. She looks forward to spending that time with this interesting young woman.

She calls Sesalie back and gives her the name Gabriel. Then she stands at the top of the hill. She watches the cloud bank drift away, revealing the setting sun as it paints the sky on the distant hill with a vibrant wash of oranges and purples and pinks.

Chapter 31

The dreams float in, and she knows she's dreaming. She's walking through the deep woods looking for basket trees in the understory. She must choose a quality tree for the basket she must make. But the ground is too dry here, the canopy too thick. The sun cannot penetrate. And the trees are silent. Even knowing the brown ash is a wetland species and she has no relationship with the trees in this unfamiliar forest, she keeps walking.

She is a trespasser, an outsider. Her ancestors have passed down a burden of shame for the theft of open lands, for the cultural genocide. Her white feet are bleeding as she walks, stumbling and falling and getting up again. She did not come from the bark of these trees. She doesn't know the language, carries no stories, knows not the difference between the male and the female.

She knows not how to harvest precious seeds for later. Knows not how to hoist the chosen tree on her shoulder. Knows not the rhythms of pounding down the length of the tree with the back of an axe. Knows not the feel of ash strips in her hands. Knows not how to weave past into present. Knows not how it feels to sit in a family circle and work the work.

Even with the sight, she cannot find the sacred trees. But she must make a good basket. She must carry it home and place it in the lap of the grandmother in the circle around the hearth fire. As her bloody feet stain the forest floor, she plunges on. The earth makes good use of her offerings, trees springing up behind her, forgiveness glimmering up ahead.

She slips and falls, rolling down an embankment. She tries to heft herself up onto hands and knees, but she sinks into layers of moist leaves. A patch of sunlight shines on the black muck oozing through her fingers.

A baby cries. A woman hums. A crow calls out. The woods go quiet.

An old woman stands in a doorway, her skin burnished by the rising sun, her hand shielding her eyes as she searches the fields beyond. The skirt of her long dress ripples in the wind. The hip-length vest she wears hangs heavy with beading. Tiny seeds stitched in rows of color spiral out from button centers.

Five children stream out of the house and race across the yard. Two younger women appear beside the elder. They watch the children at play, but Margaret knows they are also waiting as only women can wait, body wisdom guiding them.

Becoming both the watcher and the women, Margaret feels the hitch in the breath of the elder and the others leaning in.

Louisa walks toward them across the field, an ash basket riding on her right hip. One arm cradles it while the other lifts her ankle-length skirt, exposing her bare feet. A woven blanket, one colorful corner draped over the edge of the basket, swaddles the baby nestled within.

She sets the basket at the old woman's feet, turns, and walks away.

Alone now, Margaret stands under the stars on a clear night, untouched by the cold. An owl hoots. Another answers. She waits, head cocked in listening. A darkness moves toward her out of the woods. No shape. No form. Just a heaviness and then a deeper dark. It passes through her like a dusty shadow, leaving behind a residue of gray ash. Weakness wilts muscle and bone, and she loses consciousness.

Margaret sits up in bed, alert to every sound. The stirring of the dogs. The tick of the downstairs clock. The hum of the refrigerator. The spattering of rain on the window. The thrum of her heart. The echo of whispered voices. The words just out of reach.

Finally, she dresses and heads downstairs in the early-morning darkness. She lets the dogs out as the rain softens to mist, and then sprints to the barn for the sack of dog food she left in her trunk the day before.

The stench of tobacco hits her as she rolls back the door, and she's yanked inside. The door glides back in place with a bang. Sophia and Grace claw at it from the outside, barking wildly. A fist smacks her in the jaw. She falls backward, arms flailing. Her shoulder and then the back of her head slam against wood. She slides down the door, her vision blurring as her jaw screams. She wills herself to remain conscious .

"You're gonna die, bitch. No more blabbing to the cops. No more of your hocus-pocus. You fucked with the wrong people, lady." His voice is surprisingly high-pitched.

Her mind scrabbles for meaning. She tries to identify her assailant in the darkness, but nothing about him is familiar. She nearly wretches as he bends toward her, stale cigarettes strong on his breath. She tries to turn her head away, but he grasps her chin and bangs her head against the door. His fingers dig into her throbbing jaw until she cries out.

He jerks forward, his nails scraping her bruised skin, then pulls away. Her confused mind watches as he's grabbed from behind, lifted up in slow motion, and thrown on the floor.

The door rumbles open, and the girls rush in, snapping and growling at the stranger writhing on the floor. Taking up positions on either side of him, teeth bared, they snarl each time he tries to rise.

Gentle fingers at her neck trace her racing pulse. Softly, they explore the line of her jaw before opening each eyelid and letting it fall back into place.

A liquid glimpse of a bearded face framed in matted curls evokes a smile and a wince. Her body surrenders, melting into the smell of the forest after rain as she's lifted and held.

⸙

When she opens her eyes, she's lying on the hard mattress of a gurney. Shivering despite the weight of the blanket around her, she tries to focus. Flashing red lights fill the dooryard, distorting the familiar into grotesquely colored shapes and forms. A shadowed face is leaning over her.

"Margaret, it's Jay. You're safe. You're going to be all right."

Relief warms her even though the shivering won't stop. She tries to speak, but pain radiates from the hinge of her jaw, overshadowing the pain hammering her right shoulder blade.

"Don't try to talk. You're in good hands, thanks to James."

She wants to sit up but can't generate the strength to rise. Someone rests a hand on her chest and raises the back portion of the gurney.

"He's still here," Jay says, "staying out of sight but near. He wouldn't leave you. Neither would they."

As he says this, the girls whimper and two sets of front paws jiggle the gurney as they land with a click on the metal side rails. Sophia and Grace nestle their stout noses on either side of her, their dark eyes earnest.

She opens her mouth to speak, carefully this time. Her voice just above a whisper, she assures them she's all right.

"Annie's on her way over," Jay continues. "She'll stay with them while we transport you to the ER. You've already been assessed by an expert field medic, so I suspect you'll be back home later in the day with orders to rest and heal."

A hand slides into hers, smaller and softer than Jay's.

"We're so relieved you're all right," Cyn says. "And rest assured, you won't be alone when you get back. Someone will be here twenty-four seven."

She squeezes Cyn's hand in thank you and pulls her closer so she can speak.

"Dog food in the car. Keys in my pocket. That's wh—"

"I'll get it. Not to worry. We'll take good care of them. As they took good care of you."

Margaret's mind is less muddled now. Louisa's words come back to her—*Keep the girls close*—and she chastises herself for letting her guard down.

"Lessons, Maggie." Her brother's voice soothes her yet again. "Always lessons to be learned. Embody the lessons."

She winces as she smiles, and the girls nose closer before dropping down to all fours, allowing the attendants to lift the gurney into the rescue squad.

A wave of dizziness has her closing her eyes. When she opens them, Annie is framed in the doorway by morning light. Statuesque. Competent. In charge.

"I'm here. Not to worry about a thing," she says, her voice strong. "I've called John and Sesalie. They'll meet you at the hospital. Now, let these good folks take care of you."

Just before the door slams, she sees James beyond Annie's left shoulder, his brow wrinkled with concern, his eyes glistening. As she meets them, her own tears surprise her. She swallows the rising nausea as the vehicle lurches forward. Then she slips into darkness.

⚜

John eases the car up the driveway. Margaret's grateful for his care and Sesalie's thoughtfulness in bringing a plump pillow for her head. Under her shirt, her right arm is wrapped against her abdomen. The five stitches in the back of her head are covered with thick pads of gauze, and the left side of her jaw throbs despite the pain medication. The discharge nurse warned her that pain in other parts of her body would awaken as the day goes on. But nothing is broken, and she's grateful for that.

Annie opens the kitchen door, and the dogs wriggle over to Margaret. They sit inches from her, allowing her to pat their heads with her free hand. With quiet words and a reassuring tone, she sends them off for a run, then reaches for Annie's arm as an unaccustomed weakness settles in her legs. She lowers into the Morris chair, over which Annie has spread a comforter. Once she's settled, Annie tucks it in around her. She sighs and closes her eyes, surprised by the exhaustion after only a short walk.

The smell of cinnamon and apples and something she can't identify fills the kitchen.

"When you're ready," Annie says, "I have a special drink you can take through a straw. Filled with nutrients, no need to chew."

"Sounds per—"

"Nope. No need to talk either. Here it is on the arm of the chair. Later I'll have a pumpkin soup so thick, you can just slip it inside your mouth and swallow. I want to see you take a few sips of the drink. Then I'll leave you alone."

She is grateful for the creamy coolness of Annie's concoction. She rests between sips, listening to John and Sesalie chat with Annie over tea and one of her famous coffee cakes.

A knock at the door has everyone turning, and Jay enters before they can rise. The dogs rush in with him, skidding around the table and then slowing to approach Margaret's chair. Laying their heads on her lap, they sigh in unison, and for a moment all is right with her world.

For a moment.

Jay stands by the table, all eyes on him. He looks at Margaret. "Your attacker has at least five aliases and several forms of false ID. A background check nails it down to one: Derek John Whitfield."

"Whitfield. Related to Hank?" Margaret sits forward and speaks without thinking. The nurse's promised pain sizzles through her body.

"His brother." Jay walks around the table toward her, cautioning her not to speak.

Annie grabs a pad of paper and pen and places them on the arm of her chair. "Here." At Margaret's raised brows, she adds, "The less you talk, the quicker you'll heal."

"The nurse gave us this sheet of instructions," Sesalie says, handing it to Annie. "You're not to start the gentle mouth stretches until later."

Margaret rests back into the comforter, wincing anew as the stitches on the back of her head flare.

Jay pulls a chair over to sit almost knee to knee with her and looks around at the others. "This information can't leave this room."

All nod in agreement, and he resumes.

"Seems this guy is an expert forger and odd jobs man for an illegal adoption ring out of Massachusetts. For several years now, Molly, Lydia, and Clarence Makepeace have provided babies, one of a handful of rural teams in three states. Lawyers, a judge, and a network of midwives and doctors of dubious repute are involved.

"The Makepeace family likely sold babies on their own on a small scale early on. With Lydia's experience as a social worker, she and Molly recruited young women from small local colleges and tech schools like Pine Woods and Harbor Hill. They posted rooms for rent on bulletin boards and regularly visited the schools' clinics, trolling for pregnant students. Then the courting began. They offered free room, board, and medical care during the pregnancies and cash for giving up their babies at birth. But once they teamed up with Hank, things within the family got messy.

"We still haven't found their records that cross-reference the names of birth mothers and adoptive parents. We do know the background and medical information they provided was mostly manufactured, including false files about the fathers.

"Derek Whitfield is just one of the forgers responsible for false birth certificates and other legal documents. The brothers also provided the needed muscle if women changed their minds. Such was the case with Theresa Gabriel." He pauses and looks past Margaret, and she knows he's back in the room where Theresa Gabriel died giving birth to Sarah—the daughter she wanted to keep.

Margaret wanders with him to the writing on the wall along the window casing. The mother-to-be created a physical record, wanting their names written down somewhere. Even if never seen by anyone.

Jay goes on, his words bringing her back to the chair in a warm corner of her fragrant kitchen surrounded by friends. "From what we've been able to ascertain, she wanted out, they locked her in that room, and she died in childbirth."

He stops, again looking past her until an inner need to get it all out pushes him to continue. "Sometime before her imprisonment, all indications are that her older sister came looking for her. She stayed for a while, probably trying to talk Theresa into coming home. And she was killed. Whether intentionally or by accident, we're not sure. And they buried her."

Everyone is silent.

"Interestingly," he says, "we found two bunches of withered flowers tied with garden twine marking the graves."

Again, silence settles in the room, each face turned inward, each body a study in deep reverence.

Finally, Jay rises. "The search is still on for Molly and Hank, and it's clear she's neither hostage nor unwitting partner."

Margaret scribbles awkwardly on the pad.

Jay picks it up and reads aloud, "Mastermind." He nods in agreement. "Had us all fooled thinking of her as poor Molly, missing and in danger."

Margaret's attention strays. She looks up to the far corner of the ceiling at a scattering of ladybugs caught in a spider web. Lydia Makepeace places bouquets of wildflowers and echinacea on a patch of upturned earth. The old woman straightens, looks around, takes up her pitchfork, and resumes aerating the nearby compost heap.

Jay's voice again brings her back.

"Various agencies are involved in the investigation now because of the illegal adoptions and the crossing of state lines. It's kind of a mess with jurisdictional issues. One priority for all of us is the recovery of records going back several years. We found some for New Hampshire and Mass, but none for Maine so far.

"But rest assured, everyone involved will face charges. Derek Whitfield is not going anywhere anytime soon, and we'll find the fugitives. We'll work up a case so tight, it'll fit like a wetsuit. A bright orange one."

He looks to Margaret again. "John and Sesalie already found the child's grandmother through extended family networks before we had a chance to follow up on the name you gave us. Cyn is working on reuniting baby Sarah with her family, and no one had better get in her way. I've never seen her so determined." He smiles at Margaret.

She returns the smile, the discomfort tempered by joy. Then she struggles to keep the pad still as, one-handed, she asks a question.

Jay squints as he reads it. "We don't know why Mira drove up from Cambridge, but her car's navigational system tells us she went straight to Wandering Rock, no stops. When we catch up with Molly, we'll get some answers. It's a reasonable assumption that Molly asked her sister to come, they fought, and Mira was killed." He sighs. "A lot to unpack here."

"We trust you'll sort it all out," Annie says. To her offer of tea and cake, he begs off, saying he has to be on his way. "Well, you're taking some with you then."

Margaret scribbles one last note, asking him to consider giving Caitlin Hammond an exclusive interview. He hesitates, then nods with a wink. "Only for you."

As Annie hands him the cake wrapped to go, Jay assures the group that Margaret will have police protection for as long as needed. As he starts out, he turns back to her and says, "Now you do *your* part and rest. That bastard will pay for this. You can count on it." And he's out the door.

Chapter 32

The left side of her face is burning. She sits up in the wash of sunshine coming through the window. Her mouth tastes sour and her body aches; her heart is beating in her jaw and her right shoulder feels brittle inside. She tries to lift her arm to work out the stiffness, but it's stuck. Slowly, she remembers. It's strapped to her ribcage. That's when she comes fully awake with a jerk.

She's propped up on a mound of pillows on the little daybed in her office off the living room. She doesn't remember getting there or what came before.

Annie bustles into the room. "You're awake. Good timing. You've had a good long nap and you're due your pain medication."

"I'll pass—"

"Doctor's orders." She sets a tray on the nearby table.

As Margaret cups her swollen jaw with her left hand, Annie winces and continues, "He pegged you right away, sent instructions to stay ahead of the pain and not try to fight it. Pain contracts muscles. Takes longer to mend. So here." She holds out a glass of water and a shot glass with two capsules in it. "No argument. Drink up or, you know me, I'll not be letting it rest."

Margaret looks at Annie's choice of a shot glass, then at Annie.

Annie laughs. "I needed something pill worthy."

Margaret takes one pill saying, "She."

"What?"

Margaret reaches for the pen and pad on the table. *Doctor is a she*, she writes.

"Damn. Did it again. Old thinking, hobbling my journey to enlightenment!" Annie shakes her head. "Now, you can chase down those pills with a fruit smoothie and some of my world-famous applesauce. Fresh batch from the last of my windfalls."

Margaret nods obediently, although her look says, *You win for the moment and I love you but don't push it.* She writes on her pad that she needs to use the bathroom. It's a struggle to get up, even with Annie's assistance. Once standing, she steadies herself, waits for a wave of dizziness to ease, and begs off help getting to the bathroom.

Annie shadows her until she's at the door. "You better holler if you feel faint. None of that Yankee stubbornness, you hear? You can't afford another crack on the head."

Just as Margaret settles back on the daybed feeling weaker than she wants to admit, her cell rings in the kitchen. Annie calls out before bringing it in to her, "I've been fielding calls all day. Word's out."

Margaret opens her mouth. Pain slices through her intention, and she swallows the second pill instead. Annie nods approval as she comes in carrying the phone.

"It's Louisa. I told her you can't talk, literally, and—"

Margaret reaches for the phone. Annie gives her a look but hands it over.

"Oh, Margaret," Louisa says, "I should have been more forceful. The feelings were so strong. I knew something was going to happen and that the dogs wouldn't be there and you'd be alone and... I should have pushed. I'm so sorry."

"My fault," Margaret says, barely opening her mouth. That's all the movement her jaw can take, and she stops to rest.

"What's the point in knowing things if we can't stop them from happening?" Louisa asks. Quickly, she adds, "Don't answer. Your friend told me you shouldn't be talking and I—"

"Text me."

"Perfect. Okay, I will."

Margaret lies back too heavily, and her stitches sting and then throb. She has to admit she looks forward to the pain pills kicking in.

When her phone buzzes with an incoming text, she responds, her one-fingered typing clumsy and slow.

Half asleep. Let down my guard. That's on me. She wants to go on to say, *You were right. You did your part. I failed at mine. Too much in the habit of keeping my own counsel.* But she stops, brevity her best option for now.

How do I get it right AND stop what's coming? Louisa responds.

We work on that together. U game?

I'd love that. When you're feeling better.

Margaret's chest feels light, her breathing easier as she puts the phone on the table.

Annie has hovered throughout the texting and places a tray on her lap now. "Pills on an empty stomach won't do. I'll be back in a few for the empties."

Alone, Margaret sips the smoothie and slips in a few bites of applesauce before fatigue hits hard and the spoon clatters against the glass bowl. Eyes closed, she lies back, letting her imagination play. For the first time in her life, she has an opportunity to work with another intuitive, to deepen her understanding of her own abilities while exploring those of another. To be both teacher and student. Stepping back into beginner's mind and learning from a renewed perspective. A reciprocal arrangement, beneficial to both. As she drifts off, she looks down at her feet. She is wearing a funky pair of boots, ankle-high with rugged soles. She stands on a threshold, about to step off, a new landscape spread out before her.

When she awakens, the tray is gone. It's late afternoon. A chill hangs in the room along with an inviting aroma she can't identify. Her stomach rumbles as she sits up. She touches her still swollen cheek and moves her mouth around in a gentle exploration. The pain is milder. Gently, she raises and lowers her right shoulder and decides it's time to remove the restrictive bandage holding her arm in place. Time to begin those stretching exercises the hospital sent home with her. But for this, she'll need help.

Sesalie is standing in the doorway when she looks up.

"We sent Annie out for a walk earlier. It's clouding up, so she should be back soon. Let me help you."

Margaret senses the sadness sitting on Sesalie's heart and doesn't resist, knowing the act of tending to her will serve them both.

Sesalie suggests she move to the antique piano stool with its ball-and-claw feet and adjustable round seat. She removes the binding holding Margaret's arm in place, her touch gentle as a whisper.

An owl hoots. A feather drifts to the carpet, settles there, and disappears. A woman hums a lullaby.

A veil of blue-black hair falls across Sesalie's face as she leans down to scoop up the pile of unfurled bandage. Calmed by the grace of those slender fingers as she rerolls the bandage, Margaret sits forward in her chair.

She eases into careful movements, exploring her range of motion, listening to the inner cracklings of a body not used to being bound. Sesalie hands her a thick towel to cover herself and helps her out of her tank top. After rubbing her hands rapidly together, she places them on Margaret's shoulders. Warmth sinks into stiff muscles, and the slow work of a healing massage begins. Margaret sighs, her neck loosening, her head floating.

Sesalie works the left side, then moves over to concentrate on the injured shoulder area and down under the arm and along the rib cage. Her hands work in opposing circular motions, radiating heat that seeps along Margaret's spine. Remaining behind the stool, Sesalie rests Margaret's head against her chest and slides her fingers down along both sides of her face. The heat intensifies, and the jaw hinges release little by little.

Margaret feels it before she hears it. The humming. The chanted syllables she's never mastered. And the vision rises.

A circle of cloaked women, hands cupped in front of their hearts to form receiving bowls. A naked baby, a girl child, gurgles and coos as she's passed from one to the next until she's placed into the hands of an elder. Tall and straight as she must have been as a girl, she is regal. Margaret recognizes the face—the same face she saw in the cards, the woman at the window. With feathers woven into a circlet around the crown of her head, her dark hair rippling to her belly, this grandmother is radiant.

The vision fades, and Margaret sits forward, smiling, knowing.

As Sesalie helps her into a clean T-shirt and buttons a flannel shirt over it, the humming continues. All vibration. All sensation. Taken into the body as much as the mind. Straight into the bones.

As they walk to the kitchen at Margaret's request, she has to ask. "Winowa?"

"Soon."

"May I visit?"

"Tomorrow. You'll be better. She'll want to see you."

When Annie returns from her walk, a watery gust of surprising warmth follows her in before she slams the door. Grinning, she expresses delight at seeing Margaret looking better. Then she grumbles at how the shadow cast by the overhead light accentuates the dark bruise and swelling.

While she bangs pots around, preparing the final course of the dinner she's making, Sesalie informs them that she's been in touch with Detective Cyn Green. Margaret braces for difficult news, but Sesalie is smiling.

"They're awaiting final DNA results for legal verification, but there's no doubt baby Sarah belongs to the Gabriel family. She has a living grandmother, a great-grandmother, and several aunts, uncles, and cousins. They live way up north and they've been given the terrible news about the deaths of Theresa and Anita.

"I've contacted them and offered to let the grandmothers use our little studio cottage so they can come down here and take custody rather than wait for social services to get the baby up to them. Detective Green is pushing through the bureaucracy with the help of Jane-Susan Miller and Erin Irvine. Three engaged momma bears. It makes me want to weep with sorrow and joy rolled into one."

"Four," Margaret says, without trying to hold back her tears.

To Sesalie's obvious confusion, she says, "*Four* engaged momma bears." As she covers her friend's hand with hers, a line of dancing bears crosses an inner screen, each holding a sprig of bittersweet. She smiles, numb to the tears sliding down her swollen cheek.

Chapter 33

Margaret awakens to a perfect October day of sunshine and unbroken blue. The leaves on the maple out her window are a vibrant mix of orange, yellow, and red, and she wants to run to her studio and paint. But first she needs a walk in the woods to loosen the residual muscular tension and ease the sore places that have kept her from sleeping soundly. Kept her from dreaming.

In the bathroom, she surveys the yellow tinge to her black-and-blue cheek and jaw and slowly moves her mouth around, easing out the stiffness. She raises and lowers her shoulders and then alternates them in an easy figure eight. Silently, she thanks Sesalie for the healing work of her hands.

As she promised the night before when Margaret convinced her to go home to her own bed, Annie left a pot of overnight oats ready for reheating. Margaret sets a small portion on to warm and lights a fire under the kettle before stepping out back with the girls. The day is glorious, with the warmth of sun against crisp air. She sends the dogs off for a morning run and returns to the kitchen.

Her phone signals a text. Emily, asking if she can drop by in a few hours. She answers, her smile coming easily, without an accompanying wince. Eating is easier too, and she says a prayer of gratitude.

She makes a quick call to Jay, telling him she's going for a walk with the dogs. Though Jay is not happy, they finally agree the presence of the police car in her driveway and the one cruising the perimeter of her property, even though it covers many acres, should deter any unwelcome visitors, and she assures him the dogs will keep her safe.

She texts a thank-you to Annie and a promise to call when she's back from her walk. She does a quick sweep of her messages and turns off the phone. No one she wishes to talk to. And no Kenneth.

Before heading out, she takes a thermos of strong tea with honey and two hunks of Annie's coffee cake to the officer posted in her driveway. She's never met the young woman, and she introduces herself as she hands her the canvas bag.

"Officer Grady, ma'am," the woman says with a shy smile. As Margaret turns to leave, she adds, "I'm glad to see you're okay. I was here yesterday morning. You looked..." She stops. "It's good to see you up and about. You take care now. Watch yourself out there."

"Thanks. I feel as much at home in the woods as in the house, and the dogs will stay close. Thanks for being here."

This time as she turns away, she sees an old man sprinkling feed to a flock of chickens in a fenced-in yard. The coop is a miniature cottage straight out of a fairy tale, with a peaked roof and fancy fretwork along the eaves, dormered windows, and bright shutters with matching window boxes. Charlie Grady. The name comes accompanied by the whoop, whoop, whoop of chopper blades as he looks up and crosses himself.

Like so many images that float in when she meets someone new, it vanishes quickly, leaving her smiling for reasons she no longer tries to understand.

⚜

Two miles into the woods, she's feeling loose and strong. With trees surrounding her—some tall, some stretching just above her head, some to her waist—she feels protected, like she's stepped into a sanctuary. Their branches touching overhead, their roots entwining beneath her feet, they're connected. They communicate with one another and with her in subtle ways science is only beginning to understand. She imagines the early peoples living among the ancestors of these very trees, at one with them. Related beings, inseparable, fates and futures interconnected. She looks up into a flurry of colored leaves, some solid, others variegated or speckled. All the colors of October in Maine. The golden browns of the oak, the yellows of the beech, the reds and oranges of the maple, and the myriad shades in between. And she is reminded of her place in the grand scheme of things—her tiny place.

A crackling in the bushes off to her left has the girls hugging close. Fear bristles for the first time since her attack in the barn. *Damn.* A watching part of her mind expresses what the active part wants to pretend away. She's vulnerable. A human woman in a body that can be broken.

The girls soften their stance, heads cocking, tails wagging until their whole bodies are shivering with excitement. Taking its cue from them, her body relaxes, her jaw slackening, leaving but a slight ache behind.

As form separates from understory, she smiles. With a sparkling of particles, a whimsical mental image surprises her—in an instantaneous journey from dust to mass, a figure appears on the starship *Enterprise.* Joe laughs, defending his *Star Trek* addiction against her gentle teasing as she sinks into the cushions beside him. An evening of deep conversation about the nature of the universe and their place in it follows.

"You all right?" James's voice cracks as he speaks.

She suppresses the urge to throw her arms around his rugged frame. "I am. Thanks to you," she says instead.

He bends to one knee as the girls rush forward, wriggling as he runs curled fingers through their thick coats.

"You should be more careful," he says without looking up.

She notes the catch in his throat and his attempt to cover it by hawking and spitting into the underbrush.

"I know. I was careless. And I was warned. I put us both in danger, and I'm sorry. It won't happen again."

"Yet here you are. Alone in the woods."

"I have the girls, and I never feel alone out here." She puts up her hand before he can respond. "And now I realize how careless that sounds. "

There's amusement in his eyes as he nods in agreement.

She holds his gaze. "I suspect I've been less alone than I realized for a while now. I'm sure that crackling sound that alerted me to your presence was intentional. Thank you."

He rises, looking off into the trees. The dogs sit at attention before him, clearly expecting to play. He laughs, a deep raw sound, and grabs up a long stick. He breaks it over his knee and tosses the two halves in opposite directions, sending the girls scrambling.

"You stuck your neck out for me," he says. "Now you're stuck with me." This time his laugh is lighter.

"Walk with me a while?" she asks.

He falls in beside her, the leaves rustling underfoot as they step from the path and head into more uneven terrain. She lets him move slightly ahead, picking his way over jagged roots and rocks hidden under forest debris and leaf litter. Energized, Sophia and Grace skirt their route on either side, sticks in their mouths.

The terrain flattens out briefly before steepening. An outcropping of speckled granite rises to their left, and James leads her up alongside it to a stand of hemlock, pine, and spruce. The heavier scent of pine is nearly overpowering as Margaret's breathing becomes more labored, and she stops, her body suddenly weak. James waits, his breath light and easy.

She sits on a boulder and apologizes. He shakes her words away. "There's a spring just ahead," he says, "and a place to rest in the sun." Without waiting for her to respond, he grips her elbow and helps her up.

She follows, hearing the burbling water before they reach the spot beyond the trees. A flat expanse of granite stretches out before her. On it, two thigh-high boulders with smooth tops rest side by side, as if nature had created this viewing terrace bathed in sunshine as a space apart from the world below. Beyond the seats, a rock ledge rises up into the autumn sky, a spring bubbling out of its side and cascading down into a shallow pool, where the girls are already slurping their fill. A dipper fashioned from a hollowed gourd and a ceramic mug sit beside the basin on a natural shelf in the ledge.

"Sit," James says as he continues to the spring. She sits, removing her wool hat and turning her face to the sun. She closes her eyes, warmth flooding her as she breathes in deeply. Her ears tune to the snufflings of Sophia and Grace exploring new territory and the twittering of birds around their perch. Then the long scream of an eagle sends the world into stillness. She rides the sound until it disappears and then sits in the silence that follows—the gap between the inbreath and the out.

When she opens her eyes, he's standing beside her holding out a porcelain teacup filled with spring water, a cluster of violets painted on the side. To the question she asks without words, he says, "Never know when you might have company." As she takes it by the delicate handle, a woman's face appears. Younger than he by at least a decade, she has the same eyes and curly hair, the same shape to the nose but without the knot in his from a previous break. The sister John Longfeather mentioned. And she realizes this is his home place and she is not his first guest.

This terrace, looking out over miles of woods and distant fields, is shielded on three sides by trees and ledge walls. The broad extension of another granite shelf just beneath it conceals it from below. She looks around for the entrance to what must be his living quarters and finds nothing.

She lets it go, honoring his privacy. He disappears behind a thicket of young pines, and she raises her face to the sun again. She doesn't hear him return and is startled when he speaks, offering her an apple and a small knife. He sits on the other rock and alternately bites into his own and tosses chunks of another for the girls. She smiles at the distinctive crunch, the distinctive scent. High autumn in Maine.

As she cuts a slender wedge from her apple and slips it into her mouth, the juice awakens taste buds dulled until that moment by the pain of her injuries. As she savors this gift, she enjoys the chance to perch here unseen, indulging her learned need for invisibility. That thought streams into a memory. She's back at art school designing sets for the theater department and hears the director's voice. As he points out to a student that an audience can see you in the wings if you can see them, the quality of his voice stirs her. She would enjoy listening to this voice read a grocery list. Or a love poem. To another woman. When the voice moves closer, she steps back and observes the man from behind a set piece, unseen. She imagines sketching him in life studies class, trying for essence. When he steps around the corner to discuss a possible set change, she nearly runs. But she stays, and a courtship begins.

"Apologies." This single word has her turning to the man beside her. His voice is not unlike her husband's, she realizes. More gravelly from misuse, but deep and rich once engaged.

"For what?" she asks.

"Been living rent free on your land. Probably not my best idea to bring you here." He finishes with a half grin, droplets of apple juice glistening on the curls of his beard.

She laughs. "Town records may say I own it, and I may pay taxes on it, but it's not mine. My ancestors stole it. Just took it as if it were their right. I am but a steward. So are you. And you're better at it than I am. You're more a part of it all than I'll ever be."

He says nothing, and she admires that in him. No socialized dishonesty, no pretense of humility. She slices another wedge of apple and gazes out toward home. Not visible from here but out there, below and off to the right. She is comforted, knowing where to picture him as she goes about the everyday there.

When the sun has climbed enough to filter down through the mass of overhanging branches, he rises and says, "Come."

She stands up into a wave of dizziness, and a stab of pain radiates from the back of her head. As both settle into the background, a scene flashes in the foreground.

Crew cut and slender in a pin-striped uniform, his hat flaying off behind him, he runs across the outfield, eyes to the sky. He dives, catches the ball in the web of his glove, rolls back up to his feet, and throws the ball in a single fluid motion. The crowd screams and stomps the bleachers as the catcher tags the runner at the plate.

She follows him down a set of natural stone steps hugging the wall of granite ledge. Young pines crowd the narrow path, their tassels tickling her face as she descends. At the bottom, James pulls back a curtain of vines and steps through an opening in the rock wall. The dogs race ahead as they pass through a tunnel of granite. The walls are streaked with sparkling veins of quartz and speckled with minerals that give off a bluish-green light.

At the end, James lowers his head to pass under a natural archway. Woven shapes—circles, triangles, and stars fashioned from willow switches and bittersweet vines—are suspended on strings that drip from a carved ridge pole. Bits of colored glass, mica chips, feathers, and curling leaves are knotted at intervals along the cascading strings amid the dangling shapes. She stops for a moment, hand to heart, taking in the beauty of these primitive assemblages, not wanting to leave this living gallery.

When she steps through the opening at last, she is standing beside him in an enclosed garden. A combination vegetable and sculpture garden. Several standing stones are covered in lichen and moss. Leafy vines have been artfully trained to spiral down and around their sides, still alive with the orange and yellow of bittersweet, the deep purple of the wild elderberry. Surprising elements are woven among intertwining woody stems, and Margaret is reminded of the work of the earth sculptor Andy Goldsworthy. But these are unique to this environment and this artist, marrying the heart of nature to the hand of man. As she explores each nuance, each juxtaposition of hard to soft, smooth to textured, circular to linear, she is drawn deeper into a relationship with the place.

She turns toward the rock face beyond the drying stalks of corn to her left. A flickering of imagined firelight reveals the dancing figures painted there. Etched below them, a group of women circle a laboring mother. As a slant of sunlight strikes a niche in the base of the wall, she sees the chiseled figure seated on a flat rock. A child. Embedded mica chips shimmer behind her. She smiles up at Margaret, mischief on her face.

Margaret turns to find James watching her.

"This was a birthing place," she says. "But then you know that."

He answers with a shrug.

"James Harchett, elemental poet," she says, and smiles at the hint of a grin that disappears as quickly as it arises.

He turns and exits through a wooden gate, the posts carved with totems mirroring the petroglyphs on the surrounding walls. She follows.

With thick trees on the left, the path continues to hug the striated wall rising on the right with more ancient drawings overhead. Though this is part of the family land she's walked for years, she's stepped into an alien landscape. Some features are like any woodland scene, while others are steeped in mystical essence. She wishes she had her sketch pad but knows she will recall what she needs to, and her hand will easily pen the three lines that have burbled up, the words walking with her.

Silence sleeps in trees
Stillness stirs ancestral dreams
Spirit softly sings

Lost in word and image, she nearly bumps into James as he stops ahead of her. She laughs an apology then goes quiet, mouth open. Black ash trees, young and old, as far as she can see. She steps forward, standing among them, turning around slowly. A child again, eyes wet, heartbeat entraining with the thrum of the wood. She knows she's been here before, possibly while still in her bed at home. Or maybe as a child. She looks around for Mattie, cocking her head to listen. Nothing. And then the whispered word: Winowa.

James watches, Sophia and Grace at his sides. She rejoins him and searches his eyes, the violet flecks within the blue. She can see that he knows what she's about to ask.

"Bring them," he says. "The basket makers. These are theirs. They belong to one another."

With this, he turns and heads back the way they came. Before they reach the garden gate, he turns right, surprising her, though the dogs have anticipated this and run on ahead of him. A narrow opening in an outcrop leads through a passageway twice as tall as James at full height. It curves left and then right before ending at a wall of twisted vines and prickly brambles. As James reaches up and grabs a branch, she realizes it's a wooden handle. With a click, the entire mass swings away, a door opening. Wriggling with excitement, Sophia and Grace leap through and she follows them into a small clearing. Dense woods of a hardwood and evergreen mix enclose the space on all sides.

A tightly constructed cabin of narrow logs and earth and dried grasses, its crevices green with moss, is built into a hillside, part earth, part rock face. More hobbit home than cliff dwelling, it is a hybrid, a melding of the best of both.

James invites her in with a wave of the hand. Sunlight streams through skylights in recessed openings in the thick sod above. The deep earthy smell mingles with the softer aromas of herbs hanging in bundles from a lattice suspended from the ceiling and from a kiva ladder leaning against the wall of the cave-like portion of the living quarters.

She stands before the hearth. The stone and salvaged brick fireplace is yet another work of art. Above it, in the gently curving overhang, a round hole formed by centuries of water flowing through slowly yielding rock provides a natural flu. A hand-crafted cabinet beside the hearth holds cooking utensils and a few pots and pans.

She turns slowly, taking in the sparse furnishings and the raised platform nestled in the back of the room, tucked under the hillside. Over it, a single skylight bubbles up. She imagines lying in the bed, looking up into stars or rain or falling snow. As she steps closer, the fragrance of freshly mown hay left to lie in a summer field rises, and she notes the corner of a stuffed mattress under the heap of blankets and furs. Feeling like an intruder in a very private space, she steps back and nearly bumps into a bookcase against the wall, packed with hardcovers and paperbacks. A lantern sits on top alongside a wooden box of loose photographs. She recognizes a black-and-white one sticking out from under a color photo of a fishing boat. She folds her arms around her midsection to keep from reaching for it. She knows who shot this photo of a group of young men in uniform, sleeves rolled up, collars open, dog tags dangling against government-issue T-shirts. Some are grinning, some squinting or shielding their eyes from the sun's glare, one is looking away from the woman behind the camera, world weariness written on his too-young face.

She's seen this before, online, a reproduction from a prestigious magazine. She wishes again that Kasha had turned the camera in the direction of his distant gaze or zoomed in on his face. And she wonders if maybe the woman didn't do exactly that, a keepsake meant for her eyes alone.

Kasha Gula. The woman she saw in a vision walking beside him. Kasha Gula flirting, playful, sensual. The one who was embedded with his unit in a war no one would ever win. The one who came into his life in the midst of chaos and death. The woman who had taken up residence in his heart.

Margaret runs her finger along the spines of the books, pretending to be absorbed in them and not the box of photos. She wanders to the wooden rack by the front door, where she examines the curve of each bow standing there, identifies the feathers in each arrow, admires each shaft, notes the shine of the blades honed and fitted into slits along a leather strap.

"I'd like you to have these," he says, reverence in his voice.

She turns, and he holds out a lumpy bundle of cloth. Inside are three smaller bundles made from torn pieces of a bandana, and she knows the cloth is as much a part of the gift as what's inside. The first holds three triangular rocks nestled in corn silk. She recognizes them as arrowheads chiseled from stone. She holds them in her palm one at a time, each radiating heat. She feels the electricity of connection to the ancient maker, the one belonging to this land she can never own. She clears the lump in her throat and reties the bundle. As she opens the second, tears surprise her. It's a carving of Sophia, beautifully wrought, capturing the unique patch of coarse curls at the ruff of her neck. She quickly opens the third, knowing it's Grace, and is not disappointed.

She looks up at James, his face blurred by her tears. "They're exquisite. Thank you." She rewraps the gifts and slips them in her coat pocket, then wipes her eyes with both hands.

He crosses to the fireplace, his back to her. "Found the arrowheads when I was planting the three sisters in the garden."

"Ah, corn, beans, and squash."

"Right. Each sister brings her particular gifts to the soil. All three benefit." His voice is distant, although he's now come to stand beside her.

Three sharp barks pull them outside. Across the clearing, the old stag stands looking at them—Old Cyrus, motionless but for the occasional blink of his eyes. An odd sense of surprise passes through her, and she nearly laughs aloud. On some level just beneath conscious thought, she'd believed the ancient stag and Old James to be one and the same.

The girls sit on either side of James, backs straight, heads cocked. Tension crackles in their bodies—the wild urge to engage held in check by the desire to please.

James plucks two apples from a nearby tree and hands one to Margaret. He walks forward making no sound despite the crisp leaves underfoot. Heel first, he places a foot down and rolls it forward before setting the other heel down. Body loose, he holds forth the apple in the cup of his hand and stops three feet from the stag.

Cyrus extends his neck. He sniffs noisily, nostrils flaring, then settles as James steps closer. He takes the apple, leaving his head close to the man's hand.

James steps back and Margaret takes his place. She closes her eyes, savoring the warmth of breath against her skin, the flick of the rough tongue along her palm, the snort before the old stag lowers his head.

"Thank you," she whispers, and his head comes up. She fears for a moment he'll turn and run, but he remains, his face within inches of hers, liquid eyes staring into her own. The pull of connection has her reaching up to his forehead. Running her hand down that coarse old face, she again thanks him.

He lifts his head at the crack of a twig and a scuffling of leaves nearby. Towering above her, he stands frozen, a shiver rippling through his body. And then he is gone.

Not for the first time, she is left longing for more, left breathing in the emptiness of absence. Then she reawakens to the quiet presence beside her—the same odor of musk and black earth, a moist heat hanging in the air around them. The dogs dance at their feet, bristling with energy.

Telling them it's time to go is her way of announcing her need to leave.

James nods. "I'll show you a way out you can use when you return with the basket makers." He leads her through a small opening between two boulders marking the edge of his enclosure.

☙

When she reaches her backyard, she hears the girls, who have run on ahead, scuffling through leaves out front of the house. Suddenly tired, she plops into an Adirondack chair, leaning against its solid back with a sigh. She cups her cheek, aware of the mild throbbing she'd nearly forgotten. Then comes the barking and the laughter behind it.

She turns to find Emily rounding the corner of the house with the dogs. Ned follows with a lopsided gait, leaning on a cane. She leaps up to greet them, ignoring the zing of pain in her shoulder as she reaches up to hug Ned.

She ushers them into the kitchen and puts on the kettle while Emily plumps a throw pillow from the Morris chair and places it on a chair for Ned. Margaret notes the wince as he lowers himself. He recovers with a smile when their eyes meet.

She's transported to an unfamiliar room and sees him standing at a whiteboard. He points with his cane at a diagram drawn in green marker, tapping it at intervals as he talks. In the semicircle of desks around him, hands are raised. This is followed by an animated interaction with a group of engaged students. The phrase *in his comfort zone* appears first in her mind, then on the whiteboard in blue.

"So," she says as she fills the teapot with boiling water, steam and fragrance rising, "do you have some news to share?"

At first, he looks puzzled, then the light dawns. "Oh, I know what you're referring to. I do indeed have some news." He pauses, clearly teasing her. "I'm going back to work." Before she can respond, he adds, "Not in the field. Not yet, anyways. But in the classroom."

Emily is beaming. "They can't get along without him, it seems."

Margaret enjoys the interplay between the two. Emily's green eyes not leaving him, a mass of buoyant curls spiraling down her back, streaks of gold within the red. Ned's blue eyes looking from her to Margaret and back, his fair hair pleasantly shaggy after his lengthy stint in rehab. She decides it suits him, making his pale face less gaunt.

"I'm to be an instructor at the Academy," he adds. "I'm supposed to make bookwork more palatable for trainees stuck indoors for the written portions of study. Not sure I can pull that off, but it'll be good to be doing something. To not be focusing on myself all day."

Emily squeezes his hand. "You'll be brilliant." Her exuberance is sincere with no hint of the false bravado.

"You actually will," Margaret says as she pours them each a cup of tea. "You are about to discover yet another area in which you excel."

His shoulders relax and the light of hope sparks in his eyes, and she goes on. "One day soon you'll have a moment in the midst of your teaching when you realize how comfortable you feel. The witnessing part of you will be happily surprised. You'll look out at the faces of your students and know you're meant for this. You will, in short, love what you're doing." She leans forward, grinning as she stresses these last words.

"From your lips to..." he says with the boyish grin she hasn't seen in a while.

"I've seen it. So it must be true." And she winks.

"Anything else?" he asks.

She knows what lies behind the question. Will he be back out on rescues and trainings in the field? Out of doors. In the wild. Back to his former level of physicality? But he shakes his head, not wanting to hear the answer after all. Not ready to accept life without the work he's loved for so long.

"I see a life lived in joy," she answers. "Nothing specific beyond that. Just joy." She looks into his pale eyes. Various emotions flicker there before he smiles and nods.

"Just joy, huh?" He laughs. "I'll take it. Now, enough about me. What the hell happened to you and are you all right?"

She gets up and goes to the fridge. In part because she's hungry, but mostly because she dislikes feeling like a victim. Annie left two ramekins of custard, a bowl of fresh hummus with a bag of pita bread cut in triangles, and a large salad of mixed greens, thinly sliced pears, chopped walnuts, and chunks of soft goat cheese. On the counter is a bottle of raspberry vinaigrette. She fills three bowls with salad and sets them and the dressing on the table before answering.

"I'm fine. Really."

Both stare at her, waiting for her to go on. She drizzles vinaigrette on her salad and takes a bite of sweet pear, the inside of her cheek tingling with the tang of lemon. Emily and Ned put down their forks and cross their arms over their chests, letting her know they're running out of patience.

She gives them an abbreviated version of the attack in the barn and carefully chosen details about the assailant's connection to Mira Clark's death.

Both sit in silence when she's done, looking from her to each other and back. Finally, Ned speaks. "You shouldn't be alone. I know there's a police car nearby, but—"

"I haven't been alone. Annie and John and Sesalie have been with me, as well as the police watching the property. And I have the girls."

Sophia and Grace lift their heads from their beds in the corner, aware of the attention on them. They get up and come to the table, Sophia nudging Ned's thigh and Grace resting her head on Emily's leg.

"They haven't left my side," Margaret says, "but for that one foolish moment when I went into the barn in the dark and half asleep. After being warned, I might add. Big lesson learned."

Of course, she must now explain Louisa's premonition, and she's pleased that the spotlight is shifting away from her as the conversation turns to their new acquaintance. She's further pleased when they pick up their forks and begin eating, and the mood lightens.

When they tell her they tried to reach her before coming over, she's reminded that she turned her phone off while on her walk. She keeps the details of that walk to herself but smiles at the memory.

When Ned's watch alarm goes off, they explain that he has a therapy session, and they promise to check in with her later. Emily hugs her tightly before letting go. Ned struggles to get out of his chair, but then leans down for a lingering hug, his concern for her radiating through them both.

As she sees them to the door, Emily turns back. "After therapy, we're going to my place for a few hours of alone time." She smiles. "He'll be moving back to his own place soon. Once they finish with some modifications his parents arranged. I'm hoping he'll consider my house as a sort of halfway house on his way back to full independence." She winks and hurries out after him.

❧

Margaret pulls out her laptop and reheats the kettle. By the time the water's hot, she's found several articles of interest but not the one she's looking for. She sits back and sips her tea, then tries another search query. The remembered page springs into view. The photo of the boys, for it's hard to call them men, leaning back against a jeep, slouching as they squint into the sun. Grinning, their youthful expressions belying the time and place. Except for the one who looks off into the distance, body taut, wired for some certain eventuality.

The names beneath the photo are barely legible. She enlarges the page and reads the names from left to right. She writes them down on her pad, stopping when she comes to Charles Grady. She examines the boy, who looks no more than seventeen. He's leaning his head on his mate's shoulder, mugging for the camera with a goofy grin. The friend is the one looking away, identified as James Harchett.

A brief bio of the photographer, Kasha Gula, sits in the margin with a link to more information. Finally, she lands on Kasha Gula's blog, *The Circle of Least Confusion.*

In each blog post, there's a photograph and a discussion of the subject and aspects of the shoot. Margaret scrolls through the posts that go back for five years, although the photos are often much older. She stops at a stunning shot in black and white, a battle scene. Vietnam. 1964. Simultaneous explosions send dirt and debris into the air. Soldiers are lifted off their feet; others sprawl on the ground. Some are frozen in shock; others are diving for cover. Body parts are starkly visible, bloodied and detached. In the midst, a lone figure stands over a body, hands stained dark, eyes closed. A tiny cross on his bag.

Margaret closes her eyes, but the image remains. She hears the sounds of the battle and smells the acrid smoke, the burnt flesh. She wants to turn away but refuses to give in to the impulse. Instead, she opens her eyes and reads the accompanying post.

It's a tribute to those who served. Those who died. Those who were wounded. Those who survived and were forever changed. The piece is written with reverence and without sentimentality. Her prose is poetic, the language simple and all the more compelling for it.

The first sentence of the final paragraph stops her, the words enlarging and shrinking before settling back to the page. *To dear James, wherever you are.* Her heart thumping, breath shallow, Margaret reads on.

To dear James, wherever you are. I see you still, holding their hands, bending to listen, easing them with quiet words. I see you looking into your medic's bag and finding it and your training woefully inadequate to the tasks thrust upon you in the field. And I see you hunched over a table at night under the light of a hanging bulb, writing those letters no one should ever have to write to loved ones you'd never meet. Letters you chose to write with care, adding those human touches a family can hold onto in the years that follow.

I've tried without success to find you, hoping to catch the glimmer of that smile back in your eyes. Hoping we might sit and talk— catch up, move forward. I haven't given up hope for that. In the meantime, wherever you are, I hope you have found some measure of peace. No one deserves it more. Love K—

Margaret sits back in her chair, her eyes wet, her tea cold. Almost without thinking, she searches the website and finally finds what she wants. She clicks on a link and composes a brief message without giving herself time to change her mind. Then she shuts down for the day.

Tired, she takes Lucinda's journal into the living room and settles in her favorite chair. She turns the pages without intention, starting midway through. Faces. Figures. Hand-written passages. Landscapes. Seascapes. Birds. Trees. A crow on a fence. *Trust only in this other way of knowing.* The words are sharp and clear. *Assumptions hang like clouds obscuring mountains.*

She's back in the woods lying back on the Goddess Seat. It's not raining this time. The crow lands on the branch above, fanning her with a momentary breeze. When it stops, the crow leaps down to sit on her shoulder. She's again surprised by the impossible weight of it and the smell of lilacs on its breath. Lilacs.

She and Mattie are playing behind the lilac bushes, the smell strong, seeping into her skin. When Mattie speaks, the smell is on his breath.

"I hear a mommy calling," he says, sweetness blossoming in the air around them. "Louisa, Louisa, time to come in," he sings in a voice that's not his.

And then comes the answering call. "I can't, Mommy, I'm caught in the understory."

"What's an understory, Maggie?"

"It's the story beneath the story. The real story."

And she's back at the Goddess Seat on a crisp October day, the crow at her ear. "Objects in the rearview are closer than they appear."

"No more riddles. What the hell does that mean?"

She's shouting, but the crow is gone in a flapping of dark wings. So, too, the woods and the glacier-chiseled rock. She looks at the clock on the mantle. She's slept for an hour.

Chapter 34

Margaret's phone rings in her sweater pocket. It's Sesalie.

"Winowa has asked if you'll bring the girl when you come over. I'm not sure what she means, so I hope you do."

"I do. Louisa. She helped find the baby, and she came up with the Gabriel family name."

"Oh, right. Do you think she'll come?"

"I'm sure she will. I'll call her now."

She arranges for Louisa to accompany her to Sesalie's at four. Then she pulls on her coat and heads to her studio.

One after the other, the paintings flow without effort. The goddess seat. The crow. The woods. Remembered landscapes. The terrace. The garden. The stand of ash. Spring water burbling down the side of the ledge. Old Cyrus. The back of a male figure nearly hidden in the trees. The second of only two she's painted in years.

Only one haiku has arisen, and a glance at the clock tells her there is no time for more. The rattle of an engine shutting down announces Louisa's arrival. At the door, she beckons her inside.

The young woman crosses the room, taking in the triptych and puzzle on the wall. The familiar sting at the thought of Kenneth has Margaret walking to the windowed wall, a blue jay catching her attention on a branch of the oak. Bright blue against the golden brown. The only movement, the flicker of a dangling orange leaf, barely holding on.

When she turns back, Louisa is looking down into the bowl of loose puzzle pieces on the small table beneath the triptych. Fingers splayed, she dips them into the bowl and scoops up a handful. Then she lets them slip back into the bowl. Again and again, she repeats this dipping, scooping, dripping motion, her face still, and Margaret knows where she is. Knows the state from the inside out, having visited it so many times herself.

"The old woman we'll be visiting is dying, isn't she?" Louisa says at last.

"Yes. An unresolved matter keeps her here. Otherwise, she's ready."

Louisa dips her cupped hand into the bowl again. "I hear women weeping. I see women waiting. I am walking toward them carrying something." She cocks her head, squinting, forehead wrinkled. Another gesture Margaret knows from the inside. "Something filled with light."

"You are not only carrying something filled with light. *You* are filled with light. This is all confirmation for you. Breathe it in."

Louisa lifts her hand, moving her fingers so that the puzzle pieces tumble around and around in her palm. Colors flash as varying shapes with myriad arrangements of loops and tabs appear and disappear in her moving hand. She closes her eyes and lifts her head. Then, as if some inner process has reached completion, she straightens her fingers and lets the pieces slide back into the bowl. She lifts out a thick wooden one and looks at Margaret. "May I?"

"Of course."

"Oh, my God, Margaret!" Her eyes meet Margaret's for the first time. "Your face. I—"

"I'm okay. It's much better now."

"But I should have been more insistent. Should have trusted myself more."

"You were absolutely right to warn me, and I was wrong to let my guard down. I used to blame myself when folks didn't heed what I had to say, but then I learned. You will too. Honor the knowing. What others do with it is up to them."

She gives the girl a hug and indicates the table by the windows. Louisa pockets the puzzle piece and follows her.

As they pass shelves of finished works standing upright in bins, ready for packaging, Louisa stops. Margaret nods her permission and Louisa lifts one out and runs her finger over the puzzle piece placed below the painting, just above the haiku.

When she comes to the worktable, she stops again. She looks from the newest paintings to Margaret, shaking her head. "Such a mystical quality. Such depth. I want to step inside each one and go in and in and in."

She bends closer to one. "I didn't see him at first. It's him, isn't it? The one who lives in the woods."

Margaret nods.

"You've captured... You've... I don't know how to say it." Emotion thickens her voice, and she rests her hand on her heart. "He's more than *in* the woods, he's *of* the woods. He *is* the woods." She nods in answer to her own question. "And this." She picks up the picture of Old Cyrus, then holds up the painting of James beside it. "They are... They... "

She pauses, searching for words, then looks at Margaret, deep knowing alive on her face. She gasps. "Oh, my!" Gently, she sets the paintings back in their respective spots. "I should never have touched them without asking. Sorry." She steps away from the table.

"Stop." Margaret's curt response is sharper than she intends, and she softens her tone. "Don't apologize. You've given me a gift." She rearranges the paintings, putting Old Cyrus and James side by side. The old feeling comes back. *One and the same being somehow.*

As they sit at the table by the windows, Louisa takes out the puzzle piece. "I love that you put these pieces in your artwork. They add so much to the experience of them. And again, I have no words to explain it."

"They speak to something inside us, I guess. Something beyond words." Louisa holds up the piece. "I know this one spoke to me."

Margaret retrieves the bowl full of pieces and sets it on the table between them.

"For years, I had several puzzles going at once. Sometimes dozens. Gifts from friends and yard-sale finds. People dropped them off on the doorstep like they drop off cats to old cat ladies." She laughs. "And I loved finding them there." She smiles, looking off and sifting through memories.

"Part of the adventure lay in finding out if all the pieces were included," she adds. "The puzzles with gaps from a single missing piece or a cluster or a scattering were often the most interesting. They sparked the most engaging inner images or set off an explosion of visions."

"And were the visions always useful?"

"Afraid not." Margaret laughs. "Some left me puzzled, pardon the pun, for weeks, until I let them go as random elements of the great Mystery. If one came back around, I knew I needed to pay attention."

"What about the completed pictures? Were they helpful?"

"Puzzling was always about process, not the final picture. The movement of my hands, the feel of the pieces on my fingertips, the way my gaze travels, looking for connections and patterns, and the satisfaction in finding them. The interplay of color and shape and image.

"More often than not, visions came as I worked. So, puzzles were both a pleasurable pastime passed down in my family and a tool, a triggering mechanism, a way in to receptivity."

The cry of the jay out the window has her turning just in time to see a swirl of snowflakes lit by the sun. Then the sudden squall disappears as quickly as it came. She exchanges a look of awe with Louisa.

"You said you *had* puzzles everywhere."

"A couple of months ago, for reasons I can't explain, I swept most of them, in various stages of completion, into this bowl. At that same time, my artwork started to change, subtly at first. Then one day after adding the haiku to a finished painting—always a delicate process lest I ruin the entire work with a slip of the pen—I drew back and knew it was incomplete. Without thought, I dipped my hand into the bowl much as you did earlier and came out with a piece. I set it in the space between image and words, and was surprised to find it the perfect touch in both color and shape. And that further changed my process. I resist trying to attach meaning to how this added element affects the work, but interest has exploded at the galleries that carry me."

She stops. "I wonder what processes might activate your visions. How would you describe your relationship with your gift?"

"Lately, it feels more like a curse than a gift."

"I know how that feels. But I'm learning to see it differently now—to own it as a gift. Mind you, I'm sixty-two. I've come to this late. But you, you have the opportunity to get to that place early. Imagine the difference a shift in perspective might make in your relationship with it."

"When I worked for Marcella, I mainly did online research or intake interviews. Sometimes, though, I'd do a deep dive when Marcella requested it. Certain thoughts and images came, and I'd include them in my reports. I didn't realize how much my input was helping to carry her practice. Don't get me wrong. She has talent for reading people and picking up behavioral clues when something she says comes close to home, but she doesn't have the abilities she claims. I stayed because people were so grateful. Eventually, though, things she did with what I told her made me uncomfortable. When I objected, she got angry. Scared me. But I needed the money. I'm ashamed of that now."

"Don't be. We learn through experience. Would you do it again if offered the chance?"

"Absolutely not."

"Then it was valuable and nothing to be ashamed of."

Louisa considers this and finally nods.

Margaret muses out loud. "It might be interesting to explore ways to activate visions or enhance their frequency and clarity. To collaborate. Experiment together. Learn from each other as we go."

"I love that idea."

"What if we set up regular sessions that fit into your schedule?"

"That would be a godsend. *You* are a godsend."

"It's reciprocal, believe me. You have much to teach me. In fact, we could have a little fun right now."

"Oh?" Louisa's curiosity sings.

"How about we set a timer and sort pieces from the bowl, each searching for different puzzles. When the timer goes off, we talk process."

Fingers fly as puzzle pieces fill the empty space between them. Instead of it playing out as a competition, they instinctively work together. Although Louisa starts with thick wooden pieces in a neutral palate and Margaret chooses thinner ones in bright hues, each adds to the other's gatherings. As groupings form and matching colors and textures are snugged together, images emerge. When the timer goes off, they have segments from six different puzzles in progress.

Louisa sits looking out the window, her body still, her face relaxed, her mind somewhere else. With a shudder, she comes back into the room.

Without prompting, she begins. "I see little chairs in primary colors. A fluffy rug in a corner. Low shelves of children's books. Stuffed animals. Puzzles." She smiles. "Easels with pots of fingerpaints. Giggles. Laughter. Silence." She shivers. "All's quiet now. Dark quiet.

"I see a room. Door and walls of glass. A blonde woman at the desk. A couple seated opposite. An exchange." She shakes her head. "The blonde stands before a mirror. Her reflection is day to her night. Yin to her yang. A rock shatters the glass. A name like a mirror. And then there is one."

"Look around," Margaret says. "Anything written anywhere?"

Louisa closes her eyes. "I don't see any... Wait. On the door. M. Clark, Director."

"Anything else?"

"No. Another place. A storage unit with lots of file boxes. A manila folder is open. A few sheets of blank paper, cream-colored with a letterhead." She squints though her eyes are still closed. "SunLight & StarShine, Mira Clark, Director, and an address. And there's a cot with a rumpled sleeping bag. A desk with a microwave and a printer. A rack of clothing and a bag of hats and wigs."

"Anything else?" Margaret keeps her voice soft and inviting.

"A metal strongbox under the cot."

With a sudden flash, Margaret knows where the unit is. She dials Jay and Cyn and leaves a detailed message for each.

"They're not headed for Canada anymore." Louisa's words surprise her. "They're headed back down. You're still in danger." She grabs Margaret's hand. "So is..." Her brow wrinkles. "I lost it. But someone else is in danger."

"Let it go." Margaret squeezes her hand. "It'll come. You've seeded the ground, and your wise self will know what to do in good time. Often when you least expect it."

Louisa is clearly straining, reaching for more.

"Find a symbolic way to let go of trying," Margaret says. "Make a fist and release it, or picture a bird carrying your question up and away, or better yet, allow your own image to come. Then trust and let go." She pats Louisa's hand and gets up. "I need to change before we go to Sesalie's. Why don't you come and wait in the kitchen? Or take some time outside."

They leave the scattered puzzle fragments where they are.

⚜

They follow Sesalie down the hall to the open bedroom door. The room is warm and dimly lit. Candles flicker on the windowsills and mantlepiece over the fireplace. The soothing scent of lavender floats in the air along with soft flute music.

Winowa is sitting up against plump pillows, wrapped in a thick shawl. Her long hair is loose and flows across her shoulders and chest. Margaret is taken aback by the aura of radiant health surrounding her.

"You came," Winowa says. "How wonderful. But look at your poor face!"

"I'll be fine. Sesalie has taken good care of me."

Winowa smiles. "And you brought the girl." She nods to Louisa. "Hello."

Margaret steps aside for Louisa to come closer as she introduces her.

"You found the child. Yes?" the old woman says.

"I helped," Louisa says. "We both did."

Winowa lifts her hand, and Louisa takes it. Margaret's heart quickens as she watches the silent exchange between them, connected in ways beyond explanation. She is deeply grateful to be present, bearing witness.

Winowa reaches out her other hand to Margaret and motions her to the other side of the bed. As Margaret takes Winowa's hand, she and Louisa grasp hands across the quilted coverlet, and they form a linked circle. Margaret closes her eyes as the air around them crackles. Soon they are dancing, opening to a wider and wider circle, hands to hands to hands. Gnarled hands and smooth. Womanly and child-small.

As strength wanes in the old woman's grip, Margaret and Louisa hold on. Winowa settles deeper into the pillows, eyes closed. A sigh has Margaret leaning in, about to call Sesalie back into the room. But Winowa's lids flutter open, and her eyes are bright with awareness.

"You carry the guilt that belongs to your ancestors," she says to Margaret, her voice soft and rich with life. "It has served its purpose—invigorates your resolve. But you belong to the present and serve the future. Deep healing has begun. It lives in that baby girl.

"May she be taught her language. To speak it. To understand it. To be it. May she be held close against the bodies of her tribal family every day. May she learn her songs and the many ways of dancing. May she know the trees and the land as she knows herself. May she look always to the dawn."

Winowa rests, her breath quieting. Then she pulls Margaret down closer to her mouth. "Though you are our daughter, there are words and rites we haven't shared with you. You always accepted that they were meant for those of the blood. But the time has come for me to give one to you, the one meant for you to carry. The one that's been waiting. Come closer."

Margaret's chest tightens. A sense of unworthiness rises.

"Stop that." Winowa's voice is sharp. "If you did not deserve it, I wouldn't be told to give it."

Margaret flushes as she bends closer. Spoken into her ear in this familiar voice, the word, followed by a rush of warmth, spirals down into her heart and settles comfortably there.

Winowa turns toward Louisa, who is weeping. "That baby's life is forever connected to yours. You will come to her reunion with her people, yes?"

Louisa looks perplexed, and the old woman adds, "You and Margaret must be here when the grandmothers come from up north to take her home."

Louisa looks to Margaret and then back at the old woman. "I would be honored. Thank you."

Winowa again closes her eyes, and Margaret stands, reading the energy of the room. Peaceful. Fragrant. Alive with quiet joy.

"We'll leave you now," she says.

"I'll be here until the grandmothers come."

Winowa's words are barely a whisper. Margaret's heart thuds, then falls back into a steady rhythm.

⚘

In the car, Louisa is quiet. As they turn onto Margaret's road, she says, "This is the beginning of something new for me. Helping to find the baby opened a door. I couldn't turn away now if I wanted to. But I have to admit, it's a little scary."

Margaret laughs. "Ah, yes, the exciting-but-scary-as-hell part. Uncertainty your necessary companion. Welcome to the threshold of your soul's next adventure."

Louisa slows as they approach the driveway. A gaggle of reporters has returned, and they shout questions as she maneuvers her car around them. Ross Templar's voice whines above the rest. "That's the one Meader stole away from Marcella McCray. Hey, you, do you have anything—"

His words are cut off as Louisa guns the engine and the car lurches ahead. She sits taller in the seat, looking straight ahead, but Margaret feels her fear and has to acknowledge her own. Then she spots Officer Grady sprinting down the drive. As the young woman reaches the group, she directs them away from the car and motions Louisa through. She gives Margaret a quick nod as they pass.

Suddenly exhausted, Margaret wilts against the seat back. Head throbbing, she closes her eyes to the hollered questions bouncing off the window glass and apologizes to Louisa.

Annie is in the house trying to quiet the dogs. "What in the world brought those reporters back? They're more obnoxious than ever," she sputters as Margaret and Louisa remove their coats. "I tried to call and warn you, but you must have your phone off."

Margaret digs in her bag for her cell. Thirteen voice mails light up when she turns it on, and she eases into a kitchen chair. Annie takes one look and changes gears. "Never mind all that now. I've made a big pot of corn chowder." She looks to Louisa. "And you are staying for dinner. No argument." The stove timer buzzes, and in a blast of heat and doughy fragrance, she removes a tray of biscuits from the oven.

While they eat, Annie suggests Louisa stay the night and neither woman objects. When they've finished, Margaret is ready to face her phone messages. Jay has left a long one, and she plays it on speaker for Annie and Louisa.

"The DNA has proven the baby's family of origin. The police and feds have rounded up many of those involved in the scheme. They found the storage unit and are going through it, but the lockbox we'd hoped would contain the crucial files was empty. There was a burn barrel out back of the unit containing ashes." He sighs. "We're doing a press conference at six. Molly and Hank are still on the loose, so be careful. No going out alone."

Annie speaks first. "I saw a teaser on TV earlier but had the sound off. Looks like there's a lot coming to a head."

Her words spur a vision. Molly and Hank are standing in the rain in the forest. He's scowling, she's screaming. She grasps his jaw between fingers and thumb and twists. As she pulls her hand away, white indentations blossom on his tattooed skin. Lydia's face appears in close up, clouded eyes dark with fear. In the distance, Clarence rakes the ground beyond the compost heap, a sleepwalker in daytime. Then brief sensory flashes. A burst of wind. A toppling house of cards. A blue road sign—"Welcome to Maine." A gray dashboard with *Ford* imprinted on a steering wheel. Dangling keys in the ignition. The new car smell. Tension in the cab.

She's back at the kitchen table across from Annie and Louisa who are drinking tea, waiting. She grabs the pad and pen and jots what she has seen, holding on to the tingling aftermath until she gets it all down. She hands the paper to Louisa. As Margaret waits for a response, she lets her confusion surface. Why a welcome sign to Maine?

Louisa answers without hearing the question. "They couldn't cross into Canada and turned around. Headed down to Massachusetts, skimmed right by the state police. But they're coming back up here now." She shivers. "There are three in the truck. Rage is in the driver's seat."

Margaret takes this in as she opens the most recent message, a voice mail from Cyn. "Jane Susan and Erin have worked magic, and baby Sarah will be handed over to her biological grandmother day after tomorrow, the twenty-fifth."

The date stirs something. That the end of October is so close surprises her. She shakes that off and texts Jay.

Next, she listens to Caitlin Hammond's message. "Thanks for the good word with Detective Horner. I'll be reporting the latest at six."

Other messages are from reporters wanting comments and friends expressing concern. The former she ignores, the latter she saves for later. With a shake of the head, she deletes the one from the Seekers & Sages asking her to be keynote speaker at their annual conference.

Annie and Louisa set to doing the dishes, and as they chat, dishware clinking, Margaret goes into the bathroom. Alone, she listens to a message she didn't delete.

Ross Templar's snarl crackles through a faulty reception, but the message is clear. "Doing a piece on your little helper, the one you stole from Marcella. Care to comment?"

"Damn the little shit!" She takes a deep breath and looks into her reflection in the mirror. "He's not worth it. Let it go."

As she splashes water on her face, she sees Marcella driving away in her little red car, waving out the window, purple sleeve riffling in the wind.

At six o'clock, the news begins with a montage of film clips that give way to Caitlin Hammond, mic in hand, standing at the back of a large room, a podium visible over her shoulder. Reporters bustle behind her, jostling for position.

"The police are about to brief us on the latest developments in the case of the woman murdered at the site known as Wandering Rock. Channel Eight has just learned that the victim was initially misidentified as local woman Molly Makepeace. But forensics have since established that she is actually Mira Clark, Molly's twin sister. Complicating the situation, Molly Makepeace has been missing since the death of her twin, a possible second victim of foul play."

Her introduction is interrupted as several men and women walk onto the raised platform behind her. Jay Horner takes the podium, and Margaret is impressed as he lays out the facts precisely and clearly. Still, she knows he'll be flooded with questions as soon as he's done and doesn't envy him the tightrope he'll be forced to walk.

Once he's presented the basics, he announces that Molly Makepeace is now a suspect in the murder of her sister, and that she and Henry "Hank" Whitfield are considered fugitives. He holds up photos of both and explains that the couple are believed to be returning to the area in a new silver Ford pickup with gray interior. In addition, he reveals that Clarence and Lydia Makepeace, husband and mother-in-law to Molly, have been arrested in connection with an illegal adoption ring and two other murders. He emphasizes that the murdered woman, Mira Clark, is not suspected of any wrongdoing. He paints a picture of her as a personable woman, respected by her peers and loved by her employees and the parents of children in her care. He stresses that her daycare center had no part in the illegal scheme, going so far as to explain that Molly Makepeace allegedly used her twin's offices after hours for meetings with potential adoptive parents without Mira's knowledge.

As he talks, his words give Margaret an odd sense of comfort. An informed public is a watchful public, and this time James Harchett is not in the crosshairs.

When the news conference is over, Caitlin continues her coverage of the underlying story—the illegal adoption ring. Five prominent legal and medical professionals are facing multiple charges for their roles in the scheme to sell babies for profit. She reiterates that Mira Clark ran a legitimate and highly respected daycare center and was in no way involved. She describes Molly Makepeace as a central figure in the Maine-based branch of the ring, with the help of her family members.

She goes on to describe Lydia Makepeace's background as a social worker in northern Maine involved in the removal of Native children from their homes. Her familiarity with the child welfare system and adoption processes made Lydia the perfect asset for this illegal operation.

As Caitlin details the multistate operation, Margaret's heart breaks for the children lost and for the vulnerable birth mothers manipulated into giving them up. Used. Offered room, board, and care in the home of a seemingly sympathetic family.

She revisits the room in the Makepeace home and the clipboards with coded numbers standing in for names, the key to sorting it all out.

Caitlin's words bring her back to the television. "…and now two other young women are dead, their bodies found at the Makepeace farm just days ago. One allegedly died in childbirth. The other, her older sister, was killed earlier for reasons yet unknown."

A close up of Caitlin fills the screen, her eyes looking straight into the camera. "The baby business, folks. Right here in Maine, where our welcome signs says this is 'the way life should be.'"

The screen goes dark to the sound of a baby crying.

The three women sit stunned, and the dogs are on their feet rushing to each woman in turn, comforting and taking comfort.

When Annie sighs and says she's going to head home, Margaret insists she stay. "There's plenty of room. There's the spare room upstairs, and the daybed that you made up with clean sheets while I was out."

She's surprised when Annie agrees.

Louisa yawns and stretches, heading for the bathroom. At the door, she turns back. "I heard Marcella is going on tour. The same round of psychic fairs we did last year. It'll take her across the country, so she'll be away for a good long while."

As the door closes behind her, a scene from the Broadway show *Hamilton* shimmers. Jonathan Groff, King George in royal robes, scepter, and crown, minces downstage, singing "You'll be back" with a slight alteration in pronouns: "*She*'ll be back, wait and see." The lyrics have Margaret smiling despite the reference to Marcella's return.

As they say good night, Annie says, "Here we are having a pajama party and we're all pooped at seven-thirty."

As Margaret looks out the front window, her hand on the light switch, the sight of the police car in the drive reassures her. She decides to leave the lights on and goes up to bed, still smiling at the image of mad King George in all his haughtiness, balancing the too-heavy crown.

Chapter 35

Margaret awakens to a darkened room, guessing the sun has yet to rise. She sits up, pleased to be in her own bed and not her office daybed. That's when she notices the slit of light coming through the drawn curtains. She crosses to the window and pulls them open. The blast of full sunlight startles her. Late-morning sun. And the dogs are not in the room.

She throws on her robe and slippers and hurries down to find Annie knitting at the kitchen table, the washing machine sloshing away in the pantry, and a load thumping in the dryer.

"In the light of day," Annie says in greeting, "I'm feeling a little foolish that I stayed over. Louisa was up at dawn, and I sent her off with a hearty breakfast. I don't think that girl eats enough."

Margaret looks at the stove clock and is shocked. She's slept until eleven.

"Now don't go beating yourself up. You must have needed the sleep. I'll get out of your hair now unless you need something. There's a frittata with goat cheese and chives in the oven, and a fruit salad in the fridge."

Annie doesn't seem to notice that Margaret hasn't responded as she gathers her knitting bag and shrugs into her coat. "Why don't you take a day of rest? I think maybe you overdid it yesterday. But far be it from me to tell you what to do." And she's out the door.

Margaret makes a pot of tea, and as she eats, she lets the dream image that's been hanging just off to the left float into view. It bobs in front of her like a balloon, accompanied by a clacking sound. As it comes into sharper focus, she sees that it is one of the ubiquitous baby toys that have been around for decades—a set of oversized plastic car keys on a thick plastic ring. With heads of varying shapes, the keys are a rainbow of primary colors. Dangling in the air, they rattle and clack. A baby laughs. A voice shushes it. A phone dings.

Her phone, signaling a text. Louisa.

I had a funny dream this morning. I was driving a child-size bumper car. Sharing for what it's worth.

Margaret types a reply. *Anything else?*

Was writing on a plastic laptop. A fat orange one. It revved up like a car when I put a giant plastic key in the ignition. Then it sang Zippity-Doo-Dah in a creepy voice.

Margaret thinks for a moment, then writes, *Definitely something. Calling Jay. BTW Ross Templar stirring trouble. Keep your head down.*

Don't worry. Staying put, cleaning out my apartment 2 move out.

Where to?

Not sure yet.

Talk later.

A sense of urgency has her dialing Jay. He answers on the third ring. When she asks if they found anything new in the storage unit, he sighs. "No luck so far with either old-school file folders or a flash drive"

"This may be a long shot, but the files may be disguised as a toy. Back at the farm, there's that room filled with baby things. I keep seeing a ring of baby car keys."

"I know the kind. Our Benjy had a set. Bright colors, makes a racket."

"It may seem farfetched, but…"

"If you're right, she probably took them with her. But it's worth a look. My team's tied up, but I'll get over there myself as soon as I can get away. That way if it's nothing—" He leaves the rest unspoken. She gets the drift.

Then he adds, "Meanwhile, no walks in the woods until we catch these two."

"I won't. Last time I went out, though, the girls and I ran into a friend who knows his way around out there. Thought you'd like to know."

"Good. But stay home today. Please."

She hangs up, not wanting to admit to herself that she's too tired to go anywhere anyway. Maybe Annie's right about a day of rest.

The next image to arise is fresh and new. Her hand aches to put pen and brush to it, and she quickly dresses and heads to the studio, the girls racing ahead to the crest of the hill. "Go ahead, have a romp," she calls, and goes inside.

She flips on the lights. As she exchanges coat for work sweater, the image expands in her mind, and she rushes to the worktable to get it down. As she lifts the pen, a flash of sun on iridescent wings catches her eye: a crow swooping by the window. She turns back to the thick sheet of paper waiting on the easel, and a hand clamps over her mouth.

Her right arm is wrenched up behind her, pain slicing through her shoulder. "I told you not to find me. I warned you. And then you go and get the cops after us."

Margaret tries to respond, but Molly tightens her hold, fingers pressing into the already bruised cheek.

Anger trumping reason, Margaret grabs the woman's wrist and pulls her hand away. "The police found your sister's body. They thought—"

"Shut up." Her mouth is at Margaret's ear, her hand twisting her arm. "She was supposed to help me. A sister's supposed to help a sister! I asked for one simple thing. But could she frickin' do it? No. She drove all the way up here like I asked, and then she said no." She covers Margaret's mouth again, tighter this time.

"All she had to do was hide the baby at her little playpen factory for a few days until the sale was made. But no, not her. Not my own damn sister.

"Somehow she figured out I made deals right at her own desk in that shiny glass office. Smooth as glass." She laughs, a bitter sound edging toward hysteria. "The old twin switch-a-roo. No one ever the wiser."

She is strangely quiet for several heartbeats. Then she screams, "She ratted on me! Of course, I got mad. Of course, Hank had to shut her up. Then it was done, and nothing I could do about it. Couldn't bring her back. Served the bitch right. Brought it on herself. Even you can see that.

"Then you had to stick your damn nose in. And now you're gonna make up for that. If you make a sound when I take my hand away, Hank gets up real close and personal with your friend, the Jolly Green Giant who lives down through the woods. That other old lady living all alone out here."

Margaret's heart is thudding. Annie. He's at Annie's.

Slowly, Molly takes her hand away. "I need to get into the farmhouse, and there's cops crawling all over it. So you're gonna go for me."

Margaret's mind is racing, trying to figure out what to do. It settles on going slack, acting submissive. For now.

"The old cow and her damn cleaning every two minutes. I put something down, and she's tidying up behind me."

Margaret keeps her head down, letting Molly talk. She pictures the spotless farmhouse. She sees the old woman mopping up after a birth and death. Cleaning up Molly's messes. Subservient. Paying off some karmic debt for past deeds. She watches as a young Lydia leads a child by the hand. Away from family. Away from everything she's ever known. Away from who she is. Then the old Lydia places flowers on unmarked graves behind a compost heap—the graves of two young women of the same tribal blood.

Molly continues her rant. "She took the damn keys and put them in with the rest so I grabbed the wrong ones when I took off. The ones the old bag didn't pick up!" As an afterthought, she mumbles, "Or left lying around on purpose to fool me."

Margaret sees a plastic bin containing several sets of the colorful "car keys" nestled among the other toys. *Everything in its place,* she thinks. *Lydia.*

"Come on." Molly yanks Margaret off the stool. "You're going to the farm and get all the sets of baby keys. They'll let you in."

"But what will I—"

"You'll know what to say." She pushes her toward the door, still holding her arm behind her back. "Shut the dogs in the house and act normal. 'Course, maybe 'normal' is a reach for you." She slips her hand into Margaret's sweater pocket and takes her phone. "Try to warn anyone, and your friend is in deep shit. As for the dogs, you don't want to see those pretty coats all covered in blood, now do you?"

Margaret swallows the words she nearly blurts. Again she plays subservient, although the shaking is no act.

As she reaches to turn the doorknob, Molly adds, "You'll be watched, so act all nice and casual at the farm. Or else." She opens the door and pushes Margaret out.

Her body bristling, she calls the dogs. Keeping her voice light, she hustles them into the house for treats and locks them in. She walks to the barn, head down, and backs the car out with care. Down the drive, Officer Grady is leaning against her cruiser, face to the sun. As Margaret passes, she scrambles to think of a subtle signal she might make, but fear of endangering Annie and the girls stops her. She nods but can't manage a smile. In the rearview, she notes the wrinkling of the young woman's brow, but then she shrugs and lifts her face back to the sun. The reporters are gone today, having feasted on the press conference. Nothing to see here anymore.

As she rounds the curve in the road, she pulls over, her shaking nearly uncontrollable. *Think*, she tells herself. *Think*. But her mind is abuzz with overblown scenarios with horrific outcomes. She breathes herself into a calmer state and eases onto the road. When she sees John's truck coming the other way, an idea forms.

She slows and then swerves into the other lane, in front of John, causing him to brake. He jumps out of the cab as she guns it and streaks around him, afraid some accomplice might come along and see them together. She trusts John will read the danger in her refusal to stop. She watches him in the rearview. Truck door standing open, he's in the middle of the road, slapping his leg with his hat, mouth open.

At the farm, there's a police car in the yard. As she walks up the front steps, a middle-aged man in uniform comes out the front door, the name *M. Carroll* on his ID tag. He asks what she wants, his voice curt.

She adopts a helpless-female demeanor and says, "I couldn't reach Detective Horner to get him to approve it, but I need to go upstairs for a quick minute. I'm—"

"I know who you are, ma'am." His eyes search hers, his face unreadable. "I've seen you here with the detective. If I let you in without him, I'll have to make a note of it, and you'll have to sign the sheet. They've already searched and photographed everything, but you can't touch anything up there."

"I won't. I just need to look. I—"

"I know what you do, ma'am. My wife says you're the real deal. She's into all that woo-woo stuff." He smiles for the first time. "No offense."

She manages a friendly smile in return. "None taken."

"Sign here." He hands her a clipboard.

She listens to the voice that says, *Make it quick, the same time as a signature would take.*

She hands the clipboard back, following Molly's instructions to act all nice and casual. "I'm sure you'll want to double check that signature." She nods at the page. "And you probably should call Detective Horner. Never hurts to cover yourself." She flashes a smile, looking into his eyes with an intensity she doesn't have to fake.

Upstairs, she goes straight to the storage room with the baby things. Everything has been shuffled around, and it takes a minute to find the box with the keys. She digs through and finds four rings, the keys clacking as she lifts them out. The now familiar sound sends a frisson through her body.

Quickly, she examines each ring. "Hmm, what'll they think of next?" she says aloud as she discovers not one but two rings with nearly imperceptible differences from the others. Each contains one key that is plumper than the rest. One is orange, the other is green.

She fiddles with the green one. Nothing. Then she notices the rippling seam around its edges, a seam different from the other keys on the ring. She presses and pulls, nearly breaking a nail, and it suddenly slides apart. The small zip drive inside is silver.

She slips the two loaded key rings in her inside sweater pocket. The other two rings she drops in her coat pocket. Not having worked out all the logistics of her plan, she wants to keep them separated.

On her way out, she nods to Officer Carroll. Grinning with familiarity, she says, "I hope you checked that signature and got the okay. Wouldn't want to get you in trouble." And she's down the steps and opening her car door, adding a friendly wave for the benefit of anyone watching from a distance.

"All's set, ma'am. You take care now," the officer calls out.

As she pulls out of the Makepeace driveway onto the road, a dark green car gains on her quickly, kicking her heart rate up. When it catches up, it hangs back a car length, matching her speed. When she finally slows at her driveway, it sails on by. She turns in to find that Officer Grady has been replaced by an older male officer. Her heart sinks, but then she realizes it's neither a good nor a bad sign. Just time for the changing of the guard. She parks between the house and the barn and hurries to her studio as the dogs bark from inside the house.

As she enters, Molly grabs her arm and drags her to the kitchenette area. "Give me the keys," she snaps, pushing her hard against the counter. Again Margaret lowers her head, playing the submissive, cowering and compliant.

She pulls the regular sets from her pocket and holds them up. When Molly grabs for them, she swings her right elbow up in an arc, catching Molly under the chin and throwing her off balance. At the same moment, she sticks out her foot and hooks her ankle under Molly's left calf. With a swift upward motion, she kicks Molly's leg out from under her, sending her over backward with a sickening crack of the head on the hardwood floor. Grasping her ankles, she rolls the dazed woman onto her belly. Yanking an extension cord from a hook on the wall, she ties Molly's wrists behind her back, looping the cord around her ankles for good measure.

Adrenaline still pumping, she searches Molly's pockets, finds her stolen phone, and punches in Jay's number. She shouts into the phone when he answers. "I've got Molly. Annie is— "

"Safe." He cuts her off. "We have Annie. What do you mean you've got Molly?"

"I tied her up. I have to get the dogs."

"Wait. There are officers in place outside your studio. Let them in. They were waiting for the all-clear that we had Annie but you got back before we sent it. We're almost there."

Molly is swearing as she struggles to free herself, and Margaret can barely hear Jay's last words. She runs to the door and calls for help, and three officers rush in. She points them to Molly on the floor and races to the house. The girls tumble out, barking frantically. She stops them with a word before they reach the studio. Dropping to her knees, she hugs them, shivering away the remnants of the panic that had kicked her into action

Sirens scream, brakes screech, and car doors thud as Jay and Cyn come on the run. They stop when they see Margaret on the ground in a pile of wriggling golden bodies.

"Are you all right?" Jay shouts.

Margaret can only nod in response.

Jay bends to her. "We never intended for you to walk back in there with that monster. I'm so sorry. The officers here were told not to act until Hank was in custody. He somehow slipped our net and made it to Annie's *but* he never got inside. "

"So you have him? In custody?"

He nods.

"And I have two zip drives," she pulls the clacking keys from her sweater pocket. Separating out the doctored key on each ring, she says, "They should contain the names and details you need."

Jay helps her to her feet and wraps her in his arms. "God you scared me. I—"

He stops, and she glances up to see him looking past her. She turns to see Kenneth standing beyond the backyard chaos of scattered vehicles with lights flashing, doors standing open, and radios bleating. Of officers shouting orders, lowering or holstering weapons, rushing here and there. All this against a backdrop of Molly's screamed obscenities and rabid threats as she's led from the studio, and the frenzied barking of two normally friendly dogs.

His mouth is open, his brow wrinkled, a look of horror in his sea-green eyes. They connect with hers, and she pulls away from Jay. But Kenneth is already turning away. She takes a step, and he signals with his hand for her to stop. She can't be sure of the meaning of his next gesture. She hopes he's saying, *Stay put. It's okay. We'll sort it all out later.* Then he's gone. She hears Annie call to her, and turns to see her coming up over the hill.

She runs to embrace her friend, and as they stand looking out over the fields, too much in shock to speak, there's movement at the edge of the woods. She raises her hand, letting him know she's okay. She's fine. Everything's all right for now.

Chapter 36

Her sleep is peppered with short but potent nightmares. Distorted faces circle her. Snarling voices screech and taunt. Hands grab at her, fingers clawing her flesh. Her arm is twisted behind her back until the bones crack. And all the while, a baby cries.

She struggles, pulling free only to be grabbed again. Molly's voice hisses in her ear, telling her to look at what she's done. Telling her to look down. When she does, she's standing on a mound of dirt looking into a grave. Annie, Kenneth, and Jay lie in a heap at the bottom, bodies twisted, and she feels the heft of the shovel in her hands as she flings dirt on them. Molly laughs. "It's all on you. Look what you've done, bitch!"

She opens her eyes, heart thumping. She's thrown off the covers and is shivering. Sitting up, she grabs her winter robe and invites the girls up onto the bed.

⚘

After a hot breakfast and three cups of tea, she dresses in layers to go to the studio. As she steps outside, keeping Sophia and Grace close, she is surprised by the warmth of the early-morning sun. Perfect weather on tap for today's noontime ceremony.

When she enters the studio, her body stiffens, her heartrate kicking up. She hangs at the door as the girls rush around the room, sniffing in every corner, stopping where she and Molly scuffled. They look up at her, waiting for a response. Finally, her legs loosen enough for her to cross the room. She takes up a heavy long-barreled flashlight and sends them ahead of her up the stairs to the loft where they repeat the search. Downstairs again, she opens every closet and cupboard and searches the bathroom. Last, she checks the locks on the backdoor and windows at the back entrance, deciding it's time to add a deadbolt.

Satisfied all is safe, she takes out the smudge stick and lights the bundle of cleansing herbs over a bowl of sand. Slowly, she walks the main room, fanning the smoke with a cluster of wild turkey feathers, filling the studio with the fragrance of cedar and sage. Once every corner has been smudged, she settles to work at her easel, putting to paper the image that has stayed with her since the day before. Her gift for today's ceremony at Sesalie and John's.

The figures emerge with ease. The witnessing part of her mind smiles at this, a rare experience with any artwork. The journey from conception to realization is so seldom perfect, the essence of the imagined piece always remaining just out of reach. But this is that rare and welcome exception.

⁂

Margaret chooses her outfit with care. Color feels important today. Over a thermal undershirt and gray leggings, she slips a loose dress of indigo, iris, and icy blue, woven of silk and wool. Around her neck, she fastens a silver chain with a cluster of gray-blue beach stones cast in silver that sits on her heart. Then she pulls on gray dress boots with a low heel. Carrying a woolen shawl with a beach-stone clip over her arm and a roomy handbag over her shoulder, she greets Annie and Louisa in the yard. They wait as she corrals the dogs into the house, and then they head out in Annie's car.

John meets them at the door. He hugs Margaret, concern on his face. Then Sesalie ushers them through the house toward the backyard to meet the guests. As they leave the kitchen, Margaret feels the pull of connection from Winowa's bedroom down the hall. She stops, wanting to leave the others and go there.

"She asked to be left alone until she's ready," Sesalie says gently. "Hasaleen is with her and will let us know."

Margaret nods in acceptance and follows her to the backyard. Expectation hangs in the air, suspended in the evergreens and floating among the leaves and bare branches of their deciduous neighbors. She feels both the anxiety and the pulsing joy of it, the wondrous moment before possibility becomes manifest.

Although the chairs are arranged in a circle that marks the boundaries of the container in which the exchange will take place, the gathered are scattered about. Margaret hones in on the newcomers, the grandmothers from up north, and a younger woman and a very young man. Sesalie leads them forward.

She makes the introductions and steps back. The tallest of the grandmothers approaches Margaret and takes her hand in both of hers. Under her gaze, Margaret knows she is being seen, truly seen. In the woman's eyes, a profound grief rests beneath the surface. A grief that can never be separated from the woman who carries it—the woman who *is* it. This is a grief that cannot be explained away by the recent loss of two daughters or the near loss of an unexpected granddaughter. As deep as those losses are, this is deeper still and so intense, she nearly turns away. But she continues to meet the woman's gaze, knowing that nothing she's ever experienced comes close to what this woman, these people, have lived.

As if an entire conversation has passed between them, the woman bends and enfolds Margaret in her arms. The embrace leaves her feeling whole. Then, one by one, each member of the Gabriel family follows suit. When Louisa is introduced to them, Margaret gets to watch from the outside what she's just experienced. Annie is next. She opens her mouth to speak, but stops herself and simply receives each embrace.

Margaret feels the pull of connection from inside the house again, stronger this time, and turns to find Sesalie at her side.

"She's ready. It's time."

There is no need for further explanation. As she reaches the steps, Sesalie's mother and sister come down the stairs. Aiyana's smile is serene as she nods to Margaret and continues on to the circle. Sylvia's eyes are wet, and she lowers her head as she passes.

Hasaleen opens the door for her to enter the closed-in porch. She hugs Margaret and goes out the door, followed by Auntie Dawn who touches Margaret's arm as she passes. Her heart lurches in a moment of panic, but she continues toward the bedroom. As she crosses the threshold, the scent of lavender calms her and Winowa's open eyes welcome her.

She is invited to sit on the bed with a wave of the old woman's hand. As they sit in silent communion, Margaret recognizes the energy of transition in the room—the soft humming, the occasional crackling like static on a stormy night, the return of the humming. Winowa is in a hazy state. Eyes dreaming. Ears listening to something beyond the hum and crackle in the air. Spirit floating just above the bed.

She opens her mouth as if to speak, then closes it again. Margaret hears a mild bustling from down the hall, the creak of floorboards, then Aiyana enters the room with a bundle of softness in her arms. She circles to the other side of the bed and places the sleeping baby in her mother's arms, assisting her in holding it.

Winowa's eyes widen, wonder blooming there. "There, there, Little One. Look. The ancestors are hovering near." The old woman looks toward the ceiling, and Margaret sees what she sees. Faces, young and old. Eyes, brown to honeyed gold, nearly black to icy blue. Cheekbones sharp to round and wide. Smiling faces spiraling back and back and back. Fading into a soft darkness. A flickering light beyond.

Winowa looks to Margaret. "She is the healing. She is all the children ever stolen, now returned. Tell them her story, Margaret. Speak of her mother. This is a part of your great task."

Winowa's arms loosen their hold, and the baby stirs, opening her eyes. Round and dark, they look up into the rheumy eyes of the elder. One face is withered and dry, the other luminous. Margaret breathes it in. The beauty of it. The power of love pulsating in the room.

She exchanges a look with Aiyana, whose eyes are mist. A spiraling energy passes between the dying woman and the child, fresh from the light.

A quiet sound in the doorway draws Margaret's attention. Sesalie and Sylvia stand on the threshold, and Margaret rises without a word. As she leaves, the sisters slip in to take her place.

Jane Susan Miller and Erin Irvine, the women who worked miracles to make this day happen, are standing in the kitchen with Cyn Green. She exchanges hugs with all three as she passes. On the closed-in porch, she stops to collect herself, thinking back to the night the women gathered here to laugh and tell stories. She longs for a taste of that shared laughter again.

The sound of footsteps in the hall rouses her, and she steps out into the yard just ahead of Sesalie and Sylvia. She joins the flow of the scattered group arranging itself into a wide circle. A few take chairs, the rest stand. She chooses the space behind two of the cousins—Melody, her round belly the focus of much attention, and Angel.

Sesalie guides the baby's grandmothers, Helen and Frances, to stand in front of two chairs. One is Winowa's usual place in the circle, the other her oldest daughter's. On the ground in front of them, a few feet from the central firepit, presents in colorful cloth wrappers are piled on a blanket. Margaret takes hers from her bag and places it with the others.

Kalie begins a quiet rhythmic drumming, and soon the cousins, aunts, and sisters begin chanting, beautiful sacred sounds Margaret understands only on an energetic level. Louisa and Annie stand behind her, a trio of outsiders blessed by this invitation, and she is thankful for their presence. She looks toward the eastern entrance to the circle. John and the young man introduced to her earlier as Lucas Gabriel stand on either side of the granite slab. As she studies the handsome youth, she sees a little boy, hair to his shoulders, chasing a feisty girl around a basket tree—Theresa and her cousin Luke, her constant companion, at play in the fields of forever. Their laughter carries across the years to answer Margaret's need, and she closes her eyes to the sound of her own brother's laughter. Her heart reaches out to the young man, holding in his grief in a circle of strangers.

She flinches at the sound of the baby crying, and looks to the doorway as three women descend the steps. Jane Susan and Erin lead the way, and Cyn follows, holding little Sarah to her chest. As Cyn soothes her with soft sounds, nuzzling her cheek to the side of the baby's head, the baby quiets.

The drumming continues, and the chanting fades to an undercurrent as the women approach the grandmothers. Cyn hands the baby over to Jane Susan, who turns the child outward on the crook of her arm and faces out into the circle so all can see her. In the baby's wide dark eyes, Margaret sees the circle of faces around her reflected back into the space. A shiver runs through her as she senses the presence of the ancestors Winowa spoke of, lighting her way out and a child's way in.

In the next moment, as if lulled by the drumming and the voices of the women, the baby yawns and snuggles deeper into the blankets, eyes still open and shining.

Jane Susan speaks to the gathered. "In the name of Child Services, it is my honor to place this stolen child, Sarah, daughter of Theresa, back into the hands and hearts of her family, her community, her people. For too long, we have been the face of outrageous policies that tried to erase your traditions, your language, your very being. The official face of those who took your children from your homes. May this Ceremony of Return be a symbol of our intention to right the wrongs done to you. May this day mark an inflection point, a turning toward truth, and a promise to acknowledge your stories and own ours. To tell the true story of the past and not the version sanitized for the comfort of the dominant culture."

The familiar sting of guilt sizzles, followed by a flood of gratitude that doesn't wash it away but moves it toward action. Margaret is grateful for these three women—a social worker, a lawyer, and a cop—taking a stand. And she resolves to stand with these committed women to root out systemic racism. Ready to instigate change. To make good trouble.

The vision that blooms before her has her smiling. On a multisensory level, she envisions a new way of being in the art world. She sees, feels, hears, tastes, and smells a new focus and deep purpose informing her work. But more importantly, inspiring collaborative group works, engendering educational programs, and underwriting multidisciplinary projects.

A collective intake of breath brings her back to the circle. As Jane Susan places the baby in her grandmother's arms, Margaret is already painting the moment. The statuesque woman with the long dark hair looks down into the eyes of her granddaughter, her face radiant. Again, the community inhales deeply, hands to hearts.

"I am Theresa."

The words come without warning, and shocked gasps tell Margaret she has spoken them aloud.

She looks around the circle, stopping at each face. "I didn't intend to speak. Forgive me for not preparing you. But I have to believe it was Theresa's wish that this be shared."

She looks to the grandmothers for consent to proceed.

Helen and Frances nod as one.

"I bring you her words, written on the wall in the room where she gave birth to her beloved daughter."

She pauses, then begins. "I am Theresa. They may take my Sarah away, but I will always be her Mother. May she someday know who she is: Sarah, Daughter of Theresa, Granddaughter of Helen, Great Granddaughter of Frances, and so on back through the mother line. Sarah, my Morning Star, you are a part of me and I of you. I love you. Always & forever."

All is quiet but for the drumming.

"Thank you." Helen turns to Frances and hands Sarah into her great-grandmother's arms. As she does, Erin Irvine surprises everyone by stepping forward and introducing herself as the lawyer officiating the exchange.

She clears her throat and addresses both women. "This was found at the farmhouse where Sarah was born. It belonged to Theresa." She reaches in her bag and pulls out a wooden box. A scattering of stars is carved into the dark wood of its cover. One, in the upper right-hand corner, is cut deeper than the rest, a speck of mica at its center.

Helen holds the little box to her heart, then rights it and opens the lid. A tinkling lullaby lifts into the air, the same one Margaret has been hearing for the past few days, and Helen nearly crumples into the chair behind her. She catches herself as the baby gurgles softly, her eyes fluttering open. Helen holds the box closer to Sarah, and the little one becomes perfectly still, eyes alert, rosebud lips open.

As the melody winds down, Helen closes the lid and sets the box on the chair. She takes Sarah from Frances and lifts her in the air, then lowers her to sit in front of her heart.

"Our Anita was taken." Three solemn drumbeats follow. "Our Theresa was taken." Three beats echo the first. "Our Sarah was taken." Three drumbeats are followed by emptiness.

Then out of the silence, a humming grows until Helen raises the child high above her head. "And now she has been returned."

The group barks, "Aho!"

Frances steps forward and turns to Jane Susan, Erin, and Cyn. Her voice is stronger than her size would suggest. "These women have gone above and beyond in returning our Sarah to herself. And now she will grow up knowing the most sacred sounds and deepest wisdom ways. Her feet will know our dances. We will introduce her to the trees who have stood waiting for her and for all the lost children to come home. We will raise her in our homeplace to the north. She will know the night sky and the morning star. She will stand with us to face the first light of each new day. For we are the People of the Dawn."

Margaret's heart opens as the child is passed around the circle, held for a moment in each set of arms and finally placed back in Helen's lap, who has taken her seat. Handmade gifts are opened and acknowledged. When Frances opens Margaret's, the grandmothers fall silent, eyes full. They bow to her across the circle. As the delicate watercolor with the three scripted lines beneath is passed around, sobs and whisperings can be heard. As it comes round to Margaret, she bows to the grandmothers in gratitude.

She's sketched the faces of the four women sparingly—the colors soft, the features faint, every line a mere suggestion. Relative youth or age is indistinguishable, even one face from the other. In their midst, a round-cheeked child, a hint of each of the four in her eyes, her mouth, her chin, her brow, and lip. And yet it is a face all her own, wholly Sarah's.

※

As sounds of leaving stir, Sesalie takes Margaret aside. "Winowa has passed." Before Margret can respond, a cry of pain slices the air. All turn in unison to see Melody bent over, holding her belly, a puddle at her feet. A scurrying begins as sister, cousins, and aunts swoop in to attend to her. Margaret stands in the midst of the swirl, caught in a vision.

The lemniscate, a luminous figure eight lying on its side, hovers over the embers of the central fire. Winowa is standing before her, her body youthful and strong, her face creased with knowings, hands crossed over her heart. Unspoken words pass between them before she turns and walks into the vibrating figure of light, and a scene unfolds.

Surrounded by the women of her family, Melody gives a final push, and her baby slips out into the hands of her sister. It's a boy, plump and healthy, strong lungs letting the world know he has arrived.

Melody's cries pull Margaret back to the present, and she turns to Sesalie. "No time to take her anywhere. Prepare a place. This baby is coming, right here in the circle."

As she sees the panic on Sesalie's face, she takes her by the shoulders and looks into her eyes. "'All is well, and all shall be well, and all manner of thing shall be well.' His timing could not be more perfect. Two souls meet in passing, with the family beneficiary to both."

She releases Sesalie to attend the needs of her family and stands back. Louisa and Annie join her. They watch, standing apart yet a part of the broader whole. Not for the first time, Margaret envies this loving family.

On the drive home, everyone is quiet. Finally, Louisa clears her throat and speaks, her voice soft. "They'll name him Wicasa. After a boy who was put into foster care years ago and never found. They'll call him Wic."

Margaret's heart flutters, a butterfly in the center of her being, and tears come.

Chapter 37

Sophia and Grace race ahead as Annie and Margaret climb the hill. It's been a week since they were last together—a week filled with distractions and busyness—and they walk in silence.

As they enter the woods, Margaret slows. "Are you all right?"

Annie lengthens her stride, moving ahead. "Fine."

This single word response, so not Annie, kicks off alarms. Margaret quickens her pace. "You've been awfully quiet. I—"

"I'm fine. I just… I'm processing. It shook me more than I want to admit."

Beside her now, Margaret waits for more, not wanting to push.

Eyes on the ground ahead, Annie says, "I always thought I was pretty strong. After Jake's death, I worked my way back to myself, more or less. I thought I could handle anything after that, and I never felt afraid living alone. But now…"

They stop on the trail and face each other. Margaret nods in understanding, allowing Annie space to step into that territory where formless fears live, taking shape only when acknowledged.

"I came toe to toe with my mortality, Margaret. And even though Jake has gone on before me, I'm afraid. And I'm afraid to be in my own house now. Even though everything there is Jake."

She's crying now. Quiet sniffles turning to aching sobs. Margaret enfolds her in her arms as clouds pass over the sun and the world goes dark around them. Sophia and Grace are back, hanging close.

Annie pulls away. "Oh, I'm such a blubbering idiot. Sorry."

"Don't you dare. Don't you dare berate yourself. Don't you dare apologize for feeling vulnerable. For being human. He invaded your homeplace. He may not have made it into the house, but he skulked around with zip ties and a gun. A damn gun! Don't bury your feelings.

"You're not alone. I'm in that place too. You should have seen me going through my studio! Sending the girls to search every corner. Cleansing it afterwards."

She senses her friend's need to move, to immerse herself in the natural world, and turns back to the trail. "So, what are we going to do to recover our sense of safety in the world?"

Annie blows her nose, straightens, and starts forward without responding.

Margaret continues pressing, relieved to be talking about that awful day. "After this, we're going through your house with the girls. We'll smudge inside and out. Then we'll look into a security system. Sophia and Grace can stay with you until it's installed and—"

"A puppy." Annie stops, a grin brightening her face. "I want a puppy. Or a rescue dog. Or both. Yes." She dances up the path and whirls around. "I was thinking about getting a dog even before this happened." She looks at Margaret like a mischievous child with an idea. "Will you come with me?"

And the plan is drawn.

For the rest of the walk, Annie talks. Released from the fear of going back to that dark day, flushing it with light, she plunges in. She describes her horror as she looked out the window and saw Hank Whitfield mounting the porch steps. Her surprise as the police grabbed him from behind and wrestled him to the ground. Her shock when his wrist smacked the railing and the gun went off. Her panic at learning that Margaret was Molly's hostage. And her rage later when she found the bullet hole in the welcome sign Jake had made.

Her voice drops as she talks about the consequent insomnia and the racing heartbeat at every little sound at night. Then she surprises Margaret by saying, "I'm going to find a therapist. Work out some demons. Maybe become a whole new woman."

"I'm not sure I'd like that. You changing." Margaret teases. "You're my Spirit Sister. My Mystical Sidekick."

Laughing, they climb to the terraced waterfalls. The clouds have floated away, and sunlight sparkles on the water and brightens the foliage.

Buoyed by their conversation as they circle back, Annie refuses the loan of the girls. Instead, she chatters excitedly about finding a dog or two of her own.

⸓

Margaret slices a fat radish and butters a slice of sourdough as she heats the last of the corn chowder for dinner. Her plan is to settle in for an evening of rest. A chance to process the events of the past days. The knock at the backdoor has her heart racing as the dogs scramble to their feet. As they shift into playful mode and wriggle their way to the door, she relaxes.

Laughing, she opens the door, and her heart thuds.

His smile is shy, his body language tentative. His sea-green eyes hold questions. She's not sure how long the silence hangs before she speaks.

"Hello." Pleasant but casual. "How's your brother?" The genuine question slides out, and she hopes it's all right.

"He's coming along." He nods, his shoulders relaxing. "And of course, that would be your first thought. You've just been through hell and you're asking after my brother." He pauses, eyes searching. "Thanks." The boy in the man shines through.

She invites him in, though a part of her doesn't want to—is afraid to. She's not sure if she imagines his slight hesitation. When he sees her place setting on the table, he apologizes for interrupting her dinner, but before he can turn away, she invites him to join her. She ladles Annie's chowder into two bowls, then focuses on slicing another radish and more bread. She tries not to think beyond this moment. This moment of calmly preparing a meal to share with this man who she hopes is not here for a final good-bye. She arranges radish slices on the buttered bread with a sprinkling of sea salt. Then there is no more to distract her.

She sits.

"Charlie is doing better than I expected. It was touch and go, but he's a fighter. We've moved him to an excellent rehab center." He smiles across at her. His face is pale, and smudges beneath his eyes speak of his ordeal.

She lifts her spoon to her mouth, resisting the urge to reach out to him, to cup his cheek. Her fingers want to tuck the errant curl up off his forehead. Instead, she grips the spoon and slurps her chowder. Blushing, she looks up to the ceiling, laughing and shaking her head.

He joins her, his laughter full-throated as his dimple flashes in and out of sight. "I second that." He raises his spoon in a toasting gesture. "Delicious!"

The familiar teasing tone eases her. Whatever he's there to do or say or not do, it will be okay. Their connection, their friendship, is beyond choice now. She's sure of this.

His laughter quiets, and sadness darkens his face. "I'm sorry," he says. He puts down his spoon. "I've been such an ass."

When she opens her mouth, he raises his hand, stopping her. "No. Seriously. I have no excuse for not calling. None. Not my work. Not my brother. Nothing. I got caught up in myself. And then it felt like the right moment had passed. I'd waited too long and didn't know what to say. I *did* get caught up in family stuff, but I heard the awful news about what was going on for you … and I still didn't call."

Again, she wants to reach out to him, to help him. But she stifles that need and waits, opening space for him to work through what he's come to say.

"When you called after you heard about Charlie, I was a shit. You reached out—which must have been hard—and I gave you nothing in return." He shakes his head and sighs. "I should have figured out what to say before I came here tonight, but I didn't. Couldn't. I just knew I had to come." He looks up at her. "Yesterday, when I came around the corner and saw you in the midst of all that chaos, I wanted to run to you, to be there for you. I shouldn't have let them turn me away. I should have insisted."

"You're here now." She can barely hear herself. She clears her throat and reaches across to him.

He takes her hand. "I'm sorry."

"I know. It will take time to figure out what we both want and need and are capable of giving." She pushes fear aside and says, "But I'd like to take that time."

"Me too."

"So, maybe we should start fresh. I'll reheat the chowder, and we'll begin again."

He lifts his hand to stop her as she rises. "First, I'd like to address the elephant in the room. Her name is Mandy and she doesn't like the idea of us."

Margaret sits, her heart thudding again. The stark honesty in his words scares the hell out of her.

He continues. "I can't lay the blame on her for my behavior. But I did let her misgivings sneak into my thoughts. You are the first woman I've become friends with since Liza died. And before I'd begun to sort through my feelings—realized I even had feelings—she reacted. Strongly.

"It jolted me. I hadn't thought about the effect on her. For way too long I was unconscious, I guess. Just getting through day to day, habit and routine carrying me along. Then I met you and my days started getting more interesting, brighter. It didn't register at first." He looks away, a shy young man for a moment. "Then I jumped into full-blown happiness with you. Didn't even think about my daughter and her lingering grief. I owe you both an apology. There's a lot I have to do to smooth things out."

The awkwardness that's hovered since his arrival lifts. In its place, a comfortable warmth settles. Her heart is still fluttery, and she feels the youthful shyness that accompanies a new relationship that promises something more. But she knows she wants to take this journey, which may or may not lead to... She lets the word in. Love.

She refills their bowls, and when they resume talking, they agree to take this slowly, with care. Finally, he asks her about the events that concluded with sirens and cops in her yard.

It feels good to talk about everything leading up to Molly's capture. She lingers when she gets to the part about Theresa and Anita and the farmhouse, needing to tell their story aloud.

As she talks, she sees Theresa—pale, pregnant, and ashamed—hiding her condition from her family. Far from home, abandoned by the boy she thought she loved, she is easy prey for Molly and Lydia. They encourage the shame, feed it to suit their plans, use it to push her into a fatal decision.

She sees Theresa's sister, Anita, convincing her to come home and give birth on tribal lands surrounded by family.

A shiver ripples. The sisters go out to gather the morning's eggs on the day they were to leave for home. A creeping shadow emerges. Hank waits for them at the chicken coop. She wants to warn them, but she's forced to watch helplessly as he kills Anita in the coop and drags Theresa up to the locked room, its only window nailed shut.

As tears come, Kenneth kneels beside her chair, soothing her, his hand on her back, tears in his own eyes. Sophia and Grace settle on her other side, dark eyes moving from one to the other, compassion ever their offering.

Kenneth takes her by the arms and pulls her up. She leans in and embraces the simmering feelings she hasn't allowed herself to acknowledge. He holds her and lets her cry until she's exhausted, then he eases her back into her chair. He clears the dishes and sets the kettle to boil. He reaches for her favorite teapot and the tea tin labeled "Quiet" and spoons some into the basket.

She watches him work, pleased at how easily he finds his way around her kitchen. How much at home he seems.

As he pours her tea, he says, "I'd like to take you out for your birthday tomorrow. Lunch maybe? "

She looks up in surprise.

"Unless you have plans, of course. It *is* the twenty-sixth, right?"

"Yes, it is. But how did we get so far into October already?"

He stands, holding the pot aloft.

She realizes he's waiting for an answer. "Things have been so… Yes. Yes, I'd like that."

He pours his tea and sets the pot down with more of a clunk than he clearly intended.

They chat about matters light and insignificant over their tea. Finally, he clears his throat and says he'd best be on his way. Spent, she is actually relieved. At the door, she takes down her coat, deciding to join the girls in seeing him off.

They walk to the crest of the hill as the girls dive down into the moonlight, their bodies acting out the joy her tired body can't manage. And then he's holding her, pulling her against him, cradling her cheek and softly rubbing it with his thumb.

"I'm so sorry this happened to you. Thank God you're all right." He leans back, the moon shining on his open face. "Or at least you *will* be all right with a good night's sleep and a birthday lunch. And maybe a plan to go wherever the day takes us?"

More tears come, and she leans into him again. And then he's kissing her, and she's wrapping her arms around his back, receiving his mouth on hers, soft yet searching. He pulls her closer. He presses his body against her, and hers responds. The kiss becomes deeper, and then Sophia and Grace are bumping against them, wriggling for attention. And they pull apart, laughing in the moonlight.

Chapter 38

Ordinarily, I go to the woods alone …
If you have ever gone to the woods with me, I must love you very much.

Mary Oliver, "How I Go to the Woods"

Out ahead of them, the four dogs weave back and forth up the far hill toward the house. First Sophia and Grace take the lead, then Maxie and Gulliver, Gulliver ever lagging behind his brother.

Margaret and Kenneth laugh at the dogs' antics. It's been pure pleasure spending the day together, promises dancing out ahead of them under the sun. Clouds floating across the bright blue.

They stop halfway down the hill and turn back toward the woods. He reaches for her hand, and they lean into each other. Breathing as one, they take in the dazzling display of autumn in her glory. The oranges, reds, and golds. The yellows and rusts and greens. Everything shining. Exploding into the dramatic burst of color that comes just before the leaves fall and fade and give themselves back to the forest floor.

They turn away at last and continue the final leg of their walk, still holding hands. At the top of the backyard hill, they drop into the pair of Adirondack chairs. The dogs rush over, energized by the long run in the crisp October air. The crunch of tires on gravel coming up the drive has them rising. As they round the corner of the house, they command the dogs to stay close. An unfamiliar car with out-of-state plates brakes in front, rental stickers prominent on both the bumper and windshield. Kenneth's hand tightens around hers, and he takes a half step forward as all four dogs sit at attention, curiosity sizzling.

As a woman steps out of the car, Margaret senses she's seen her before yet knows they've never met. Wondering if she's press, she prepares herself, straightening.

The woman raises her hand to shield her eyes and smiles. Her face is lined, especially around the mouth and light-blue eyes. Her fair skin has a translucent quality. The shoulder-length hair dancing around her head in the breeze is the bright white of a once true blonde.

As Margaret searches to place her, the woman speaks, her accent thick.

"Margaret?"

Stepping out in front of Kenneth, Margaret nods, breath held.

"Hello. My name is Kasha. Kasha Gula. I understand we have a friend in common."

I wish to thank

My editor, Elizabeth Barrett.

My publisher, Tom Holbrook and Kellsey Metzger.

Jodi Paloni, founder of Maine Coast Writers Retreats & Workshops.

The Jodi-inspired community of writers.

Becky Karush, creator of the delicious literary podcast *Read To Me*.

Chris Upton at the Freethinker's Corner for his Author Talks.

The Maine Writers & Publishers Alliance.

Libraries everywhere.

My readers for embracing Margaret et al.

My family and friends for their unwavering faith and support.

Made in the USA
Las Vegas, NV
26 April 2024

89173939R00239